Nina and Minerva

Cy Cross

Copyright © 2022 Cy Cross
All rights reserved.
ISBN-13: 978-0-578-35766-9

Contents

Chapter 1

ALIENS HAVE INVADED th' Earth, but humans are still killin' each otha. Why am Ah not surprised?

Mah tattered shoes clap against th' cold wet cobblestone path. Behin' me Ah hear th' scurried march o' th' Chosen scum, an organization dedicated tah killin' scavengers on th' Surface. Th' cans o' food in mah backpack rattle against one anotha as Ah run along. Ah keep th' grip on mah axe tight as Ah zip 'round a corner, nose blarin' steam. Ah swear tah God Ah ain't dyin' tahday!

Ah turn 'round—

"Oof!" Ah crash intah th' corner o' a large blue dumpsta, clippin' mah chin on th' filthy lid. Mah brain rattles. Ah crumple, takin' in quick, nasty-ass breaths. Th' hard, jagged concrete stabs intah mah back as Ah roll round in pain claspin' mah throbbin' head. Cold moon light drifts down from th' bleak black sky, bathin' th' alleyway inna eerie silver glow as Ah scramble tah mah feet. Long ominous shadows stretch out from 'round th' corner, an' Ah realize Ah ain't got time tah run.

'Spose Ah'll jus' haftah hunt th' hunters.

A Chosen darts outta cover wit' his pistol raised. Mah arm flashes forward inna blur o' silver, an' th' next thing y'know his arm is on th' floor an' mah bloody axe is embedded intah th' brick alley wall.

Th' shorthaired blonde man wit' deep, shimmerin' blue eyes wails in agony, clutchin' his right shoulder as a burst o' crimson explodes from th' empty socket. His arm flops 'round on th' pavement like a fish on land, then it's drowned by th' flood o' red fluids comin' from th' body it used tah be attached to.

Th' folk 'round th' corner gasp, but they ain't got time tah be surprised. Ah run up tah th' wall, grip mah axe wit' mah right hand, then bounce off wit' a swift, clean swipe. Ah flinch back as an intense red spray pours ova me froma brown man's throat, his thick goatee pointed skyward as his head starts unhingin'. Ah wince as he collapses, now a howlin', twitchin' geyser while a green-eyed woman wit' straight black hair like mine swipes a metal bat at mah head. Th' cold steel blasts mah hair sideways as Ah crouch, yank mah knife out from mah waist holder, then spring upwards, left fist clenched tight 'round th' knife's handle as Ah *jam* it unner th' woman's chin. Warmness splatters ontah mah left hand as mah wrist judders wit' finality.

Th' woman stumbles backwards, hands claspin' th' handle. She takes in pained, wheezin' breaths, eyes rollin' intah th' back o' her head. Ah yank out th' knife, makin' blood jet from her chin like an eruptin' inverted volcano. She sways on th' spot, then slithers tah th' floor, body shudderin' wit' wet coughs.

Ah'm tremblin' all ova as Ah inch backwards. Th' back o' mah ankles slip out from unnerneath me, makin' me bust mah ass on th' diamond hard floor. Unnerneath mah ripped blue-jeaned thigh is th' unarmed blonde guy, who's still inna a world o' hurt. Ah scurry offah him wit' a yelp, then raise mah axe up high an' cleave it intah his forehead.

He goes still as th' axe's wooden handle vibrates in mah grip. Ah dislodge th' axe from his handsome, split-open face, revealin' a thick, bloody red rope that glues th' axe an' his face tahgether. Ah tear th' axe away from th' crimson web as both halves o' his face slide apart from one anotha. Mah stomach twists intah knots, but Ah ain't got time tah be sick.

Sumthin' squeaks nearby. *Shoes skiddin' 'cross th' floor?* Ah burst intah a sprint, sparin' a quick glance ova mah shoulder. Three Chosen are on mah ass, one o' 'em dashin' ahead o' th' rest wit' a burst o' speed. He clasps his hand 'round mah backpack's shoulder strap, yankin' me backwards. Mah stomach falls as Ah take inna hissed breath then slam th' back o' mah head intah th' bastard's nose.

He sputters, "Bitch!" but keeps his grip on mah backpack.

Ah ain't gotta choice, huh? Tears pourin' from mah eyes, Ah stomp on his foot, reach mah arm back an' cut through th' straps. Th' hateful strangah lurches backwards, still clutchin' mah backpack, but Ah'm freed from his grip, blastin' forward like a deer 'scapin' fromma net.

Ah sprint intah th' next corner, then take anotha corner at lightnin' speed. Ah catch mahself against th' green dumpsta's edge 'fore Ah slam intah it. Aftah a quick dart o' th' head from side tah side, Ah creep th' lid open. It smells like a corpse bathin' in skunk spray, but it seems empty. Ah slither inside, but right when mah feet hits th' slimey wet floor, mah heels slip out from unnerneath me, makin' me bang th' back o' mah head against th' dumpsta. A dull *clang* echoes throughout th' hollow interior an' Ah take inna sharp, pained breath.

Definitely th' smartest thing Ah've done.

Th' rank smell o' death ovapowers mah nostrils. Ah cover mah mouth jus' as vomit bursts from it, th' lumpy liquid oozin' 'tween mah fingers. Ah keep an iron grip onnit, tryin' tah stay as quiet as possible as footsteps thud outside. A nail o' pain stabs me in th' third eye as Ah choke on th' vomit, cryin' silently.

"Hey, you guys hear something?" a gruff voice asks.

"I don't know, *jackass*," a deep female voice says. "I can't believe you let her get away."

Anotha female lets out a high-pitched giggle. "Don't be so hard on Zack. He's an old man, y'know? Besides, if you're going to blame anyone, blame Logan and his squad. They let one girl take them all out!"

Mah insides freeze. Above, th' dumpsta's lid creaks, an' a thin strip o' light pierces th' darkness. It reveals th' mangled Feral corpse lyin' 'cross from me. *Oh, God.* Its dark-blue skin is riddled wit' deep red gashes. White, squirmy maggots crawl 'cross th' thing's split open insides.

"Oh, jeez, *gross!*" th' bubbly voice says, an' th' lid whams shut. Th' strip o' light disappears as if it neva were, trappin' me back in th' rank darkness. Th' footsteps continue onwards, passin' me up. "Smells like rotten shit in there."

"Relax, ladies," Zack says. "Logan's group didn't die in vain. We'll find her."

Ah wait there fer God knows how long, head poundin' sumthin' fierce. *Shit. Shit!* Ah punch th' air in silent fury, still chokin' on th' stench. They took mah food. *We're fucked.*

Once Ah can't hear th' footsteps no mo', Ah carefully open th' lid an' crawl outta th' hell inna box. Mah sobs stop me from 'ppreciatin' th' *relatively* cleaner air.

Oh mah God. We're gonna die.

Guess we finally ran outta miracles. Fer a secon', Ah'm so ovawhelmed wit' sorrow that Ah get an image o' me lyin' on th' cold floor, paralyzed wit' tears fer hours. Ah shake th' vision off, a sob stuck in mah throat. No sense lyin' 'round cryin' here. Might as well spend what lil' time Ah got left wit' mah brother. A gust o' bitin' cold wind slashes through me, makin' me wince an' cradle mahself. Mah hair flutters in th' cuttin' breeze as Ah emerge from th' alleyway an' look at th' endless desert an' th' sea o' blackness ovahead. Th' moon's pale silver glow goes ova mah shoulder an' lights th' path home. Teeth chatterin' sumthin' fierce, Ah inch forward, walkin' intah tahmorrow.

Chapter 2

"Minerva?" an angelic voice calls. "Wake up, please."

I clench the heavenly soft covers around myself, pretending not to hear her, but a sudden *click* makes me crack open an eyelid. The intense glow bursting from the light bulb on the ceiling stabs me in the eye, making me groan. I wince as the sleepy haze encompassing my brain is blown away, revealing my dearest friend standing at the entranceway to my room. Even though her arms are crossed and her foot is tapping relentlessly against the metallic grey floor, she still graces me with a small, patient smile. "You going to stare at me all day, or are you going to get out of bed?"

"Ugh..." I roll over, turning my back to her. "Sarah, it's only..."—I check my clock—"11:30. A lady needs her beauty sleep, yes?"

"Well, it's not like you need it."

"That's the funniest thing I've ever heard."

Bombastic footsteps clap from somewhere behind me. "Don't be like that. Come on, you're already late for class. The teacher sent me to fetch you." My mattress shifts under her weight as she sits down. "Again."

"Mmm..." I roll over to look at her, marveling at the golden waterfall tumbling down her shoulders. I grab ahold of a few strands and wrap them around my finger, resisting the urge to glare at the wooden cross hanging from her neck. "The world has gone to hell outside, my dear. Who cares about education? I'd rather just lie here, make a warm cup of tea and do some reading. After I sleep a few more hours, of course," I give a content sigh, then snuggle back into my blankets. I love my room! The walls I painted sky blue never fail to put me at ease, and being surrounded by my favorite novels is a delight.

I start thinking about what I'm going to read today when Sarah says, "Minerva, your laziness never seizes to surprise me. What happens if we get out of here sooner than we think? Queen Amity will need you—we all will need you on the Surface."

"Well, to be honest..." I stretch myself out with a tight smile, a pleased squirm slipping from my lips. I let go of my darling's hair and let my hand rest on the warm, soft mattress. "I don't believe we'll ever leave this place. The Feral outnumber us a hundred to one. We'll never entirely defeat them, if you ask me."

A storm awakens in Sarah's azure eyes. "We *will* defeat them. You of all people can't have that kind of attitude. What if someone overhears you talking like this? They'll lose all hope of ever getting out of here."

I have the decency to look guilty, and Sarah purses her soft lips.

"Now get off your rump, you lazy bum." She gives me a playful shove. I giggle and roll out of my fluffy sanctuary, dragging my silk covers over me along the way. "Minerva, we don't have time for your silly little game."

"Game? Whatever are you talking about? This is no game." I use my powers to become invisible, wrap the covers around myself, then stand up and make a ghostly moaning sound.

"For the last time, Minerva, ghosts don't wear tacky shades of blue," Sarah says, shaking her head with a laugh. "They wear *white*." I notice she's gripping her left side with her right hand. My eyes narrow. "Besides, a real ghost would have eyeholes."

"I'm a ghost. I don't *need* eyes," I huff. "Besides, I'll have you know that saying we only wear white is quite an offensive stereotype, and I refuse to listen to you slander my sense of fashion any longer. Come at thee!" I tackle her to the floor, tickling her ribs.

"Minerva, stop it," Sarah cries, though she is pink with laughter.

I just tickle her harder. She giggles until my hand grazes her left side and she gasps, forehead creasing in pain.

I stand up, turn visible again, then throw my blankets off to the side. "That imbecile hit you again, didn't he? Only this time he tried to be subtle about it."

Sarah looks down, ashamed. "How'd you know? You can't read minds too, can you?"

"No, but while invisibility may be the only ability I have that is inherently super, it is not my only power by any means. Intuition, reading body language, and common sense is just as useful." I grab her hand and gently pull her to her feet. "I'm getting off the sidelines."

I storm over to my restroom, my insides fried from the fiery anger dancing in the pit of my stomach. I toss on a pair of wrinkled blue jeans and a spaghetti strapped white t-shirt, then open my cupboard and grab the electronic shock bracelet I ordered from overseas. I shove it in my pocket with a grimace. I initially bought the bracelet to help control my bad eating habits, but it looks like I'll be using it for a different reason starting today.

I open my closet and greet my beautiful silver rapier, the one given to me by the Queen when I was knighted. I like to call it The Blade of Justice. The sword's cup-hilt is royal blue and golden, and the blade itself is thin but incredibly sharp.

Nice to see you again, darling.

I sheathe the blade and attach it to my waist belt, then walk out of the bathroom. Sarah's standing at the entranceway with crossed arms and a fierce scowl. "Minerva, you can't solve all of my problems."

"Oh, but I can, dear. Just watch me." I walk to the door and open it.

"Wait!"

I turn invisible. "Oh, right, you can't." I giggle to myself as I close the door, but I don't exit the room. It's a trick that's worked dozens of times when I've needed information from people, and a trick I expect to work now.

Sarah deflates, sinking back to the floor. "Oh, William, what are we going to do?" She looks down at her stomach and cradles it gently, almost... lovingly.

Oh, my. Did he... Is she...?

"How are we going to raise you in a cage?" She asks no one.

My friend is crying. *I'm going to make that lowlife pay.*

I open the door and close it slowly behind me, careful not to make any noise. "Right then, time to chop off his balls."

Chapter 3

AH WANNA CRY, but Ah can't 'till Ah get unnerground. Th' world is a cruel place, an' it gets crueler every day. Any sign o' weakness ya show *will* be exploited full heartedly. So Ah keep mah face hard as Ah creep towards th' stairwell that leads down tah th' metro station, passin' up two rotted heads on a stick an' th' *Stay Out!* sign Ah made ages ago. As always, Ah'm scannin' th' area fer threats like a robot. Th' only weapons Ah have on me are mah knife an' axe, so if Ah run intah a Feral out in th' open like this, Ah'm probably dead. Well, even deader than Ah already am.

Lucio an' Ah had already scavenged th' area fer miles, but there ain't a drop o' edible food anywhere nearby. We haven't had an actual meal in at least a month, survivin' offah rats an' water alone. Lucio had gotten weak from hunger three days ago, so Ah left our base tah search fer food. Ah vowed tah return wit' sumthin' fer him tah eat, no mattah how long it took.

Ah've failed.

Ah descend down th' metro's stairwell. It's funny, in th' ol' days, Ah wuz scared o' th' dark, but now Ah find it mo' comfy than a warm blanket. Darkness hides ya from harm, see, while all light does is *expose* ya tah danger. Th' shadows are mah best friend, an' th' light is mah worst ene—

Mah left foot lands on sumthin' slippery an' Ah lurch sideways. Ah trytah grab th' wall but end up tumblin' down th' stairwell, bouncin' off th' sharp concrete steps in th' dark. Ah break mah fall on mah now bleedin' an' throbbin' elbow. *Ah 'spose that philosophy is complete bullshit.*

Ah struggle tah mah feet, supportin' mah bleedin' appendage as Ah hobble down th' tunnel. Mah footsteps echo through th' chamber an' th' blood tricklin' down mah arm creates a drippin' sound when it hits th' floor. *Clip-clap, drip-drip, clip-clap.* Ah'mma one woman band. Ah laugh fer th' first time in days, 'till a fierce wave o' hunger makes me cradle mahself, like sumhow self-embrace will stop th' stabbin' pain rippin' through mah stomach.

Eeyup. That there settled it.

Ah'm gonna die soon.

Mah legs get heavier than elephants. Every step could be mah last. How will Ah find th' strength tah move forward when mah demise is so close?

"Nina," a bright voice calls out in th' darkness, "is that you?"

Ah break intah a sprint an' enter th' crack in th' wall that leads tah our secret alcove. Ah find mah angel lyin' on th' tattered mattress we found at sum dump 'bout a year ago, a lil' while aftah th' invasion. In th' light o' th' two candles beside him, his brown face is lifeless an' waxen, his once bright hazel eyes dull. He gives a shaky smile as Ah run tah him, then pick up his featherweight body an' envelop it inna hug. Allah his hair has fallen out, an' his fingernails have been chewed down tah th' stubs. He shivers even though his forehead is beaded wit' sweat.

"Brother, Ah failed ya," Ah choke out. "Ah found food but th' Chosen—"

"Hush, sis. Ya made it back tah me. Thas' what counts."

Ah hug him tighter, an' he groans.

"Yer hurtin' me," he murmurs, "but itsa good hurt." He tries tah hug me back, but Ah can barely feel it. "Ah'm 'bout tah see our folks."

His anguished face becomes a messy brown blur, but Ah wipe mah eyes. "Ah'm comin' wit'cha, Lucio."

"Naw," he says wit' a small smile. "Ah'm weak, but yer strong. You've always been. You can an' *will* survive."

"Whas' th' point o' survivin' when yer only family is leavin' ya?"

Lucio grips mah wrist. "You gotta find anotha family. No mattah how long it takes."

"Bu—"

"*Promise me* you'll find happiness."

"Ah'm as close tah joinin' Mom an' Dad as you are. There's no food fer miles, our water supply is finished—"

Lucio's grip tightens, an' Ah'm amazed how he's summoned so much strength when he's practically a walkin' skeleton froma cheap horror movie. "Nuh-uh. No excuses. *Promise me!*"

"Ah... Ah promise," Ah say.

His sharp eyes study me intensely fer one long secon', then he nods wit' evident satisfaction, eyes glassy an' unfocused again. "Good. Could ya do me one last favor?"

"Anythin'."

"Take me tah th' Surface. But first, pack yer things. Use mah backpack. There's nuthin' left fer ya down here."

He's right. Ah nod, then gently lay him back on th' bug infested mattress. At least he won't haftah sleep on that anymo'. Ah grab his backpack an' stuff in mah favorite books, a map, sum arrows, a bundle o' rope, a buncha throwin' knives an' th' trusty hatchet Pa gave me. Ah pick up mah hand-crafted bow an' sling it ova mah shoulder. Ah walk back ova tah mah brother, put one arm unner his knees an' anotha unner his neck then lift him up.

Ah carry him intah th' hallway an' towards th' stairwell, which seems impossibly tall now that Ah have all this extra weight.

Lucio says, "This is nuthin' fer you. Yer stronger than ya think ya are."

"How'd y'know what Ah wuz thinkin'?"

"Sis, Ah know ya betta than y'know yourself."

Ah take th' first step up th' stairwell, intah th' thin reedy light shinin' down from th' entranceway above. As we ascend, mo' light fills th' chamber, an' mah tears drop ontah Lucio's face. Memories o' our time tahgetha blurs mah eyesight. Ah remember Pa teachin' th' two o' us howtah hunt, Ma tuckin' us in an' readin' us bedtime stories. Ah remember us fightin' ova toys as children, an' th' dark times where we fought ova scraps o' food when our hunger got th' betta o' us. But mos' o' all Ah remember that th' two o' us always stuck tahgetha, no mattah how bad things were, no mattah how hopeless things got in th' past few months.

An' now he's leavin' me.

Mah body is wracked wit' sobs, but Lucio jus' shushes me. "Don't cry. Can'tcha see? Dawn is breakin'."

We reach th' Surface. Th' sun greets us wit' its bright an' beautiful glow, risin' up 'tween two collapsed buildin's in th' distance.

"Y'know," he says, "as th' last thing Ah'm eva gonna see, Ah can't ask fer anythin' betta."

His eyes start closin', an' mah heart rips itself apart. "Don' leave me, brother. Don' leave me alone."

"Ah..." He tries tah open his eyes. "Ah can't stay. Ah'm sorry."

Ah roll mah jaw, close mah eyes, then take a deep breath 'fore respondin' inna soft voice: "Don' 'pologize fer things ya got no control ova,".

We cradle one anotha one las' time, then he puts his hand on mah cheek. "Ah love you, sister."

"Ah love you too, mah lil' angel."

His smile gets warmer. "Remember yer... promise."

Ah kiss his forehead. "Ah will, don' you worry now."

"You're beautiful, sister..." His body goes limp, an' th' hand on mah cheek falls.

Ah wanna scream, but that will only bring th' Feral tah me, an' then Ah'll neva be able tah make good on mah promise. Ah fall tah mah knees an' place mah angel on th' ground, hopin' mah parents are welcomin' him wit' open arms in Heaven.

Ah'mma 'bout tah break down when Ah hear a squawk 'bove mah head. Ah look up an' see a grand eagle flyin' right ova me. Ah scramble tah mah feet, grab mah bow, notch an arrow, an' drop tah one knee.

Ah fire. Th' projectile soars through th' air 'fore... bullseye. Th' eagle tries tah flap its wings, but seein' as an arrow's stuck in its throat, it ain't goin' nowhere. It gets out one mo' flap 'fore it nose dives, crashin' ontah th' ground wit' a snap.

Ah run ova, grab it by th' wing, an' yank mah arrow out wit' a sticky *squelch*.

Why couldn't this damn thing have flown by an hour ago? Ah'd have had plenty grub tah feed Lucio. But mah brother had already flown away, off tah bigger an' betta adventures. An' Ah wuz still here, grounded, still hungry, an' wit' a body that needed its fill.

Ah gettah work on makin' a fire. Mah brother needs tah be cremated too, but aftah that, Ah'm gonna find mah happiness. Sure, Ah'll make good on mah promise tah find a new family; but that can wait. Lucio said he wanted me tah be happy, an' that happiness involves slaughterin' *every single one o' th' Chosen* an' th' cowardly Queen that commands 'em. They killed mah brother, an' all o' 'em are gonna pay wit' their lives.

Ah take out mah axe, a heavenly plan comin' tah mind. Ah jus' had tah find sum Chosen an' track th' bastards back tah th' hellhole they came from. Ah laugh lifelessly, tryin' tah ignore th' gapin' hole in mah heart as Ah chop off th' bird's head wit' a single stroke.

Chapter 4

I *stroll down the halls of the vault, my bare feet rustling the grass. Fluorescent lamps cling to the ceiling, serving both as a visual aid and as a means of keeping the grass healthy. The previously gray walls have been painted over with pictures of trees and plants. It's the Queen's attempt at creating an outdoor atmosphere in the underground cage we're trapped in. It works, or at least I've convinced myself it has.*

Other young adults in shorts and T-shirts populate the hall alongside me, talking amongst themselves. Some are heading towards the gym room, others the library, and others their own personal chambers. The lunch bell rings. What superb timing. William will most certainly be there.

Most of the students change their route and head in the direction of the cafeteria. My stomach rumbles loudly.

Oh my... most unlady like of me.

Flames lick my cheeks, and I'm grateful that I'm still invisible.

I skip towards the cafeteria, resisting the urge to pull pranks on people I'm not fond of or swing my blade around like a child imitating the sword fights they saw in the Star Wars prequels.

Being a knight was rough sometimes.

I arrive at the lunchroom within a few minutes. A muscle-bound boy with a seemingly permanent scowl opens the door for his girlfriend, and I enter the room before her.

"Why, thank you," I exclaim, patting his cheek.

The boy yelps, eyebrows reaching the heavens in shock. "Wh-who's there?" he shrieks in a high-pitched voice.

"Um, me?" his girlfriend says with a confused smile. "Are you OK?"

"I-I-I..." he shudders, as if a cold breeze had flown by. "I think I need to sit down, sweetiums." It takes everything I have not to die laughing. I'm terrible.

A love story plays on the giant screen overlooking the long row of tables with small round seats. The screen never goes dark: it runs films all day, back-to-back. The Queen got her hands on just about every DVD in London before the Nuke hit, so we've never seen the same film twice unless it's requested. As bad as it is to not have everyday necessities like smart phones or the Internet anymore, I must admit we've got it pretty good under here under the circumstances.

The food ranges from bad to mediocre depending on the day of the week, but I suppose even a lady with my standards can't complain too much. Today's menu consists of beef stew and carrots. It smells delightful, but I mustn't let myself get distracted.

I look for William. That scumbag is in here somewhere. He always does his upper body work-out in the morning, so he wouldn't be in the gym again already, and he's far too stupid to be much of a reader, so I know he can't be in the library. Unfortunately, he's also too ignorant to know that no one wants to see his despicable face, so there's little chance he stayed in his chambers.

I find him lounging at the end of one of the tables. His shiny bald head glistens in the light while his glazed-over brown eyes stare transfixed at the beer can he's crushed between his hands. I must have a word with the kitchen staff. Whoever is supplying this man-child with alcohol needs to be punished severely.

As I approach the table, the imbecile snaps out of his drunken daze by burping loudly. His idiotic friends congratulate the non-confirmative bodily function with laughter and pats to the back of his wheelchair.

I grab the back of his icky head and plunge it into his bowl of stew. A splash of gravy and food erupts, splattering me and his mates. It takes every effort not to squeal at the top of my lungs. I *hate* stains.

"What's gotten into ya, mate?" one of his friends asks, stripping a thick piece of beef off of his lovely silk shirt.

I almost feel sorry for the friend, but being mates with someone like William negates any sort of sympathy I would have had otherwise. Shame about his darling top, though.

When I let go of the back of William's head, he flings himself from the bowl. His face is coated in brown juices so thick an onlooker may believe it's another substance entirely.

"Ugh..." he groans, "who did that?"

"You did!" his mates yell in unison.

I giggle to myself. Being invisible made for an endless possibility of pranks. It's a good thing my power is a secret; otherwise my reputation as a Lady would be completely tarnished. Speaking of which... I hastily wipe away the stain on my shirt before anyone notices a floating brown spot moving around.

William says, "Jimmy," but before he can finish I grab ahold of his arm and swing his fist across his mate's face.

The black-haired boy stands up slowly, ripples of angry testosterone flowing off him in waves.

I back away, blending in with the crowd of teenagers behind me who are already screaming, "Fight! Fight! Fight!"

"You wanna have a row, mate?" Jimmy growls.

A boy with shaggy brown hair restrains Jimmy, but he spits at William, "Oi mate, for the last time, just 'cause your legs got bitten off don' mean ya getta be an ass tah everyone. I oughta let Jimmy here knock ya head off!"

Everyone around us yells in approval, and while they're distracted I crawl underneath a nearby table, turning visible with a smile.

William starts apologizing to his friend, but I emerge from underneath the table before he can say much. I make sure my rapier is still invisible, though. "William! Sarah wants to speak with you."

I grab his chair's handles and start rolling him out of the cafeteria.

"Hey! I don't want to go anywhere with you," William protests. "You can't force me."

"Oh?" I ask coolly. "Watch me."

The crowd behind me demands bloodlust, but I turn and give them a glare so sharp they all close their pathetic little mouths. My scars made me hideous, sure, but boy did they come in handy for intimidating people.

We exit the cafeteria and I start rolling him down the hall at a leisure pace. As we walk, I consider how to propose my threat. Sarah must see *something* in this despicable human being, perhaps I should appeal to his sense of reason?

"Could you hurry it up?" William barks. "I've got things to do."

Oh, wait, I forgot. William is an imbecile. So it makes perfect sense that I treat him as such. I wheel him near the restroom and tell him that I will be right back.

"Couldn't you have pissed *before* you grabbed me?"

I walk in, turn invisible, and then walk out. William is already rolling back towards the cafeteria. I suppress a snort, and then dart ahead of him, keeping my footsteps inaudible. I open the supply closet in front of him with perfect horror movie-esque slowness that only one with years of experience pretending to be a ghost can achieve. He stops in front of it, shock and awe plastered across his face. "Wh-what th-"

It would be interesting to see how he would react to this situation. I am constantly fascinated as to how humans attempt to explain the unexplainable. But, unfortunately, I do not have time for such games. I roll him backwards, turn him to the side, and then roll him around the door and inside the closet. He's full on freaking out now, twisting his head from side to side, but as far as he can see, no one is there. I put my blade to his throat. He can't see the cold steel, but he can most certainly *feel* it. "Don't scream," I murmur in an otherworldly hollow voice.

"Argh—"

"Be silent, or you'll lose your tongue."

William whimpers like a kicked dog, and a tear slides down the side of his cheek. "Who are you?"

"I am your unborn child's guardian angel."

"B-bullshit, mate. I don't believe in angels. I don't believe in God!"

I let him turn around fully so he can see for sure I'm not here.

His mud-brown eyes widen. "This isn't real! It's just a shitty dream." He smacks his head. "Damn it, William, wake up!"

I stifle a giggle. "Not real? Can't you feel the Blade of Justice cutting into your Adam's apple, just enough to make you bleed?"

William, being an imbecile, starts struggling in my grip and I'm forced to yank the blade away so the little chicken doesn't slit his own throat.

I walk around him, murmuring, "I have seen you sin greatly against the child's mother. Give me a good reason why the Blade of Justice shouldn't run you through and be done with it."

William starts to sob, and through wracked breaths he says, "I'm s-s-so sorry."

I'm so surprised that my burning anger dies instantly, as if a gust of sympathy flew by and extinguished the fire in my heart. With years of being a fly on the wall, I can judge people's character really well. William's reaction feels genuine, in every sense of the word. *How quaint.* Not that I can let that stop me.

"'I'm sorry' doesn't cut it, I'm afraid." I cough to stop myself from laughing. I'm terrible.

"It can't end here. I'm not gonna die some alcoholic loser!"

William whirls around, fist drawn back. I flinch as my back hits the door, my palms held out. My heart surges with intense energy, and the sound of thunder roars in my ears.

I close my eyes tight, but I'm not hurt? I open my eyes and see a purple inverted triangle hovering in front of me. William has his fist pressed in the triangle's center, eyes shut in pain.

Did I just create a force field?

Wait, when did I become visible? I shroud myself again as William wheels himself backwards, banging the back of his head against the door just as the triangle shatters into smaller triangular fragments that disintegrate into nothingness. His hand goes for the knob, but I step forward and draw my blade. The weapon's gleam becomes visible even in the darkness.

I poke the tip at his nose. "Any more sudden moves and this work of art will make your brain a shish kabob." *Oh my, now I'm even hungrier.* "Are we clear?"

William nods slowly and swallows, his Adam's apple bobbing.

"Y-you really are an angel, aren't you?"

I withdraw and sheathe the blade, willing it to become invisible as I do so. "But of course."

He swallows again.

"I must admit," I say, "attacking an angel takes courage. Your eyes... they tell me you seek redemption."

His eyes becomes stronger than steel. "I will be redeemed—even if that means never touching a drop of alcohol again."

"Alcohol isn't the central problem, even though you *do* need to stop drinking. The problem, my dear, is that you're using alcohol to run away from yourself. Why did you start drinking in the first place, and why is it so hard to stop? These are the questions you must answer if you wish to achieve redemption."

William looks at the floor, his face solemn. "Before the invasion, I was a football player. I wasn't all that good, but football has been my passion since I was a lad. The feeling of dribbling the ball between your feet, moving at a million miles an hour while you dodge the enemy... nothing can beat it. Now that my legs are gone, it doesn't feel like anything matters anymore."

"Sarah matters."

William jerks back and hits his head on the door again. "Of course she does. She was my girlfriend even before the invasion, and she's stuck with me even though I'm a bloody bugger. I'm just saying I never found anything as meaningful to me as football."

"Instead of focusing on what you *can't* do, why don't you *do what you can?*"

William goes still, visibly digesting what I said.

"Take care of your girlfriend," I say. "Make yourself a man for your unborn child. Become the best possible you, a pillar of strength for your family. Gain self-esteem through their love and your hard work."

William nods, a determined scowl on his face.

Wow, he's really getting into this. "Right now, you are a caterpillar. You can blossom into a butterfly, or you can remain trapped in your self-deprecatory cocoon. What will you do?"

"I'm going to become a *butterfly!*" he says, his fists clenched against his wheels.

I nod, stifling a giggle, but then remember he can't see me anyway. *Are you sure William is the imbecile here?* "I'm going to give you one last chance, William, but know I'll be watching you. If I have to intervene again, next time I won't be so kind." My hand goes to the electronic shock watch in my pocket, and I rub my thumb across its face. "Promise me you'll do everything to protect your family, even if that means protecting them from yourself."

William scoffs, as if my previous sentence went without saying. "I promise. I'm outta here, mate! I'm gonna go apologize to Sarah, then I'm going to hit the library. Sure, I've got these guns"—he flexes his arms—"but my mind is my sword, and it needs to be sharpened if I want to help my family."

"You're learning, William. Before you go, give this to the boy I made you hit. I believe his name was Jimmy?" I throw an arcade ticket into his lap, one that can be traded in for delicacies such as tea and ice cream. "I thought he was an idiot for being around someone like you, but if you've blown up on them before and they're still your friends, they have more strength than I accounted for."

William nods solemnly. "It's true. Everyone's been so supportive of me, and I've just been drinking myself into oblivion. I'm going to achieve redemption, and you can bet on it!"

I find myself skeptical. "It won't be so easy, you know."

"If I focus on the people I love, it will be." He looks at the ceiling. "Thanks for giving me a second chance. You won't regret it."

I turn around and open the door for him. When I turn back around, I have to fight off a gasp. He's made perfect eye contact with me. I step out of his path, my arms crossed with satisfaction as I watch him roll down the hall.

That went surprisingly well.

I look at my hands, remembering the shield I'd accidently created when Will was about to hit me. Maybe there is more to my powers than I initially thought?

My stomach rumbles again, and all thoughts concerning my metahuman biology diminish. I hurry to the cafeteria, but at the door's entrance stands the Queen, in all of her beauty and elegance. She looks up when she hears my footsteps.

"Minerva, I know you're around here somewhere. We need to talk."

Chapter 5

AH RIP APART th' eagle's heart wit' mah hands an' shove th' squishy organ in mah mouth. Ah chew ravenously, an' th' thick, juicy blood an' veins slidin' 'tween mah teeth gives me th' strength tah take anotha bite. It's th' single mos' delicious thing Ah've eva tasted. Every mouthful fills mah stomach an' makes mah body all warm. By th' time Ah'm finished wit' mah meal, Ah'm tinglin' wit' relief.

"Lucio, that wuz th' mos' amazin'..."

Mah smile dies an' mah vision blurs. *No! Ah ain't gonna cry!* Ah wipe away th' tears, but seein' as though Ah'mma dumbass, blood gets in there. Then Ah try an' wipe th' blood out, but like Ah said, Ah'mma dumbass, so Ah only get mo' blood in.

"What am Ah even doin?"

Ah clench mah sticky fists tahgetha, mah jagged, filthy fingernails stabbin' intah mah palms.

Ah need tah find sum Chosen, but where should Ah even start searchin'? All Ah see in frontah me is a massive barren orange wasteland. Ah turn 'round. Way out in th' distance, Ah can barely make out the delipidated London Eye, half-submerged in th' dirt an' castin' twisted shadows 'cross th' sand.

Where haven't we searched? Ah close mah eyes an' think.

Lucio said a week ago that he wanted tah revisit th' museum. Said we mightah missed a few supplies there th' last time we went, seein' as though we'd been chased out by th' Feral 'fore we could get much done. Ah had passed by there earlier this mornin', but a couple o' scavengers were already there. They had guns, an' Ah didn', so Ah wuzn't gonna mess wit' 'em. Assumin' they're still there, Ah guess Ah could use mah bow tah defend mahself. Hell, maybe Ah could find sumthin' they missed, an' maybe getta clue on th' whereabouts o' th' Chosen.

Sure, why not? Where th' fuck else am Ah gonna go?

Ah start mah journey through th' destroyed city, climbin' ova wreckage on occasion. Man, it used tah be so pretty here. Ah could neva get enough o' seein' all th' gorgeous lights on th' elegant buildins' at night. Way back in th' deep southern asshole o' Texas, as Pa called it, Ah wuz used tah quiet nights on th' farm wit' mah family. Now don' get me wrong, every now an' again we'd go out 'round town an' see a movie or sumthin', but we mostly kept tah ourselves.

Pa didn' like us leavin' our reservation much, see. Told us mos' Americans didn' take too kindly towards our folk. But on our vacation here in London, he let us go whereva we wanted. *It blew mah mind* that there were so many things tah see an' do that *didn'* involve physical labor. Sure, Ah missed harvestin' th' crop an' makin' mah own food aftah a hard's day o' work, but havin' others cook fer me while Ah did nuthin' wuz its own typah treat.

Come tah think o' it, Ah dunno if it wuz good luck or bad luck that th' aliens invaded while we were here. Fer all Ah know Texas is an even *worse* place than London. Ah guess it don' mattah. Either way, mah entire family is still dead.

Ah reach th' natural history museum, a huge brown building wit' lotsah busted windows. On opposite ends o' th' rooftop lies miniature twin towers wit' a UK flag stuck right 'tween th' two. Th' flag flaps in th' wind as Ah jog up th' long set o' sandy stairs tah th' broken-down set o' doors.

"Don' mind if Ah do..." Ah say as Ah let myself in.

Ah decide tah head towards th' dinosaurs. They were always Lucio's favorite. Ah pass by th' statue o' Charles Darwin an almos' smile. Sum jokester had spray painted a big black dick on his shiny white forehead.

Ah approach th' destroyed statue o' a T-Rex. Scavengers have stolen th' bones, probably hopin' tah use 'em as weapons or fashion 'em intah materials. Ah put mah hand on th' small podium in frontah th' exhibit an' close mah eyes.

Lucio jumps up an' down like a rabbit as he drags me towards th' ultimate dinosaur's exoskeleton. Th' darned thing is so huge Ah gotta crane mah neck up jus' tah get a good look at it.

"Didcha know that th' T-Rex's bite mightah contained almos' five thousand pounds o' force," he asks excitedly.

"Nope."

"Didcha know that th' female T-Rex's were bigger than th' male ones?"

"Nope."

"Didcha know that they had 'round two hundred bones, roughly th' same amount o' bones *we* have?"

"Nope."

"Consarn it, sis, are ya even listenin' tah me?"

"Ee*nope!*" Ah scoop him up an' rub mah knuckle intah his thick skull. "That'll teach ya not tah try an' educate this here hick!"

"Argh, stop it!"

Ah'm smilin' tah myself, but th' distinctive *clip-clap* o' loud footsteps takes me outta mah memories an' throws me back intah reality.

Ah duck behin' th' podium, crouchin' 'mongst th' destroyed bones. Mah heart is goin' a *thump thump thump* as Ah draw mah bow an' notch an arrow.

Ah miss th' ol' days, when ya could talk tah strangahs without bein' 'fraid o' 'em slittin' ya throat when ya turn yer back tah 'em.

There's this squeakin' noise not too far away from th' podium, followed by a thud. "Get up, Jamie! They're comin—"

Th' sound o' molten hot lead bein' ejected at ova a thousand miles an hour echoes through th' room twice. Mah grip on mah bow tightens, but Ah make sure not tah move an inch. Mah heart is beatin' so damn loud Ah'm half-'fraid Ah'll give myself away. "Nice shots, Zack," th' same deep, feminine voice Ah'd heard this mornin' says.

Mah face flushes wit' rage. Th' hot, wicked emotion chases mah fear away like a dog chasin' a cat uppa tree. Zack wuz th' bastard who took mah backpack this mornin'. If it weren't fer him, Lucio might be...

"We lost three Chosen to that burnt bitch because of my poor marksmanship," th' monster named Zack says. "I'm not going to let any other survivor catch us off guard."

"Good for you, but I'm still pissed she got away."

"Who cares? We got her shit. She was pretty damn thin... she probably already died from starvation."

"Yeah, but I feel kinda bad," th' bubbly voice says. "I'd hate for her to suffer. We could have at least made it quick, right?"

Ah'm clenchin' mah bow so hard it nearly bursts intah splinters. Ah whisper tah myself ova an' ova again, "Ah can't attack yet, Ah *can't* attack yet."

"The Queen didn't choose her like she chose *us*," Zack says. "There's no way that brownie was born here. Who gives a shit about her?"

"We could at least have *some* human decency," th' bubbly voice argues.

"Get that bullshit 'I'm a good person' shit out of here, Grace," th' deep feminine voice growls. "Whether they die slow or not, we're still killing these people for supplies we don't even need."

... *What?*

"You said shit twice," Grace says flatly. "Besides, that's not true. We can't beat the Feral. Not alone. Who knows how long we'll be underground? We need all the resources we can get."

"At the expense of others, eh?" Zack asks. "Just admit it, you don't give a damn about the people we kill. All you're doing is putting yourself on moral high ground to make yourself feel better. The truth is, you're just as sick and twisted as we are. I bet you enjoy the thrill of the hunt more than we do, you fucking freak."

Grace grunts, but doesn't say anythin'.

Ah hear 'em shufflin' 'bout, probably ransackin' th' people they jus' killed.

"Aw, these brats don't even have anything useful," Zack says. "Waste of bullets."

"Waste of life..." Grace grumbles unner her breath.

Y'know, Ah think Ah hate Grace. Ah think Ah'll kill her first.

"No," th' deep voiced woman says. "We'll burn their bodies. Less food for the Feral."

"Roger," th' otha two say.

Ah peek mah head 'round th' corner. As 'xpected, there's only three o' 'em, all wearin' gas masks an' strapped wit' armor that wuzn't there this mornin'. So it's three people wit' firearms versus one woman armed wit' a bow, sum throwin' knives, an' th' almighty element o' surprise.

Ah like these odds.

Mah eyes scan th' room as Ah start plannin' mah attack. Ah need sumthin' tah distract 'em wit' first. Ah find a light bulb in frontah 'em, one off tah their left. Ah hurl a knife at it. Th' sound o' explodin' glass makes th' little piggies jump. They whip their heads towards th' sound, an' while they're distracted, Ah sneak ova tah a nearby podium, one off tah their right side. Then Ah raise mah bow, notch an arrow, an' fire. Ah'm already dartin' tah a podium in frontah 'em when th' arrow bursts through th' back o' Grace's head.

Th' remainin' Chosen swing 'round tah where Ah wuz a secon' ago, gaspin' in fear an' exposin' jus' enough flesh. Ah hurl a knife intah Deep Voice's throat, right 'tween her armor an' gas mask.

She collapses tah th' side like a cow without hooves. Blood gushes from her wound an' splatters all ova Zack's gas mask. He tries tah wipe off his faceplate, but Ah'm already in frontah him. Ah grab his shoulders, drop tah a squat, an' spring upwards, crackin' mah knee intah his chin. Th' worm lets go o' his gun an' collapses tah his knees, arms drooped. Ah snatch up his gun an' aim it at his forehead.

"Yer gonna show me where ya live, Mistah Zack."

"Not happening," he tries tah say bravely, but he's cowerin' away from th' nozzle.

Ah *smack* th' gun against his temple. He falls ova tah th' side, catchin' his fall tah th' floor by bracin' th' ground wit' his right hand. Ah smile, steady mah grip, then blow his pinkie finger clean off. Th' ensuin' *bang* makes mah ears ring sumthin' fierce as Zack falls ova, howlin' in agony. It... it feels like mah heart's dancin'. "Squirm lil' piggy, squirm!"

"*Argh!*" Blood splutters from his finger stump an' his entire body trembles wit' shock. He bursts intah a dazed, desperate sprint tryin' tah escape, an' it's so adorable Ah can't help but laugh.

Ah rip out mah lasso, twirl it 'bove mah head, an' toss it ova him. When it falls tah his ankles, Ah yank it backwards. Th' sound o' Zack's head crackin' on th' cold, hard floor echoes through th' entire museum. He groans in agony as a thick red puddle drizzles ontah th' floor unnerneath him.

Ah pull up his shoulders, makin' him get tah his knees. Behin' th' remnants o' his gas mask issa pudgy clean shaven bald white guy wit' muddy brown eyes an' a tight, swollen red face.

"If you're going to kill me, just do it," he says. "Don't waste my fucking ti—"

Ah kick him full in th' face, imitatin' a soccer—Ah'm sorry, a *football* player takin' th' winnin' goal. His gas mask shatters, sendin' orange glass flyin', an' he collapses inna twisted jumble o' limbs.

Ah take out mah knife. "Didn' Ah tell ya you were gonna show me where ya live?" Ah stomp on his left wrist, then yank up his right hand an' jam th' knife intah his pinky's hole. Ah dig th' knife in an' twist it 'bout as Zack explodes in agony, stompin' his feet against th' floor. His scream reaches an unholy apex while Ah smile wit' glee. His pain sounds like a chorus o' angels.

Ya hear that, Lucio?

This is fer you.

Chapter 6

*T*he Queen, in a lovely dark purple shirt with an all-black jumper dress over top, struts vaguely towards me. The power of her presence makes me take a few steps backwards, and the sound of my cowering retreat is enough for her to home in on my person even without seeing me. She seizes my wrist. I'm so surprised by the hardness in her springtime eyes that I become visible. Why is she acting so serious?

"You are aware that you missed school *and* a meeting this morning, correct?"

My worry dissipates like vapor. "I am," I say with a smile.

The Queen rolls her eyes and pulls me along down the hall. "What did I miss out on this time?" I ask. "Did you and the knights finally decide what wallpaper we're going to use to decorate the halls this winter? I'd personally recommend the one with the Christmas trees. It'll get people in the festive mood early."

"Very funny, Minerva," the Queen says dryly, even though she's fighting a smile. "But this is serious. Come. I think you'll need to sit down."

She drags me to her chambers. She's acting *quite* solemn this afternoon. What could they have discussed at the meeting?

We approach her chambers. I open the door for her, and then bow my head. "After you, my lady," I say.

The Queen's stiff upper lip falters and she graces me with a small smile. "Thank you, my dear."

The smile reminds me that while I have grown much taller than her over the years, she would always feel bigger than the world to me.

I enter the room after her, relishing in the texture of the soft purple carpet and basking in the warmth of her yellow walls, which are covered in arts-and-crafts projects made by children, pictures of previous Queens and Prime Ministers, and a massive map of the London underground littered with sticky notes.

She lets go of my wrist. I'd much prefer it if she had held my hand, but any contact with my Queen is a supreme delight.

"Please, sit," she says. "I'll make us a spot of tea."

I oblige and sit at the desk in front of the map. There's already two empty cups on the desk. I turn the seat around so I can watch her work, resisting the urge to fiddle my thumbs or brush my hair or floss my teeth or—

Is it getting hot in here or am I just parched? I use my hand as a fan and go to sip my tea. *Ugh, I am an idiot.* The cup is *empty.* I put down the empty cup and shake my head.

My oh my. I'd been alone with the Queen in her chambers before, but I never fail to get nervous. What if something actually happens this time? What if she and I...

My heart punches my insides and I roll my eyes, trying to ignore how hot my face is.

She's the Queen. She's not going to do anything with her hideous monster knight.

But the heart wants what it wants, and I can't get over how magnificent her posture is, how every movement of hers is deliberate and precise, how her blonde French braid gently sways in the light...

The unmistakable sound of liquid gushing into a cup snaps me out of my trance.

"My dear, you mustn't stare. It is *most* unbecoming of you."

It takes effort not to become invisible. "Ahem, yes... quite."

I lift the steaming cup to my lips and sip the sweet honey chamomile tea. *Too hot.* As I return the cup to the table, my jittery hand sloshes tea onto my knee. I wince at the burn but manage to keep my expression serene as I ask, "What is it you would like to talk to me about?"

The Queen gently pats my burned knee, sending an icy lightning bolt rebounding up my thigh. "Minerva, you of all people know how dangerous the Feral are."

I find myself touching my scarred face. "Obviously," I say, much more aggressively than I intended to.

The Queen purses her lips, and the only thing keeping me from staring at them for longer is the heaviness of her words. "When the Feral first invaded, I had the entire kingdom's finest scientists converge at a facility under Edinburgh. They vowed to discover the Feral's weakness within a year's time. That year has since passed."

"Have you tried to contact them via radio?"

"I'm not *four*, Minerva."

I resist the urge to smack my lips.

"We need to figure out what makes the Feral tick and how to stop them as soon as possible. The other knights and I met up this morning to figure out who is best suited to travel to the Surface, reach

Edinburgh, and uncover the truth behind the Feral once and for all."

"And you all chose me."

The Queen nods. "Yes. The other knights have powers suited for offence or defense. You, my dear, are a rarity, with powers suited for stealth and our success. If anyone can go on this journey and come back alive, it's you. Will you accept this quest?"

I look into my Queen's eyes, and within them I see a Feral raking its claws across my face. Those monsters destroyed my society, killed my family, and *made me ugly*. The Surface and the Ignored frightened me, but the idea of obliterating the wretched beasts responsible for all this with my own two hands gives me the strength to nod my head.

"Excellent. You'll be provided with a motorcycle and two weeks' worth of supplies. That should be more than enough for the trip to the lab and back."

If I want to survive, I have to be confident. If I pretend to be a brave hero, I *will* be a brave hero. "It'll be easy."

The Queen shakes her head. "I appreciate the bravado, but let us not fool ourselves. It *will not be* easy."

"I'm a knight. We cannot be defeated in combat."

"You do not know as much as you think you know."

"What? Have you been keeping secrets from me?"

"You think you're the only one who knows how vital confidence can be? Sometimes we must keep secrets, and this one of those times."

"So what then? One of our knights was defeated?"

"Correct."

"Who? How? When?"

"It was Sir Tyrone, about a month ago. He was traveling the Surface with the Bell Brothers, looking for supplies in the metro stations, when he came across two Indian teenagers. He still can't tell me the full story, but I bet if it weren't for his powers, he would have died too."

The Bell Brothers were Tyrone's only friends. *No wonder he's been so depressed lately.* "How could you cover this up?"

The Queen takes a long sip of tea, evidently choosing her words carefully. "It's quite easy to control information if you're the only source the public has to it. All my citizens know is that I sent the Bell Brothers on a 'secret mission' last month." She takes another long sip. "Do *not* glower at your Queen, young lady. I'll have you know that their family will receive word that they died for Her Majesty within due time."

But not until it's convenient for you to reveal the truth, hmm? "Are you going to cover up my death too if I don't make it back?"

"You'll make it back. I wouldn't be sending you if I didn't have the upmost confidence you'd survive. No knights have died under my command, and that's the truth."

That has more to do with our competence then yours, my lady. I bite my lip, not wanting to be chastised for backtalk.

"I just want you to know that there are many things out there that might surprise you," she says. "Be confident, but realize there's a lot out there we haven't seen. Keep your guard up."

"Well, I'm sure having another knight or Chosen squadron up there with me would help tremendously. Who will be accompanying me?"

"No one. You'll be all on your own up there."

The mask falls off. I swallow dry spit. "Why must I be alone?"

"This is a solo mission, and for good reason. You can turn invisible, and with your perfume on, you will be *completely* invisible to the Feral. Adding more people to your scent is dangerous. The more people you have with you, the more likely you'll be spotted by the scavengers on the Surface. The Feral's weakness *must* be discovered if we are to have a future. An entire nation's survival now rests on your shoulders. Do not let her down."

The words sink in like a wounded animal being consumed by quicksand. "When do I leave?"

"You have three days. We will spend that time re-iterating your survival training. I *do* hope you've been reading your material and practicing your basic cooking skills like you promised."

The world has gone to hell outside, my dear. Who cares about education? "Ahem... yes, quite."

The Queen sighs, walks to her closet, and pulls out a tin of beans. "I want you to cook this for me."

I walk confidently to her and grab the tin. I dig my fingernails into the side of the top, but I can't get the bloody thing open. "Um, how do I open it?"

The Queen smacks her forehead.

Chapter 7

AH SHOVE TH' knife further intah Zack's left eye socket, movin' slower thana sloth wakin' up fer brunch. "This is th' *last* time Ah'm askin' ya: Are ya positive th' Chosen are holed up at Camden Town Hall?"

Zack screams as Ah twist in th' knife jus' a wee bit mo'.

"Ah'm sorry, Ah didn' catch that."

"Argh!"

"Silly me. There's a knife stuck in yer eye! Ah didn' notice." Ah rip out th' blade. A red geyser bursts from his split-open socket. Th' blood splashes 'cross mah face an' runs down mah cheeks. Ah smile as Zack shrieks like a man on fire. Th' unfathomable agony on his face makes me feel alive. He can't even move—his arms an' legs limbs are bound wit' mah rope tah an empty exhibit podium that used tah hold th' statue o' a Microraptor. Ah've got th' bastard hogged up tighter thana sasuage inna pancake, but he keeps thrashin', an' in his panic he cracks th' back o' his head against th' pillar. Ah stifle a laugh as he lurches forward—but 'fore he can hit th' floor mah ropes hug him tight, forcin' him upright. He stands there fer a minute wit' his head hung 'fore Ah grab him by th' shoulder an' slam him backwards.

His fully ruptured eyeball stains th' right side o' his face wit' thick crimson tears. "Please, stop. I have a family!"

You're beautiful, sis.

"Ah don' got time fer tears an' such," Ah growl. "Ah had a family too, but ya killed him."

Cripplin' sadness courses through mah vains, but 'fore Ah'm sucked intah despair, Ah draw mah leg back an' stomp on his face, grindin' his head against th' expired exhibit.

"Now Ah heard an engine earlier," Ah lie. "Where didcha park yer ve-hicle?"

"I..." he rasps, "don't have a *vehicle*."

"Don' ya lie again, Mistah Zack. Ya mustah gotten that fancy shmancy armor from sumwhere aftah y'all ambushed me this mornin'. An' Ah doubt that sumwhere is close enough fer ya tah have gotten there by foot. That armor is 'bout as shiny as spiderweb, Ah know ya didn' jus' take that from anotha survivor."

Ah put mah foot down as Zack looks away, suckin' his teeth. "We found the armor at an abandoned police station on our way here."

"So ya jus' happened tah come 'cross three sets o' fresh armor, didcha? No mo' lies." Ah clasp mah right hand 'round his sticky, sweaty neck an' start squeezin' th' life outta him. His face goes red an' he starts strugglin', but itsa lost cause an' he's gotta know it. He grits his teeth, then his lips contort an' he spits me full in th' mouth. Ah swipe mah tongue at th' glob o' spit, enwrap it in mah own ball o' saliva, an' then spit th' metallic tastin' mess right back at his face. He flinches back in disgust, eyebrows scrunched tahgetha.

Ah stroke his bald head wit' a tender touch, smearin' red everywhere. "Don'cha want this tah stop?" Ah coo.

"Motorcycle... parked it in the exit stairwell. Door's hidden behind a dirt curtain."

Ah hold out mah hand in frontah Zack's face. "Keys."

Tears slide down his chin as he tries burstin' through mah ropes. *"I'll kill you, bitch!"*

Ah chuckle. "OK, OK. Which pockets are th' keys in?"

Zack stops strugglin', but his jaw is set harder than graphene.

His noncompliance ain't amusin' no mo'. "Ah done asked you a question, now."

"It's... it's in my left pocket," he spits.

Ah swiftly kick him 'cross th' face, slice open th' ropes 'round his legs an' reach intah his right pocket tah yank out th' keys.

Zack's single eye is aflame. "Don't scratch Her!"

Guess even a psychopath needs a hobby otha than killin' people. Ah toss th' keys up 'fore catchin' 'em. "Don' you worry now, Ah'mma good driver." Ah raise mah knife an' point it towards his right eye. "If yer lyin'..."

Zack tries tah wail, but anotha kick tah th' rib cuts him off.

"Y'know, Ah jus' can't trust ya. Yer gonna haftah come wit' me tah yer hideout." Ah'm pretty good at tellin' whether on not sumone is lyin', an' Ah'm pretty sure Zack ain't, but Ah ain't feelin' too confident in mah lie detectin' skills at th' moment. Th' emotional weight of Lucio's death might be throwing off that logic-based ability. Besides, it wouldn't hurt tah have a hostage wit' me in th' likely scenario that things go south.

"No."

Ah laugh. "Ah didn' say ya had much o' a choice in th' mattah, did Ah? Look here, Ah'mma go get that cycle. Ah would tell ya not tah move, but sumhow Ah don' think thas' necessary, yeah?" Ah cackle an' slap mah knee. "Whewee, Ah kill mahself sumtimes. Mistah Zack, sit tight, ya hear? Be back in two seconds." Ah jog towards th' entrance o' th' museum.

"Y'know thas' mathematically impossible, right?"

"Shut up, Lucio!" Ah turn 'round tah rustle his hair, but no one's there.

Ah break intah a sprint, thinkin' that if Ah run hard enough mah despair won't catch up.

Ah reach th' exit stairwell near th' main entrance an' descend tah th' lower level. Th' sun greets me wit' an' intense glare as it hangs in th' desolate gray horizon. Ah cover mah eyes, then get off th' flight o' stairs. Ah turn tah mah right an' see a dim corridor 'tween stairwells. Bingo.

Ah start walkin' down th' corridor. Th' sun laughs at mah back, burnin' mah neck an' givin' me a melted shadow. Ah stare at th' blank, hazy silhouette that is me, then follow mahself intah th' darkness. Wit' every step Ah take, mah shadow gets smaller an' smaller. Ah squint intah th' abyss, but when a gust o' hot wind pours intah th' corridor, Ah can jus' make out traces o' cloth flutterin'. By th' time Ah reabsorb mah shadow, Ah can make out th' dirt curtain hangin' ova th' dusty wall. It's taped down, but Ah pull at it 'till it rips away. Th' thick brown cloth hits th' ground wit' a whump, an' in it's place lies a metallic steel door. Ah rip it open, smellin' th' remnants o' what had tah have once been a supply closet.

Two motorcycles are hidden here. One has a muted gray coat wit' curly dark pink stripes, an' th' otha is a sea o' black wit' splashes o' blood red. Its ape hangers are painted tah look like bones, an' th' engine has a picture o' a buncha skeleton-warriors. There's a gleamy shine tah th' machine that jus' gets mah nether regions all tingly. Th' bike is sleek, dangerous an' sexy, an' Ah know it wuz Zack's baby.

An' now it's all mine!

On tahppah th' awesum purple seat is a helmet. Ah grab it tah 'spect it closah. Th' side is decorated wit' crazy red an' orange flames, an' on th' back are two bloody swords—one vertical an' th' otha horizontal—comin' tahgetha tah make a cross symbol. Ah draw mah head back an' spit on th' helmet's visor wit' a satisfyin' *puh*. Sum elbow grease wipes off mah saliva inna jiffy an' when Ah'm finished, th' helmet's gleamin' right alongside th' cycle.

Ah put on mah new headgear an' look up th' long stairwell. Ah snort. Ah can see why they decided tah leave th' cycles down here. Guess Ah'll go up there, grab Zack, then hoist him up on this arousin' piece o' machinery.

Wearin' th' helmet, Ah walk back up th' long set o' steps an' intah th' dinosaur corridor where Zack is restrained—or *wuz* restrained.

Mah ropes are in tatters at th' feet o' th' pillar.

Ah whip 'round, but he's nowhere tah be seen. How did he escape, an' where could he have gone?

Ah draw mah pistol an' carefully search th' exhibit fer trails o' blood, but th' stuff's *everywhere*, includin' in mah nose, on mah hands, an' all ova mah body. Th' quiet is shattered by Zack's unmistakable howl bellowin' intah mah ear. Ah jump back, aimin' mah gun... but no one's there. *OK, Ah'm trippin'*.

Ah back up, tryin' not tah freak out, but now Ah'm noticin' jus' how thick th' blood on mah arms is. It's almos' like a secon' skin. Ah close mah eyes, tryin' tah think o' Lucio, but all Ah see is th' blood squirtin' from Zack's eyeball.

"Whew wee," Ah chuckle. Th' world gets wobbly, an' a stabbin' pain pierces through mah stomach, makin' me drop tah mah knees. Meaty vomit bursts from mah lips, coatin' mah face inside th' helmet. *Ah can't breathe!*

Ah drop mah pistol an' throw off mah helmet wit' a yelp. Mah face is drippin' wit' sick. Th' smell ovapowers me, an' Ah fall tah mah knees, heavin' once, twice—urgh. A torrent o' half-digested eagle heart splashes ontah th' floor wit' an explosive *ca-plat.*

Ah kneel there, claspin' mah stomach. It feels like mah intestines are bound up inna tight knot. Ah'm 'boutah fall ova an' lie next tah th' pool o' sick when Ah hear shoes skiddin' 'cross floor tiles. Ah grab th' gun, look up an' trytah aim, but blood or sick or *sumthin'* gets in mah eye. Ah fire th' gun three times: *Bang! Bang! Bang!*

"Don' come any closah! Ah'll kill ya, Ah swear it!"

Mah ears are ringin', but Ah can hear th' footsteps gettin' further away. Looks like Ah scared th' bastard off. Ah can only hope one o' those bullets hit home.

Ah use th' back o' mah hands tah wipe off mah face, coatin' mah knuckles in red vomit an' blood. Ah walk ova tah Grace's corpse an' smear th' blood ontah th' back o' her rough armor. Heh. Guess Zack wuzn't th' only psychopath in th' museum.

Ah force mahself tah take a closah look at what Ah'd done. Ah use mah foot tah flip th' son o' a gun ova on her back. Th' arrow has pierced through th' back o' her skull, makin' her a unicorn wit' a drippin' red horn. Behin' her shattered gas mask are her wide open, shocked brown eyes. Lady didn' even know what hit her.

Ah look at Deep Voice. Th' knife that went intah her neck tore open her throat. Her jaw hangs limply tah one side, an' her hands are clasped 'round th' base o' th' blade. She'd spent her final moments tryin' tah get it out.

Mah mind flashes back tah when Ah blew off Zack's finger an' stabbed him in th' eye. Ah'd tortured a man, an' mah actions would scar his mind an' leave him half-blind fer th' rest o' his life, assumin' he wuzn't already dead.

Ah'd convinced mahself that Ah needed tah torture him fer info, but Zack's words tah Grace 'bout bein' honest wit' yerself haunts me like a bad memory. Ah'd enjoyed th' killin' an' torturin'.

Lucio told me tah find happiness. Is revenge really th' answer Ah'm lookin' fer?

Eeyup.

Th' moral conflict settled an' all, Ah figure Ah betta get th' hay outta here. That gunfire might draw survivors or th' Feral tah me. Ah open mah backpack, shove in th' vomit-soaked helmet, then hurry back tah th' cycle.

By th' time Ah'm back on th' road, th' sun is blocked by a sea o' gray clouds. Th' road is bumpy as all hell, an' Ah'm havin' a lil' trouble adjustin' tah th' speed o' th' ve-hicle. Back at home, Ma had a cute lil' cycle she'd use tah cruise 'round th' farm aftah chores were done. She taught me howtah ride it, but she neva let me go fast cuz she said it wuz too dangerous.

Now, goin' too slow would be too dangerous. Funny how that silly rule worked out. She wuz jus' tryin' tah protect me, an' now mah lack o' 'xperience at ridin' at high speeds could cost me mo' thana drunken night at a Las Vegas casino.

Th' barren wasteland blurs past mah vision like Ah'm ridin' a cocaine-snortin' horse. Ah'm 'fraid Ah'll hit a rock, go flyin' an' bust mah head open. Ah hope Ah'm at least goin' th' right way. Didn' have much time tah study th' map 'fore headin' out.

Th' closah Ah get tah th' buildins on th' horizon, th' mo' Ah feel that sumthin' ain't right. But everything seems normal. Too normal?

Then Ah notice th' changes. Th' jagged, cracked road Ah'm drivin' on is smootha now. Th' buildins' ain't completely trashed, an' there ain't rotten skeletons litterin' th' street.

Ah mus' be enterin' th' Chosen's territory. Ah've gotta be even mo' careful from now on.

When Ah see this huge steel-framed stone buildin' standin' a bit taller than th' others... Ah know thas' gotta be Town Hall. Ah look 'round fer a good place tah park an' hide mah shiny new ve-hicle, but as mah head turns Ah see an arrow flyin' straight towards me. Ah lean tah th' side right as th' arrow whizzes *jus'* by mah ear. Ah swerve from side tah side. *Gotta regain control!* Once Ah've regained mah sense o' balance, Ah look up tah see a waterfall o' arrow's rainin' on me from th' rooftops.

Ah swerve one-eighty degrees an' stomp on th' gas pedal. Th' beast unnerneath me roars like a lion, an' th' ensuin' burst o' speed is so great mah heart almos' falls through mah ass.

Th' arrows behin' me hit th' ground so hard Ah can hear *pings* even as Ah'm zoomin' away. It's rainin' steel. "Shit! Shit! Shit!"

Ah tell mahself tah calm down, but Ah *can't*. Ah'm picturin' an arrow goin' through th' back o' mah skull, jus' like how Ah did Grace.

Don' look back. Ya can't look back!

Ah'm blazin' down th' highway so fast th' spotted white lines on th' road turn intah a single line. Aftah thirty seconds or a minute or an hour, Ah realize Ah've *gotta* be outta their range by now. Ah want tah wipe th' sweat off mah brow, but that'll haftah wait.

If Ah can't reach th' Chosen's hideout, Ah can't execute mah plan, an' can't have mah revenge. This entire aftahnoon wuz pointless. Sure, Ah took out th' ants that killed mah kin, but sumone else's brother is gonna be killed by those bastards if Ah don' take out th' Queen.

Th' giant orange ball in th' sky starts tah drop, tauntin' me wit' its dyin' light. It's gettin' cold an' worse yet, hard tah see. If a single Feral caught me out in th' dark... Ah've gotta find sum shelter, *now*.

Ah drive on down th' road, hopin' every bump won't be mah last. Ah can't glance back tah see if th' Chosen are chasin' me, but it don' even mattah. Ah'm gonna go where no one else will dare.

Ah have a lil' trouble findin' out where tah go without mah map, but Ah eventually roll up tah th' House o' Sinners, an infamous abandoned church. Th' buildin' used tah be all white an' sparkly, but now people have tagged it wit' demonic graffiti. On one side o' th' buildin', men wit' horns an' blood-red skin drink crimson wine 'round a poker table, only difference is they're bettin' wit' eyeballs insteadah chips. Painted on th' large cross on tahppah th' buildin' is an image o' a crucified Jeezus Christ. A bullet has gone through his thorny crown, makin' trails o' smoke wisp 'bove his corpse.

Th' place has always freaked me out. 'Cordin' tah th' legend told 'mongst survivors, literally dozens o' Chosen came tahgetha here tah throw a crazy party, knowin' full well they would attract th' attention o' th' Feral. Th' resultin' carnage wuz enough tah paint th' walls red.

Lucio an' Ah had hid here on th' odd occasion we'd wander too far away from th' metro stations in our daily quests fer grub an' supplies. An' here Ah am again, 'xcept this time Ah'll be spendin' th' night all alone.

Ah open th' door an' wheel mah cycle intah th' church. It's quiet, dark, an' smells like rotten cotton, but Ah already know where tah go. Ah hide th' cycle flat on th' ground 'tween rows o' seats an' walk tah th' nursery. Ah open th' door, walk intah th' pitch-black room an' close th' door wit' mah foot.

Ah stumble towards th' nearest bed an' collapse ontah it. Th' bed here is much softah than th' mattress Ah'm used to, only problem bein' that all th' dried blood soaked intah it can make ya itchy sumtimes. But Ah'd rathah deal wit' blood than bugs any day.

As mah head sinks intah th' bed, Ah consider reachin' intah mah backpack tah nibble on sum eagle wing, but mah stomach squirms in response. Ah pat mah tummy an' rub it wit' a wince. Aftah throwin' up th' proud beast's heart, Ah guess Ah don' got much o' an appetite.

Ah toss an' turn, cradlin' myself. Ah've neva felt so cold, figuratively an' literally. If Lucio an' Ah eva found ourselves trapped on th' Surface at night durin' a supply raid, we'd cuddle up tah keep each otha warm. Now that he's gone, am Ah even gonna last th' night? It's... it's hopeless. He told me tah find happiness, but happiness is a resource even scarcer than food. What am Ah 'sposed tah do?

Ah bite mah bottom lip an' slam mah eyes shut, tryin' tah keep th' tears in. *If mah angel's still watchin' ova me, Ah can't let him see me cry.*

Ah lie awake fer what has tah be hours. Tah think it went from chilly tah downright freezin' so soon. A full body chill goes through me, an' mah breath comes out as fog. *Ah wish it wuz mornin' already. At least then Ah could read mah books.* Ah trytah think o' th' grand adventures in mah stories, how mah heroes always succeeded in th' end. *Surely Ah'm th' hero o' mah own story, an' mah success is right 'round th' corner?*

But that don' make no sense. *Lucio wuz th' hero o' his own story too, an' that didn' help him one bit.*

Why would God do this?

Ah purse mah frozen lips tahgetha, shakin' mah head furiously. Images come tah mah head: Lucio smilin', Grace wit' th' arrow through her head, Deep Voice's torn open throat, Zack's eyeball explodin'—

Ah clutch mah head. *Ah haftah stop these images. Ah haftah stop 'em right now!* Ah grab mah gun—

Creeeeeeeeeekkk.

Mah heart does a triple front-flip.

Don' move. Don' move an' they won't see ya! Ah yank th' nozzle away from mah temple an' aim it at th' door. "Don' make me kill ya, strangah," Ah whisper. *Ugh, would mah heart stop beatin' so fast?*

Th' footsteps come closah.

Ah leap tah mah feet, drawin' mah gun. "Get outta here or Ah'll blow a hole through yer head!"

Th' door bursts open. Ah pull th' trigga twice, but no one's there. *Th' hell?*

Mah ears are ringin' from th' shots, but Ah hear sumthin' rollin' on th' floor. Sumthin' taps against mah foot.

Oh shit! Ah trytah cover mah eyes, but it's too late. A bright light slams through mah eyeballs, blindin' me. Mah pistol slips from mah hands an' Ah stumble backwards, fallin' back ontah th' bed. Ah hit th' mattress, but use th' momentum tah fling mahself back tah mah feet. 'Fore Ah can even swing, cold steel is pressin' right up against mah forehead.

Chapter 8

I run out of the kitchen coughing and sputtering, letting a massive cloud of smoke enter the theatre room. I rest my back against the nearest wall with a sigh. No one ever told me how much work cooking was!

"Minerva, get back in here," Sarah says, walking out of the kitchen in a flowery apron, her hair tied up in a neat bun. "You think you can survive on the Surface without knowing how to cook a *can of beans?*"

No. "Yes, actually!"

"You're impossible." She shakes her head and turns to storm off.

"Ah, wait!" I grab her wrist. "My apologies, Sarah. I'm just stressed. I cannot be-*lieve* I'm going to be out there in only three days."

She walks back into the kitchen, dragging me along with her. "You never listened to my warnings, and now it's coming back to bite you on the bum. I've been telling you this whole year that you'd have to go back up there sometime."

"I just didn't expect that sometime to be happening this soon." I take in deep breaths. "How will I possibly stay groomed? I won't even be able to shower up there. The only thing I'll be able to do is... *floss!*"

Sarah slams a gigantic white chef's hat onto my head. "Let's just focus on keeping you alive, yes?" She tosses another can of beans at me, which I catch. "Let's try this again."

I successfully operate the tin opener, a procedure that took me over twenty minutes to get the hang of earlier. The tin opens with a satisfying *click*. The smell of beans makes my stomach wiggle. Drat, I haven't eaten since yesterday. "So… William visit you this afternoon?"

Sarah's proud smile at seeing my cooking skills take a half-step from non-existent towards basic competence disappears. "He did. He told me an angel had convinced him to stop drinking."

I don't bother stifling my chuckle as I pour the beans into a cooking pot. "Oh?"

Sarah sighs. "Minerva, you can't go around making people religious based off of lies and half-truths."

"Isn't that what pastors do?" I place the pot on top of the stove and turn on the heat. I glance at her, and the look in her eyes is enough to make me stand at attention. "Oh now don't give me that look, Sarah. You know I'm just being facetious."

"I *told* you I didn't want you to intervene."

"What would you have done if I didn't? He was just getting worse."

"I don't know, and I don't care. You shouldn't have intervened. You should have respected my wishes—"

I wave her off. "It's far too late for that, dear. So, what does Sir William intend to do now that he's been saved by the Holy Spirit?"

Her glare intensifies like a beam of concentrated sunlight. "He said he's going to start his spiritual journey in the library. He's starting with the Bible and wants to branch off into fiction."

I wasn't aware the Bible didn't count under the fiction category. "Excellent. I'd be glad to recommend him some titles—"

"What makes you think you have the right to turn my boyfriend into something he's not?"

I sniff the air for a moment, a foul scent invading my nostrils. What was that smell? I shake my head in a futile attempt to get rid of the stench, then say, "I needed to give him a plausible explanation as to why an invisible being was toying with him, and an angel was the best thing I could come up with. Honestly, dear, I thought this would make you happy!"

Sarah grabs her cross and presses it against her chest. "Faith is not blind, Minerva. Tricking him isn't the right way to show him the way of God. He has to see it for himself."

"How long would that have taken? Listen, there is no need to be upset. It is not my fault that some people lack the empathy necessary to be a civilized human being. Religion, on the other hand, has all-mighty deities that will punish them for their actions in the afterlife, ensuring that believers follow moral guidelines they otherwise wouldn't. That's what makes it such a useful tool in dealing with imbeci—"

Sarah flashes forward, hand drawn back. A shimmering purple triangle materializes in front of my face right as she swings. Her open hand hits it with a *whump*. She bounces back from recoil, palm smoking from impact.

I unsuccessfully fight the urge to giggle. "Careful, sweetie, you might get yourself hurt." I can feel my powers getting stronger. Maybe I can survive this journey to the Surface after all. My powers make me untouchable, after all.

I hear a high-pitched whine from behind me. Sarah ignores it and spits, "I hate you."

A rusty nail goes through my heart. I try to summon a barrier around my ears, but no supernatural ability can protect me from the destructive power of words.

"You always complain that no one wants to be around you because your scars scare them off," she says, "but you're wrong. No one cares about your scars; the reason nobody wants to be around you is that smug attitude. You may know everything about history and psychology and all that, but the fact that we're having this conversation proves you know nothing about how humans feel. You can't even tell when you're making your only friend upset." She turns her back to me, storms towards the exit, then looks back and hisses with venom, "I hope you never come back from the Surface."

"Sarah, wait!" I shout, but she's already left me alone in the room with a shattered heart. She's gone... Behind me, the whining gets even louder. I spin around, irate. "What is that horrid noise!"

The cooking pot is shaking, a column of smoke sneaking through the lid. I turn off the heat and remove the top, only for a thick black cloud to slam right into my face. I jerk backwards, flailing my hands as the burnt fumes sting my nostrils.

I make a run to the fire extinguisher, grab the heavy red can, and whirl around to blast the pot's interior with sodium bicarbonate. Oh, confound it all. This is the third can of beans I've burned today.

Ugh... I hadn't realized how rude I was being to Sarah. I have to make things right with her. I throw away the smoldering pot. Survival training will have to come later. I must find William.

I check the library and then the gym, but he's not in either. He must have decided to call it an early night. Suddenly I find myself standing outside his door, paralyzed.

Were my earlier shenanigans really alright? I feel like I've stooped to the Queen's level, hiding the truth for my own agenda. I can't let this hypocrisy go unchecked.

The words "I hate you." echo in my head. I try to drown them out by knocking on the door.

No answer. I wait a minute, then knock again. Still no answer. Hm. I turn the knob, and, to my shock, the door is unlocked.

"William? It's Minerva. I'm coming in, OK?"

I step inside his chambers and examine his room. Posters of familiar-looking football stars plaster his walls while trophies with bronze, silver, and golden footballs rest on his nightstand. Some Chosen scavengers must've helped him accumulate this impressive collection over the past year.

Poor William. His lifelong passion was ripped away from him. No wonder he started drinking. Not that his tragedy excuses what he did to Sarah.

An intense gurgling sound from what must be the bathroom makes me jump. For a moment I think William is simply having digestive issues, but then the gurgling turns into gagging. I run to the source of the noise, barging through his bathroom door.

My foot hits the floor with a splash. I look down. My shoe is submerged in lumpy brown vomit.

I almost scream, but I manage to keep my composure. I'm standing in a trail of sick that leads to the toilet, where William has his head down the bowl.

At the wheels of his wheelchair is an ocean of half-empty alcohol bottles. He lets out a strangled cough that turns into gurgling.

He's choking! I wheel his chair backwards, get in front of him then lift the muscle-bound slob out of his chair. Holding him up, I twist him to face the toilet then perform the Heimlich maneuver. He sputters and coughs, then hacks out a thick wad of brown mush that splashes against the rim of the toilet.

I drop him back into his seat. "Yuck!"

He slides back into his chair like a slug, sighing deeply. When he looks up, his hazy eyes widen.

"M-Minerva! What are you doing here? Did that angel send you again?"

"Ah, about that..."

"You should have just let me die," he groans.

"And then what?" I ask through clenched teeth. "Who would take care of your child? What would happen to Sarah?"

"They'd be better off. I can't beat the booze. Even if I could—*hic!*—control my anger and not take it out on them... I'd just weigh them down. I'm worthless." He turns away from me, staring down the toilet bowl.

"You're worthless *because* you *choose* to be worthless. The only one stopping you from being the best you you can be is *you.* Stop running from your problems. Confront your fears, confront yourself, and you'll be one step closer to being the person you inspire to be."

"You make it sound—*hic!*—easy."

"That was never my intention. I—the angel told you it would be tough, and you didn't believe it. Not even eight hours have passed and you're already in this position. Look at yourself! Do you have even an *ounce* of restraint?"

William's shoulders tense. "You have any idea how hard it is to quit cold turkey? I got the shakes, bad. My heart was beating so fast... I felt like I was going to die unless I got a drink."

Oh my. "I didn't realize you were such a heavy drinker. My apologies. We should have some beta-blockers in the health wing that will help you fight the urge, and I'll have one of the doctors keep a look out for you too. William, I will do everything in my power to help you, but in the end your destiny is in your hands. If you don't fight harder, you'll never crawl out of that hole of misery you're in."

He clenches his arms. "I'm so scared."

"Of what?"

"I—*hic!*—dunno."

"I do," I lie. "You're afraid that even if you're strong enough to kick the alcohol, you still won't be strong enough to be a father."

"... Maybe."

"William, if you stay the way you are, you'll always have that convenient excuse for being a loser. 'Oh, I would have been a good father but I have an alcohol problem.' Do you really want to go down in history as *that* person?"

He turns to look at me, jaw loose. "Nooo."

"You intentionally cripple yourself with alcohol so that when you fail at life, you can blame the booze instead of your own incompetence. You're so busy protecting your ego that you lose sight of the only thing that can keep you alive during times like this."

"My—*hic!*—family and friends." His eyes brighten, like someone just plugged him into an outlet. "How did I forget? They're the source of my strength. That's how I can fight the booze!"

I purse my lips. We *just* went over this a few hours ago. Would this little pep talk help at all long-term? There was no way to be sure, but I had to try regardless. "Without them, you have nothing. Humans, Meta or otherwise, are social creatures at heart. Solitary confinement has been a punishment for thousands of years, and for good reason. There is nothing more painful than being alone." I lean back against the wall with crossed arms in a vain attempt to cover up the Jupiter sized hole in my heart. "I would know. If you don't get yourself together soon, you'll end up just like me."

"Like you? A knight who everyone looks up to? W-why wouldn't I want to be that?"

"That's not *me!*" I say, voice cracking. My cheeks burn, and I waft the air near my face to cool them, burning up. "Ahem. It's time you know the truth."

His eyes narrow. "What truth?"

I turn invisible right before his eyes. "There was no angel."

William nearly falls out of his chair and grabs ahold of his shower curtains for support. "I thought you didn't have powers!"

I reappear at the wall across the room. "Well, I do. I lied to you, by the way, about the angel thing. I wanted you to believe there would be a divine repercussion if you didn't behave yourself."

His face goes red as he rolls towards me, muscles bulging. "You... you tricked me! I told you *everything!*"

I calmly step back, wondering if I'll have to beat him into submission. "It was wrong of me! I'm sorry, but I just wanted to protect my best friend."

"I can't believe you did this! What gave you the right—" He flinches, then shakes his head and sighs. "No. I can't run away from me anymore. I—hic—know I needed to stop. But couldn't you have just told me the truth from the start?"

"Well, for one, I'm leaving for the Surface in three days, so that takes away any external incentive for you to behave. Secondly, I didn't know if you'd blame Sarah for my involvement and have another excuse to get violent with her. Thirdly, if you had known it was me from the start, you would have just told me to bugger off and we never would have had this heart to heart."

William crosses his arm, frowning deeply. "Fine, I get it. So why are you telling me the truth now?"

"Because Sarah found out, and she told me it wasn't right to trick you into believing."

"What?" William hiccups. "She's been trying to get me to go to Church with her for years, even before the invasion. I'm surprised it wasn't *her* idea to begin with."

"She said you needed to see the path to God for yourself."

His eyes widen with awe. "She did?"

"She did." I look at my feet. "Now she hates me for tricking you."

"... I'm sure she's just upset. I'll talk to her for you, yeah?"

Am I really being consoled by an abusive alcoholic? I shake my head. "It doesn't matter. I'm leaving, and then you two won't ever see me again."

"I—*hic*—wouldn't be so sure. You're a real pain in the ass, Minerva. You're... you're like a piece of gum stuck to the bottom of my shoe." He shakes his head with a small smile. "I can't seem to get rid of you. You'll make it back, even if it's just to spite me."

I can't let the boy who beat my Sarah make me smile. "Charming."

"That's what I'm here for." He hicks, then says, "Hey, let's get out of here and hang out somewhere that doesn't smell of piss, shit, and sick."

Drat.

I walk back into his living room, hearing his wheels grind against the floor tiles as he follows me. "It's been a long day. Why don't you take a seat? I'll put on an audio book and make us some tea." He rolls over to his kitchen and opens the pantry. "I should have just enough tea bags for the two of us."

He's willing to share the last of his tea with me? I almost blush. "Not to worry. A true lady is always prepared for a tea party. I will provide the beverages, and you shall provide the entertainment for the evening. Deal?"

"Deal."

I grab his kettle, fill it with water, then turn up the heat. I snag cups from his cabinet, place them on the counter, then toss in my favorite tea bags: Celestial Uprising.

William snorts. "You carry around tea bags everywhere you go? Where do you even keep them?"

I wink at him. "A lady must keep a few secrets."

William laughs as he rolls around his room and sets up a small grey battery powered stereo system. He ransacks his cabinet for CDs as I absentmindedly wonder how many batteries we have left. Then he says, "A year ago, I could have just connected my phone to Bluetooth speaker without even having to move. The things we took for granted..."

"Hey, William?"

"Hm?"

I turn to look at him. "Are you my friend?"

He gives me a lazy smile as he puts a CD into the system then closes the top. "Listen Minerva, you may have lied to me, tricked me into revealing my darkest secrets, barged into my chambers without my permission, and seen me at my lowest moment, but I've never seen anyone try so hard to help someone they hate."

"I don't *hate* you."

"Well, not now, obviously." His lazy smile dissipates, and the slur in his speech becomes almost unnoticeable. "But I know you used to. I've seen the way you look at Sarah. Bad enough seeing the girl you love date someone else, even worse seeing them date someone who's hurting them."

He pauses, looking at the floor. "I'm not a good person, and I'd wager I'm worth hating. If you'd chopped my balls off, well, I wouldn't have blamed you."

"I came somewhat close, you know."

"But you didn't do it. You talked things out with me, tried to make me a better person. That's more than I'd have done for you if I were in your position."

I grab the kettle and pour the steaming water into the cups. "If Sarah wouldn't give up on you, I couldn't either. She loves you."

William smiles. "Got the answer to your question now? Yeah, we're friends."

His words are molten steel, poured right into the hole in my heart. It doesn't quite fill the hole, but... it helps. It really does. I hand him his tea and melt into my seat. "I worry for you, dear. Will you be alright? Soon enough, I won't be around for these pep talks."

He inhales the tea's scent with a smile. "Don't worry, mate; I've got a secret weapon." He pushes the "play" button on the radio.

"In the beginning," the recorded voice says with an epic, booming tone, "God created the heaven and the earth. And the earth was without form, and void; and darkness was upon the face of the deep. And the Spirit of God moved upon the face of the waters. And God said, Let there be light: and there was light."

William leans back in his seat and takes a sip while I raise an eyebrow with a wary smile. *Faith is not blind, hmm?*

Chapter 9

TH' STRANGAH PRESSES th' pistol intah mah forehead, an' right when Ah think he's gonna pull th' trigga he reaches intah his pocket an' takes outta bright orange lighta. A flick o' th' thumb latah an' Ah realize he's a she: a middle-aged white lady wit' short, messy black hair inna ballet bun. She's wearin' a battered green hoodie an' torn-up black jeans.

She lowers th' gun. "I'm sorr—" she starts.

Ah slug her in th' chin, slam mah left forearm intah her throat, an' pin her against th' wall. Ah whip out mah knife an' press th' tip o' it against her stomach. "Gimme a reason why Ah shouldn't gut ya like a pig."

She holds up her hands, but she's lookin' at sumthin' ova mah shoulder. "I could have just blown your brains out, but I didn't."

Ah glance backwards tah make sure no one's 'round, then look at her razor sharp blue eyes. "Why didcha point th' gun at me in th' first place?"

She laughs like she's mo' embarrassed than afraid. "I apologize. My men and I were chasing a white Chosen who fled here. I thought you were her until I saw your skin color."

"Shoot, you don' like th' Chosen either?" Ah take mah forearm offah her throat. "Ah reckon that makes us friends."

"A wise decision, my young warrior," she says, rubbin' her neck. "Rest assured, you shall find me to be a powerful ally."

"Tah be sure, ya made a nice entrance wit' th' flashbang an' all... butcha don' seem all that powerful tah me."

"Oh? Reveal yourselves, my friends."

Ah raise an eyebrow. "Have ya gone hooey? This ain't no ninja film—"

Shadows burst intah th' room from th' door, th' windows an' even from th' flippin' ceilin' wit' a *whish*. Dozens o' silhouettes roll tah attention then give th' woman a powerful salute wit' a "Ma'am!"

Th' woman says, "A light, please."

A lit torch gives birth tah a bright orange glow. Ah'm surrounded by a buncha people, way mo' people than Ah've seen in one place inna while. Ah start sweatin' sumthin' fierce, but not cuz o' th' new company. Thanks tah th' light, Ah can see jus' how terrible th' room looks. It looks fifty times worse than what Ah'd done tah th' Chosen at th' museum. Th' blood splatters are so thick that th' white walled floor an' wall is coated wit' dark red . If th' Feral were drawn tah th' noise an' th' smell o' all th' fresh blood, there'd be anotha massacre, an' this time Ah'd be a victim. Ah had tah get outta here, Ah had tah—

"Ah, madame," a deep voice says above me.

Ah look up, an' there's a one-armed black guy 'bout ten stories tall. He's smilin' wit' pearly whites so shiny it's like sumone's holdin' a flashlight in his mouth. Normally Ah'd be afraid o' sumone so big managin' tah sneak up on me, but those big an' gentle hazel eyes put me at ease.

"Zere is no need to be afraid," he says, nudgin' me on th' arm. "Ze Queen merely has a flair for ze dramatics, no?"

Th' Queen? She don' look like Queen Amity. Hell, if this lady wuz Queen Amity, she'd have blown mah head off th' moment she saw mah brown ass on her soil.

A petite Asian lady wit' brown eyes, a cut jawline, an' a bandage on her nose barges through th' crowd o' people an' glares up at th' tall man, "Do not tease Her Majesty, you burnt French fry!"

Th' man's smile gets brighter. "My vertically challenged companion, I would advise you to—how do ze kids say it?—check yourself before you vreck yourself, yes?" He pats th' lady on her head hard, makin' her knees quake.

Ah wonder if Ah'll haftah stop mah new friend from crackin' th' foolish gal open like an egg, but she jus' cracks up alongside everyone else in th' room 'xcept me.

These people... they almos' look like ordinary folk you'd see 'fore th' invasion. They're a diverse, banged-up bunch o' comrades playin' ninja fer their leader. Ah can tell they mean me no harm, an' it looks like they're strong enough tah fight any Feral that might come by. Wit' so many people in th' room, it ain't so cold no mo'. Fer th' first time since th' invasion, Ah feel *safe* 'round otha people. Now this jus' ain't natural.

"Look, this is nice an' all," Ah say, "but now Ah'm even mo' lost. Will sumone *please* tell me what in tarnation is goin' on here?"

"Haven't you realized it yet?" th' 'Queen' says. "We're members of the Ignored."

"Th' who?"

Th' woman's hands go flyin' backwards like a child touchin' a hot oven fer th' first time. "My word, have you been living under a rock?"

"Eh, sumthin' like that. Why do ya 'spose Ah haven't heard o' you fellers by now?"

"I'm not so sure; I just assumed word of our efforts would have rippled here by now. Oh well... maybe the survivors thought we'd vanished. How many survivors are left anyway? I can't help but wonder what the population count is like in dear old London. "

"Uh, far as Ah know, pretty much everyone but th' Chosen are dead. There are lil' pockets o' survivors here an' there, butcha don' come 'cross folks often 'less ya go lookin' fer trouble."

"I see. It appears that my sister has really done a number on the place."

"Yer sister?"

"Queen Amity, ruler of the Chosen, my *beloved* sister," she says, voice drippin' in sarcasm. "I am Queen Adelia, leader of the Ignored, the organization that will crush the Chosen under our just boot."

"Yer sister?" Ah say again, th' gears in mah head turnin', turnin' an' turnin' 'till...

Click.

A balloon o' anger expands in mah chest, makin' mah breathin' heavy. "What is this? Whas' goin' on here?" Ah grab her by th' scruff o' her collar an' shake th' shit out o' her. "This siblin' rivalry o' yers cost me mah brother's life!" Hot tears spring tah mah eyes as everyone 'round me tries tah pull me offah her, but Adelia jus' shakes her head calmly an' no one moves.

"What happened to your brother?" she asks.

"He's dead. Your sister an' her men killed him."

Adelia stiffens at that, an' then hangs her head. "Let me go, please."

Ah've released her 'fore Ah even have time tah think 'bout it. Where'd mah anger go? Adelia drops tah one knee, then hangs her hand ova her heart. "Nina," she says all serious, lookin' up at me wit' shimmerin' blue eyes. "I'm sorry."

"Whaddya doin'? Get up." Ah grab her by th' elbow an' hoist her tah her feet. "No person should bow before anotha."

Adelia grabs her left arm's middle wit' her right hand, lookin' away wit' a sniffle. "You are correct. However, the fact that my incompetence has led to the death of yours and countless other people's families puts me in a position less than that of a person."

Ah put mah hand on her shoulder. "Stop th' self-contempt nonsense an' jus' tell me what happened. Why are ya fightin' yer sister?" Adelia sighs. "It's a long story, but I'll tell you, Ms...?"

"Mah name is Nina Eagleheart. Jus' call me Nina."

Adelia manages a small smile. "Very well, Nina. As the eldest, my sister was granted the throne from birth; however, within a few years of her rule, she faked her death to relinquish the crown."

Ah snort. "Why go through all that trouble? Sounds tah me like th' mos' convoluted way tah quit yer job."

Th' Ignored laugh, an' Adelia says, "The reason my sister was so desperate to leave her role was because the gap between the rich and the poor had become too large... she simply couldn't deal with the people's anger. When I became the Queen of England after she relinquished the crown, I too struggled connecting with the people. Because we were born into our position, people felt they had no reason to respect us. While we were learning how to sip tea properly, our citizens were struggling to put their children through school and pay the bills."

"Ah'm surprised yer willin' tah admit yer privilege. A lotta people back in Texas try an' pretend that everyone's born on equal footin'."

"Do not be mistaken. It took me quite awhile to see it. While I was striving to become a better leader, my sister went underground. She bought a new identity and worked her way up through politics to become a candidate for Prime Minister. I saw through her reconstructed face from the beginning, and while royalty is supposed to be above politics, my sister was truly the most qualified person for the position, so I elected her instead of the other candidates. Once she revealed her true identity to the public, the people were so in love with her they called her the Queen again. I tried to regain control over the nation, but my sister said that the people had spoken."

Ah spit outta th' shattered window. "Mustah sucked seein' people choose her ova you."

"Indeed. For a little while, my sister and I engaged in petite political squabbles, fighting over who controlled what. But when a metahuman with time-traveling powers turned up to warn us about the forthcoming alien invasion, my sister grew terrified and—"

"Wait."

"What is it?"

"Didcha jus' say a metahuman wit'—Y'know what? Why am Ah even surprised? We're dealin' wit' *aliens* here. O' course time travel is involved too." Ah shake mah head.

Adelia snorts. "My sister thought that due to our limited resources, it would be better to run and hide instead of helping me come up with a plan to fight the aliens. She decided to name citizens born here the Chosen and allow them live in underground colonies she'd built all over the country. If a citizen could not produce evidence that they were born here, they were not allowed inside the colony."

"Her logic issa load o' horseshit."

"Agreed. To make things worse, she decided to stock up all the country's resources inside the colonies, leaving non-citizens to die of starvation. I tried to fight her, but my efforts didn't accomplish anything. She had the will of the people, and as the eldest, she also had the right to the throne. She had all the power again, and I had nothing. I fled to Ireland to see what leverage I had there, but that's when the aliens invaded. After the ensuing nuclear blasts, I gathered up citizens who weren't Chosen and formed the Ignored. We began fighting the Chosen with the goal of reclaiming the country's resources and fairly distributing them amongst everyone. Will you join us?"

Ah think back tah what Ah'd done tah Zack an' th' otha Chosen this aftahnoon. Ah can't have done all that awful stuff fer nuthin'. Th' Chosen had tah be stopped. "Darn tootin'!"

Adelia holds out her hand. "Welcome to the Ignored, Nina." Ah give her a handshake mah pops wouldah been proud off. Adelia warm expression disintegrates intah a scowl. "I swear to you, your brother's death will not be in vain."

A blonde guy wit' a surfer hairstyle pumps his fist. "Sweet, a new member! Everyone, like, welcome Nina into the Ignored!"

Ah'm bombarded wit' handshakes, high fives, an' hugs as they welcome me intah their clique.

"Ah don' wanna hear no mo' o' this mushy business," Ah say, face burnin' an' chest warm. "Now y'all seem like a fine group an' all, but th' Chosen outnumber you a million tah one. First things first, we need mo' men."

Adelia laughs. "You underestimate us. These are merely my knights. We have plenty more soldiers making their way to London as we speak. We scout ahead to make sure the coast is clear before our companions follow behind us, risking a few for the sake of many."

"Why are you apart o' th' scoutin' party? If you die th' Ignored won't have a leader anymo'."

"Zat's vat ve've been trying to tell her for avhile now," th' black guy from earlier says, shakin' his head.

Adelia snorts. "How can I expect to lead my men if I don't stand alongside them?"

Seems tah me like this lady values honor ova logic. "If you say so. When do ya wanna attack?"

"That's yet to be determined. We know there's a Chosen colony in this area, but we haven't pinpointed its location."

"Y'know, Ah think Ah can help y'all wit' that."

"Wonderful. Now then, let's—"

Th' unmistakable sound o' a gunshot next door bursts our cherry atmosphere. Everyone goes straight intah battle mode, whippin' out weapons an' hurryin' towards th' exit. Ah let out an annoyed sigh an' draw mah pistol. Guess things couldn't be peaceful fer mo' than two seconds, huh?

"Everyone *relax*," an Ignored Ah can't see shouts. "Nobody's attacking us. While Queen Adelia was welcoming our new member, I found the Chosen we were chasing. She was hiding under the seats next door, and she killed herself before I could get my hands on her."

The Ignored all start calmin' down, sum o' us lookin' a bit flustered.

Adelia nods. "A wise decision on her part. Shame we missed out on interrogation, though." She hooks her arm 'round mine. "Come now, Nina. Let's get you cleaned up—you smell like fried shite."

<h1 style="text-align:center">Chapter 10</h1>

AFTAH A GHETTO but 'ppreciated shower from water bottles, we end up chillin' inside an abandoned gym. It's th' only place we could find that could hold *all* o' us. Even then, every half hour, a dozen mo' Ignored come inside, introducin' one anotha wit' grim smiles. Even aftah a year o' not bein' used th' gym still smells o' sweat an' desperate testosterone.

"So whas' th' deal wit' Amity," Ah ask Pete, th' big an' friendly French guy wit' one arm.

"You know her deal," Chinwei, th' petite Asian chick holdin' hands wit' Pete, says. "Her sister betrayed her and—"

"I'm afraid zat's not what ze fair lady meant vhen she asked, 'vhat's ze deal'. She's vondering if she can trust ze queen, and I assure you zat you most certainly can."

"Why should Ah?"

"I believe ze better question vould be, vhy *shouldn't* you," Pete says. "If she vanted to kill you, you vould be dead already."

"Why shouldn't Ah trust her? Her sister played a hand in killin' mah whole family! Thas' a pretty big reason tah be untrustworthy, don'cha think?" Tah be honest, Ah can't say that Ah don' trust Amity already. Ah know at th' very least she's not a bad person. But whether or not she's capable o' leadin' this assault is a whole other story.

"Mmm, I see why you'd be cautious," Chinwei says. "Alright, let me tell you a story. After the nuke, one run in with the Feral told me I wouldn't survive for long on the Surface alone. I tried to get into a Chosen colony, but they wouldn't let me in. I found a few friendly survivors, and we decided to stake out the colony. We hid at the entrance, waiting for someone to show up and ambush. The opposite happened. A flash bomb stunned us and they knocked us out soon after. I woke up to the sound of one of my comrades gagging. Two men had him pinned to the floor, raping him from both ends."

"Oh, God..." Ah say, feelin' ill.

Chinwei clasps her stomach lookin' sicker than a puppy wit' heartworms as she says, "I will never forget when one of them turned around and said that me and my friends were next. The rest of us were shaking from head to toe with no way to move. I struggled as hard as I could against my chains—then, my hands started vibrating so hard my shackles fell right through them."

"Yer a metahuman?"

"Yes, and this is my thrilling origin story," Chinwei says wit' a light chuckle. "I didn't know what the hell was going on, but I stumbled forward and drove my fist through the back of a rapist, literally. I screamed, he screamed, then my fist vibrated and his entire body exploded into bits. The buckshot of human flesh sent me tumbling backwards. I tripped on my shackles and hit the floor, sobbing in distortion. When I managed to wipe my eyes off with the little bit of dry skin I had, a Chosen had a shotgun aimed at my face. But before he could pull the trigger, a mace slammed into the guy's face," Chinwei exclaims, jumpin' at th' word 'slam' an' throwin' her arms out. Is she American too?

"I could see the mace dig into an eyeball, and with one strong yank, it was ripped from the socket! It was the most righteous thing I'd ever seen, and what made it even better was that the one who saved me was this little lady barely five feet off the ground, needing both arms to even swing."

"Hm," Ah say, "she sure *sounds* tough."

"You don't know the half of it, dude," Chinwei says, sharin' a quick smile wit' Pete. "After Queen Adelia saved me, we freed the other survivors, snuck into their food cabinet, grabbed as much as we could and got the hell out of there. The Queen led us to a safe place, where I got myself cleaned up. She'd been resting at the colony when she heard rumors that some foreigners were kidnapped by the guards. That's when she came to our rescue. She had no back-up and no real plan; she said she just couldn't let such injustice stand."

"That's pretty brave," Ah admit. "Stupid, but definitely brave."

"She told me her plans to stop Queen Amity, and her plans to form a rival organization called the Ignored. She asked me to join, and I said yes immediately."

"Voman, you sure love to run your mouth," Pete chuckles. "It is my turn to tell ze story, alright?"

"Hollup, Ah wanna know what happened tah th' fella who got raped. Is he still here? Can Ah talk tah him?" Fer what? So Ah can say, "Ah'm sorry you got raped"? Whas' goin' though mah head, a misguided case o' sympathy that'll jus' make him feel worse?

"Sorry Nina, but he killed himself a few weeks later." Mah heart takes a nosedive as she says, "He kept having these intense nightmares. He was always up in the middle of the night screaming, and then he'd spend the rest of the day apologizing even though no one ever got mad at him for it. One night, we heard a bang instead of a scream, and no one was surprised when we found his corpse with no head."

Ah ain't got nuthin' tah say tah that, so Ah jus' hang mah head. Fer one secon', Ah get so angry that th' world jus' goes black. But then Ah roll mah jaw, close my eyes, take a deep breath an' get scary calm. Ah'm gonna kill a lot o' Chosen tahmorrow anyway, so there's no reason tah get mad.

"Now zats a downer if I've ever heard one," Pete says.

"Hey, she asked what happened to him," Chinwei says, raisin' her hands up as if tah say, 'sue me', but her voice has gone all tight. Pete starts rubbin' her back, an' soon enough, Chinwei's rigid body structure relaxes.

"Let us talk about somezing a bit more cheerful. I vas actually accepted into a Chosen colony right avay."

"You tellin' me they aren't all racist assholes? Well, Ah'll be damned... maybe this attack ain't such a good idea aftah all."

"Ah, my impulsive friend, I vish zings vere zat simple. You see, zis colony vas one of ze few zat vas on ze Surface. Zey lead us into zis huge varehouse. Ze moment I valked inside, I knew I vas in trouble. In ze corner of ze building, many minorities vere in shackles. I vas knocked out before I could even react. I awoke in chains bleeding from my temple and terrified for my life. Rifles surrounded me from all sides. Zey told me zat I vas zere slave now, and if I didn't vant a bullet in me I'd better get to vork. I told zem zat ze shackles vere entirely unnecessary, zat all zey had to do vas ask for vhatever zey needed and I vould have helped regardless. Zey told me zat if my, ahem, 'monkey ass' spoke out of turn again, I'd lose a tooth."

"Bastards..." Ah hiss. "What did they even want yer help wit'?"

"I used zese massive muscles of mine to rip tiles from ze floor. Once ze dirt vas exposed, ve planted fruit and vegetables. I vas honored to help build a garden, but being a slave vas about as terrible as you'd imagine. Ze only zing I could do vas make ze best of my predicament. I made friends wiz ze ozer unpaid laborers, and ve decided to bide our time for ze next few days, looking for an opening to exploit.

"Living conditions vere avful. Ze only time ve veren't chained up vas during food or restroom breaks, and even zen ve had guns pointed at us. Ze concept of privacy didn't exist to zose monsters. Ve veren't even given plates or silverware, zey just tossed food on ze floor. Seeing as zough I am a chef and the personification of sophistication and class, I refused to eat at first. Of course, ve all know how hunger can make you do zings you normally vouldn't..."

Ah nod darkly. "What a load o' horse shit! There hadtah be sumone there that could help ya. Th' Chosen there weren't all slavers, were they?"

"No. But zey mostly pretended not to see us. Vasn't too hard—ve vere separated from everyone else. Early on, zis elderly gentleman tried to tell off ze slavers, but zey shot him dead before he could even get two sentences in. Everyone ignored us after zat... except for ze children. Late at night, zey'd spoon feed us soup and give us vater. As humiliating as it vas to have eight year old's vipe your face off after a meal, I have to admit zat zose little angles vere ze only zing keeping me from doing a suicidal charge at ze slavers. Zankfully, it vas only a few days before ze Queen came to our rescue."

Chinwei says, "The Queen had rescued us only a week or two before all of this happened. We were doing some recruiting in the area, and a new member mentioned that they'd heard some Chosen in the area were using minorities as slaves. The Queen would not let such injustice slide.

"Once we learned of the colony's location, the Queen infiltrated their warehouse immediately. Usually, they demanded identification from anyone trying to get in, but pretty white women seem to be an exception to the rule. As she waited for night to fall, the Queen told me that the few hours she spent there made for one of the worst experiences of her life."

"How th' hell can she say that when there were *slaves* right 'cross th' buildin' from her?"

"Zhat's ze zing, Nina. For zose few hours, she vitnessed ze vorst of humanity and dozens of people do absolutely nozing to stop it. Seeing her citizens act so dishonorably in ze face of fear devastated her. She told us zat she vould have raided ze place immediately if it veren't for ze fact she vould have lost men and put us all in danger. So she bid her time, even as it broke her soul to do so." He smirked. "Tell me zat's not a sign of a great leader."

"So she waited 'fore attackin'. Big deal," Ah say, though Ah dunno if Ah wouldah been able tah do th' same thing. "Don' mean Ah can trust her."

"Patience, ze story isn't over," Pete says as his smile grows wider. Did he see through mah not-lie? "Late zat night, Ze Queen approached us wiz no vords. She simply produced a key from her pocket and freed us from our chains, one by one. Ve vere at a loss for vords for ze longest time. Vhen she had freed us all, a single sentence broke ze spell of shock ve vere under: 'Let's get ze hell out of here!' I vas filled wiz so much enzusiasm I vanted to vhoop and yell, but common sense told me to stay quiet. Ve snuck out of ze varehouse and took in ze freshest breath of air for vhat felt like years."

"We parked right in front of the warehouse in a military jeep we'd nicked from the Chosen," Chinwei says. "I was on the fifty cal, pumped and ready for battle. But then Pete walked outside looking sexy as hell with those big, sweaty muscles and that tight, raggedy t-shirt full of holes and dirt—"

"I appreciate ze compliments, Chinwei," Pete says, "but perhaps you can leave ze steamy details for anozer time, yes?"

Ah give Pete a look-ova. Y'know, he *is* pretty handsum, so Ah can see why Chinwei would be happy tah see him. Ah gotta admit Ah'm jealous. Ah don' reckon Ah'll eva met a strong, smart, kind feller like him on Th' Surface. Chinwei got lucky.

"Fair enough," Chinwei says, throwin' an apologetic grin mah way. "Anyway, the slavers wouldn't let their precious 'property' be taken quite so easily. We were only a few minutes away from the warehouse when they started chasing us in their own car. They shot at us with pathetic aim. They had a clear shot at my head, and the best they could manage was this." She points tah a shallow scar that cuts a small line 'cross her cheek. "I made them pay anyway. I blew out their tires with the .50 cal the moment they were making a turn. Their car flipped a dozen times before exploding."

"Damn, this is sum action movie shit."

"Except her spectacular display of marksmanship had tremendous consequences," Pete says.

"True," Chinwei agrees. "After the explosion, a herd of Feral started chasing us."

"... How th' hell are y'all alive?"

"Two words: Ze Queen."

"I was the first to see the herd," Chinwei says. Funny, her eyes were livid when she described th' explosion, but now they're lookin' at th' floor. "Scariest sight I'll ever see, I'm sure."

"Ah don' doubt it. Hope Ah neva come 'cross one."

"As do I," Chinwei says. "I was so freaked out I started shooting the .50 cal. Like always, the bullets reflected right back at us, and this time it was *our* tire that got punctured. As we slowed down to a stop, a tall Feral ran to the head of the pack. It was at least seven feet tall with claws bigger than Pete's dick, which should speak for itself."

"... Really, Chinwei? Zat's ze best analogy you could come up wiz?" Pete sighs while Ah laugh so loud people 'round us startah look.

"It's the first thing that came to mind, Petey. Anyway, the thing had to be an Alpha Feral, the leader of the pack. He—she—they—whatever, grabbed a smaller Feral next to him and chunked him at me like a missile. I ducked under the tornado of teeth and claws then uppercut it through its chest," Chinwei says, punchin' th' air. "I was dislodging my arm from its body when another Feral leaped aboard. Before it could attack, a mace crushed its skull wide open!"

"Adelia savin' yer hide again, Ah take it?"

"That's *Queen* Adelia, and you got that right!" Chinwei chirps. "She helped me get my arm unstuck, and then we leapt from the car together, hit the floor with a roll and came up fighting."

"I joined ze fight as vell."

"How'd ya fight when you were unarmed?"

"I ripped off a Feral's arm and used ze claws as a makeshift sword."

"Whoa," Ah say.

"It vasn't very effective, zough. I scratched one on ze cheek, zen it kicked me right in ze chest. I hit ze floor avaiting death, but instead of slicing my zroat open it cut zrough my arm bit by bit. Zen it snapped ze vhole zing off." He twists from side tah side, makin' his empty right arm sleeve flutter.

Ah wince. "Why do ya think it didn' kill ya?"

"Oh, it vas going to, but I suppose it has seen me, ahem, *disarm* its comrade and vanted me to see vhat it felt like. Made me feel like a bit of a brute in retrospect. Makes me vonder if ze aliens aren't smarter zan ve give zem credit for."

Don' mean ya can't manipulate 'em, though.

"Vhezer or not it sliced off my arm to prove a point or just to take pleasure in my pain, it only gave me a few moments to shriek in agony before opening its mouth." He shudders, makin' Chinwei rub *his* back in circles. Seein' 'em reciprocate those gestures makes mah heart hurt. Ah'd neva been inna relationship before, but at least Ah'd always had mah family tah fall back on. Now they were all gone, an' Ah had no one.

"I do not hesitate to admit zat seeing all zose teeth up close and personal made me pee pee and poo poo my pants instantaneously."

"Hey, at least ya wouldah gave th' fella a bad aftah taste."

Chinwei makes a face while Pete erupts wit' a belly laugh. "It appears as zough you and ze Queen share a similar sense of humor. Speaking of her, before ze Feral could eat me alive its body vas engulfed in flames, courtesy of a Molotov cocktail zrown by her. She pulled me away before ze flames could eat me alive," Pete says, gettin' all chocked up. "I'd just lost my arm. Blood vas *pouring* out of me. I told her she vas vasting her time, zat she should save herself. But she didn't give up on me, just told me to shut up. She dragged a two-hundred-and-forty-pound man away from danger wiz one hand, lobbing grenades overhead wiz ze ozer. She risked *everyzing* to save a total stranger."

"Alright, Ah trust her," Ah say, an' Ah mean it. Ah done neva heard o' sumone so brave. Looks like she's come a long way from strugglin' tah connect wit' her people. Her citizens respected her an' then sum. Seems tah me she earned it.

"Story isn't even over yet," Chinwei says, snugglin' back intah Pete's side.

"Ze grenades exploded wiz astounding force—body pieces vent everywhere—some Feral, some human."

"Damn. She mustah been mighty desperate."

"We all were," Chinwei says. "We lost a quarter of our men within seconds. The grenades were a last minute gambit, but even with the collateral damage, it was the only way we got out of there alive."

"Don' tell me a couple o' grenades were enough tah take out an entire herd," Ah say, crossin' mah arms.

"No. Zis next part is a little hard to believe, but, please, bear wiz us."

"C'mon Pete, supahpowers an' aliens are a part o' our daily life, what could be hard tah believe nowadays?"

Pete an' Chinwei share a look.

"OK, vell," Pete says, "Vould you believe me if I told you zat ze only reason ve survived is because ze Queen negotiated wi—"

"Bahahaha," Ah cry, laughin' so hard tears come outta mah eyes. "What, yer tellin' me she brewed a cup o' tea fer th' Alpha Feral, an' one sip latah he decides tah leave y'all alone? Ha!"

"No," Chinwei says, "She grabbed a box of grenades and threatened to blow us all to hell if he didn't leave us be."

"What th—" *She's actually serious!* "An' it *worked?* Wha—how—ya tellin' me th' Feral speak English or sumthin'?"

"No, but zey do have common sense. Little green orbs go 'boom', and too many of zem at once, 'mega-boom'. Ze Alpha Feral almost charged, but zen it looked to both sides. Seeing all ze bodies of his clan must have had *some* effect on it."

Ah take a big sigh, rubbin' mah throbbin' temples. "So yer tellin' me a herd o' *hungry aliens* left y'all alone jus' cuz ya threatened tah blow 'em up?"

"Not completely," Chinwei says. "The Alpha Feral clicked and croaked to its underlings, and they all sat cross legged. The Alpha valked forward slowly, glowering at each of us." She starts rubbin' her palms on her pants, leavin' behin' a slick trail o' sweat. "I only looked up after it passed me by, and nobody dared to move as it approached the Queen."

Even though Ah know everything turned out OK in th' story cuz they lived tah tell it, Ah still find mah heart rate increasin'. Crazy how a good story can do that tah ya, even one wit' a foregone conclusion.

"I vas still bleeding out, using ze Queen's feet as a pillow. Vhen I saw ze Alpha coming closer, I zought I vas hallucinating. Zen it grabbed my ankle and started to drag me away." He smiled a smile that wuzn't a smile. "After you shit yourself, you really don't zink zings can get much vorse, but zey did. But before I could have a heart attack Ze Queen flashed forward and *slapped ze Alpha in ze face.*"

"Wha-what?" Ah stand up. "*What?*"

"Are you *mad*," sumone Ah can't see yells. "Shut up, some of us are trying to get some sleep!"

Ah take a deep breath an' sit back down, face toasty.

"It's true," Chinwei says, gigglin'.

"Ze Alpha must have been just as surprised as ve vere because it let go of me and just stood zere for ze longest time vhile ze Queen said somezing along ze lines of..." Pete trails off 'fore clearin' his throat, then, speakin' inna shitty impression o' her, says, "You take him, and I'll blow us *all* to hell. I know your people are hungry, so you can take our dead. But I vill *not* allow you to take anozer one of my citizens away from me. Are ve clear?"

Pete returns tah his normal voice while Chinwei shakes her head. "Even wiz countless gestures, ze Alpha evidently didn't learn to speak English in a matter of seconds, so ze Queen made a point of having everyone vho could move drag ze corpses of our dead to ze herd. It was ze closest zing to a peace offering ve could manage."

"Having to drag the corpses of people I had grown to consider family over the course of a few weeks was miserable," Chinwei says, "but it's not like we had a choice."

"Ze Alpha growled at Ze Queen, and a huge drop of drool splashed next to my face. Ze Queen just raised ze box of grenades, so ze Alpha valked away. But before it left, it surprised me one last time. It clicked and clacked at its followers, and zey all rose simultaneously. Zen, zey picked up ze bloody pieces of zeir own before leaving us alone, backs all hunched over."

"Even though they killed my friends, as they dragged the corpses of their own away from us, I couldn't help but feel sorry for them."

"Feelin' sorry fer th' aliens who ruined our lives… yer sumthin' else, Chinwei."

Pete nods in agreement, holdin' her close. "Zat she is."

Ah get up, stretchin'. "Well it's been a pleasure talkin' tah y'all. Really. Haven't had a conversation wit' anyone who wuzn't named Lucio in quite awhile."

"Was that your brother's name?"

"Eeyup," Ah drawl, chest feelin' like Ah jus' bench pressed a bull.

"I'm sorry for your loss," she says, while Pete nods sympathetically in tandem.

"Ah 'ppreciate it. Lissen, if y'all are up fer it, Ah can tell y'all 'bout him latah tahnight."

"Absolutely," they say.

"Thanks, y'all," Ah say, shuttin' mah eyes real tight tah keep from cryin'. Guess Ah ain't so alone aftah all. "But first Ah wanna talk tah 'ze Queen'." Ah say, butcherin' Pete's French accent wit' mah southern drawl. Chinwei laughs as Ah ask, "Do y'all know where she is?"

"I saw her go into what used to be the manager's office," Chinwei points tah a closed door tah mah left. "Make sure you knock before going in!"

"Yes'm." Ah get up. "Thanks fer openin' up, both o' you. Mustah taken sum courage tah face them memories head on like that."

"You decided to go along wiz a group of total strangers after losing someone dear to you. You are ze one wiz courage, Nina."

Ah trytah shake their hands, but they get up an' wrap me in th' warmest hug Ah've had in years. Fer jus' a secon', jus' *one* secon', Ah let 'em hold me tight. Then Ah push 'em away wit' a grin. "All right now, les' not get too mushy here," Ah say, voice crackin' in spite o' mahself.

Th' couple smiles at me. "We'll be waiting for you when you come back."

Ah turn away from 'em, wipin' mah eyes as Ah head fer th' Queen's chambers. Ah watch otha members o' th' Ignored along th' way. They're all jokin' round, drinkin' tahgetha, playin' board games, readin' books aloud an' passin' it inna circle fer th' next person tah read. Y'know, Ah feel like comin' along wit' these folks wuz a great idea. Maybe one day, Ah'll be able tah call these people mah family.

Ah knock on th' door tah Adelia's chambers, surprised that mah heart's poundin'.

"I've been expecting you, Nina. Come inside, please."

"Pardon mah intrusion," Ah say 'fore headin' on in. Th' room is nearly empty, probably been scavenged an' stripped clean long ago. Adelia sits cross legged on th' floor, a small, scratched up wooden table in fronta her. "Please, sit down."

"Sure," Ah say, takin' a seat. On each end o' th' table are rose-scented candles, an' they smell damn good. "How'd y'know it wuz me?"

She chuckles. "Unfortunately, even with my quote, unquote, Royal Blood, I lack any foresight into the future, and it would have been *very* embarrassing if you turned out to be someone else. But my sister is responsible for a great deal of your misfortune, so it would make perfect sense for you to visit me. Did I sound mysterious and cool, even for a moment?"

"Ah'd say so," Ah say, smilin' at her. "Ya sure know howtah break th' ice."

"A worthy attribute for a leader, I believe. So, how can I help you? Perhaps I can alleviate your concerns in some way?"

"Pete an' Chinwei told me ya negotiated wit' th' Feral an' won. It amazes me thatcha managed tah pull that off."

"Believe me, you're not the only one."

"Why were ya willin' tah gamble wit' hungry aliens?"

"I didn't have much of a choice, Nina. We couldn't fight off that many, not at all once."

"Thas' not what Ah meant. Ya wouldn' let th' Alpha take Pete. Ya were willin' tah sacrifice everything an' everyone tah save sumone ya jus' met. Why?"

Queen Adelia closes her eyes an' takes a deep breath. "That was one of the hardest decisions of my life. It was an entirely selfish one, mind you, and it probably wasn't the right one, if there even *is* a right one. It's just... I couldn't let someone who was enslaved by my citizens be killed on the first day of his freedom. I couldn't save many of them, but I am glad I was at least able to save Pete."

"Ah really like that answer, but sumthin' tells me ya ain't bein' entirely truthful here."

She raises an eyebrow. "My my, you've got a remarkable bullshit detector. Very well, I'll tell you my philosophy. It's never won me any favor in the past, and many people have used it to call me old fashioned. But I've used it to guide every decision in which it was applicable. It goes like this: We all stand together, and we all fall together. My sister believes in the 'greater good' which allows her to let hundreds of people die for the sake of thousands on a daily basis with a clear conscience. She's willing to shut people out of colonies because we might run out of resources too fast, then we'd all starve to death.

"A fair point, granted, especially if the Feral are unbeatable and we'd have to live off of the country's resources for who knows how many years. But that doesn't excuse her actions one bit. We all stand together, and we all fall together. *No one* gets left behind or abandoned. You always do the right thing, saving as many comrades as you can, no matter the consequences. *That*, Nina, is my philosophy. Do you think me a fool?"

"Eeyup." Her smile dips a few centimeters. "Ah'd neva sacrifice everything fer sumone Ah jus' met. That said," Ah stretch out mah hand. "Ah'd gladly follow ya intah battle. Ah can't help but respect sumone wit' moral fiber as strong as yers."

She takes mah hand wit' both o' hers, her rough hands boastin' a soft grip that contrasts wit' mah hard one. "Ah've neva been fond o' political figures, a lotta 'em screwed ova mah people back home. 'Spose yer an exception tah that rule."

"I suppose my friends weren't exaggerating when they said you Texans have a firm grip. Ah, you are a Native American from Texas, correct?"

"Darn tootin'."

"It amuses me that you refer to the near complete genocide of your people as being merely 'screwed over'. That's a light way of putting it."

"It is what it is. I used tah get furious thinkin' about it, but no amount o' anger will change th' past. As fer improvin' things in the present, well, assumin' there's any semblance o' society in America aftah th' invasion, it seems tah me like there's too much old blood in th' government fer any ordinary person tah make a difference. Ah jus' don' see any amount o' protestin' stoppin' those in power from doin' whateva they want, even if achieving what they want comes at th' cost of people's lives or th' death o' th' planet itself."

"That's depressing," she says with a sigh and a frown. "It's like you've completely given up hope on change."

"Back home, maybe. But people like you, Queen Adelia, make me want tah have faith again. I can tell you care about people, and it seems tah me like you've fully earned yer title. Ah wanna help ya stop yer sister in any way Ah can. She's torn apart mah family an' Ah'll do everything Ah can tah stop her from tearin' apart others. But whaddya plan tah do wit' her once we have her captured?" Ah kinda want her tah say we'll kill her, but at th' same time th' idea o' makin' her kill her own sister makes mah stomach flip.

"I... I'm not entirely sure. Regardless, I truly appreciate your support as well as your respect. That said, I was wondering if you had any ideas in attacking the colony tomorrow? I am sure the fortress is extremely well guarded, and I'd like to keep casualties on our side to an absolute minimum."

"Ah've gotta idea that'll work. Question is, are ya willin' tah follow through wit' it?"

Queen Adelia purses her lips, leanin' forward an' restin' her chin on th' back o' both her hands. "I'm listening."

Chapter 11

"**W**ake up, *Scarface*."

I grunt and sit up, protecting my eyes with my left hand. A demon with slime green eyes and snow-white hair and has turned my ceiling light onto its brightest setting. "What are you doing my chambers, Angel?"

She blocks my vision of the light bulb with her head, casting a shadow across her weasel face. "Sparring exercise. Report to the gym in five minutes."

"I wouldn't dream of it. Now get out of my room before I make you."

She sneers. "Someone's feeling brave today."

Out of bed. "Someone's feeling stupid today."

Her maw opens, and the sound of a dying animal slithers out of her throat. She whirls around, walks to my door and opens it. Then she flips me the sideways peace sign. "See you in *five*, Scarface." *slam!*

I clutch my only lover and am about to beat the living stuffing out of it, but manage to keep ahold of my composure like a true lady.

"Don't let that creature get under your skin. If she gets you upset, she wins." I set the pillow down and say this to myself over and over as I head to the shower, but when my eyes meet my reflection it's hard not to cry. "You're a knight." I take off my underwear, and then step into the shower. I turn the knob until I can no longer take the heat. "You're a knight."

Warmth is indeed a welcome distraction, but the word *Scarface* echoes around in my skull. I grab a bar of lavender soap and a gentle towel, and then get to scrubbing. *Not to worry, after you thrash them you can take as long of a shower as you want. Continue forward, Minerva! An old and unoriginal insult such as that can't stop you, especially when you'll be heading to the Surface in only two days.*

I exit shower jam tooth brush in mouth dry off with towel brush brush gurgle-spit put on purple and white jumpsuit grab blade of Justice electric shock watch purely on the hypothetical chance Queen will let me use it on Angel. I run out of the restroom... then I run back in, grab my floss and leave my chambers all together.

A true lady should always have the time to freshen herself up. This is so unfair. I look ugly enough with make-up on, even worse without it! I'm cutting the corner next to the gym when I slam into someone. My cotton stuffed head hits the floor. The stranger and I groan, sucking our teeth in pain. I'm tempted to stay there and moan, but an image of Angel makes me spring to my feet. I shake off the pain and brush myself off. "How clumsy of me! I'm sorry, dear." I hold out my hand to help the stranger up, but when the person looks up I gasp. "Sarah!"

I expect her to smack my hand away, but instead she takes it and I help her to her feet. She holds my hand with both of hers, making my face prickle. "Minerva, William told me what happened yesterday. I can't thank you enough for what you did for him. I'm so s—"

I put my index finger to her soft lips. "Don't you dare apologize. I was completely in the wrong. All those things I insinuated... I should have *never*—"

See you in five, Scarface.

"My *dearest* friend, my *sincerest* apologies, but the Queen called for an emergency training exercise and I really must be on my way. We shall make up later!"

"Aw. Well, when you're finished, come by the kitchen! I'm not losing my best friend because she couldn't cook a meal for herself!"

She slams me with a hug so warm I find myself teary eyed. "Thanks again."

I want to hug her back, but I am afraid of what I might do once my arms are around her. I settle for an awkward pat on the back. "No thanks necessary, dear. See you in a few hours."

She lets me go. "Bye!"

I run into the gym, an expansive room with wooden floors and blue walls. The Queen is sitting cross legged on the bleachers, wearing a long white skirt and a purple blouse. Three other knights are present in the center of the room, doing various warmups on a blue wrestling mat. Tyrone, a black man with low cut hair and warm hazel eyes, is doing push-ups. Mark, a spectacle bound warrior with spiky black hair, is stretching his legs. Angel is shadowboxing, fists in a blur of movement.

"Right on time, my dear." The Queen says with a smile of approval. My heart flutters. "Are you ready to begin?"

I give a small bow. "As always, my Queen." I stroll towards the other knights, winking at Angel when she catches my eye. She pounds her fist into her palm.

I step onto the mat with confidence. "Who shall taste my blade first?"

"Ah, you won't be using weapons today." The Queen says, studying my reaction. "And you'll be facing all three at once."

"Sounds reasonable," I say, setting down my weapon a few feet away from the mat. "Let us begin."

Angel whirls into action with a spin kick. I turn invisible and duck. The force of the hit blows my hair backwards. With Angel's intangibility powers, she could avoid any physical attack. When she expected it, at least.

"Show yourself, coward," she spits.

My left fist goes across Mark's face. He hits the mat like a kid eager to make a snow angel. I creep towards Tyrone, but his palm comes up. I turn away right before a bright flash fills the room with intense light. My eyes sting as little fireworks of pain explode in them.

I stumble backwards, trip, and sink into the rubber floor. Tyrone swings haymaker blows with grunts, hitting nothing but the air above my head. I stifle a chuckle, and then flip to my feet. I catch his arm in the middle of a punch, slip behind him, and then twist it into an unwieldy position. "Yield," I say loudly.

A crackle in my ears makes me smile and turn my head. Angel has her fist pressed against an inverted purple triangle. I'm no longer invisible, though. I suppose I cannot make barriers and remain invisible simultaneously, but it hardly matters.

Angel starts to say, "What the fu—", but I let go of Tyrone, spin, crouch and spring upwards, stabbing my knee into Angel's gut. She tries to gasp, but a swift elbow to the jaw cuts her off. Her shoulder hits the edge of the mat, making her head *thunk* on the wooden floor. She doesn't move.

Tyrone thrusts his palm at my face. I wave my hand, and a small, transparent purple barrier shimmers to existence and blocks the blow. He smiles.

I start to close my eyes, but it's too late. Intense light sears my retinas. I blindly roll to the side right as a train of momentum hurtles past me. I stay absolutely still, trying to locate Tyrone by sound.

Interesting... now we both can't see each other.

I shout, "Over here!"

"Do you expect me to run over there so you can trip me? I'm not stupid, Minerva."

I strain my ears, barley detecting the sound of Tyrone's footsteps. "No, but if you don't approach, you will lose the only advantage you have." I back off, staying on my tip toes.

Even though I can't see him, I imagine Tyrone shaking his head. He must know that I'm right. We start circling each other; at least I'm pretty sure we are. I can hear him, but I don't know how far away he is. This continues for twenty seconds before my vision starts coming back. He's maybe ten feet away, arms out and eyes closed. He's heading in the right direction, unfortunately for him.

I hunch my shoulders up like a cat arching its back, creeping towards my foe. Tyrone's eyebrows scrunch up, confused. He must know I'm getting closer, but he has no idea where. He holds his hands out like he's pushing an invisible wall. I shut my eyes before he can blind me then throw a punch. I feel him slap my punch aside, then—

I taste blood as my head flies sideways. My knees wobble from the weight of the punch, but I don't fall. I look up to see Tyrone thrusting his palm at my face. I close my eyes and feel a punch to my gut that lifts me off my feet, but this time I'm ready. I grab his arm, twist behind him, and then jerk his wrist upwards. A sharp cry slips from his lips. "Yield," I growl. "In a real fight, your arm's broken."

Tyrone grunts. "You're right. I lost."

I let him go. The Queen claps her hands together with a bright smile. "Well done, Minerva! I had no idea you could create force fields."

I wink at her, standing tall even though it feels like I've got a sack of rocks in my stomach. "I'm full of surprises."

She smiles and stands up a little straighter, her hands behind her back. "Tyrone, that was really clever using your powers to flash her through the force field. You were also the only combatant to go against Minerva, score a hit and maintain consciousness. Impressive work!"

I smile at him in agreement, but his face is stone. "Sure." He turns and walks towards the exit, nodding to the Queen as he makes his way towards the door.

I made a new friend for the first time in a year yesterday. Who's to say I can't make another one today? Tyrone is a quiet man, so I never really know what he is thinking. But what I do know is that he must be lonely after losing his only friends to those savage Indians. I'm going to talk to him! "Where are you going," I ask.

"Breakfast."

"May I join you?"

"...Uh, sure?"

"If you do not want my company, you merely have to say so."

"No, I..." He coughs. "I'd like that, actually."

"Onwards, then. To the cafeteria!"

He smiles and holds open the door for me. I start to follow him out when the Queen catches my eye. "Tyrone, Minerva will meet with you in the cafeteria. I must have a word with her for but a moment."

"OK." He leaves the room.

I approach the Queen. "Yes?"

"I do ask that you pull your punches next time," she says. "I don't know if you saw, but you elbowed Angel so hard her head hit the floor. She has a concussion."

"Yes, I did that on purpose."

"Excuse me?"

"... I said I did that on purpose."

"And may I ask why exactly you did that, Minerva Henswood?"

"S-she called me Scarface."

The Queen purses her lips, but her piercing gaze softens. "And you decided to take matters into your own hands instead of just telling me what happened? I could have *helped.*"

"No, you could not. This has been going on for awhile. She's smart enough to not act up when you're around. Besides, this is between me and her, not *you.* It is not like you can solve all of my problems for me. That would be a rather insulting proposition, no?"

... I can't believe Sarah forgave me.

"I see you aren't hesitating to take advantage of your short leave," The Queen says, pursing her lips.

I gasp melodramatically. "I wouldn't dream of it, my lady!"

She sighs again, but she's smiling now. "I haven't said what I'm about to say because I thought it would be obvious after all the time we've spent together. Minerva, you're my *friend.* I would crush the stars for you, dear. I care for you more than you will ever know. You're one of the only reasons I have to smile nowadays. Sending you to the Surface has been the hardest decision I've had to make in my life."

"Really?" I croak out, feeling like something's stuck in my throat.

"Really. I want nothing more than to avoid putting you in harms way, but you are truly the only one who can do this." She shakes her head. "I tell you all this because I want you to know you can talk to me about anything. Please don't let our professional relationship get in the way of our personal one. Now come here and give me a hug. I'm sure Tyrone is getting hungry."

I eagerly run into her arms and embrace her. She feels so warm and big even though she's smaller than me. I realize that I used to hug my mother like this. I almost feel like a little girl again in her arms. Was our relationship always so familial, and I just didn't notice because I was blinded by loneliness and infatuation?

After a moment of bliss, she pulls away. "Good luck with your *date.*"

I shake my head with a laugh. If only she knew... I start to exit the gym, then think better of it and turn around. "Can I ask you for a favor?"

"Anything."

"I recently found out Sarah's boyfriend William is an alcoholic. He could use some medication to help him fight the urge to drink."

She nods. "Understood. I will ask a doctor for assistance in this matter, and I will also keep a closer eye on our alcohol. I suppose I've been a bit too lax guarding our supply."

"Wonderful. Thank you, my Queen."

"The pleasure is all mine!"

I exit the gym, smiling all the while. It makes me so happy to hear that the Queen values me just as much as I value her. I must make sure I don't let her or the rest of England down!

I enter the cafeteria. Sitting at the table in front of the door is Tyrone, with two separate trays of biscuits and oatmeal. His meal remains untouched, even though his hand is at his stomach. "My my, you're quite the gentleman, aren't you?" I must be smiling hard because Tyrone looks like he's about to blush.

He grabs a spoon and gets to work on his oatmeal. "I just didn't want to start without you."

I tear open a warm, fluffy biscuit and spread on strawberry jam. "I appreciate it."

We're both silent for a few minutes, trying to regain our energy. Using superpowers always made us knights hungry!

I start to feel awkward when the entire meal has gone by and there's been no conversation. Did I make things weird by calling him a gentleman? I thought I was being nice.

Tyrone devours his last biscuit. He snatches up his orange juice, downs it, and places his now empty cup on the table with a lazy smile. He throws his head back and produces a mighty belch. "Ahem. Excuse me."

I laugh, relived.

When Tyrone raises an eyebrow, I tell him, "I was afraid I'd said something wrong."

"Why?"

"Because you were silent the whole meal. I thought you were mad at me or something."

"Meals are for eating, not conversation. Besides, if I didn't want to eat with you, why would I have waited at the entrance solely so you can see me when you walk in?"

"Good point."

"Why did the Queen make us jump you?"

Did he miss the meeting yesterday morning as well? Perhaps I am not the only slacker here! "I'm leaving for the Surface in two days. She probably wanted to teach me something along the lines of, 'You're going to encounter scenarios you can't predict. Always be prepared.'"

"Where are you going?"

"Edinburgh. The Queen wants me to figure out the Feral's weakness by obtaining some scientist's research."

"Hmph. That's a dangerous mission, even for you. Who's going with you?"

"No one. The Queen says more people would just attract the Feral to me." I take a deep breath, ignoring my pounding heart. "What do you think my chances are?"

"...I'm not sure. You're tough, but there are some people up there that may be even tougher. As for the Feral... I mean, if you can sneak past them, great, but fighting even one of them is really risky. And if there's a group of them... How long can you keep yourself invisible?"

"Quite awhile. But I do get tired eventually. I'm not so much worried about the Feral as of now; I've got some heavy perfume that will throw them off my scent. But you worry me when you say there are *people* up there who may be tougher than me."

He looks around for a bit, and then leans in, his palm covering half his face. He whispers, "Listen, the Bell Brothers aren't on a secret mission for the Queen. They're dead." I'm not entirely acting when I gasp at his words. He *trusts* me with classified information? But why? "We were, uh... scavenging the metro stations for supplies when we came across an Indian boy in a cowboy hat. He looked, I dunno, twelve or thirteen. The Bell Brothers charged him against my orders when they saw him holding a knife, trying to 'restrain' him. Then an arrow went through Harry's stomach."

My spoon slips from my fingertips and clatters to the floor.

"Barry fired his gun, but we couldn't see anyone in the dark. I told everyone to stop fighting and used my powers to light up the room. An Indian woman with these big, beautiful green eyes, bountiful freckles, straight black hair like silk dipped in ink and toned arms—"

"Really?"

"Ahem. She charged Barry, but Barry pointed his gun at the boy and told her to back off. Then she threw her tomahawk." He winces. "Barry's gun hit the floor along with the hand still holding it. I—I watched him scream as his knees slammed into the floor, blood squirting from his stump. I blinked, and the next thing I knew she was kicking me in the throat. By the time I could open my eyes, Barry's head was rolling across the floor."

Deep breaths darling, deep breaths.

"There was nothing I could do. This woman was just too fast. She asked if I was a threat, and I told her no. Then she told me to leave, and said that if any of other Chosen were to hurt her brother she would kill us all."

I purse my lips, my heart dropping in shame. I had referred to these Indian people as savages earlier, but the fact is that my people were the ones who instigated the conflict in the first place. I was being a racist idiot. I vow to make sure I don't assume things right off the bat in the future, then another thought comes to mind. The only reason why I'm going to the Surface is because I hate the Feral. My hatred fuels my courage to kill every last one of them. If my parents had been killed by people instead of the Feral, I would have directed all my hate towards them instead. And I most certainly would have killed everyone responsible.

Tyrone and I make eye contact in mutual fright. Who was this woman, and, if her brother dies at the hands of a Chosen, will she have the power to make her vengeful dreams a reality? As if God could sense our terror, the sound of a metallic baby shrieking in agony wails from above. Flashing red lights burst from the ceiling, making Tyrone and I jump up while everyone in the cafeteria screams and runs towards the emergency exits.

"Minerva," The Queen cries from the intercom, "report to my chambers at once! Tyrone, gather the other knights and get ready to defend our home."

I shake Tyrone's hand and shout, "Thanks for telling me what happened. That must have taken a lot of courage."

"No problem, mate. I needed to talk about it; I just needed someone who would listen."

We exchange smiles, nod, and go our separate ways.

After slipping through the panicked crowd I find myself in the Queen's chambers. She tosses me a backpack, which I catch and sling over my shoulder. "What's happening, my lady? Did you stub a nail?"

"This is no joke. Turn invisible and get out of here as fast as you can. I'm sorry, but it looks like you'll have to make the journey by foot."

I scoff. "And leave you and my friends behind?"

"I'm not asking you. Find a way to stop the Feral. Free us from the cages I trapped this great nation in." She clutches my wrist and she pulls me to her. A soft but warm pressure presses against my cheek. I almost fall to the floor in bliss, but the Queen keeps me upright with an embrace. "Stay safe, my child. I will miss you."

I hug her back so hard I lift her into the air. "I will miss you more. I will return, rest assured!"

The Queen squeezes out, "Go!"

I let her go with a wink then disappear. I want to pull my privacy trick, but there's no time. I leave her chambers and blaze through hallways until—what? A petite Asian woman covered in a bloody trench coat zips past me with a snicker.

"Hey!" I turn around to follow, wondering how this intruder got in, when I notice that she's leaving behind a literal trail of hacked off limbs. My insides clench together at the horrible sight. I turn back around, looking at where the trail began. Down the hall, right next to the doorway of the stairwell that leads to the Surface, lies my worst nightmare.

Something with a frog's skin and a lanky figure is crouched there; sniffing a curved nose at a cleaved off leg. Cold and heavy claws extend from its webbed hands. It's wide, snake-like yellow eyes sees me, and then narrows. It opens its mouth, revealing a long, massive bloody tongue and several rows of sharp teeth. The tongue shoots out of its mouth, just like when Father...

No!

I briskly step to the side. The pink spear impales empty space before I slice it in half. The Feral screeches so loud the shockwave blows me back a few feet. What's left of the tongue flops to the ground. Red blood oozes out of the open wound. The Feral gives out on an unearthly groan as blood pours from its mouth and paints the grass red. Then, it leaps into the air, drawing its awful claws backwards.

"Not this time!" Instead of backing up, I *step forward,* then slash open its right leg. It flops to the floor gyrating madly. Left claw swipe? I duck and slash upwards, slicing through its left leg. The Feral turns around and tries to hop away, but I get behind it and stab it through its stomach.

The Feral's vocal sack opens and fills with blood, then the bubble explodes. I summon a barrier to keep the splatter from drenching me—if other Feral smelled me, I would be a target.

I'm breathing heavy as I lurch the blade out of the beast's gut. It slithers to the floor as I ask, "How did you get in here?"

The door to the stairwell bursts open. One by one, dozens of Feral bounce into my home.

I scream, turn around, and run as fast as I can down the hall. A tongue almost wraps around my ankle, but I fling my hand back and block it with a barrier. I glance back when I hear a peculiar sound. Oh no. There's a large crack in the triangle. If that had been a direct hit, it would have shattered my only defense.

I can't hold them off. It's the end of the world. This can't be happening. "Run to the emergency exits!" I shout to everyone as I dart into a populated hallway. They shriek and run down the hall, but I had a head start. My chest burns with shame as I sprint past them. But if I were to die, who would stop the Feral?

A little red-haired girl running alongside me trips and falls. I screech to a stop, and then turn around to help her, but a sharp tongue has gone right through her chest. Her blue eyes go wide, and then her body zips backwards. She flies towards a Feral's wide open mouth all the way down the hall. I turn away before I hear the digestive process begin. This can't be happening.

When I reach the central hallway that connects to every area underground, I find a row of armored knights bracing themselves for battle. When I catch Tyrone's eye I stand by his side, raising my blade at the approaching enemy.

"To the death, comrade," I growl, tears burning my eyes.

"It would be an honor to fight alongside you, Minerva, but you've got to get out of here. Find a way to stop these beasts once and for all. We'll be fine."

"Bu—"

Angel, her head wrapped in white bandages, shoves me hard in the chest. She grips her sword and spits, "Get lost, Scarface!"

I bite my bottom lip as I run to the emergency stairwell on the other side of the complex. Queen Amity, Sarah, William, Tyrone, even you, Angel... I'm sorry I couldn't do more. Please, please be safe!

I open the door and begin my journey towards the Surface. Every time I take a step upwards my heart tries to leap into my mouth. Was I ready for this? Was I a coward for abandoning my friends? Would anyone survive?

I twist open the vault door on the ceiling blocking the underground facility from the Surface. Immediately, the air feels different, tainted. I climb out of my home and enter the brand-new world, a world I haven't seen for over a year.

I'm now standing in the middle of a musty old bedroom with wooden walls. The vault door has the same design as the floor, and the metallic wheel is hidden underneath a pile of scrap. No one would know there's an entrance into the facility without having insider knowledge. I leave it open in case anyone else from below needs to make a quick escape.

I open the door and walk outside. Seeing the wide-open grey sky makes me cry. Where'd all the color go? It feels stuffy and hot, like the summertime allergies from my youth have come back to haunt me. Heat waves distort my vision, ahead of which rests a destroyed children's park in the shadow of Camden Town Hall.

Basketball goals are sticking halfway out of the ground, football nets are rotten and decayed, and the slides look like melted ice cream. It's like a wave of death has swept over the world. All the grass is brown, there's no green *anywhere*. Earth, or rather, this part of it, is a dead piece of land, and it's not going to recover anytime soon. The clash between past and present shatters my brain and I remember my mum carrying me here after my face got sliced open.

Hah. That's funny. I can almost hear the motorcycle she rode right now...

Wait, what?

I walk down the street and look down the destroyed road.

"Bloody hell."

A red silhouette streaks towards me. To call what she was riding a motorcycle would be a disgrace to the elegance of her vehicle. It was a something the Grim Reaper would die to ride *once*. I recognized it instantly. Zack couldn't go five seconds without bragging to everyone about how much he loved it. He wouldn't let anyone touch his bike without dying for it first.

I run back to the entrance of the cabin, then turn around and stand my ground. My backpack hits the floor. I will not be intimidated. I am a knight. I am a knight!

The Killer screeches to a stop at the entrance of the park. She's a brown skinned woman with tattered blue jeans, a dusty orange jacket and a bloody white t-shirt underneath. A bow is strapped to her back. She steps off the motorcycle, not bothering to take off Zack's skull like helmet.

She grabs ahold of the black utility belt on her waist and adjusts it. So many weapons... "Figured you bastards had two ways outta that lair."

"... Did you lead the Feral here?"

"Eeyup."

"Who are you?"

"Jus' anotha one o' yer victims. Yer a Chosen, ain'tcha?"

"I'm the Queen's knight, *fool*." I draw my blade. It shines even in the dead sunlight. "I'm not asking again."

Her hand hovers over a pistol as a heat wave passes between us. For a second, her figure is distorted into a blurry haze and she looks like a demon from hell.

Can I make a barrier strong enough to reflect a bullet? I have to try!

The creature studies my reaction, then yanks out her tomahawk instead. "Ah'm th' gal who killed ya."

We charge. Her hand goes to her waist—a silver blur? I slip, turning invisible as I fall. Something sharp skims past my right ear.

"Knew there wuz sumthin' weird 'bout you." I stumble into dead bushes as the Killer skids to a stop, my heart pounding and ear throbbing. "Makes me no difference. Yer still gonna die."

She grabs her bow notches arrow then fires! The projectile flashes through the space I was a second ago. Sweat forms on my brow, but I keep still. One wrong move and...

The killer's bow turns slowly to the side before stopping to point right at me. *How?* "Gotcha!"

I dart to the side, dodging the arrow, then unsheathe my blade and charge her now visible. She rears her arms back and throws a storm of throwing knives. I deflect one after another with a few twists of my blade, but one of them slips by and rips across my thigh, drawing blood. The burning pain hurts, but not enough to stop my retaliation swing.

My sword bursts into the side of her helmet with a powerful screech. Glass goes flying as the side of her visor shatters and she spirals to the floor. She lands with an "oof" so I try to stab her stomach, but she kicks the blade away then kicks at my face. A hastily made barrier blocks the blow, so the Killer grunts, retracts her leg, springs upwards and smashes the barrier with a single swing of her tomahawk.

"Ah!" I scramble away from the Killer just as her ensuing swipe almost takes my head off. I pick up my blade as she bounces to her feet.

"No mo' playin' 'round." She yanks off Zack's helmet, revealing cold emerald eyes, a plethora of angry dots one would call freckles, and a face chiseled from concrete. She's got short, straight, and dead black hair. Bits of black glass are nailed into her temple, soaking the side of her face in blood. She grabs a knife and clenches it in her free hand, bringing it over her tomahawk's handle to make an X. Her lean muscular arms and shoulders are tense with trembling fury.

The girl from Tyrone's story! "Wait!"

She charges again. I curse; then create a barrier across my forearm. The makeshift shield blocks the knife while her axe meets my blade. Clash! My shield holds strong, making her knife bounce across the dirt, so I smack her across the face with it. She stands her ground, opens her mouth, *bites off a chunk of the barrier* and then spits it at my forehead. It hits with serious stopping power, making me stumble backwards, but I get a retaliating slash in as I retreat. Blood explodes from her arm like a bloody water balloon. The arm goes loose and she cries out, shutting one eye in pain. Still, with gritted teeth, she throws her tomahawk horizontally with her freehand. I duck my head only for her to introduce her knee to my face.

Stars explode in my eyes and blood bursts from my nostrils while my back hits the floor. Killer drops to her knees, raises the knife above her with both hands and plunges it towards my chest, but I make a barrier between my palms. Before the knife makes contact, I realize she'll break them like the Feral if I don't enforce it. I focus on the barrier and imagine it being as hard as steel. My brain stirs and the barrier becomes a deeper shade of purple right as the knife clashes against it in an explosion of sparks. We both grunt in concentration, me flexing my mind while Killer flexes her arms, a power struggle ensuing. A sound like static television screeches through the air as the knife cuts deeper and deeper into my barrier. It's the only thing between the knife and my throat.

"Stop strugglin'," Killer growls, smiling with rotted yellow teeth. "It'll all be ova soon."

It's like my brain is being torn apart. I've never been in so much pain. If I just relax...

"An entire nation's survival now rests on your shoulders. Do not let her down."

"I'm a *knight!*"

My heads throbs as the barrier turns black. Killer's knife shatters into nothingness.

"Wha—"

I relax my mind, making the barrier disintegrate, then shoot my hands towards her dirty greasy neck and *choke*. She gurgles, but before I can completely cut off her air flow she grips me by the bangs, pulls me up then slams my head to the floor. Even as my brain rattles I keep choking her, a surprised thrill coming to me as she starts gagging. *I'm not going to die after all. I'm going to kill the Kill—*

My head hits the floor again, and it stuns me so much that I can tell this fight is far from over. I slam my foot into her chest, kicking her off me. I reach my hand out, grab my sword, flip to my feet then charge. I swing my sword downwards, but Killer twists to the side and stabs at my temple. I drop the blade and flip into a cartwheel, making my ankles crash into her jaw. She sways but doesn't fall.

She grabs her knife and lunges. I leap into a spin kick that knocks her face sideways. She sways but doesn't fall, then throws a small black stick at my feet. I kick it to the sky. The flash bomb explodes in midair as Killer leaps forward. She sweeps my legs from beneath my feet.

I create shields above me as I fall. The wind slams from my lungs when I land. Killer stabs through the barriers like paper, and the sound of shattering glass echoes through the landscape. My heart leaps as I roll to the side then flip to my feet breathing hard. Two knives are stabbed into the dirt I just lay in. Killer lurches them out of the ground. I run around her, snatch up my blade, then turn to face her. I have the worst headache of my life.

"You just... you just don't give up, do you," I huff, trying to catch my breath.

She wobbles forward, doing the same. "Yer one tah talk."

"I'm not letting you pass."

"Thas' funny, cuz Ah'm gettin' past ya if it's th' last thing Ah do."

"A duel to the death, then." I stab my rapier into the dirt. "No more weapons. No more powers. Let us end this fight like civilized women."

She examines her knife, then drops it alongside her toolbelt. They hit the dirt with a small *whump*. "Sounds interestin'."

She's smiling at me with blood-soaked teeth. Even though we've been trying to kill each other I can tell a part of her is having fun. "Ah've neva had a mo' worthy enemy. Ah want nuthin' more than tah end this fight wit' mah own two hands."

Had the circumstances been different, I would feel bad for what I'm what about to do. Her smile has proven to be infectious—I'm smiling too. Her naivety is charming, and I must admit... "You're also the worthiest opponent I've fought. Usually my invisibility is enough for me to win every fight, but you countered that *and* my barrier ability instantly, all seemingly without any powers of your own..."

"Thas' right, Ah'm jus' a normal human."

"I'm impressed, but I'm still going to stop you."

We smile at each other before regaining our seriousness. I won't let her kill people who had nothing to do with her brother's death. I will defend my home no matter what.

The Killer scowls at me, countering my willpower with hers. "Les' finish this."

We charge once more. Right before she swings I turn invisible and crouch. Her mighty punch misses me by a mile, and then I spring upwards. My fist cracks into her chin. She soars backwards then crashes to the floor, squirming in agony upon impact. I tower over her fallen figure, now visible. She glares at me with half-lidded eyes, then croaks, "Ya... cheated..."

I don't have a response, but I don't need one. She's unconscious.

My whole body is sore and shaking when I walk back down the street, retrieving my sword and backpack. I walk back to Killer, then point the Blade of Justice at her nose. "You did well. I know the Chosen did you wrong, and I'm sorry for that. But I can't let you hurt my home any more than you already have. I'm sorry, but this is goodbye."

I raise the blade... and sheathe it. The Blade of Justice would not cut her flesh again. Killer isn't just a killer. Killer is a victim. Even though that little girl and who knows how many others died by her hand, surely Killer doesn't deserve to die?

I raise the blade when the little girl's dying screams echoes in my brain... then sheathe it once more. There must be another way. But the little girl—

I fight down a lump of vomit. *Deep breaths, Minerva!* I reach for the Blade of Justice once more, but then shake my head. I can't kill this woman. She's not just a victim.

She is me.

But I can't just leave her here. When she wakes up there might not be any Chosen left for me to save when

I get back. *Fine. I don't want to do this, but I don't have a choice.*

I take the shock bracelet out of my backpack. I wasn't killing her, but I couldn't let her kill anyone else. She is going to have to come with me. She will redeem herself, and together we will stop the Feral once and for all!

I clasp the bracelet on her wrist.

Chapter 12

AM AH SLEEPIN' onnah marshmallo'? Ah yawn an' stretch. *Man oh man, that hadtah be th' best nap Ah've had all year.* "Am Ah in heaven," Ah mumble, turnin' ova an' sinkin' deeper intah th' mattress.

"I am afraid not. But you are somewhere safe."

Ah flip outta bed. Ah'm inna small an' sparse cabin. A massive fan rotates 'bove me. On th' opposite side o' th' room is anotha bed, an' a door's next tah it. Th' scarred warrior, th' one taller thana skyscraper wit' sapphire eyes, struts intah th' room. She's wearin' a white martial arts jumpsuit wit' purple lines stretchin' down tah th' sides. Th' Bruce Lee wanna be has a mean lump on her forehead an' two bandages 'cross her nose.

Ah charge her, drawin' a fist backwards. "You cheatin' bastard!"

"Don't come any closer!"

Ah'm 'boutah punch her in th' throat, but she raises a remote an' presses a big red button. A gabillion volts o' electricity rebounds through mah bloodstream, makin' me bite back a cry an' collapse on th' floor. Ah smile bitterly. *Damn, is this how steaks feel on th' grill?*

"Oh my." Mah enemy says, her eyes softenin' fer th' first time. "That looked quite painful. Do pay heed to my warning next time, dear. Are you alright?"

"What... how...?" Ah look at th' origin o' that concentrated Hell. A small an' tight silver bracelet wit' a single blue stud in th' middle is bound tah mah wrist. Ah trytah pry it off, but it's stuck on me like a leash onnah dog. Mah entire body goes cold. "Oh no."

She looks away, makin' her luscious curly blonde hair bounce. Ah wanna rip it off an' expose her scalp, then drive mah knife through her skull. "I'm sorry, but you left me no choice."

"Get this damn thing offah me!"

"Why would I do that? You'd just try to kill me."

"There wouldn' be no 'try', you'd jus' be dead. Ah can't believe you." Ah shake mah head. "When we were fightin', Ah thought fer one secon' Ah'd found an honorable Chosen. But yer even worse than them! All they've eva done is trytah kill me, an' here you are tryin' tah make me yer slave!"

"You are not my slave. In fact, I want you to be my partner."

"Partners don' put shock bracelets on one anotha, fool!"

"They don't, typically," she says, walkin' towards me wit' an angry pep in her step. "But, typically, *murderers* are executed for their crimes! You are an exception." If Ah wuzn't so pissed off, Ah mightah found her intimidatin'. Three jagged red lightnin' bolts streak 'cross her face from bottom left tah upper right at a forty-five degree angle, tearin' deep gashes intah her otherwise perfectly symmetrical face.

"You people killed mah little brother, an' yer tryin' tah act all high an' mighty?"

She rolls her jaw, closes her eyes, an' then takes a deep breath. Now she looks... calm. Still a lil' scary but, she definitely ain't angry no mo'. Funny, Ah do th' same thing when Ah'm pissed an' wanna calm down. Wait, what th' hell? Ah don' have anythin' in common wit' this bitch. "Tell me everything you know about the Chosen."

Ah don' wanna tell her shit, but it looks like Ah don' got much o' a choice. "Y'all travel tah th' Surface lookin' fer survivors tah kill fer supplies ya don' even need."

She laughs. "That's preposterous. I've been in the food cellar myself; we've got enough food to live down there for years. Why would we kill you for supplies when we already have more than enough?"

"'Cuz y'all dunno how long y'all gonna be unnerground, an' you greedy pigs want all th' supplies ya can get yer hands on. Y'all think y'all can deprive th' Feral o' food an' starve 'em out, least thas' what sum Chosen said 'fore Ah sliced her fuckin' throat open."

Her laugh falters. "You're lying. The Queen would *never—*" she pauses fer a long moment. *Whas' she thinkin' 'bout?* "... Perhaps I don't know my Queen as well as I thought I did."

"Damn right."

She sighs again. "Did we really kill your brother?"

"Ya think Ah'm lyin' or sumthin'? He starved tah death aftah yer friends took th' only food Ah'd found in months!"

"I'm so sorry, Stranger."

"Ah don' want yer sympathy, Ah want mah brother back!"

She looks even mo' pathetic now, so pathetic that Ah wanna rip her apart, but God damn it, even though she's shackled a shock bracelet on me her eyes are shimmerin' wit' whas' gotta be true sympathy. Mah face mustah softened or sumthin' cuz she tries tah put her hand on mah shoulder, but Ah smack it away.

"Don' you fuckin' touch me!"

"*Hmph!* It appears that I am not the only one in need of a reality check. Do you really think I was the only one who *didn't know* what the Chosen who ventured to the Surface were doing?"

"What're ya tryin' tah say?"

"I'm saying that a lot of *innocent people* who had *nothing* to do with your brother's death died today because you were foolish enough to think that the actions of our Queen and her soldiers equated to the will of every single Chosen. Most of us had no idea what her plans were. You unleashed viscous aliens on a *colony of civilians*, not some military base!"

Ah feel woozy.

She stamps a foot down, creatin' a loud hollow echo. "I've had enough of your ignorance! Who helped you plan the attack? The Ignored?"

Zack had said sumthin' 'fore Ah stabbed him in th' eye. What wuz it?

"Ah don' believe ya."

"You don't? Then why are you swaying on the spot! My friend—"

"Ah ain't yer friend!"

"—I saw, with my own eyes, a Feral's tongue going through a little girl's chest." She glares at me 'fore shudderin'. "I don't doubt other children suffered the same fate."

What wuz it? What did Zack say? *"I have a family."*

Th' world won't stop spinnin'. "Yer lyin'!"

"I am not lying. You killed innocent people today, and that's the honest truth."

Ah stare her down, but Ah can already tell she ain't lyin'. Damn it, she ain't lyin'! Th' way Ah feel when Ah think 'bout Lucio... Did Ah really give that feeling tah sumone else? Tah people who didn' even deserve it? Ah think... Ah think Ah'm gonna be—

Mah knees hit th' ground wit' a clang. Ah dig mah fingers intah th' cold metal floor, then Ah throw up everywhere. Mah stomach is on fire. Every horrible thing Ah've done since Lucio died has only hurt otha people. No justice has been served. All Ah wanted tah do wuz stop otha families from bein' torn apart. Ah ended up jus' doin' th' opposite.

Th' gruesum images from yesterday come flyin' back—me killin' Grace an' Deep Voice, then torturin' Zack—but now Ah know mah actions have caused even worse things tah happen, things Ah can't even imagine. How many people have Ah killed? How many families are ruined cuz o' me? Th' pain is too much. Ah gotta stop it.

Ah'm gonna stop this pain.

"Are you alright, dear?"

Ah reach fer th' knives on mah tool bet, but they're not there. That blasted gal... wait a sec. Wuzn't Ah bleedin' durin' th' fight? Ah touch mah face, but Ah'm clean. Th' bad cut on mah arm is patched up too. Ah snort. So what? It wuz jus' a trick.

Ah barge past her. "Where're mah knives?"

"Sit down. I'm cooking dinner. Don't you dare say you aren't hungry."

"Ah'm askin' ya—"

"I don't care. Sit. Down." Her hand hovers over th' remote. Ah sit down. She smiles tah herself. "Good." She starts tah walk out, stops, then turns 'round. "By the way, I just so happen to have a clean t-shirt in my possession that's not my size. I have placed it on the edge of your bed, please change into it before we eat."

She walks out th' room while Ah glare at her every step o' th' way. Ah hate her.

No, no. Ah ain't gotta reason tah trip. Ah'm gonna wake up from this nightmare. Ah look fer mah backpack, but it's nowhere in sight. It mus' be wit' her in th' otha room. Ah groan. *There's gotta be sumthin' Ah can use!* Jus' when Ah'm 'bout tah give up, Ah see mah shinny new ve-hicle restin' against th' back wall. Ah massage th' handlebars lovingly. There's sum rope bound 'round th' seat. Wait. It's *mah* rope. Guess she gave me a makeshift seat belt 'fore she drove us ova here. Whateva.

Ah grab th' rope, an' then look at th' ceilin' fan spinnin' 'bove me. It's perfect. Ah place a chair unnerneath th' roatin' blades, then stand onnit tah turn th' fan off. Then, Ah wrap th' rope 'round mah neck. It's scratchy as all hell, but it's not like Ah'm gonna feel anythin' soon anyway. "Dinner's ready," mah slaver calls from th' kitchen.

Shit. Ah lasso th' opposite end o' th' rope 'round th' staff that attaches th' fan tah th' ceilin'. Guess Ah'm all set. Mah slaver walks intah th' room, but Ah'm already dead. "Don't—!"

Ah kick th' chair out from unnerneath me. Ah fall tah th' floor, waitin' fer th' decisive tug that'll take me outta mah misery, but Ah'm jus' too heavy. Ah tear th' fan away from th' metallic ceilin', then mah back hits th' floor wit' a *clang*. Ah wince, an' when mah eyes pop open in pain, Ah see th' fan bouta crush mah skull open. Ah wait fer th' pain tah finally stop.

"No!" Th' entire room trembles as if cryin'.

Ugh, why am Ah still not dead? Ah open mah eyes tah see that th' slaver has her open palm raised tah th' destroyed ceilin'. Th' moon smiles down on us, makin' th' room glow gray as dust particles fly 'bout. A large triangle made o' purple light is floatin' 'bove th' bitch's hand, which, sumhow, is holdin' up th' entire fan. She looks down at me, eyes wide wit' whas' gotta be genuine concern. "Are you alright, dear?"

Ah punch her in th' face. Th' barrier 'bove us shatters. Th' fan crashes intah th' spot mah slaver wuz a secon' ago. She's hit th' floor across th' room. She's gonna be OK. An' so am Ah.

Ah run intah th' kitchen. "Where are ya where are ya where are ya?" On one side o' th' room there's a small brown table wit' two full plates restin' onnit. On th' otha side o' th' room there's a stove an' a fridge, where mah backpack is restin'. Ah snatchup th' backpack, open it, grab a knife an'—

A lightning bolt slams through mah wrist. Ah scream as th' world bursts intah white hot blindin' pain. Ah find mahself on th' floor, mah knife only a few feet away. Ah reach fer it, but a foot kicks it away. Mah slaver has returned, lookin' scarier than eva.

"Do you *enjoy* being tortured? What in the Queen's name is wrong with you? I'm trying to save your life!"

"So Ah can be yer slave? No thanks, bitch."

She raises th' remote. "*Language,* dear."

"*Fuck you!* Can'tcha see Ah don' wanna live anymo'? Ya can't force me tah live if Ah don' wanna. Jus' let me die in peace!"

"No. That would be too easy. I've got much better things planned for you."

"Like *what?*"

"I'll tell you everything after you sit down and finish the meal I made for you." Ah scream an' lunge at her. She raises th' remote. Every muscle in mah body locks up. "Be quiet. You need to eat. A supermodel has more meat on her bones than you."

"Stop playin' these games," Ah growl. "Jus' let me die, *please.*"

"The next time you try to kill yourself, I will shock you with this thing for *hours.* I'm not asking you again, Ms...?"

Ah snort. "Aftah all th' shit you've done tah me, ya think Ah'm gonna jus' tell ya mah name?"

"All I've done for you? Spare you in battle, dress your wounds, *save your life?*"

"Ya shackled a damn shock bracelet on mah arm, moron!"

"Hmph. No matter. My name is Minerva. You will reveal your name to me within due time. For now, you will go next door and change out of that filthy shirt immediately. Then you will come back in here, sit down and eat dinner with me. Any objections?"

Ah wanna argue, Ah wanna fight, but her thumb is hoverin' ova that red button. This *bitch.* "Fuck, alright, alright! Fine."

"Be quick about it. If you're in there too long or I hear signs that you're hurting yourself, you know exactly what I'll do."

Ah storm intah th' bedroom wit' narrowed eyes an' a heavin' chest, then shake mah head. Ah take off mah shirt. Ah hadn't realized how disgustin' it is 'till Ah get an eyeful o' red. Mah nostrils sting wit' th' stench o' death as Ah rip it off. Ah pick up th' shirt on th' bed an' slip intah it. Itsa lil' big fer me, but whateva. Ah scowl at th' case o' floss that wuz hidden unnerneath th' shirt, then take it an' throw it on th' ground.

Minerva flings th' door open wit' her thumb up high ready tah press th' switch, but when she sees th' floss skiddin' 'cross th' floor she jus' shakes her head. "Hmph. I suppose I can't force you to be hygienic. Come, let's eat."

Ah follow her outside wit' a clenched jaw, then sit down at th' table, body still twitchin' from th' last shock. Ah pick up th' spoon an' get an image o' me shovin' it down mah throat, then Ah shake mah head. Eternal sleep sounds sweeter than apple pie, but eternal sleep ain't worth bathin' inna pool o' fire fer hours on end. If Minerva sumhow stopped me from chokin' tah death, she'd definitely make me pay. But when she falls asleep...

Minerva is starin' at me hard. "You're still thinking about killing yourself, aren't you?"

"Ye—shut up!"

"Hmph. Very well, I will stay up until you promise not to do so. You being the honorable type, I will be able to tell if you're lying."

Ah scowl at her. "Ah hope yer ready tah be up fer awhile. Soon as yer body collapses from exhaustion Ah'm outta here."

"We'll see about that. Now hurry up and eat."

The button is within her arm's reach. Ah sigh, then use mah spoon tah scoop up sum beans an' swallow. They're tart, warm, an' juicy. In th' old days Ah'd probably think they were nuthin' special, but Ah'm so hungry they taste amazin'. Ah scoop up anotha spoonful, but now Minerva's lookin' at me all intense an' it's pissin' me off. "*What?*"

"Is it good? Do you like it?"

"Uh, it's OK Ah *guess*, but that *ain't* on account o' yer cookin' skills. Didn' these come straight from th' can? 'Sides, mah brother wuz workin' th' stove when he wuz six. That boy wuz sumthin' else."

"I'm so—"

"Look, if ya really didn' know what yer Chosen friends were goin' on 'bout 'bove ya, then ya had nuthin' tah do wit' his death. So stop apologizin'."

She looks down at her plate. "I'm so—Alright then."

We eat in silence fer awhile. Ah starta feel a lil' betta as th' meal goes on. Every bite is a simple joy. Th' beans remind me o' a hot summer day back in Texas. Ah imagine mahself sittin' on th' porch, feet propped up on th' fence, a piece o' wheat 'tween mah teeth, Pa's stetson on mah head, an' a good ol' book in mah hands. Ah pick up th' sandwich an' take a bite. Then Ah start laughin'.

"What's funny?"

"Nuthin'," Ah say, but find mahself chucklin' anyway.

"I want to know!"

Mah eyes go half-lidded. "Ya gonna shock me if Ah don' tell ya?"

She bares her teeth. "No, I will not. I've only shocked you if you were a threat to me or yourself. I am *not* a bad person."

"Yer a *cheater!*" Ah hiss.

"Oh, come over it! If we had kept fighting *both* of us would have died."

"So? You were th' one who said we should fight tah th' death in th' first place."

"I lied, you bloodthirsty buffoon. It's your fault for believing such an obvious trick."

It's like she jus' set me on fire, Ah'm so mad. "'Xcuse me fer thinkin' you had a code o' honor. 'Xcuse me fer thinkin' a knight wasn't jus' another backstabbin' liar." She flinches at that, which makes me smile. *That mustah hurt. At least now Ah know she feels bad 'bout trickin' me.*

"Y-you have no one to blame but yourself! You didn't have to agree to my obviously unbalanced terms of agreement. You could have kept your weapons, but nooo, you just had to have a good old-fashioned brawl. You act like your revenge was righteous, but even if it was, you prioritized a good fight over your ultimate goal. I didn't, which is why I won our battle and why we're *both* still alive."

Th' fact that she's right pisses me off even more. Ah can hardly breathe at this point, but before th' heat o' mah anger can suffocate me Ah redirect it right back at her. "Yer jus' a hypocrite. Ah ain't eva tellin' ya mah name."

She sighs. "I'm sorry I tricked you, but I didn't have much of a choice. It's obvious that we've got far greater problems to face than one another. Like, for example, the *bloody Feral.* We shouldn't be fighting. We should be working *together.*"

Ah raise th' bracelet. "Yer not workin' wit' me!"

"Are you on drugs? That bracelet saved your life twice and possibly even mine. It stopped you from trying to kill me when you woke up. Without it one of us could've died in the ensuing fight, and even if we both walked away from that relatively unscathed, you certainly would've succeeded in killing yourself when I revealed the impact of your actions."

"But Ah don' even wanna live anymo'! You took that right away from me, an' yer applaudin' yerself fer it?"

"Now *you're* the one lying. I know you still want to live. I saw that look on your face when you were eating. You were enjoying yourself. Now that I think about it, you were enjoying yourself during our fight as well. You were having such a good time living on the edge and pushing yourself against a worthy foe that you forgot all about your precious revenge." Ah purse mah lips, so Minerva continues, "If you died, you'd never get to eat or fight again. That would be dreadful, would it not?"

"Maybe so, but even mo' dreadful is walkin' 'round knowin' Ah killed people who meant me an' others no harm. Minerva, ya patched up mah wounds but Ah'm hurtin' worse than eva. Ya have tah finish me off. Ah know ya wanna, ya got this keen look in yer eyes when ya told me Ah killed a kid. Ah know ya wanna do it. Jus' make it quick," Ah whisper.

"... Perhaps I once had the urge to take your life. But that urge has gone away."

Ugh! "You're worthless." Ah shake mah head. "Maybe Ah hit ya too hard. Anyone else wouldah killed me by now."

"My head is perfectly fine, thank you. I knew someone like you once, you know."

Ah roll mah eyes. "Guess its story time."

"He was an alcoholic. He did some terrible things to people who cared about him, and he wanted to die."

"An' ya didn' let him?"

"No."

"Why do ya keep intrudin' in on otha people's business?"

"He got my best friend pregnant. I wasn't going to let him slack off in Hell while she raised his child by herself."

Hmph. "So how'd ya keep him alive?"

"I reminded him he had something to live for. I thought I had made a positive impact, but when I went to check up on him a few hours later I found his head down a toilet. He was choking on his own vomit, trying to drink himself to death."

Ah grunt sympathetic like. "Mah Uncle drank himself tah death durin' one crazy night at Las Vegas. Pa said that he looked like he wuz inna lot o' pain in his final moments. It mustah been an awful sight."

Minerva gives a solemn nod. "It truly was, but I managed to save him and we had another talk. I'll never know if I ever had a lasting impact on him, but we became friends that night. I hope he's alright."

Wait, is that it? That story went nowhere. "Fer sum reason, Ah thought you were tryin' tah convince me *not* tah kill mahself."

"Don't you see? You're just like him. You have something to live for too. The same reason he has."

"Mah entire family is dead. Ah killed innocent people. There's nuthin left fer me here."

"Oh? You don't seek *redemption?*"

Ah snort. "Redemption? This ain't *Dragon Ball Z.* Nuthin' can bring back th' people Ah killed."

"You're right. But you can't let them die in vain. It's time you know the full truth. I came to the Surface on the Queen's orders. She has a mission for me, one I want your help on."

"A mission from th' Queen? Ya really think Ah'd help th' witch that betrayed her own sister, th' one who started all o' this? Ain't happenin'!"

"You haven't even heard what the mission is yet!"

"Golly-gee, whose fault is that?"

"Yours, obviously. Perhaps you should stop interrupting me?" Ah cross mah arms. "Thank you. As I was about to say, she wants me to go to Edinburgh. A group of scientists there think they've discovered the Feral's weakness."

"They *what?*"

"You heard me full well."

Ah grab mah chin. "If we can stop those bastards, there'd be nuthin' stoppin' th' Chosen from sharin' th' food wit' everyone."

"And then the Ignored will have no reason to attack us."

"Wowie. This mission o' yers could end th' alien war an' th' civil war all in one swell swoop."

"So you understand how big this could be. Will you help me on this Quest?"

"Do Ah really got much o' a choice?"

"Yes. If you don't want to come with me, I will let you go."

"This ain't a trick?"

"No."

"Ain'tcha 'fraid Ah'll trytah kill ya?"

"No, because if you did, I wouldn't show you any mercy." Ah suck mah teeth at that, then she says: "But if you don't want to come with me I won't force you. What will you do?"

Nuthin' can take back what Ah've done tahday. But if we can stop th' Feral, how many lives will Ah be able tah save in th' long run?

Ah smile. Minerva said Ah had a choice in th' mattah, but Ah really didn'. There ain't no way Ah'm dyin' a coward who didn' at least trytah make up fer her mistakes. "Yeah, alright then. Ah'm comin' wit'cha. Now get this damn thing offah me."

"Ah, I am afraid that's not possible at this point in time."

"*Why?*"

"I don't trust you yet. If you relapse and kill yourself on my watch, it'll be my fault."

"If Ah really wanted tah kill mahself, ya couldn't stop me."

"I've stopped you twice so far."

"Thas' cuz ya were right next door. Ya really think ya can keep an eye on me at all times? How're ya gonna stop me in yer sleep, or when ya go piss—"

"We are *eating.* You will speak like a lady at this table at the very least."

"Ah'm gonna speak how Ah'm gonna speak! Now where's that remote? This thing is comin' off, *now.*"

Her face tightens, makin' her scars contract. "You *assaulted* me after I saved you from being crushed by the fan you tried to hang yourself on. Can you really ask me to trust you so soon after that?"

"So ya really are jus' scared o' me."

Minerva smiles. "I am friends with a knight you encountered awhile ago, you know."

"Th' black fella wit' th' freaky light power?"

She raises an eyebrow. "How do you know about Her Majesty's knights?"

"Back at Texas, we've got a few supahheroes o' our own. Ah dunno if you've heard o' Samurai Kid an' Th' Cube?"

"How can I *not* know them? They were the first metahumans. What does that have to do with the knights?"

Mah stomach squirms, so Ah take anotha bite o' mah sandwich. "Mah brother wuz a big fan o' 'em, so when mah folks started plannin' a vacation here he wondered if th' UK had any supahheroes o' their own." Minerva glares at me, eyein' th' wads o' chewed food that flies outta mah mouth as Ah yap. "Thas' when he researched th' hay outta you fellas. He became a fan o' you guys too, an' when we came here he wanted tah get an autograph. But o' course, everything went tah hell pretty soon. Th' aliens invaded. Mah folks joined th' volunteer military tah fight 'em off, but then th' Nuke hit an' they died."

"I'm so—"

"Lucio an' me survived unnerground in metro stations an' sewers. We were harmin' no one, jus' mindin' our own business when yer friend an' his goons got on our turf."

"Your turf? How were they supposed to know that?"

"We made a sign that says 'Stay Out!' right at th' entrance."

"Ah. Carry on then."

"We heard 'em shufflin' down th' stairs so Ah got ready tah fight. Lucio said we didn' need too, cuz he recognized th' black fella as a knight. He went ova tah say hello, an' th' white folk attacked. So Ah killed 'em all. Ah only let th' knight live cuz he tried tah stop 'em in th' first place."

"Tyrone, the knight in question, made me aware of your exploits before our battle. He called you powerful, so powerful he specifically pointed you out when referring to people who may be stronger than me. You're strong, and while that's an asset for a partner, you may still be a threat to yourself and I should you lose yourself in sorrow once more. So you see why I can't just let you go, correct?"

Ah groan. "Ah'm gettin' mighty sick o' talkin' tah ya 'bout this. Seems like you've made up yer stupid mind, so Ah'll stop arguin'. But 'till ya let me go, Ah ain't tellin' ya mah name."

"Fair enough. Now, what exactly made you laugh when you bit into your sandwich earlier?"

Ah shake mah head, suppressin' a grin. "Yer still on that? You've gotta be kiddin' me."

She smiles. Y'know what? She don' look so scary no mo'. "My conversation skills are akin to a sporadic taxi driver. I may take an obscure route, but I will eventually reach my destination."

Ah let mah guard down an' smile back at her, jus' this once. "Ah wuz jus' rememberin' th' time Ma made Lucio one o' these when he wuz a lad. He cried an' said he wouldn' eat it, on account o' there bein' crust on th' sides."

"One of those picky eaters, hm?"

"Darn tootin'. Not that he could afford tah be picky out here. We ate everything we could get our hands on—rats, cockroaches, you name it. Wheneva we hadtah choke down th' varmints, Ah told him a good ol' steak wuz right 'round th' corner, that soon enough we'd be eatin' like royalty once we were rescued."

"A rescue that never came." She's startin' tah look green.

"Eeyup." Ah drawl, finally turnin' mah attention back tah mah meal. Ah rip through th' rest o' mah sandwich like a wolf then lick up th' bean sauce. Ah burp loud an' proud.

Minerva shakes her head. "I know you were hungry, but licking the plate? *Most* unladylike."

"As if Ah care 'bout yer standards. When Ah wuz still a squirt, Ma wouldn' let me leave th' table 'till mah plate wuz white as snow. Mah folks were famers, see, an' Ah wuz raised not tah waste any food an' enjoy every bite o' it. Ah'm 'fraid Ah ain't got much interest in bein' 'proper' an' boring as all hell like you."

"You're assuming quite a lot about someone you just met." Minerva says, though she's still smilin'. Mah face heats up, but why? "Either way, your belches would put a man's to shame."

"Golly gee, ya sure know howtah make a gal blush," Ah roll mah eyes. "So, what do we do now?"

"We're going to call it in for the night. You were out for awhile. The drive over here was *quite* exhausting. Besides, this is the last underground safe house for miles on end. Might as well sleep in a bed while we still have a chance."

"Yer th' boss," Ah half-heartedly growl.

"So, we have a deal? You promise you aren't going to kill yourself?"

Tch. "We gotta deal."

She studies my reaction, realizes Ah'm tellin' th' truth, then gives me a satisfied smile that makes my heart stir. "Good, I'd much like some sleep after a day like this."

Ah nod, tryin' not to think o' mah poudin' heart as Ah walk ova tah mah backpack. "Hey! What are you doing?"

Th' warm feeling in mah chest goes cold. "Didn' Ah *jus'* say we had a deal? Ah'm grabbin' a book."

"So those were yours, hm? I didn't take you for a reader."

"Whas' *that* 'sposed tah mean?"

"Ah, it's just... you really like fighting. And the accent threw me off..."

"So cuz Ah like a good brawl an' talk differently than folk like you Ah'm illiterate? You like fighting too, an' from mah perspective, yer haughty voice sounds funny as hell. But Ah guess that means Ah should assume your pampered ass doesn't like reading, huh?"

"You're right, forget I said anything."

"Ah will, jackass." Ah walk back intah th' room, movin' 'round th' collapsed fan before Ah dive ontah th' cloudlike bed. Ah sink intah th' mattress, flip open mah book, an' grin. Soon enough

Ah'm not in th' cabin. Ah'm not even thinkin' 'bout all th' people Ah killed, or 'bout th' people Ah might be able tah save, or even 'bout how much Ah wanna die—instead Ah'm in th' shoes ova teenaged boy wit' magical powers, th' fate o' a country on his shoulders, not mine. Ah smile at th' warm, comfortin' dialogue Ah'd read thousands o' times before. Sum books were so good ya could read 'em ova an' ova again an' still have yer funny bone tickled.

Th' pit o' mah stomach goes cold. If Ah had killed mahself, Ah wouldah neva gotten th' chance tah read anotha book. Shit, maybe that wuzn't such a good idea aftah all. Ah almos' want tah thank Minerva fer stoppin' me, but thas' not happenin'. Th' bracelet is cold on mah wrist.

Ah hear a door close an' look up. Minerva yawns as she walks intah th' room. She flops down on her bed like a suffocatin' fish. "A shame there's no running water. I would love a shower right now."

"Ah'm jus' happy tah be sleepin' onnah bed thas' not caked wit' dried blood or infested wit' critters."

"Sounds awful."

"Welcome tah th' Surface, hope ya enjoy yer stay!"

"Hilarious."

Ah go back tah mah book. "Thas' jus' how it is up here, lady."

Time moves slow now, 'least it feels that way. Seconds, minutes, hours... how long have Ah been up? Th' sentences start tah mesh tahgetha, an' Ah find mahself re-reading th' same paragraph ova an' ova. Ah don' wanna stop readin' anytime soon, cuz Ah know mah dreams are gonna be torture, but at th' same time, Ah'm gettin' tired and less comfortable by th' minute. Minerva's havin' a rough time too, tossin' an' turnin' but neva stayin' too still fer mo' than a few minutes. Ah grunt, shuffle 'bout, lick mah dry lips then finally ask, "Do ya want me tah turn off th' light?"

"No, it's fine, I can't sleep anyway. Besides, the moonlight will be there even if the light goes off."

"Thas' true," Ah admit 'fore goin' back tah mah book. Ah finally digest the paragraph Ah've been stuck on, then flip th' page.

"Hey, Stranger?"

Ah look up from th' book, then turn tah look at her. "Yeah?"

She's biting her quivering bottom lip. Her eyes are red and her nose is running. "I'm sorry. For everything."

Ah go back tah mah book. "Thanks."

Chapter 13

1wince at my reflection. I've brushed my hair as best as I can, but my face is still my face.

"Are ya constipated or sumthin'?" Stranger yells from the main room. "Hurry up!"

I start to yell back, but I bite my tongue. I'm really not in the mood to argue so early in the morning. Besides, I *have* been in here for awhile. It's not like Stranger would appreciate any cosmetic efforts on my part, anyway.

I step back into the main room. Stranger has her back against the wall next to the exit, jaw set and arms crossed. She really does look better when she's wearing a shirt that isn't coated in blood, though her mood hasn't improved much since last night.

"What?" I ask.

Her frown makes me feel guilty, almost like the time my parents caught me watching gay porn. "Yer 'sposed tah be leadin' this mission, but it's almos' noon. We shouldah left hours ago!"

I resist the urge to destroy her and say, "According to the map, we won't come across another safe house for at least two days. Why wouldn't I relish in the opportunity to sleep in a bed one last time?"

Stranger looks at me like I'm wearing uggs in the summertime. "Th' longer we spend here th' mo' daylight burns. Atta certain point we're gonna haftah stop travelin' an' start lookin' fer shelter. We lost a lotta daylight foolin' 'round here, which means we lost a lotta miles. Now our journey's gonna last anotha day."

"I saw people get eaten alive yesterday. Excuse me for wanting to sleep in."

Stranger flinches back as if she'd been jabbed. "... Ah'm sorry."

I believe this person is genuine. I don't know why, but I do. "I accept your apology, but that doesn't change the fact that you are trying my patience. We're in this together, alright?" She nods her head in affirmation. "Right then. Let's go."

I grab my backpack, but then realize it's too heavy to ride with, so I unpack most of our canned food and put it in a bag on the bike's luggage rack alongside my brush and floss. I zip up our supplies, then sling my lighter backpack over my shoulder while Stranger ties her bow to the back of the backset's headrest with rope.

I nod at Stranger to tell her I'm ready, and then open the front door for her. She wheels Zack's motorcycle up the stairwell leading back to the Surface. I yank on a thick black cord protruding from the wall. The ceiling cracks open like a set of double doors being pushed outwards, then hits the dirt outside with a *clang*. The sound makes me wince, and I turn invisible instinctively. "Wait here," I say. "I'll peak outside and make sure we aren't walking into an ambush."

She nods, so I poke my head out and look around. There's no one in sight. I walk up the stairs, and then emerge outside. My feet are on the Surface once more, but this time my trip won't be so temporary. It smells like rotten rat corpses, though I'm surprised to say I'm already getting used to the stench. Just another part of the Surface I suppose. I turn back to Stranger, visible again. "We're clear."

"Am Ah eva gonna get used tah that?" Stranger asks as she steps outside, smiling at me despite our earlier argument. I don't know when, but she definitely used the floss I gave her last night. The dim grey sunlight adds a little shine to her messy black hair.

"Probably not," I say, smiling back at her.

The road ahead is stretching on for miles. My head pounds as I calculate the distance. This is going to be a long journey. I really, really don't want to drive right away.

"I'll drive, if you don't mind," I say with enthusiasm.

Stranger grabs mah shoulder and whirls me around. "No. Ah'm drivin', an' thas' final!"

I suppress a smile. "Very well then, if you insist." *Oh, the wonders of reverse psychology.*

Stranger gets on Zack's cycle, and I sit behind her. I wrap my arms around her waist, feeling a little awkward. The cracked road ahead seems impossibly long. It's all I can see for miles ahead. *Are we really going to be this close the entire ride?*

"Hold on tight, missy."

I'm only blushing because of the hot and stuffy air. "I am!"

She looks back with a toothy grin. "Suit yerself."

A burst of speed sends us flying down the bumpy road. I shriek and squeeze her tight like an infant clinging to their mother.

"Where to, yer highness?" Stranger yells. The wind rushing past my ears makes it hard to hear.

"Just—*ugh*—straight ahead! And please avoid further potholes on the road!"

"Whose drivin' this beast again?"

"That doesn't mean—gah—I'll have you know I helped design this so-called beast with its creator!"

"What does that have tah do wit' who's drivin'?"

"You wouldn't be driving it without me!"

"Lissen here, ya fussy... look, we're gonna be on th' road fer awhile! This bickerin's gettin' ol'. Why don'cha tell me 'bout yerself? Feels like Ah did all o' th' talkin' last night."

"Nonsense. I couldn't keep my mouth closed for more than two seconds."

"Ya might wanna rephrase that! Sumone might get th' wrong idea."

"How crude!"

"Thas' what Ah'm here fer. Now get back tah that backstory o' yers."

I stifle a giggle, clinging to her waist a little tighter. "I am afraid there's not much to tell. Before the invasion I spent most of my life as a model. It may be a shock to you, but I used to be quite pretty."

"Actually, no."

My eyes pop open like I just drank a gallon of coffee, giving me an eye-full of wind as consequence. "Wait, what?"

"Look, don' make things weird, alls Ah'm sayin' is that those scars o' yers don' make ya look quite as ugly as ya seem tah think they do."

"Hmph. I *suppose* I'll take that as a compliment."

"Take it as ya like. Continue!"

"I was at the park doing pull-ups when I saw a diamond the size of a meteorite break through the atmosphere. It hurtled towards me with incredible speed."

"A chunk o' Supah Meteorite, Ah take it?"

"Do you want me to tell you the story or not?"

"Take that stick outta yer—"

"Everyone screamed and ran. A pair of twins ahead of me tripped, so I grabbed them and ran for our lives! The Super Meteorite hit the ground behind us with a shockwave that knocked us off our feet. The supernatural rock shattered into shards of power—"

"Shards o' power? Lame."

"—Three such shards stabbed me in the back. Fortunately, my body was able to act as a shield, and I was able to protect the children from harm."

Gah, my throat is getting hoarse from all this yelling. I don't know if she can feel my heart pounding against her back or what, but Stranger slows down. The wind stops rushing past my ears quite so hard. Excellent, now we can talk without making our diaphragms explode.

"I awoke in the hospital feeling better than I ever had. Queen Amity received word of my heroic exploit and visited me in the hospital. Seeing the ruler of our nation visit me personally was just too much for me to bear. I wished I could turn invisible... then I couldn't see my hands."

"Heh. Th' thought o' you actin' shy is hilarious. Ah done neva seen an Amazonian shrinkin' violet."

"Couldn't go too long without interrupting, hm? Still, I suppose a full sixty seconds is a big achievement for you."

Stranger laughs while I look ahead. The melted corpse of a flipped over 18-wheeler is lying in the middle of the road, blocking our path. "Lady, you dunno what Ah'm capable of."

She sends us veering off road. I squeal in terror as the uneven terrain makes our bike bump all over the place. We shred around the 18-wheeler, dirt spilling behind our rear tire. When we swerve back onto the road, I slap her shoulder, making her laugh even more. "Don't ever do that again," I growl, but my heart isn't in it. That was fun!

"No promises," she says. "What were you sayin'? Sumthin' 'bout ya turnin' invisible in frontah yer so called Queen?"

"Oh, yes. Upon seeing my immense metahuman potential, the Queen asked me if I wanted to be a Knight. I accepted, and the rest is history. I became somewhat of a celebrity after that."

"Really? How come Ah haven't heard 'bout ya from Lucio then?"

My feelings are not hurt. "The Queen kept my powers a secret. As far the public knew, I was just an abnormally powerful Normal like you. If your brother were only interested in the metahuman knights he wouldn't have heard of me."

"So yer like her secret weapon?"

"… I suppose that's one way of putting it."

"Ah wuz 'xpectin' a snooze fest, but that wuz actually a pretty good story."

"I couldn't tell by the way you kept interrupting me like some brute."

"What? Ah can't help it! Sumtimes ya gotta talk durin' th' movie is all."

"You talk during films? You really are a brute!"

We share a laugh together for the first time as the road slopes upwards. When we reach the hill's peak, I can see just how endless the desert is. We're in the middle of a grainy ocean, with sand stretching out for miles and miles. Even amidst the decayed buildings on the horizon, the bloody cars littering the side of the road and the extinction of the color green, I realize there's still beauty in this world.

A crack of sunlight bursts through the grey clouds above, bathing us in its holy light for a single instant. Stranger looks back with a warm smile, her emerald eyes twinkling. I smile back as fireworks pop in my stomach, but she turns around before I self-combust.

We drive for awhile in a comfortable silence. All you can hear is the roar of the engine and wind. Eventually, Stranger slows down and coughs. "So, uh, if ya don' mind me askin', what happened tah yer folks?"

A fresh wave of pain ripples through my body, but I push it away with a sigh. "My parents and I were watching Dr. Who at home when the aliens invaded." The irony makes me laugh just as much as it makes me cry. "We got in the car and sped towards Camden Town Hall when a pack of Feral started chasing us. They slashed our tires out and sent us veering off road. We crashed and ran for it, but not fast enough. A Feral's tongue went through my father's back." I wipe my eyes. "We couldn't recover the corpse for the funeral."

"Man..."

"We made it to the hall, but I fell near the entrance. I got to my feet right in time for a Feral to raise its claws at me. I jumped backwards, but I underestimated its reach. That's when I got these scars. I fell down screaming, so my mother picked me up and got me inside. The Chosen tended to my wounds, but mother got sliced in the stomach saving me. She bled out before they could do anything."

"Thas' rough, Minerva."

"It is. But they spent their last moments protecting me. I will always carry on their wills, no matter how hard it gets."

"Dyin' tah protect yer kin is th' only way tah die wit' honor."

"Then I can proudly say that both of our parents were very honorable people. Yours sounded especially brave; joining the volunteer army even though they weren't citizens here must have been a difficult choice to make."

"Very brave, an' very stupid."

"How could you say such a thing?"

"Well they ain't here, are they!"

I open my mouth, and then close it.

"They left Lucio an' me all alone, all cuz they wanted tah be brave. An' what good came from their deaths? Nuthin'! Lord knows Ah love mah folks, but they were complete fools!"

I don't—and can't—say anything. After awhile, Stranger chuckles. "Ah didn' mean tah blow up on ya like that."

I sniffle. "Not to worry. We're all dealing with our own demons."

"Ah reckon so."

"Stranger, I think I know a little too much about you to keep calling you that. Do you have a nickname or something you could tell me?"

"No."

"Fine," I spit. "I'll just call you Partner."

"Call me whateva ya like, jus' don' shock me, Masser."

"Hmph."

We ride along in silence for the next few hours. All the time I spent underground I wondered how the world above had changed. I do not like what I'm seeing. The death and decay I saw when I first came to the Surface hasn't gotten any better the further away I get from home. It was as if the beautiful scenery I saw on the hill earlier was nothing more than an optical illusion cooked up by my hormones. For a second, I actually thought that the Surface wasn't so bad.

We pass by destroyed buildings and ride through dead forests as the sun slowly goes down, still trapped behind those ever present grey clouds. My mind wanders towards yesterday's events.

How many people died? Was the Queen still alive? Sarah? William? Tyrone? Angel? "Partner?"

"What is it?"

"You never answered my question yesterday. Were the Ignored involved in your attack on my home?"

"Yup."

"What did you plan to do with the survivors?"

"Keep 'em prisoner. Provided th' Feral Ah sent down there didn' eat 'em, yer friends should still be alive."

"... I see. Oh!"

The engine whines like a tea pot at high pressure. I swallow dryness as the awful scenery blurs by.

"Partner, remember that I'm here with you. If you die, I will too."

Partner eases up on the gas, and I release a breath. "No one's gonna die! Stop makin' assumptions."

I hold my tongue, opting instead to wipe the sweat from my brow. In a short distance is a seemingly abandoned house on the side of the road. I say seemingly because I can hear someone screaming for help at the top of their lungs.

"Park next to that house."

"Pardon mah intrusion, but does that house have a closet that'll transport us tah Edinburgh?"

"Perhaps not. It wouldn't hurt to check, though."

She groans but still brings us to a stop. "Ah agreed tah be yer pardner in stoppin' th' Feral, not in helpin' every person who pretends tah need it." I get off the bike and walk towards the house. "Ah'm warnin' ya, itsa trap," she says, walking in step with me as she throws her bow over her shoulder, carrying it by the bow string.

"But what if it isn't? What if someone really needs our help?" I unsheathe the Blade of Justice and slice through the decayed door. "If it's a trap, we'll handle it." I walk inside, feet creaking on the loose floorboards.

"Ugh—don' say Ah didn' warn ya!"

The home's interior looks like a drunken giant stumbled over everything. There are cracks in the floor and walls with no furniture in sight. This place must have been raided at least a hundred times. "Help," I hear from the room next door.

I catch Partner's eye. I point to the rotted door, give her a 'come hither', and then put my index finger to my lips. She nods. I turn invisible and creep towards the entrance. Partner darts past me and kicks the door down. I facepalm, then run in behind her with my blade drawn.

The room is mostly empty, but over Partner's shoulder is a tattered turquoise couch. "Come out, or Ah start shootin'!"

"No, please," a soft voice calls from behind the furniture. I grab Partner by the wrist and divert her aim as a bald Asian girl with penny eyes steps out of cover, hands in the air. "Don't kill me, please!"

"We—we're not gonna hurt ya, youngin'! We're here tah help. Are ya in trouble?"

The girl's eyes focus on something behind me, then her face scrunches up together like a balled-up tissue paper. A whining noise escapes from her throat, making Partner holster her gun. "Ah'm not gonna hurt ya, promise!" She walks towards the girl slowly, hands up in peace.

What was she looking at? I turn. A man in a tattered black shirt and pants creeps towards Partner, his hand clenched around a knife. A single horizontal swipe slices his arm open. He yelps, his knife clattering to the floor. I smash an elbow into his stomach. He doubles over, so I pull up my sword and drive my hilt into his temple. His head lurches to the side, and then he hits the ground with a thud.

I turn visible, run over to the girl and swallow her in a hug. "Don't worry, darling. Mama won't let the bad man get you!"

"You—you saved me," the little angel squeaks.

I let her go, then turn around and wink at Partner. She shakes her head. "I did, didn't I?" I hold out my hand and the angel grabs it, enveloping my fingertips in marshmallows. "Let's get you someplace safe. Where are your parents?"

Partner chuckles darkly.

"What's so funny?" I ask.

"She'll tell ya." The little girl is looking at the floor. "Go on, tell her th' truth youngin'."

The little girl looks at the floor, eyes hollow. "My parents are... gone. I've only been hiding here for a few hours when that man attacked." Her entire body shudders. "He was so scary."

She's all alone.

I grab my chest, trying to pull out the spike of pain that just impaled my heart. Well, that settled it. "Looks like we just made a new partner, Partner."

Partner shakes her head again. "This is bullshit." She walks over to us with a sigh, then squats to look our new friend in the eye. "Whas' yer name, kiddo?"

"I'm C-cho..."

"Ah'm Nina. Pleasure tah meetcha!" She holds out her hand, and after a beat Cho takes it. The two girls shake while I smile.

"Nina, hm? I quite like that name."

"Les' pretend ya didn' hear that, Minerva."

"I decline that offer. Come. Let us leave this retched place!" I start to walk out, but Nina grabs my shoulder and whispers, "Get her tah th' cycle. Ah'll make sure this fella causes no mo' trouble."

I gasp. "You will do no such thing!" I grab her wrist and drag her out of the room. She shakes her head as we walk to the exit. "Ah don' think ya unnerstan' how things work up here, girlie."

"You will not call me *girlie* ever again. I am a *lady*, and we ladies expect to be treated like one. Isn't that right, Cho?"

Cho giggles. "You two sure are fun! I wish we could spend more time together..."

"Whatever do you mean, dear? Our time together has only just beg—"

?

I whirl around. The man from before has his knife raised. He plunges it towards my heart, but I wave my hand and create a barrier that blocks the stab.

I slash at his head, but he's gone? My feet are swept from underneath me, making me hit ground with a *whump*.

"You motherfu—!" I hear a *thwack* and a grunt. Right as I'm getting up, Nina smacks into me, knocking us both over.

"Bye girls! It's been fun." Cho waves, smiling brightly.

Nina bounces back up. "Get back here ya thievin' vermin!" She hurls her lasso, but the rope catches nothing but air as the duo speeds down the highway and into the horizon. I stare at their disappearing silhouettes, unable to believe what I'm seeing.

Nina sucks her teeth. "Toldcha it wuz a trap."

My chest burns. "What was I to do? I thought someone was in trouble!"

"But th' only ones in trouble turned out tah be us. Lissen, jus' cuz ya got powers don' mean ya can be a hero. Not in this new world, anyway." She gets up and starts walking down the road.

I want to cry. Almost all our supplies... gone, just like that. Could we even afford to eat tonight? I only had a few cans of food in my backpack; everything else was strapped to the cycle. And where were we going to sleep? How would we get to Edinburgh now? I collapse onto my knees, cradling my face in my hands. Queen Amity trusted me with a mission that could save the entire country. I've failed on the very first day. What kind of knight am I?

Right when I'm about to break down, I hear Nina call out from far away, "Are ya gonna sit there an' sulk all day?"

I look up to see her hazy figure. She's dozens of feet away from me down the road. "Where are you going?" I yell.

"Edinburgh!" She yells back. "You comin' or what?"

"Wait for me," I plead, running after her. When I reach her, my tears are wiped away, but more are threatening to fall at any moment. "Aren't you mad at me?"

"Ah already wouldah beaten th' shit outta you if this bracelet wuzn't on me. But Ah recognize that Ah fell fer th' trap too. 'Sides, whoopin' yer ass ain't mah main priority right now. We gotta find shelter, an' we gotta find it *fast*."

I find the courage to smile once more even as the weight of my mistake threatens to make me vomit. "I... I didn't realize you had such a practical side, Nina!"

"You can't call me that!"

"Why ever not?"

"Far as you know, 'Nina' wuz jus' a name Ah gave Cho so she would feel betta, if 'Cho' is even her name."

I cross my arms. "I take back what I said about you being practical."

"Too late fer that. C'mon, les' pick up th' pace. Trust me, ya really don' wanna be caught on th' Surface aftah dark."

We run alongside the destroyed road as the sun starts its slow descent and the air begins to chill. Time mercilessly marches forward to the beat of our footsteps, unconcerned with humanity's mortal problems. Despite the fact that my feet are throbbing, despite the fact that I lost us our transportation, despite the fact that we've been running for hours with no shelter in sight, I find myself smiling.

"It's been quite awhile since I've had such a good run. We've got—or had, perhaps, a gym with a treadmill underground, but it's not the same as feeling the sun on your back and the wind through your hair."

"Yer an intrestin' character, y'know that right?"

"Why do you," I catch my breath as I stumble over a crack in the road, "say that?"

"Neva thought a fussy gal like you would be intah exercise."

"F-fussy?"

"Yup, fussy. Ya spent like, what, twenty minutes in th' restroom this mornin'? Ah wuz half-'fraid we'd neva leave. What were you doin' in there? Needed tah get yerself off or sumthin' 'fore we left?"

"... Why, I *never*! If you continue to be so crude, I will not grace you with my magnificent time-obliterating conversation skills."

"'Course ya will. Ya ain't got no one else tah talk to."

"... I was freshening myself up. You are lucky I had to leave the colony in such a hurry, otherwise I would have been putting my makeup on for what you would consider to be ages."

"But *why*? Who ya tryin' tah pretty yerself up fer? Ya think yer gonna meet sum swell guy up here or sumthin'?"

"I'll have you know I was prettying up myself for *myself*, and that I'm into women."

Ugh, why *did I just say that?* It is not as though I am ashamed of my sexuality, but such information is usually on a need-to-know basis.

"Well Ah still don' get it," Nina says, not even flinching, "yer prettyin' yerself up 'cuz it's fun or sumthin'?"

"Well, it *is* fun. But think about it. Even before the invasion the world could be quite a bleak place. It has always been my duty to brighten the world with my beauty, and that hasn't changed since I became ugly. My hair is still marvelous, after all," I say proudly, flicking it back.

Nina was shaking her head in amusement, but frowned when I said "ugly". She groans, and then says, "Lissen, ya ain't ugly, alright? Ah wuz jus' givin' ya a hard time earlier cuz you've got this damn bracelet on me."

"Mm, I find that quite hard to believe," I say. *She's just being nice to me because we're becoming friends.* "Nevertheless, I appreciate you being polite."

"Ah ain't bein'—"

"It is *quite* the shame we lost Zack's bike," I say. The earnest tone of her voice is making my throat tight. I want out of this unfamiliar territory before my insecurities make made me do something mortally embarrassing. "I left my hairbrush in the luggage rack!"

"So, les' jus' ferget 'bout th' fact that we can starve up here, les' curl up an' cry ova a *hairbrush*. Ya really are fussy!"

I shake my head. "You couldn't possibly understand. My face is ruined. But I can at least make my hair look nice. At least I *could* with a hairbrush."

Nina groans. "Ah'm *tellin'* ya ya ain't u—"

kkkrrooooookkk!

It feels like I've jumped into a bathtub full of ice. Looking down the road I spot a single Feral hopping over a hill in the distance. It's the biggest one I've ever seen, easily over eight feet tall with claws as long as a tractor and a single, large eyeball in the middle of its head.

"What in the bloody hell is that," I hiss.

"Oh, *shit*. It's an Alpha Feral!"

Every nerve in my body tells me to run, but my brain isn't accepting the signals.

"Don' freak out. This guy is scary, but w-we might be able tah take him. Les' jus' hope our friend didn' bring any otha—oh mah God."

One by one, dozens of Feral hop over the hill and into the street. Soon enough, we're looking at an entire herd of hungry aliens heading straight towards us. Have they already caught our scent?

"Shit," Nina snarls. "Shit!"

I rip open my backpack, tear it open and yank out my perfume. I drown the two of us in its heavenly scent grab Nina's wrist and then turn us invisible. We hurtle towards the dead forest we've been running alongside. We stumble over broken sticks, fallen trees, and half-mutilated animals as we make our way deeper into the decayed habitat.

Ewewewewewewew

The Feral croak behind us. Did they catch our scent?

"I must keep calm," I whisper to myself. "I must keep calm."

The sounds behind us are getting louder. I pick up the pace, but I know we're done for.

"This is it," Nina murmurs. "Ah'm sorry, Lucio."

I trip over a beheaded deer with a small squeal, and then pick myself up. "Our journey is far from over. We'll get through this."

kkkrrooooookkk*!*

I don't believe my own words. Right when my façade is about to shatter I see an abandoned car crashed into a large tree just ahead of us.

"There!" I try to point at it, but Nina's already hauling me towards it. In the driver's seat rests the fresh corpse of a woman. Her head is busted open. Bits of her skull are embedded into the cracked windshield. "She—she killed herself!"

"Brilliant de-duction Sherlock." She yanks open the backseat door and drags me inside with her. I gently close it behind us. Outside the car, Feral are sniffing around. A small one with no claws picks up a dead bunny and bites off an ear. The young alien spits the ear out a second later, and then lets its bloody tongue hang out in what I suppose is disgust.

There's a *thud* on the roof. The entire car shakes.

"Ah don' wanna die," Nina whispers.

A pink spear goes through the driver's front seat window and into the dead woman's temple. Bits of sharp glass land on my body. My hand goes from Nina's wrist to her hand. The dead woman's head yanks to the side, then the rest of her body is ripped out the vehicle and into the mouth of the Alpha Feral. Hot plasma sears into the window next to my face. A pink sponge splashes against the glass and mops up the blood with a sickening twirl. The Alpha Feral's orange reptilian eye glares at us from outside while Nina squeezes my hand back.

"It can't see us," I hiss to reassure myself and Nina. But my scars are on fire. And I can't stop shaking. And I really have to pee.

It stares at us for one long moment, then hops over to the young alien and opens its mouth. The other Feral gather around the two of them in a circle, croaking and clicking their tongues. The young alien's mouth goes wide as the Alpha Feral's teeth start spinning. A torrent of blood, flesh and bones cascades into the young alien's open mouth. "Ah'm gonna be sick."

"Not in here you won't!"

We watch as the bizarre ritual reaches its conclusion. The young alien licks up the blood around its mouth while the Alpha pats it on the head. The weird chanting finally stops, and the aliens resume their search for food.

A few Feral creep in our direction. I try to slide down in my seat, but my legs are cramped as it is. If I were just a little shorter! "Where are they going," I whisper, using my free hand to cover my eyes.

Nina doesn't answer. She's still not answering! Right when I'm about to explode, she says, "'Round us.

W-we might be safe. They'll probably leave once they find mo' food. We jus' haftah wait it out."

"No no no don't tell me we'll have to spend the night here?"

Nina pushes her finger to her lips. "Shh! Yer hokeyness will get us both killed!"

I fight down a squeal. "But that means no shower, no pillows, no blankets! This is positively dreadful!"

"Would ya rathah be outside?"

I swallow. "Duly noted."

Nina lets go of my hand. My heart plummets for no particular reason while she takes off her backpack. A book is produced moments later.

I lean my head against the cold window with a groan. The condensation from my breath makes the glass foggy. Just how cold does it get out on the Surface at night? Would we freeze to death? I groan again, begging my brain to stop thinking of the worst possible outcome, but it doesn't help much. "This is going to be one long night."

"Ah hear that, pardner."

Chapter 14

"COCKADOODLEDOO!"

Ah flinch, open mah eyes an' look 'round. Mah head is sore from restin' 'gianst th' window all night, but there ain't a Feral in sight. Ah'll be damned, we actually made it! Ah find Minerva lyin' on mah shoulder, droolin' slobber all ova mah shoulder sleeve.

Ah smile. It had gotten so cold last night we had no choice but tah cuddle up. It wuz... nice, inna way, tah have sumone tah sleep next tah again, even if th' situation wuz life an' death. Ah turn mah head back towards th' window. Th' risin' sun's glow illuminates th' mutilated forest; bits o' flesh hang from dead trees all 'round us. Mah jaw drops in horror while Minerva snores quietly. Ah dunno whether tah laugh or cry, but Ah know that this is a moment tah remember.

Mah stomach rumbles sumthin' fierce, so Ah gently push Minerva offah me then open th' door. Ah try gettin' out but she's gotta death grip on mah hand. Ah pry mahself free, then go outside. Mah feet sink intah th' grass wit' a *squish.* Ah lower mah eyelids an' sigh. Mah shoe is soaked inna puddle o' blood. Ah slosh through th' forest an' grab th' least blood-soaked logs, then get tah work on makin' a fire. It feels humid tahday, almos' like summertime back in Texas.

Mah subconsciousness grabs th' steerin' wheel while mah brain buzzes loudah than a swarm o' bees. Ah hate tah admit it, but it mightah been a blessin' in disguise that Cho stole our cycle. Ah wuz ridin' that thing mighty fast. If we kept goin' at that speed, we mightah ran right intah th' herd an' not had enough time tah get away. Minerva's pops died froma tongue stab tah th' back. We came mighty close tah her sufferin' th' same fate.

Ah sure as hell hope Cho didn't.

Smoke takes flight as th' growin' flames consume th' wood Ah gathered. "Thanks, Pa."

Ah go back tah th' car, open th' front seat an' then th' trunk. Inside Ah find a tire iron on tahppah a spare tire. Ah grab it wit' a grin, then go tah th' backseat an' grab a can o' green beans from Minerva's backpack. Ah rip off th' paper labels an' cut sum holes through th' top wit' a knife, then Ah place th' can on th' outskirts o' th' flames. Ah twirl th' tire iron 'round in boredom, watchin' breakfast cook wit' half-interest. Tahday is gonna be anotha tough one.

Ah hear a car door close, an' sure enough it's Minerva steppin' outta th' vehicle. When her foot sinks intah th' grass she squeals, "EEEEEEEK," an' hops right back in th' car. Ah hear her scrappin' blood ontah th' car mat, body shakin' all ova like a leaf.

"C'mon out Minerva, th' water's jus' fine."

"How can you kid around at a time like this? This is the most horrifying thing I've ever seen in my life!"

"Thas' 'xactly why Ah gotta joke 'round 'bout it," Ah say. "Now ya ain't bein' logical here. This blood can't hurtcha. It ain't gonna go away no time soon. Ya might as well come out now an' get it ova wit'."

"No."

"Suit yerself. Guess Ah'll eat all th' breakfast."

"I'll have you know we still have a few cans left!"

"How're ya gonna cook it from inside a car? Ah know yer pampered ass don' wanna eat it cold."

Minerva inches a foot outside, but then goes, "Nina, I can't do this!"

"Ya fought me an' lived tah tell th' tale. Ya can handle this, pardner. Jus' pretend its water." She nods slowly, takes a deep breath, then gets out o' th' car. When her foot sinks intah th' warm wet grass, she winces like sumone is 'boutah hit her. But she still takes a delicate step towards me, lookin' me right in th' eye as she does so. Her endless blue eyes quiver like a hurricane o' turmoil is stormin' inside o' her, but when she takes anotha deep breath an' lets it out slowly, they've stilled a bit. "Feelin' a lil' betta?"

"Only a little."

"Ya wanna start ova an' pretend this neva happened?"

"That would be wonderful." She coughs lightly intah her wrist. "Good morning, Nina!"

"Mornin'!"

Every step she takes makes a *squish.* "This forest is positively dreadful. What do you suppose happened while we were asleep?"

"'Side from you droolin' all ova mah shoulder?" Minerva reddens, but remains silent, so Ah chuckle an' say, "We mus' not have been th' only ones hidin' in th' forest. There mustah been a fight 'tween th' Feral an' th' survivors, an' this is th' result o' that fight."

"I see. Well, I for one am glad last night wasn't the end of our blossoming friendship."

"We're friends?" Ah raise mah bracelet, scowlin'.

"Why, of course we are!"

"Prove it."

"I shall!" She turns 'round an' squishes her way back tah th' car. She returns wit' her backpack an' th' remote tah th' bracelet. Her thumb hovers ova a button fer a long moment, makin' me snap.

"Are we friends or not?"

"Of course we are, dear, but... yesterday, when we were on the motorcycle..." Mah stomach drops as she says, "I asked you what the Ignored planned to do with the survivors. After you answered, you started driving really fast. Were you going to...?"

"M-maybe th' thought crossed mah mind fer an instant. Butcha heard me yesterday. Ah don' wanna die. Ah didn' live through last night jus' so Ah could off mahself tahday."

"I suppose that logic makes sense." She swallows, but when her eyes meet mine. "Very well, I shall put my trust in you. That is what friends do, afterall." She presses th' button, makin' th' cold pressure 'round mah wrist relent. Ah rip th' blasted device offah me then stomp onnit fer good measure.

Ah approach Minerva, mah hand clenchin' th' tire iron tight. Her eyes narrow, an' aftah a long moment, she slowly clenches th' hilt o' her blade. "What are you doing, dear?"

Ah glower at her, starin' her down even though Ah'm lookin' up at her. "You put a shock bracelet on me."

Th' gentle giant stands her ground. "Indeed I did."

"Would ya do it again?"

"Unfortunately, yes."

Ah give her a long stare, then nod mah head in approval. Ah toss th' tire iron intah mah left hand, then hold out mah right. "Ah'm Nina Eagleheart."

She smiles. "I am Minerva Henswood. It is a great pleasure to be properly introduced to you!" Hm. Ah can see how she used tah be a model. She takes mah hand an' we shake. Her palms are calloused, but when our hands withdraw Ah feel her jus' how soft her fingertips are. When our eyes meet again Ah haftah look away. Mah face is burnin' sumthin' fierce. Why, though?

"All righty then, les' eat!" Ah use th' tire iron tah drag th' can outta th' flames.

"Wait, before that, I really have to use the ladies' room."

"Heh, alright."

She goes off an' does her business. Ah take a seat next tah th' flames, watchin' 'em dance in th' heat. A question comes tah mind right as Minerva returns.

"No plates or silverware... I suppose we'll have to eat this measly meal like cavemen."

"Welcome tah th' surface, enjoy yer stay!"

"That joke is even funnier now than it was two days ago," she says.

Once th' can cools off, we pass it back an' forth tah one anotha, slowly regainin' our energy. Ah keep mah ears open fer danger, makin' sure a Feral ain't gonna sneak up on us an' make us breakfast. Then Ah remember what Ah wuz gonna ask her. "Hey, why didcha have that bracelet in th' first place?"

Minerva winces. "It's dumb. Promise you won't laugh at me?"

"Nope."

She sighs an' shakes her head. "I wanted a strict way to control my diet. So I ended up ordering this online. I even had them make the shocks stronger. Whenever I ate something unhealthy, I gave myself a shock."

Ah wince. Jus' th' thought o' th' shock hurts, Ah can't even imagine doin' it tah *mahself*. "Yer crazy."

"Maybe so, but the bracelet helped me obtain my desired weight. Anyway, how far away do you think we are from Edinburgh?"

Ah kinda don' want th' conversation topic tah switch so easily, but she looks embarrassed enough as it is, so Ah decide tah let it drop. "Ah have no idea. You grew up here, not me! But lookin' at th' map, even though we covered a lot o' ground thanks tah Zack's bike we probably still have a few days walk ahead o' us. Mattah o' fact, how much longer do ya think our food will last us?"

"Roughly the same time frame if we limit ourselves to two cans a day."

"Then that settles it. We need tah do a supply run."

"With all due respect I think that Edinburgh should remain our first priority, especially since my dillydallying lost us our transportation in the first place."

"Minerva, ya still don' unnerstan' how things work up here. Mah brother died o' starvation, remember?" Th' pang o' loss hurts more than Ah 'xpccted, but Ah push past it wit' speech. "Th' Feral an' otha humans ain't th' only threats tah yer life up here. Makin' sure we're well stocked on food an' water has always gotta be our first priority. 'Sides, you realize how lil' food two cans a day is? Thas' basically one can fer each o' us fer a whole 24-hour span. When wuz th' las' time you ate that much food inna day? Do you realize how hungry yer gonna be?"

"Alright, I see your point. Very well then, we shall leave once we finish eating. Where are we headed?"

Ah point towards th' forest. "We gotta go explorin'."

She shakes her head, makin' her curly hair go flyin'. "But it's so icky out there!"

"Through that ickyness may be all th' supplies we could eva want. Think 'bout it. There's blood all 'round us. There mustah been a massacre last night, which means lots o' people, an' lots o' people means lots o' supplies. See mah logic?"

Minerva groans. "I hate today already."

"Up here, tahday always hates you. Butcha haftah be stronger than tahday if you wanna live." Ah rub mah throat. "Dang, Ah'm already gettin' thirsty. Les' hurry."

Minerva tosses me a water bottle. Ah catch it, then stand up. "Thanks."

"Not a problem, dear."

Ah take a swig, swish it 'round in mah mouth fer a bit then spit it out ova th' fire. Th' flames extinguish wit' a *hiss*.

"You are truly the crudest fire fighter I have ever met."

"Les' jus' go. We gotta hurry. If Ah'm right, an' sum o' th' blood here belongs tah th' Feral, anotha herd may not be too far behin'."

Minerva stands up, stretchin' her arms ova her head. "It's adventure time, I suppose. How dreadful!" Ah'm startin' tah stare at th' way that jumpsuit o' hers hugs her body in all th' right ways, so Ah look away an' walk deeper intah th' forest. "Wait for me!"

We walk through th' sloshy grass, seein' mo' signs o' yesterday's fight. Feral corpses litter th' walkin' path, sum o' 'em wit' hands stickin' outta their mouths or weapons stuck through their skull. "It's like I-day all ova again."

"I can only imagine."

"Ya don' haftah. This here is exactly what me an' Lucio saw, 'xcept twenty times worse wit' corpses fer miles on end."

Minerva trips ova a pair o' legs. Ah grab her hands, gettin' a brief taste o' those cloudlike fingertips as Ah help her up. "Thank you, dea–AHH!" She's finally noticed that them legs ain't attatched tah no torso.

Ah cover up her screechin' mouth. "Shaddup girlie! Don' draw attention tah us."

"Too late," A strangah's voice says. From th' shadow o' a bloody tree stands a pregnant black lady wit' fiery hazel eyes an' long dreads. Ah trytah draw mah pistol, but th' rifle she's got pointed at us makes me reconsider. "I wouldn't do that if I were you."

Ah holster th' pistol an' put mah hands up.

"You two are coming with me."

"Lead th' way."

"And leave my back exposed? This ain't my first rodeo sugar, and I suspect it ain't yours either. You know the drill." Ah sigh an' walk ahead o' her, then she presses th' rifle's barrel intah mah back.

"No one threatens my friends," Minerva growls, her hand goin' tah th' blade strapped tah her waist. "Put that wretched thing away within three seconds or I shall *destroy* you!"

Ah squint mah eyes at Minerva, wonderin' why she's flippin' out while th' lady says dryly, "You can destroy me all you want, but good luck saving your friend with a bullet through her heart."

"Three."

"Minerva, Ah really don' think—"

"Two."

"Are you *insane*? I'll really kill her!"

"On—"

Ah spring forward an' slam Minerva intah th' nearest tree wit' mah forearm. She hits th' wood wit' a *thud*, then glares at me like Ah'm Judas reincarnated. Ah whisper quick like, "Ah 'ppreciate yer defense, but we really outta go wit' her."

"But—"

"Jus' trust me, pardner."

"Ugh, *fine*," she whispers, then says loudly, "Unhand me, you ruffian!"

Ah let her go. "Sorry, Ah'd rathah not start th' day off wit' a bullet through mah heart."

Th' pregnant lady grabs me by th' arm, then jams th' rifle intah mah temple. "You better make damn sure Scarface over there behaves."

Flames burn through mah veins, but Ah keep walkin' forward. "You betta make damn sure you don' call her Scarface again."

Minerva coughs, her face flushed. "Not to worry dear, petite and unoriginal insults such as that no longer phase me."

"Shut the fuck up," th' lady growls.

"As you wish, oh round one."

Ah flash Minerva a grin... then th' back o' mah head explodes. Th' world splits intah two, makin' me see double. "Ugh..." Ah startah collapse, but Minerva catches me 'fore Ah can hit th' floor. She grits her teeth so hard it sounds like steel scrapin' against concrete. Th' lady matches her glare, levelin' th' rifle back at us again.

"It's... OK," Ah whisper, slumpin' 'gianst Minerva as Ah take anotha step forward. "She'll get hers."

We keep walkin', eventually comin' 'cross three walkin' trails. Ah shrug an' go tah th' left, but a poke tah mah back tells me Ah'm goin' th' wrong way. Ah turn tah glare at her, but she jus' points at th' middle path. A few snakes slither by as Ah walk forward. Minerva squeaks, "Eep!" an' grabs mah shoulders. Ah roll mah eyes an' keep walkin'. We follow that trail fer a bit, then take anotha turn. We find ourselves outside a large white house aftah maybe five minutes. Yup yup, a plain white house knee deep inna forest soaked in blood. Sumthin' ain't right here, an' it looks like Ah'm 'bout tah find out jus' what.

"Open the door," th' lady says. Ah open it, then hold it open fer Minerva.

"Ladies first."

Minerva grabs me by th' wrist, pulls me tah th' entrance, then gently pushes me inside ahead o' her. "You've become quite the flatterer, dear."

Mah cheeks get warm, an' not cuz o' th' heat. "Looks like Ah ain't th' only one."

We smile at one anotha, an' even though mah head feels like chopped beef Ah couldn't be happier. Then th' gunwoman cocks her rifle. "Hands in the air, back against the wall. *Now.*"

Minerva supports mah wobblin' self as we walk further intah th' house. Ah look ova th' livin' room. "Whoa nelly!" They gotta *workin'* HDTV 'gianst th' wall! Th' brown carpet is stained red. Not from blood, but from juice. There are cups all ova th' floor, along wit' dozens o' books, comics, an' DVDs. Ah 'spose they were in th' middle o' throwin' a hoedown when th' Feral crashed their party.

Ah see a kitchen on our way tah th' back wall. Loads o' unwashed dishes are piled up in th' sink, an' a bowl o' half-eaten popcorn rests on th' counter. Mah stomach roars. *Damn it, why didn' they eat it all? Wasteful bastards!*

Ah put mah back against th' wall, takin' mah place next tah Minerva. Th' pregnant lady aims her rifle at us. This ain't th' first time Ah've been held at gun point, but that don' mean Ah ain't scared.

Minerva grabs mah hand. Ah can't believe Ah'm sayin' this, but Ah'm glad Ah got her by mah side. Ah trytah catch her eye, but she's lookin' right at th' gunwoman, face harder than bark.

"You two wanna tell me what you were doing in *my* forest?"

"Hidin' from th' herd, thas' what. You wanna tell me why yer holdin' two innocent people hostage?"

"Well, I knew *someone* had to lead the Feral to us. Now I know who."

"How dare you accuse us," Minerva spits.

"There's no other way. Herds are nothing to us. We're so far off road they've never caught our scent. Until now."

Minerva's grip loosens as Ah say, "W-we were jus' tryin' not tah get, y'know, *eaten alive*. How where we 'sposed tah know you an' yer kin were hidin' back here?"

"I... maybe there was no way you could have known. But *I don't care.* My husband and the rest of my family are dead because of you two! I can't shoot the aliens, but I sure as hell can shoot you." She raises the rifle. "Last words?"

Minerva's grip turns iron. "You don't want to do this. If you shoot—"

Th' lady takes aim. A ripple o' black energy shimmers in frontah us, thena crack o' thunder makes me flinch. Ah await eternal darkness, but Ah can still hear sumone screamin'. Th' scream is cut short, an' Ah open mah eyes tah see th' lady's head snappin' back. She hits th' floor wit' a crash.

Wait, what?

Ah pat down mah entire body. Ah ain't dead. Why? Ah look at Minerva. She's standin' perfectly still, body stiffer than a muddy stick, but there ain't a hole in her either. Ah walk ova tah th' gunwoman. A sticky red gapin' hole has replaced one o' her eye sockets.

"... Guess ya weren't kiddin' when ya said she didn' want tah do this."

Minerva don' say nuthin', jus' stares at th' bloated corpse in frontah her. Ah put mah hand on her shoulder. "Hey, Ah unnerstan' what yer goin' through, but we gotta start packin' their supplies 'fore th' aliens come back. We can talk 'bout this latah, Ah promise."

She takes a step towards th' corpse. Then anotha, an' anotha, movin' slowa thana sloth. Her knees hit th' floor when she reaches it. She puts her hands on its belly. Her head sways from side tah side... then hits th' carpet wit' a *whump.*

"Uh, Minerva?"

kkkrroooooookkk!!!

Ah look at th' ceilin'. "Are ya kiddin' me?"

Ah run ova tah Minerva an' trytah pick her up. "Damn, why ya gotta be so heavy?" Mah muscles are cryin' harder than Lucio aftah he saw Bambi's Ma bite th' bullet, but Ah manage tah heave her up.

Ah wobble up th' stairwell. Every step is a stab tah mah knees, but Ah keep on walkin'. Ah kick open th' nearest door, but it's jus' a bathroom. Ah groan an' hobble towards th' *next* nearest door. Ah kick this one open, an' itsa bedroom. Perfect.

Ah lay her down on th' bed on her side, then take off her backpack so she can lay down flat. All 'round us are pictures o' th' dead woman an' her family, plus posters o' Michael Jackson an' Th' Beatles. It's too bad a family wit' such swell musical taste hadtah die so we could live.

Ah open th' closet an' find sum ovanight bags. Ah grab 'em an' startah run back downstairs, but then stop. A thought comes tah mind, an' 'fore Ah know it Ah'm in th' bathroom lookin' fer sumthin' stupid as all hell. But Ah find it soon enough, so Ah throw it intah th' bag then run back downstairs an' intah th' kitchen. Ah open th' cabinet, an' th' sight o' rows upon rows o' canned food an' bottled water makes me teary eyed. *Ya ain't got time tah be sentimental!* Ah sweep inna few armfuls o' supplies intah th' bags, then zip 'em up. Fer th' first time, there's too many supplies fer me tah carry. *Oh well.* Ah pick 'em up, but they're heavier thana pregnant pig. No way we can go on an adventure carryin' this much shit.

"OK Nina, stay calm an' jus' think," Ah murmur, joggin' back intah th' livin' room. Ah look ova th' corpse, shrug, an' then search its pockets. Mah fingers touch silver. Ah pump mah fist. Ah look 'round tah make sure no one saw me, then smile harder than diamonds as Ah pull out th' car keys. If this ain't th' mos' lucky break Ah've eva had, Ah dunno what is.

Ah run 'round th' house like an idiot, tryin' tah find th' garage. Ah come 'cross a heavy door in th' kitchen an' then fling it open. Sure enough, there's a white SUV restin' here with a "baby on board" and paw print car stickers plastered on the windows. Ah open th' backseat, run back tah th' bags, pick 'em up an' wobble ova tah th' car. Ah haul 'em intah th' backseat, then close th' door. Ah wipe mah forehead. Now Ah jus' gotta grab Minerva an'—*crash!*

"No," Ah whisper as Ah run tah th' garage door. Ah creek it open an' see a Feral hop through th' broken front door, then anotha hops in, then anotha an' anotha. Soon enough eight Feral are in th' house, an' they probably got sum friends not too far behin'. Ah shut th' door.

Eenope. Sorry pardner, Ah can't fight off that many. Ah snort. *'Sides, Ah've only known her fer like two days, an' one o' those days she had me shackled up like a dog. Ah ain't riskin' mah life fer sum ovadramatic gal. She'd be safe if she hadn't decided tah jus' faint. She's a wimp an' a burden. Ah'd be betta off goin' tah Edinburgh without her.*

Ah walk tah th' car door. Sapphire eyes stare intah mah soul from th' front seat window.

"No one threatens my friends!"

Ah shove th' car, pissed as hell. "Damn it all."

Ah creep back ova tah th' garage door an' open it again. Two Feral are lungin' towards th' corpse while anotha starts bouncin' towards th' stairs. Ah raise mah bow, heart leapin' intah mah throat. Ah notch an arrow an' pull th' string back.

Shoot th' damn thing. Ah wanna, Ah haftah, if Ah'm gonna save Minerva. But mah hands are shakin' so bad Ah can't even aim right. An image o' Queen Adelia pops intah mah head. She fought off an entire herd tah save th' lives o' people she'd jus' met. If she could do that, then fightin' eight aliens tah save a friend is nuthin'.

Ah take inna deep breath, then let go o' th' string. Th' arrow snags th' creature mid-hop, piercin' through both eyeballs an' pinnin' it against th' wall. *Thas' one.*

Th' rest o' th' aliens look at their dead friend, then at me. They howl. Th' combined shockwave sends me flyin' outta th' kitchen an' intah th' garage. Ah hit th' floor on mah back then flip tah mah feet, winded but alive.

A Feral bursts through th' garage door, so Ah notch an arrow an' shoot. Th' Feral swipes it's tongue, knockin' it tah th' floor. Ah roll unner th' tongue, an' when Ah'm upright again stab it in th' belly.

Its throat bubble thing expands an' fills wit' blood, but Ah'm already outside when Ah hear it explode. *Two.*

Ah run through th' broken front door. Two o' 'em are still tearin' through th' dead woman's stomach, makin' a thick red puddle ooze ontah th' carpet. Ah'm boutah take th' shot but a shockwave throws off mah aim. Th' arrow impales th' wall at th' back o' th' house. Th' Feral eatin' look up. Two sharp tongues go flyin' one aftah anotha while half-chewed baby finger spills tah th' floor.

Ah ready mah tomahawk, duck, chop off th' first tongue, then sidestep. Th' secon' tongue impales th' air next tah me, so Ah grab th' slimy wet muscle. Th' Feral gags an' retracts its tongue, sendin' me flyin' towards its wide-open mouth. *Thunk!* Ah dig mah tomahawk intah its forehead. *Three.* Ah grab th' beast's shoulders an' whirl it 'round. Th' Feral next tah us takes a swipe at me, but all it ends up doin' is rip open its comrade. A spray o' red splashes intah its eye, makin' it roar an' thrash 'bout wit' its claws.

Ah fall off th' dead Feral, then roll when its corpse hits th' floor next tah me. Ah put mah foot onnit an' trytah yank out Pa's axe, but it's stuck in there good. Ah'm pullin' an pullin' when a shadow at mah feet gets huge. Ah hurl a knife upwards then roll tah th' side. A Feral lands at th' spot Ah wuz a secon' ago wit' a *crash.* Blood sprays from its torn open throat. Th' stealthy bastard collapses while Ah shoot th' blinded Feral through th' back o' its webbed head. *Four an' five!*

Ah look 'round fer mah next target, but there's not an alien in sight. "Shit!" Aftah a few more strong pulls, Ah finally rip out Pa's axe an' run upstairs. Two o' 'em look like they're sniffin' th' air, but th' third one is slashin' through th' door thas' blockin' Minerva from 'em. Ah send three arrows through its skull. *Six.*

Th' last two Feral blast me wit' their shockwave. Ah stumble backwards but lose mah footin' midway. Ah tumble downstairs heads ova heels. Mah butt hits th' carpet an' Ah scoot backwards wit' flailin' feet. A pink spears stabs th' ground 'tween mah legs. Ah scramble tah mah feet an' run tah th' kitchen. Ah twist on th' stove, then turn tah face th' chargin' Feral. Ah swing. It leaps backwards. Mah right arm bursts open. A spay o' crimson splatters 'cross mah face an' a wave o' agony sweeps ova mah body, but Ah keep mah grip on Pa's axe wit' gritted teeth.

Its tongue comes flyin'. Ah run forward an' roll 'tween its legs, then chop intah its flabby ankle. Th' Feral screeches so loudly a nearby window shatters. Ah leap up, then shove th' alien ontah th' stove. Ah grab th' back o' its head an' slam it intah th' flames. *Hisssssssss!*

Seven.

Ah leap offah it 'fore it can get anotha swipe in. It whirls 'round an' lumbers towards me, but flames are eatin' away its eyeballs. They melt, its wide, waxy orange eyes shrinkin' in unimaginable pain. It takes one mo' wobbly step 'fore it collapses on th' carpet. "Shit!" Ah trytah stomp on th' flamin' beast, but anotha pink spear makes me roll tah th' side. Th' carpet is fully on fire now, an' th' flames are growin' quick. Ah gotta get Minerva outta here!

Th' last Feral retracts its tongue 'fore shootin' it again. Ah roll, reach fer mah toolbelt, snatch outta small silver ball, then hurl it intah th' Feral's open mouth. Ah charge it right as th' bomb explodes. A huge cloud o' smoke fills up th' Feral's bubble thing, makin' th' alien croak an' cough. Ah jump onnit, usin' its knees as steps an' steadyin' mahself by grabbin' ontah its left shoulder. Ah bring up Pa's axe.

Thunk. Thunk! *THUNK!*

Th' Feral's head rolls offah its shoulders.

An' thas' eight.

Ah leap offah it, then run upstairs. Ah dart tah th' room Minerva's in, leapin' ova th' dead alien. She's jus' lyin' on th' bed, lookin' bout as peaceful as a dove onnah lake. Ah sling her backpack ova mah shoulders then pick her up, right arm soakin' th' side o' her jumpsuit in blood. Ah'm sore all ova, an' this gal still weighs heavier than an elephant on steroids. So how am Ah findin’ th’ strength tah carry her downstairs?

Th’ entire lower floor is on fire. Th’ livin’ room is bathed in flames. There’s no otha path tah take. “Fuck me.”

Ah take mah first step downstairs. It feels like Ah’ve stepped ontah a billion micro needles an’ all o’ ‘em are on fuckin’ fire. But th’ secon’ step don’ hurt none, nor th’ third, or th’ fiftieth. Th’ flames are literally makin’ a path fer me tah walk through unscathed. It’s almos’ like there’s a barrier—

Ah look at th’ scarred warrior in mah arms. She snores.

This gal...

We pass by th’ dead lady’s burned, torn open corpse on our way tah th’ car. She smells worse than shit, but Ah still tip mah metaphorical hat tah her. “Sorry fer th’ intrusion. Thanks fer th’ grub.”

Ah take us back tah th’ car, open th’ door, then put Minerva in th’ passenger seat. Th’ engine starts aftah a few twists o’ th’ key. Mah head is a two-ton brick, mah right arm feels like Hell, an’ Ah really wanna take a nice long nap. But Minerva ain’t in no shape tah drive, so Ah don’ complain an’ whip us outta th’ garage. We’re already a good ways intah th’ forest when Ah see th’ house collapse in th’ rearview mirror. At th’ rate th’ flames are movin’, th’ whole forest will burn down.

“Too bad we couldn’t get anymo’ supplies. Ain’t that right, Minerva?”

She snores.

Chapter 15

*O*h, God damn it!"

A car engine? I open my eyes. Nina is in the driver's seat, smashing her fists against the wheel. I'm right next to her, seatbelt secure. We're back on the road, but we're not moving.

"Whoops. Sorry, Ah didn' mean tah wake you up."

"It's quite all right dear, but may I ask you why your arm is ripped open?" Three deep gashes with a familiar pattern streak across her arm. The same pattern is mapped across my face.

"Oh, this?" *She raises it and oozes even more blood over the seat. A smelly puddle sloshes around on the car matt.* "This ain't nuthin'. That cut ya gave me th' otha day hurt worse than this." *She opens the door and motions to leave.*

"Where are you going?"

"Ah gotta check th' starter."

I almost hyperventilate. "You are *bleeding*. Now is not the time to play mechanic!"

"Minerva," *Nina says with a pause, voice weakening for an instant.* "If we can't get this thing started soon we'll be stranded on th' road. A-gain. Ya really wanna risk runnin' intah anotha herd?"

"Sit. Down." She plops back in her seat with a grunt and wince. "Did you manage to grab my backpack?"

"Who do ya think Ah am?" *She jerks a thumb to the backseat, where my backpack is. Its lower half is burnt to a crisp. I grab the smelly thing with pursed lips and open it. I take out my transparent emergency care kit and our last bottle of water.*

"Woah, you are nurse or sumthin'?"

"Of course not, but all Knights are trained in basic healing techniques."

"H-how do Ah know them needles are clean?"

I resist glaring at her. "The Queen of England does not supply her Knights with inadequate resources."

"Oh, so that bitch gave you this junk?" I bite my tongue. "Now Ah definitely ain't lettin' ya stitch me up."

"I'll have you know I used some of this so-called junk on you after our fight."

"Not with my permission!"

What *is the problem here?* "At least let me clean the wound out."

"... Fine."

She holds out her arm. I uncap the bottle and slowly pour water across her arm. A drizzle of red floods the car matt and makes the smelly puddle smellier. Nina is grinding her teeth together so hard I can hear the crunch. "Sorry."

"What Ah tell you 'bout 'pologizin' fer sumthin' ya had no control ova?"

I purse my lips as the last of the water drips from the bottle. "I wish we had more. This may not be enough to clean the wound."

"Check those bags Ah got in th' backseat."

I crush the now empty bottle, throw it in the backseat and reach for an overnight bag. I unzip it, and its contents make me gasp. "This will last us at least a week!"

"It betta last us *two weeks*," Nina mumbles. I grab a few more bottles and rinse the wound thoroughly. I nod, satisfied. I'm ready to stitch the wound!

"Hold out your arm."

"No."

"I am not asking you anymore. You'll die if I don't stitch that wound *now*."

I grab the emergency health kit and prepare the needle and thread. Then I take out the latex gloves and stretch them on with a look of disgust. The texture always felt, I don't know, *icky* to me. "Let us get to work. As you said, we don't want to be out here forever."

"Ah told ya Ah ain't—"

I reach for her arm, but she throws a fist. A barrier shimmers to existence and blocks the blow. I stare at her for a long moment, then ask very carefully, "Do you really think you can fight me in that condition?"

"N-now that wuz an accident!"

"*Calm down.* Let me help you, dear. Now hold out your arm before I punch you out again."

She holds her arm out once more. I give her a long skeptical look, then shake my head and prepare the needle again. When it touches her skin, her entire body quivers. "I've figured it out!"

Nina snorts loudly, trying to keep her pride intact. "What am Ah, a puzzle?"

"Of sorts, yes. You're afraid of needles, aren't you?"

"A-Ah ain't 'fraid o' nuthin'!"

"Then *stay still.* I wasn't kidding about punching you out."

It takes a bit of arguing to calm her down, but after awhile the needle finally pierces her skin. She quivers but bites her lip and keeps her composure like a true lady. I never realized how adorable she is. Wait, did I just call her adorable? *Ugh*, I did not just think that.

Here we go again. If I were to have a superhero name like those gentlemen in Texas, it would be Love Struck Fool.

I shake my head and start stitching the wound. Nina's left hand has a death grip on the wheel. She's too tense. If she starts shaking again, things could get even worse. *Take her mind off the needle.*

"So are you going to tell me what happened when I was unconscious?"

"No."

"Ahaha, excuse me?"

"Ah said no."

"Whyever not?"

"Cuz ya don' wanna know."

"Yes, I do, in fact."

Nina raises her left eyebrow slowly. "Do ya really?"

"Yes. No. Yes."

"OK, well... you saved our lives. Twice. End o' story."

Thread by thread, stitching it together... "You're an awful liar, Nina."

"Ah ain't lyin', but Ah ain't tellin' ya th' whole story neither. Ah'm jus' tryin' tah spare yer feelin's."

"I appreciate your goodwill, but I simply must know the truth if I am to get a good night's rest. Stay perfectly still, dear, this will sting." The needle and thread close part of the wound. Nina winces again. "Sorry." She shakes her head with a small smile, but remains silent as I continue stitching. "...Hem-hem," I cough lightly.

No response.

"I'm waiting for my answers, dear."

"... Y'know, Ah read a lot."

I glare at her. "I am aware. So do I. Do not change the subject."

"Ah ain't, ya gotta lissen tah where Ah'm goin' wit' this."

I sigh. "Very well."

"One o' th' books Ah read talked a lot 'bout memories. It said that th' brain sumtimes gets rid o' bad memories tah protect yer ego."

"And the point of this psychology lesson is…?"

"Ya don' remember what happened cuz yer brain made ya ferget."

"So you're going to make me remember." I finish stitching the first gash. The second needle pierces Nina's skin.

She scowls. "Yer stubborner than mah ol' granny."

"I suppose we're more alike than what was initially assumed," I shoot back.

"Ya wouldn' be mistaken." I look up from the middle gash to see her smiling at me, making her emeralds twinkle in the sunlight. I look back down quickly; face burning as I get back to work.

Nina sighs, and I can practically hear her smile wither away and die a slow death. "Looks like ya ain't takin' no fer an answer. Ah'll tell ya th' truth then. That woman tried tah shoot us. You deflected th' bullet wit' yer powers. It ricocheted an' put a hole through her head. You walked over tah her corpse, put yer hand on her belly, then ya fainted." I keep stitching the gash, but it's hard to see through blurry vision. "Ow! Stop shakin' now, that thread hurts."

"I-I killed a pregnant woman?"

"A pregnant woman who wuz 'bout tah kill us, yeah." My stomach feels like I ate glass for breakfast.

The car starts to shrink inwards. *We're going to be crushed!* A hand reaches out, but my barrier stops it from making contact. "See, this is why Ah didn' wanna say nuthin'." She shakes her head. "Neva mind that. Jus' take deep breaths, gal. Everything's gonna be fine."

I reach to roll down the window, but something stops me. *You'll contaminate the gloves and get Nina's wound infected. Keep it together, at least for now. You're a knight, and even the lowest of knights can stitch wounds.* I use my elbow to press the button instead. I poke my head out the window and take in deep breaths. After one long moment I get back to stitching. It feels like I'm making good progress despite my blurry vision. Then I see a burst of red and a head flying back. *Oh my God. I really did kill someone.* "T-this is *your* fault!"

Nina snorts. "So its mah fault *you* deflected a bullet?"

"If we had just *left* the forest instead of going further into it, we never would have run into her!"

"You wanna play that game? If you hadn't lost mah damn bike, we neva wouldah been stranded on th' road, an' we neva wouldah hadtah run intah th' forest in th' first place!"

My face burns with rage as I finish stitching the second gash and get to work on the third. "That wasn't your bike. You stole it!"

"Jus' shut it! 'Sides, if we hadn't ran intah that lady we neva wouldah found all these supplies."

"So killing people is OK as long as you get to take their stuff afterwards?"

"Thas' not what Ah'm sayin' an' y'know it!"

"Then what *are* you saying?"

"That... oh, Ah dunno! But that lady wuz bad news. She had a death wish—she wuz gonna die anyway."

"You're just saying that to make me feel better. How can you say such a thing? I killed an unborn child and its mother, do not make light of the issue!"

"Naw, think o' it as you killin' a parasite an' its murderin' host."

I glare at her like it was *my* baby that got killed. She has the dignity to not look me in the eye. "'K, maybe that wuz outta line. But y'know exactly what Ah mean when Ah say that she wuz gonna die anyway."

"Elaborate."

"You said, 'If you shoot—', right 'fore she cut ya off mid-sentence, by, y'know, *tryin' tah shoot us.* If she hadn't interrupted ya, what were ya gonna say?"

"I... I believe I was going to tell her that if she fired, the sound of the bullet and the smell of our blood would have drawn the Feral to her."

"Exactly. Y'know what that means, right?"

"Are you insinuating that she planned to kill herself?"

"Duh. She lost her whole family inna single night. Her husband, maybe sum siblings or grandparents, maybe even another son or daughter. There wuz a lot o' blood in that forest, an' we know it wuzn't all from th' Feral. She'd gone cuckoo, Minerva, an' Ah'll tell ya why. If she wuz jus' gonna kill us from th' start, why didn' she jus' ask us questions in th' forest an' shoot us dead? How come she dragged us all th' way ova tah her house when she wouldah been helluva lot safer jus' shootin' us in forest an' goin' back tah her house?"

"Because…because…"

"There ain't no otha reason. She led us tah her house so that aftah she killed us, th' Feral wouldah killed her too. An' even if Ah'm crazy, an' there's sum othah reason why she brought us ova there, *she still wouldah died anyway.* Ah didn' get this wound pickin' flowers! Aftah you fainted, eight o' 'em came burstin' through th' front do—Ouch!"

"Sorry! It's just, that's, well, bloody unbelievable! How did you escape and rescue me at the same time?"

"Well, Ah gotta backtrack a bit. Aftah ya fainted Ah took ya upstairs, then used sum overnight bags tah get as much supplies as we could. Ah found a car key on th' lady's corpse an' threw everything in th' backseat. Ah wuz 'bout tah go back inside an' grab ya, but thas' when th' Feral arrived."

I finish stitching the third gash. Her arm is still caked with dried blood, but at least she's not at risk of bleeding out anymore. Nina graces me with a smile. "Thanks, gal. Sorry fer freakin' out."

"Not to worry, dear. But I'm even more confused now. How did you sneak past eight of them?"

"Y'know damn well no one can sneak past eight o' 'em damn things. Even *you* would have a hard time doin' that."

I take in a sharp breath. "You went through a house full of aliens just to save me?"

"Uh, yeah?"

My vision is wavy. "Nina, it took all of my courage just to fight *one* of them. I can't even imagine…" Raw emotion tightens my throat. "You could have left me behind, but you didn't. Why?"

Nina looks out the window, her chin resting in her palm. "Ah—Ah dunno why Ah saved ya, Minerva. Ah sure as hell wuz 'boutah tah leave ya once Ah saw all o' 'em come inside. Ah didn' think Ah could pull it off. Mattah o' fact, Ah still dunno how Ah pulled it off. But when Ah wuz 'bouta leave you, Ah saw yer eyes lookin' at me from this here window. Thas' when Ah realized sumthin'." She turns to look at me, her springtime eyes blossoming in the sunlight. "Ah care 'bout ya. Alot. Yer th' only friend Ah've got left in this world, Minerva. An' Ah sure as hell ain't gonna lose you too."

Something large and heavy gets stuck in my throat. Nina chuckles as my mouth flips and flops open like a dying fish. No words are coming out. Why can't I speak?

"Hey, uh, 'fore we left, Ah got ya sumthin'." She reaches into one of the overnight bags in the back seat, and then slaps a purple hairbrush into my palm. "Thought ya might want this."

My mask shatters. Tears fall from my eyes faster than the water streaming down Cautkey Spout. My chest heaves as I take in deep breaths, unable to fill my lungs with enough oxygen. Gratitude at having my life saved by such a true friend makes me weep tears of joy, but the weight of taking two lives from this world threatens to destroy my heart. I am ecstatic, but I am devastated. My chest is warm and cold at the same time. I am a whirlwind of paradoxical emotions. I take in a shaky breath, and for one moment I am calm. Then I sob even harder.

Out of the corner of my eye, a brown hand stained with blood reaches for my person. No supernatural barrier shimmers to existence, but before she makes contact with my shoulder she pulls away as if my body is spewing flames.

"Ah, uh, Ah betta go check on that starter. Call me if ya need anythin'."

I try to say, "Of course, dear," but all that comes out is a series of strangled intelligible words. Nina makes a swift exit.

If I hadn't killed it, what kind of person would that baby grow up to become? Would they grow up to make this desolate world a better place, or would they follow in their mother's footsteps and be swallowed by the angry beast that dwells within us all? Was it even possible to raise a child, a ray of hope, in a world as dark as this? I suppose I'll never know.

The car's hood pops open, blocking my view of Nina. My thoughts do a one-eighty. Nina saved my life. She went through *eight Feral* just to save me. She even went through the trouble of getting me this hairbrush, a trivial item that shouldn't have even crossed her mind in the very definition of a life-or-death situation. We went from worst enemies to the best of friends in a matter of days. For our relationship to progress so much in so little time, for such terrible events to occur and give birth to such a beautiful friendship... as awful as the past few days have been, I wouldn't take them back for anything.

The engine stutters, then roars to life. The car's hood slams down, and I'm greeted by Nina's beautiful smiling face. "Edinburgh, here we come!"

Chapter 16

"OH, GOD DAMN IT!"

Th' God damn car engine is stutterin' like a God damn stutterin' car engine, but Minerva is havin' a God damn gigglin' fit. "Ya realize we're stranded in th' middle o' a city? We were safer out there on th' highway than we are here." Minerva hugs herself an' giggles even harder. Has she gone nuts? She's been flippin' 'tween happy an' sad eva since she woke up, almos' like she's got a God damn split personality disorder. "Now there ain't nuthin' funny 'bout this. We could run intah sum real sickos out here!"

"No, dear, it's just, nnnhghghgh!"

Ah sigh an' roll mah eyes. "All right all right, whas' tickilin' yer funny bone?"

"You are, without a doubt, the bravest person I have ever met. But you're, but you're—hahaha!"

"You makin' fun o' me?"

Minerva sticks her bottom lip out an' makes those ocean orbs go big. Gee, if they got any bigger Ah jus' might drown in 'em... wait a sec, Ah'm still pissed off, right? Ah bare mah teeth at her, only cuz Ah dunno how tah swim.

"I'm only teasing. Please, do not take it personally. It's just... the idea of a fearless warrior whose bested human, metahuman, and alien alike, cowering over a little needle..." She laughs so hard she grabs her belly, an' Ah can't help but smile at th' sight. "Nina, you couldn't get cuter if you tried."

Ah sling on mah backpack an' get outta th' car, tryin' tah ignore th' fact that it feels like sumone dipped th' tip o' mah ears in lava. "Ah'm many things, Minerva, but Ah ain't cute." Ah cough. "Th' ovanight bag is too heavy tah carry wit' us. We'll haftah leave it here fer tahnight. Hopefully no one steals it." Ah close th' door right as she opens hers, grinnin' all th' while.

"You realize denying it only makes you cuter?" Ah shake mah burnin' face from side tah side then walk off. Ah hear her close th' door behin' us an' scramble tah catch up. "Wait for me!"

We walk down th' clustered street. Dozens o' cars wit' bloody interiors block our path further intah th' city. What a pain in th' ass. Would Ah have even been able tah drive us outta here if th' car hadn't broke down?

Ugh, walkin' is gettin' tough. Startin' tah feel woozy. Gotta keep goin', can't collapse here...

"Oh my... now I see why you didn't want to be here."

"This..." Ah take a deep breath, "ain't why Ah didn' want tah be here. Yer gonna see horrible stuff like this everywhere ya go, it's jus' unavoidable. Ah'm jus' 'fraid o' runnin' intah othah people."

Ah toss a glance tah mah side, but she ain't there. Mah heart *pounds* fer one long, evalastin' secon', but then Ah see her. She's lookin' intah a pink van wit' shattered windows. A teddy bear wit' no head lies on th' car mat, its brown fur soaked in blood. Minerva covers her mouth, then her eyes start tah water, makin' mah chest ache. Ah grab her warm hand an' gently pull her away. "Everyone wuz tryin' tah leave th' city all at once, an' it made 'em an easy meal fer th' Feral. Ain't nuthin' no one can do 'bout that."

Ah've pulled her from one atrocity, but that don' mean nuthin'. There's horror stories whereva ya turn. Minerva has gone quiet. Ah look back tah make sure she's still there, an' she is, but she's cryin' again. We pass by a car wit' a bloody carriage, an' when Ah look back at her this time her face has gone blank. "Jus' keep yer head down. Ah'll get us outta here lickity split, don' you worry now."

"I will not look away."

"Why're ya doin' this tah yerself?"

"To remind myself I wasn't the only one who suffered because of the invasion. To not give into hopelessness and instead surrender myself to outrage, the outrage that will give me the will to *destroy every last one of those monsters.* I swear, I won't rest until they're all—"

Ah chuckle. "Yer so dramatic."

Minerva's eyes go half-lidded, but at least now she's jus' unamused insteadah 'boutah blow a gasket.

"Either way, ya can't go on no rampage onnah empty stomach, or wit' outta good night's rest."

Minerva sighs deeply. "I suppose you are correct. Let us find shelter, then."

Ah look 'round. "Found it!"

She yelps as Ah drag her through th' maze o' cars tah reach th' massive brown stoned hotel in th' distance. Ah lead us in frontah th' buildin'. It's got a few shattered windows an' sum o' th' stones are cracked, but otha than that th' place is in great shape considerin'. A sign wit' big, rusted gold-colored letters says 'The Apex Hotel'. "This looks like a good place tah spend th' night. Whaddya think?"

She lets go o' mah hand. "It seems too... normal. What if this place is already occupied?"

"There ain't no 'stay out' sign an' there ain't a corpse nearby. Ah think we're good."

She squirms like she jus' drank sum bad milk. "I don't know about this."

Ah shrug. "Ah unnerstan' why yer cautious, but Ah'm too damn tired tah care. Ah need a bed tah sleep in. That car ain't gonna cut it tahnight."

"You *did* lose a lot of blood. Sleeping here would be quite convenient, all things considered. However..." She frowns.

"Look, don' ova think this. All ya gotta do is turn us invisible. We'll go intah th' nearest room an' lock th' door. We're probably safer in there than out here when ya really think 'bout it."

Ah keep movin' towards th' entrance. Sure enough, Minerva falls in step wit' me aftah a few moments.

"Oh, alright. I hope you realize you are the only person I'd follow into a place like this."

"An' tah think two days ago ya didn' trust me wit' a knife. Fer shame!"

"You were going to—"

"Oh, have a sense o' humor."

"Just because I do not laugh at your grotesque jokes does not mean I lack a sense of humor, it merely means your jokes are unfunny."

"If ya don' learn tah laugh at this awful place an' th' things it'll push ya tah do, yer gonna have a hard time comin' up wit' reasons tah smile."

"I wouldn't be so sure about that, dear." She winks at me.

A wave o' chillin' heat sweeps through mah body. Ah jus' stare at her while she opens th' door fer me. "Heroes first."

Ah push her inside, finally findin' mah voice again. "D-didn' Ah tell ya ya saved our lives twice earlier?"

"Any particular reason why you're stammering, dear?"

Whas' happenin' here? Mah heart starts tah pound... "N-now thas' besides th' point! Look, Ah'll tell ya th' whole story once we're inna room. Fer now, les' act stealth like."

Minerva grabs mah hand an' turns us invisible. Ah'm glad she can't see me anymo'. Whas' she doin' tah me? She's makin me feel... off. So why am Ah lookin' forward tah hangin' wit' her mo'?

Th' hotel is dark, but not really scary. Ah can almos' hear a gentle *hum* comin' from sumwhere that puts me at ease. It's hard tah see much o' anythin', but Ah guide us tah what Ah'm pretty sure used tah be a receptionist desk. Ah swipe a rusted paper clip from th' cabinet then lead us upstairs. We approach th' nearest door, but when Ah trytah open it th' knob won't budge. Ah sigh. Guess Ah gotta let go o' her hand now.

Ah give Minerva a nudge, an' she takes th' hint. She lets go o' mah hand, an' Ah find mahself lookin' at her frownin' face. We share a grin in th' darkness. Maybe, jus' maybe, Ah wuzn't th' only one who didn' wanna let go. Ah shake mah head. Th' longer we're out here visible, th' mo' danger we're in. It don' take me long tah unlock th' door wit' th' paper clip. *Click.*

"Marvelous work, dear!" Ah almos' walk in ahead o' her, but Ah hold it open fer her instead. Minerva giggles. "Are we going to do this every time we encounter a door?"

"Ah dunno, maybe."

She motions tah push me in, an' Ah stumble backwards intah th' room. She trips an' collapses on tahppah me, two hunned pounds o' toned muscle crushin' mah thin bones. Hah. Ah'm glad th' floor is carpet, othawise this cutesy shit wouldn' be so cute. "Oof!"

Th' soft, warm weight goes away. Ah'm surprised by how disappointed Ah am. "I'm sorry!"

Ah groan. "Damn gal, ya weigh mo' thana rhino!"

She stomps on th' ground, then locks th' door behin' us. "That is simply *not* true!"

"Yer jus' too tall." Ah get up, wobble towards th' bed, then dive ontah it. Mah body bounces up an' down a lil' 'fore Ah'm nice an' comfy. "Ya ruined everything, see. We both fell on th' ground at th' same time. This wuz 'sposed tah be th' part where we look intah each otha's eyes an' kiss, butcha jus' flattened me like a pancake!"

Snort. "It's too dark to see anyway. I'd end up snogging the floor!"

We laugh. "Ah neva did finish tellin' ya 'bout how ya saved us both a secon' time earlier tahday."

"Carry on, then!" Ah hear her start shufflin' 'round.

"When Ah wuz—" *Click.*

Ah blink, stunned at th' light that jus' turned on. "Wow," Minerva says. "This place still has electricity!"

An alarm bell goes off in mah head. There's no way a vacant hotel has electricity, right? Sumone has to be here maintaining th' place. Ah'm considering havin' us leave, but th' bed is stupid warm. 'Sides, its dark outside an' we've been invisible almos' th' entire time we've been in here. How could anyone have seen us? Plus, th' door is locked. "Huh. They mustah installed a generator sumwhere." Th' carpet is brown an' th' walls are light green. Itsa nice lookin' place wit' a round brown table in th' livin' room an' a small kitchen off tah th' side.

"Anyway, when Ah wuz fightin' th' Feral, Ah set one o' 'em on fire. By th' time Ah grabbed ya from upstairs, th' flames had already consumed th' whole lower floor."

"No wonder my backpack smells burnt."

"Ah thought we were done fer, but th' flames started movin' away from us wit' every step Ah took."

Minerva grabs her head "I... what?"

"Ya made a barrier 'round us tah protect us all while ya were asleep. Yer amazin', Minerva."

She smiles sadly. "Oh, I'm nothing special."

"How can ya say that? There ain't no one else on this planet that couldah pulled off what ya did, metahuman or othawise."

"Tell me, dear. If I did all of this while I was unconscious, how does that make what I did special? If you had my powers, the same built-in defense mechanism would have activated. I didn't do anything to warrant acclaim. On the other hand, dear, you deserve all the acclaim I am capable of giving, if not more."

"Cuz Ah killed sum Feral? Thas' got mo' tah do wit' luck than skill, Ah guaran*tee* it."

"One cannot boil down the act of killing a house full of aliens to simple luck."

Mah eyes are gettin' heavy. "A-Ah jus' did."

"You're impossible," Minerva giggles.

"Whateva ya say. Lissen, Ah'm plum tuckered out. Do ya think ya can cook tahnight?"

"Absolutely! Leave it all to Mama Minerva."

"... Please don' eva say that again."

"Oh, wonderful!"

Her raw enthusiasm wakes me up a bit. "Didcha find any fresh food? A bushel o' apples, by chance?"

"Of course not. But I did find some plates and silverware. There's even a working stove! We shall eat like royalty tonight."

Mah eyes are heavy again. "Well thas' jus' great," Ah drawl.

"Indeed!"

Is this gal unaware o' th' concept o' sarcasm? Ah shrug. "Jus' wake me up when dinner's ready."

"Will do."

Ah grab a book from mah backpack, but Ah'm only a few paragraphs in 'fore th' world 'round me has faded tah nuthin'ness. An instant latah, a stench invades mah nostrils, takin' me outta th' tranquility that is sleep an' throwin' me back intah a harsh reality. "Whoa, wuz that smell?"

"My awful cooking."

"How'd ya manage tah burn a can o' beans? Ya cooked 'em jus' fine two days ago."

"I am afraid that was merely a fluke. I only learned how to operate the stove a few days ago. Cooking is not a skill I grasp easy."

Ah snicker. "Ain'tcha named aftah th' Roman goddess o' wisdom?"

"The irony is not lost on me."

"So ya can talk fancy, make force fields, an' turn invisible, butcha can't cook a can o' beans without burnin' it?"

"*Most* amusing."

"Am Ah irritatin' ya?"

"Yes."

"What're ya gonna do 'bout it?"

Minerva's turns away from th' stove, eyes flashin' wit' determination. "I suppose I'll have to *shut you up*."

Ah stannup as she starts movin' towards me. Mah heart has jumped right intah mah throat. *Oh God, what've Ah done? Is this really 'bout tah happen?* She's killin' distance fast. So many thoughts are goin' through mah head right now, but they all go quiet once Ah look intah those eyes. Ah dunno whas' gonna happen next. All Ah know is that Ah wanna get as close tah those eyes as possible.

Ah grab her by th' waist an' pull her in. Our noses bump, makin' us giggle like school gals. Minerva's lips pucker. Shit. Ah done fergot howtah breathe.

All Ah haftah do is move forward. Ah wanna kiss her, really Ah do, mo' than anythin' Ah've wanted inna long time. So why ain't Ah leanin' in? It's like sumone dumped a bucket o' supahglue right on tahppah me, rootin' me intah place.

Minerva's sapphires start glistenin'. "What's wrong, dear? You don't want this? Have I misread things?"

Th' answer rams me like a bull. "Ah'm scared." Ah let her go an' back away, body quiverin' like a baby experiencin' its first winter. "God, Ah'm so scared."

"Of what, darling?"

"O' *losin' ya*, idiot! Mah brother told me tah find sumone who makes me happy. Ah ain't ashamed tah say that yer that sumone, Minerva—but if Ah lose ya too, Ah jus' dunno what Ah'll do."

Minerva don' say nuthin', jus' walks forward an' holds out her arms. "A-Ah miss him so much."

"Shh." Her soft an' nimble fingers stroke through mah hair as she rubs mah back. "It'll be alright."

Bein' this close tah her feels too good tah be true. It'll make losin' her all th' worse. Ah push her offah me. "No it won't! Sooner or latah one o' us is gonna die, an' th' otha will be left all alone." Mah tears are hot an' bitter. "It ain't fair."

"It isn't fair, Nina. But let me ask you something. You loved your brother, correct?"

"No shit."

"He's gone now, and his loss still hurts. Chances are it will for the rest of your life. But if he had never been born, you never would have felt this pain. If you could erase his existence, would you?"

"Hell no."

"Why ever not?"

"Cuz even though he's gone, Ah still have th' memories Ah made wit' him. Nuthin' can take that away from me." Minerva gently grabs ahold o' mah cheek an' brushes away a tear wit' her thumb.

"I want to make more memories with you."

Ah can't look her in th' eye. She'll suck me in. "Th' memories ya already made can't be that great. We've only been on th' road two days an' so much awful stuff has happened."

"You're wrong. Last night should have been the worst night of my life. We were trapped in that car for hours and it was so cold. The day's almost over and I *still* can't get the smell of blood out of my nose. So tell me why that was the best sleep I've had in years?"

"... Come tah think o' it, Ah slept pretty good too." Ah smile despite mahself. "Bein' snuggled up wit'cha wuz nice."

"Please, look at me." This time, there's no mistake. Ah'm drownin' in those ocean eyes. "I feel safe next to you. I feel like I can tell you anything. I feel closer to you in a span of 48 hours than people I have known for years." She rests her forehead against mine. "I do not care that one of us will die one day. Right here, right now, I just want to be closer to you."

Ah wrap mah arms 'round her an' bring her in tight. Minerva squeezes back, but then grabs mah shoulders an' gently pushes me away.

"*Nina*." Sumthin' 'bout th' way she says mah name sends chills down mah spine. It's like her eyes are lookin' right intah mah soul. Ah've neva seen her look so damn serious before, not even when we were tryin' tah kill each otha. "Are you ready?"

Ah want tah call her ovadramatic, but all Ah can do is nod. Ah close mah eyes an' startah lean in.

Click.

Ah push Minerva away hard as th' door bursts open. A wave o' men rush intah th' room. Ah grab th' pistol, but—

A punch to the face knocks my dear flat. As soon as she collapses, seven men crowd around her, caressing her body all over, reaching into her shirt, her pants—

One of them shrieks in pain, and through a blur of bodies I see a knife sticking from his gut. "Back away, she's mine!"

A viscous brawl ensues as I watch from the shadows, eyes steeling with rage. An explosive step shoots me across the room. The Blade of Justice yearns for blood!

"Hey, isn't there supposed to be another girl here?" A burly blonde man hollers above the commotion. "Where'd she go?"

"Right here," I hiss, grabbing his hand then slashing through his fingers. A red arc splashes onto my jumpsuit as I burst the hilt of my sword into the back of his head. He goes limp, his mutilated hand twitching as he collapses.

I stab a long-haired spectacled man in the ankle from behind. His head flies back howling. I stomp on his front toe so I can lurch out the blade, then I yank his hair backwards and slam him onto the floor. A nasty crack makes my stomach squirm, but even so, I grab an olive-skinned arm reaching for Nina, then slam my knee through the front of his elbow. He wobbles backwards with an ear-piercing cry, his arm hanging limply to the side. I flash forward and stamp my blade's hilt into his eyeball. He falls as sticky blood drizzles down my hand.

I approach another man from behind, but a blur of silver makes me jump backwards. A familiar tomahawk is cleaved into the side of his throat.

Another fierce chop sends his head rolling off his shoulders in a geyser of crimson to reveal a blood-soaked Nina, her jaw set and her eyes piercing.

I turn visible. Nina gives me a stern nod, and the two of us turn our attention to the last man standing, a large, built person wearing a sweat cap. He backs up slowly, his baby face unable to hide the fear in his soft eyes. Wait a moment...

I narrow my eyes. The man turns to run, but Nina throws a knife into his thigh that stops him flat. He topples to the floor and the sweat cap falls off, revealing wavy brown hair. "You're a woman! How dare you help these retched men commit such a foul act?"

She yanks the knife out of her leg with a grunt, then crawls backwards, a desperate grin on her face as blood spills from her thigh. "We were watching you two on our cameras. We're more alike than you think, you know. Pussy just hits different." Her hand has almost grasped Nina's dropped gun. I stomp on her fingertips and then hack off both of her opposable thumbs.

Her horrified screams make me look past the haze of rage I'm seething in. Nina approaches me with her arms outstretched. Even though we're both soaked in blood, her touch manages to comfort me a little. We embrace momentarily, and then she gently pushes me away. "Thanks fer th' help, pardner. Now ya might wanna 'xcuse me fer a moment, Ah don' think ya wanna be 'round fer what happens next."

"On the contrary, dear, I'd prefer to be present for this."

Nina shrugs. "Suit yerself." She walks over to the woman on the floor. Her life's essence oozes from the stubs that used to be her fingers. The sound of her pain and the look of agony on her face makes sympathy's cool grip calm my blazing heart. She's human, just like us. "Wait, Ni—"

Ca-thunk! "Nuthin' to it, Minerva. Notta one o' these freaks are gettin' outta here alive."

"The Feral are our enemy, not our fellow humans."

"Ya sure 'bout that? Seems tah me," ca-thunk! "like our alien friends are jus' hungry. Ah done neva seen two Feral fightin' each otha either. But this filth you call our fellow humans jus' tried tah do sumthin' unspeakable. Ah'd say" ca-thunk! "they are the real enemy."

"Dear—"

"Even if ya don' agree, if we let th' rest o' these freaks go, they'd jus' bleed tah death. We ain't got no hospital tah take 'em to, an' Ah sure ain't gonna patch 'em up mahself." She draws back the tomahawk. I grab her wrist. She turns to me, eyes wet. "They touched me. Let me do this."

"This hell turned these people into monsters. I won't let the same happen to us."

"They chose tah become monsters. Ah've been up here a year an' Ah ain't no monster!"

"No, but if you saw the expression on your face when you chopped off that man's head, you'd agree with me. I never thought someone so cute could look so scary."

"Ah'd probably say th' same fer you, 'xcept Ah'd use th' word 'beautiful' insteadah cute. Too bad Ah couldn't see ya while ya were slicin' through these men

like sum tornado o' justice. It mustah been pretty sexy."

"Sexy is the last word I'd use to describe my actions," I say, recoiling at the fresh memories, "but I wasn't going to let those savages do something they would regret later."

"Don'cha see they ain't gonna have a 'latah'?"

"Just like I am going to stop you from doing something you'll regret later."

"Ah neva regret mah kills," she looks down suddenly, a crestfallen expression coming across her face. "Th' ones Ah intended, anyway."

"Are you sure about that? I'd wager you aren't as desensitized to your actions as you say you are."

"Honestly? Ah—" her eyes zone in on something behind me, then her arm becomes a blur. I hear a strangled cry and turn to look, but Nina grabs ahold of my chin. Little droplets of blood trail down my neck and onto my breasts, making me shiver. "Ya don' wanna see where that knife went. But Ah can't lie tah ya sugah, Ah do regret sum o' th' things Ah did."

"I'm listening," I grab her hand and try to pull her out of the room, away from the last survivor—the olive-skinned man with the broken arm and busted open eyeball. Wow. Did I really do that to someone?

Nina stands rooted into place, her face telling me that she "ain't buyin' none o' mah bullshit". "Th'…" She coughs as if to clear her throat, "Th' mornin' Lucio died, Ah went lookin' fer his killers, th' pack o' Chosen that stole th' food that mightah saved him from me. Ah saw 'em at a museum right aftah they'd killed sum survivors. That wuz when Ah found out th' truth behin' th' Chosen, how they kill people on th' Surface tah try an' starve out th' Feral."

My stomach shrinks. Did I ever eat a meal taken from the dead hands of a survivor?

"Now that weren't yer fault, so stop makin' that face. Yer breakin' mah heart, seriously."

"My ap—carry on, then."

Nina nods at me with an impressed smile, then says, "Ah shot one o' 'em through th' back o' th' head, then sliced open anotha one's throat. Then Ah tortured Zack, but he got away 'fore Ah could kill him."

"… I believe you can spare me the grotesque details."

"Ah did!" I roll my eyes. "Anywho, seein' their corpses didn' make me happy."

"Why do you suppose so?"

"Ah dunno. Maybe Ah jus' felt like shit 'bout everything aftah Lucio died. But Ah think it wuz cuz that wuz th' first time Ah killed sumone an' it wuzn't self-defense. Even aftah seein' 'em kill innocent people without battin' an eyelash… when Ah looked at th' gurl Ah shot in th' head, seein' her glazed ova eyes jus' rubbed me th' wrong way.

"Ah guess Ah can't say Ah regret killin' 'em, cuz Ah would probably do it 'gain. But torturin' Zack, an' then not even havin' th' courtesy tah finish him off… that Ah regret. He probably stumbled 'round th' wasteland fer hours 'till he bleed out. Even though he killed mah brother, Ah really don' think anyone deserves a drawn-out death—anyone, that is, 'xcept that evil Queen o' yers. Allah this mess is *her* fault."

I purse my lips and cut off my reply to the contrary. Nina raises an eyebrow, but she seems to let my hesitation slide.

"Anywho, thas' a helluva long winded explanation as fer why Ah'm gonna kill this here rapist."

"Nina, *please*. Don't do this."

"Now ya ain't thinkin' straight. Look, Ah'm sorry ya hadtah hurt these folks tah save me, but keepin' this guy alive won't change th' fact that he's already dead, jus' like his friends were 'fore Ah killed 'em. Ya broke his arm an' left him half-blind. Killin' him is th' only humane thing tah do at this point."

I look at the pathetic excuse for a human. The poor thing's trembling in a fetal position; his broken arm twisting in a way I didn't think was possible. God, what in the bloody hell did I do to these people?

Nina is right. None of these people could have survived on the Surface in the condition I left them in. All that was left to do was finish the job.

"Very well then, I suppose we have no choice."

"There's always a choice. This is jus' th' right one." She takes a knife from her belt.

"I am afraid I will have to take the, um, honor, as it were, from you this time. This is *my* sin to finish, not yours. I apologize for being too cowardly to finish what I started."

"Ain't no shame in not wantin' tah kill sumone. Butcha ain't gonna live up here very long if ya don' do whatcha gotta do."

"I will not deny that there is a small part of me that is looking forward to this." I unsheathe The Blade of Justice. "No one touches *my* darling and gets away with it."

Nina sucks her teeth. "Damn, that wuz hella sexy. Ah hadtah stop mah hand from smakin' that fat ass o' yers."

I gasp, horrified. "I do not have a 'fat ass'!"

"Ya sure as hell do from where Ah'm standin'. If Ah had a smartphone Ah'd snap a pic so ya could see fer yerself."

"Surely we aren't discussing the size of my rear end in the presence of a man I am about to murder?"

"It's like every step ya take makes yer booty go BAM BAM."

I shake my head and turn to face the suffering man on the floor. He looks up at me, tries to say something, and then winces tightly. "You have last words?" I ask. "Take your time."

I cross my arms and look down at him, hoping I look as impatient as I feel. "You fags …done talking? Just… get it over with already!"

I raise the Blade of Justice. The man flinches and curls up in a tighter ball. "On th' verge o' death an' yer still talkin' shit," Nina says from behind me.

"Men are so confusing," I say.

"What… are you waiting for?"

"Before I kill you, I would like to ask you something."

"I'm… not talking."

"You aren't?" I tap his broken arm with my toe. He shrieks. "Don't you want this to end?" *What am I doing? What am I doing?*

"Ahh! Fine."

"I want to know why you tried to rape us."

Nina groans from behind me. "Y'know damn well why he tried to rape us. He's horny as sh—"

"Because *I don't give a shit*. After… the aliens invaded, I… me and my friends knew we were going to die soon. So we figured we might as well go out getting as much pleasure as possible. Isn't... isn't that the whole point of living anyway?"

I turn to Nina. "Would you like me to stab him in the heart or the brain?"

Nina shakes her head. "Neither. Chop off his dick."

"Sounds reasonable, dear." I raise my blade...

"Wait! That wuz a joke. Jus' drive yer sword through his forehead. That'll probably take this fella outta his misery quicker."

"You were right, Nina."

"'Bout what?"

"Everything. Especially about this man already being dead." I close my eyes and stab the sword downwards. My wrist vibrates with finality. Tears fill my eyes, and I turn around to embrace my darling. She opts instead to grab my hand.

"Les' get you outta here, sugah."

Nina pulls me out of the room and back into the lobby. Now that the lights are on, I can see that this place looks quite fashionable despite a year of being occupied by rapists. The walls are a glossy white, and the floor is made up of shiny brown tiles. The numbers to the hotel rooms are gold plated and shiny. Maybe they kept everything so clean to deceive passersby such as ourselves. Or maybe they just needed something to do.

"Now how 'bout that kiss, hm?" Nina asks.

"You *cannot* be serious. We are not having our first kiss soaked in blood."

"Ex-actly. Now get that fat ass intah a shower pronto! We're probably workin' wit' runnin' water here!"

I laugh, which shouldn't be possible because I just killed someone, again. "Keep that crude mouth closed, dear, something might go in it."

"Yer tongue?"

"No, my foot."

"Ah didn' know you were intah that sorta thing!"

"I—you—"

"Ya can come back wit' a comeback latah! Fer now, jus' pick th' lock tah one o' these doors. Ah left sumthin' in this room."

"Hurry back. I'm not going in there alone."

"O' course."

AH GO BACK inside th' room wit' a sigh. It really stank o' blood an' bodily fluids in here, an' Ah don' doubt th' same smell is on me. Th' brown skinned fella is still curled up like a baby. Minerva's sword is stickin' outta th' floor right next tah his head. It takes a few tough pulls, but Ah manage tah yank it outta th' tile. "Mighty thankful ya didn' say nuthin' tah mah gal 'fore she left th' room."

"You were, ugh, going to step on my arm if I said anything, wouldn't you?"

"Eeyup." Ah finish th' job, then Ah wipe her filthy blade off on th' bed an' fling it ova mah shoulder. Ah grab our backpacks, then take one last look at th' room. Th' burned pot o' beans is still restin' on th' counter. Ah shake mah head an' walk out.

X X X

Aftah we eat, Minerva spends th' rest o' th' night cryin' on mah shoulder. "How many more people are going to die on our journey? How many more people are we going to kill?"

Ah stroke her beautiful hair. "As many people as it takes tah protect this." Ah kiss her forehead. Minerva hugs me tight an' starts bawlin' her eyes out even harder than before. Ah chuckle unner mah breath but keep on strokin' her hair. *Eeyup. Ah ain't gettin' no kiss tonight.*

Chapter 17

I awake wrapped around Nina like a lovesick snake. Even though I spent the whole night crying on her shoulder, she's smiling. Hm. Interesting.

I untangle myself from her right as images of yesterday's events fly back to me. A hurricane of butterflies storm my stomach when I recall my near-kiss with Nina, but the gruesome memories of me slicing through fingers and breaking arms puts a lump in my throat. I played a role in about eight deaths yesterday, one of which was an unborn child. How will I continue living like this, knowing full well I may be forced to do such awful things on a daily basis if I am to survive?

Sunlight slowly bleeds through the window. I get out of bed and look out of it, absentmindedly brushing my hair all the while. In the far distance, past collapsed buildings, past the literally bloody cars, past the rotted corpses of men and Feral alike, the sun starts its steady ascent. The flaming orb of life kisses the horizon, painting the normally dreadful grey sky a vivid combination of orange, pink, and red. My, oh my. You definitely can't see that in the colony.

Nina flinches on the bed and bolts upright. When we make eye contact, she breaks into a grin. She raises her hands over her head, stretching. Through a pleased groan she says, "Mornin' sugah!"

I approach her, hoping I'm smiling majestically. I gently place my prized hairbrush on the counter, then give her an enthusiastic, "Good morning, dear! May I ask how you managed to go to sleep with such a wonderful smile on your face after a day as awful as yesterday?"

"Th'..." She yawns with a lazy grin, "... gal Ah wuz sleepin' wit' is jus' so swell, Ah completely fergot 'bout all th' lives Ah took yesterday. An'..." Her smile dips, "... well, y'know."

It hurts to say, "That I do."

Nina coughs. "But really though, th' kicker is that even though all that shit went down, Ah still didn' get no kiss at th' end o' it."

"Close your eyes."

A lump goes down Nina's throat, but she complies. Her hands are clenching the covers we slept under. I get on the bed behind her, then start messaging her shoulders. Nina gives a surprised, "Mph".

"Relax, dear. There is nothing to be anxious about."

"Ah am rela—" I blow behind an ear. She quivers while I giggle with supreme delight. "Consarn it, stop teasin' me!"

"Shh. Let me have my fun! We only get one first kiss, you know."

Nina groans. "It's jus' a kiss. Stop makin' such a big deal outta it!"

"If it's, 'jus' a kiss', why is your heart beating so fast?"

"Ah'm three seconds away from grabbin' th' steerin' wheel."

"Oh, fine. I suppose I can no longer delay the inevitable. Turn your head."

She complies. I stroke her smooth face. "You really are the cutest little thing."

"Ah done toldcha Ah ain't cute."

"Allow me to prove it to you, then."

Slowly, gently, I press my lips against hers. My brain hops right on an elevator ride up to pleasureville. I don't even have time to think about how that makes no sense whatsoever, as Nina has grabbed my shoulders and is pressing deeper into the kiss. My back sinks into the mattress as Nina's light body straddles my waist. "Mah turn, sugah."

Butterfly kisses grace my neck, and a sluggish path towards my chest begins. I want to tell her to slow down, but the waves of happy hitting my brain make it hard to form coherent sentences.

"Ah'm sorry, yer speakin' gibberish."

"I—said—" I push her back with a giggle, "are you going to let me speak, or are you going to keep kissing me?"

"Which would ya prefer?"

"The latter of—haha-haha! Stop it!"

"What wuz that?"

"I—hahahahaha—" Stomach gurgling? Oh, my. *Poot!*

Nina cackles so hard she rolls over and hits the floor, laughing herself half to death. "Oh Jeezus, ya even fart like a princess!"

"I do not fart; I merely *pass gas,* as it were." I turn invisible, then hop out of bed and lunge for her ribcage. Nina immediately yelps with laughter.

"Yer killin' me, sugah. G-get offah me!"

"I shall give you what for, dear!"

"Ah'm serious!"

"Not a chance!"

"*Stop!*"

Ugh! I hit the floor on my rear end hard, turning visible upon impact. Nina is hugging herself tight, gritting her teeth so hard I fear her jaw will shatter.

What have I done? "I'm sorry! I thought we were playing a game."

She's shivering now. "N-naw, *you didn' do anythin' wrong.*"

My stomach feels like a cauldron of mixed emotions. "Oh."

"A-Ah'm—" She covers her mouth like she's about to be sick, then manages to say, "Ah'm gonna go take a shower real quick. Be right back, OK?"

I look at the floor, a galaxy sized hole in my chest. "Alright then. I shall await your return."

Nina lumbers towards the shower. My heart sinks, but before it can plummet I get to work on cooking breakfast, trying to distract myself from the tornado of emotion currently ripping oxygen from my lungs. I do not know if I am angrier than I am sad. I wish I could vow to kill the people who hurt my Nina, but they're already dead.

By the time breakfast is done and the table is set properly, Nina is out of the shower. She's wearing a pair of blue shorts and an orange shirt, treasures we found in this room's closet last night. She's got on the bravest smile I've ever seen even though her eyes are rimmed red. She takes the seat in front of me. "Smells great. Glad tah see ya retained yer cookin' lesson from last night." I grab her wrist before her hand grabs ahold of silverware.

"May I kiss you?"

Nina's smile disappears. "Ya don' eva haftah ask that question, sugah."

I lean across the table and gently press my lips against hers. When we break apart, Nina's got a grip on her temple. "Whoa, that wuz a gud one."

"Listen to me," I say, caressing her cheek. "If you need to talk about anything, or if you need something done—"

"Yer here fer me," Nina says, her voice tight.

"That I am. Do not hesitate to tell me anything, anything at all."

"Ah 'ppreciate it."

I grab my spoon and feast on my yams. They're sweet, sticky, and mushy all at the same time. Nina takes a few spoonfuls of chicken noodle soup, and then pokes at her bowl of sliced peaches. I frown. I want to tell her she should eat more, but I don't want her to throw up everywhere.

We eat in silence for awhile until Nina says, "When we finish eatin', we should search this place fer mo' supplies. Those freaks we killed mightah had sum mighty useful stuff lyin' 'round."

"I suppose not thinking about what happened yesterday won't change the fact that those events did indeed occur."

"Don' worry sugah, as bad as it sounds, you'll get used tah it. Th' killin', Ah mean."

"That day will never come, mark my words."

"Whateva ya say." She sets her silverware down and rolls her jaw. "So, uh, now that we're together... we are together, right?"

I roll my eyes. "No, we are merely friends with benefits. Of course we're together!"

She smiles at that, and I find myself smiling back. Then she gets all serious. "Well, while Ah wuz in th' shower Ah wuz thinkin'... couldn't we jus', y'know, *not* go to Edinburgh? Ah'd really rathah jus' spend time wit'cha away from all th' aliens an' murderers an' rapists."

"As wonderful as that would be, dear, I am afraid I am not content with spending the rest of my days snogging with you while the country goes to hell. The Feral aren't going to go away, and with them around, society has no chance of rebuilding."

"Didcha see th' people we ran intah last night? Society ain't gotta chance tah rebuild."

"That is where you're wrong, dear. You cannot give up on humanity so easily."

"Sure Ah can."

"Yes, you can, but you may miss out on some amazing opportunities. Say for example I killed you after our fight just because you made a simple mistake. I would never have gotten to know such a wonderful person."

Nina purses her lips, so I say, "Your circumstances led you to make an awful decision, and I suspect the same applies to the people we met last night. Besides, I'm sure you haven't forgotten the initial reason why you agreed to accompany me in the first place."

Nina sighs. "No, but a lil' procrastination neva hurt nobody."

"Didn't you tell me that you grew up on your family's farm? Surely you say that in jest?"

"But o' course, dear!"

I slap her shoulder. "Oh, stop it!"

X X X

We emerge from the hotel, our foreheads dripping with flabbergasted sweat. "Well, that was the most

190

disgusting thing I have ever had the displeasure of seeing."

"Ah know that gal said she wuz watchin' us on them cameras but Ah didn' think they would be…"

My stomach screeches. "I'm going to be sick."

"Hey, it ain't so bad. Maybe we should go back in and grab a toy or two. Could be fun!" Lumpy fluid bursts from my mouth and paints the pavement orange. It's the sweetest vomit I've ever tasted, which makes me even sicker. "Jeezus, gal! Are ya alright?"

I wipe my lips and manage to stand, chest tight with pain. "Never, ever, *ever* make a joke like that *ever* again."

"Ah liked that spiked purple one. Ah bet Ah could do sum serious damage wit' that."

"Why do I continually kiss someone with a mouth as filthy as yours," I ask with a wince while Nina laughs.

"Cuz yer a naughty gal, thas' why."

"I am going to do something very naughty if you don't be quiet," I growl.

"Does it involve them toys? Cuz if so, Ah'd be ready an' willin' sugah."

"This conversation is officially over."

I storm away, but Nina just jogs behind me with an irritatingly charming chuckle.

"Hollup now, yer fergettin' sumthin'."

"What have I forgotten?" She grabs my hand and our fingers interlock. "Ah, I see."

Nina snickers. "Yer skin looks th' same color as a baby pig. Ah'd say yer th' cute one, sugah."

"That is a ridiculous analogy. Nevertheless, we shall keep the flirting to a minimum whilst on the road.

Getting wrapped up in romance is not the best course of action out in this wasteland."

"Are ya sayin' ya wanna kiss but don' feel safe lettin' yer guard down?"

"Perhaps."

We go back through the maze of vehicles to reach our gray car. Nina gets in and twists her head to check the backseat. "Whewee, our grub's still here!"

"That is fantastic news! I suppose fate cannot be unreasonable all the time."

"Ain't that right? Now les' check out that engine..." She jams the key in the ignition and twists. The automobile responds with a roar weaker than a baby lion's. Nina opens the door, her head hung. "Ah don' 'spose y'know howtah fix a transmission?"

"I am afraid they never taught us that in knight academy."

"They sure as hell don' teach that onnah farm either. But even if they did, we'd still be screwed. It's not like we have any car parts lyin' 'round."

"Is walking to Edinburgh really that great of a task? It may be as dreadful as it sounds, but we shouldn't be *too* far away at this point, at least according to the map. A few days' walk, at most."

"Whoa, yer really up fer walkin' that far? Ah figured you'd be complainin' th' whole trip."

"Oh, I would be complaining. Quite a lot, actually. Nevertheless, with you around, I suspect everything will turn out to be fine in the end. And I'm not just talking about our journey to Edinburgh."

Nina cracks a wonderful smile. "Shucks, thank ya sugah! Still, without transportation we'd lose a lot o' our supplies. We can't carry all o' it wit' us by foot.

An' it ain't like our adventure is gonna end once we get there. There ain't nuthin' betta than bein' well-stocked up here, Ah guarantee it."

"I am sure you are correct. Hm. It appears as though we have gotten ourselves in quite the pickle."

"Darn tootin'. Th' chances o' us findin' a workin' vehicle out in this hellhole is slim tah none. But th' odds bein' against me is th' norm. C'mon, Ah saw sum o' them cars still had keys in th' ignition. Might as well start sum o' 'em an' see what we're workin' wit'."

X X X

"... And my clothes are bloody again."

"Not really. You've gotta few flakes o' dried blood on ya, but thas' not so bad. 'Sides, havin' blood on ya is a good sign o' a hard day's work up here on th' Surface!"

"Surely you're joking."

She snickers. "O' course. Stop takin' everything at face value."

"Perhaps we should start walking to Edinburgh now? I feel like we've checked every car in the city. Most of them don't even have keys in them, and the ones that do never start. And *all* of them are disgusting, horrifying, et cetera."

Nina wipes sweat off her brow. "Yer right. Ah guess itsa lost cause at this point. Ah jus' hope those science fellers are well stocked. C'mon. Les' go back tah our ol' car an' stuff in as much supplies as we can."

"Sounds fair."

When we get back to the car Nina says, "You get th' water, Ah'll get th' cans." I'm finished packing within a moment, but Nina is glaring at me. "Pack as much as ya can carry. We might not make it back here 'gain."

"Oh, fine."

Once we're done packing everything, I slug my two-ton backpack over my shoulder. "Ugh, it's so heavy."

"Ain't as heavy as you."

"Some ladies can be quite sensitive about their weight, dear. Remember I used a shock bracelet just to control my diet!"

"Don' be stupid. If Ah didn' think ya looked tastier than a glass o' lemonade onnah summer day, Ah wouldn' have kissed ya. Ah jus' know ya can handle this without bein' a wimp 'bout it. If mah skinny ass can carry 'round these supplies, so can you."

"You raise a fair point," I say after a beat. "Still, you're being awfully aggressive about this. Why?"

"Its jus', well, runnin' outta supplies has gotta be mah worst nightmare."

We hobble towards the city's exit as I absentmindedly wonder if it's scientifically possible to shrink a few inches due to carrying excessive weight. "Worse than needles?"

"Ah ain't playin'. Lucio an' Ah once fought ova a dead rat, we were so hungry. We almos' killed each otha."

I can't think of anything to say other than, "Oh."

"Hunger will make ya do things ya didn' think you were capable o' doin'. Ah ain't too comfy wit' th' idea o' us fightin' again either."

"Rest assured, I will not lay another finger on you ever again, so do not worry about that."

Nina smiles sadly. "Ah hope we'll neva haftah see how well yer morals hollup when yer starvin' tah death. Either way, that last bit 'bout not layin' a finger on me is pretty dissapointin'."

"My dear, I said I would not lay a finger *on* you, I never said I wouldn't put a finger *i—*"

"Didn' ya *jus'* say sumthin' 'bout keepin' th' flirtin' tah a minimum?"

"Come now, you walked right into that one. Besides—"

"All of my life!"

"What th'—"

"I've been searchin'!"

The singing is coming from a blown open house a little way ahead of us. From outside, you can see into an elderly man's homely living room. He's got a microphone in his hand; eyes jammed shut with passion as he continues singing, "*For a girl! To love me, like I, love you…*"

"This idiot is gonna get himself killed."

"But let me tell ya now!"

"Perhaps we should say hello? Maybe he could help us out?"

"*Every girl I've ever had…*"

"How?" Nina grabs my hand and pulls me along. "Not happenin', Minerva."

"*…Breaks my heart and leaves me sad…*"

"We ain't runnin' intah no mo' freaks. Feels like everyone we met ends up screwin' us ova or we end up havin' tah kill 'em."

"*What am I, what am I, supposed to do? Oh-oh-oh-oh-ohh Anna…*"

Sharp pain stabs my chest. We killed around eight people yesterday, but when you factor in how our presence caused the death of the pregnant woman's family, the numbers would undoubtedly reach the double digits. "You are correct. Very well then."

I let her drag me past the house, but once we pass by the singing stops. Nina grabs her pistol and aims it at the door that opened with a pleasant jingle. At its entrance stands an old man with sunglasses. He has on an orange Hawaiian shirt, a fisherman's hat, and khaki shorts. He gives me a warm smile. The mole under his lip reminds me of my deceased grandfather. "Oh, you can put that gun away!" *he says.* "I mean you ladies no harm, and as you can see, I am thoroughly unarmed."

"Thas' all nice an' well sir, but Ah'm sure y'know why Ah can't do that."

"Unfortunately, I do. Not a problem then, you are still welcome inside for a cup of tea. I'll have you know it is *quite* delicious. It is, how they say, 'Slap yo mama good'."

He laughs, to which I respond with a confused smile, but then he starts laughing even harder, so hard that he grabs his belly and bends over.

Nina and I look at each other with raised eyebrows, and then Nina says, "Take off them sunglasses." *He perches the shades on his forehead, revealing glazed and bloodshot eyes.* "Eeyup, yer higher than a hot air balloon. Minerva, les' get outta here."

"Who cares if I'm high? It's the end of the world! Why don't you two come inside and humor an old man? I'm ever so lonely..." *He tries to take a step towards us, but Nina aims the weapon right at his* forehead. I put my hands on the cold steel and aim the weapon at the floor before she can blow his brains out.

"Nina, you are being *beyond* rude. Put the gun away."

"B—"

"I mean it. This man means us no harm, and even if he did, you know as well as I do that bullets mean about as much to me as they do to the Feral. And unless you want to argue that he can best the two of us in hand-to-hand combat, there is no reason why you shouldn't put the gun away."

"Oh, fine." She holsters the weapon.

"Marvelous! Now, you two lovely women wouldn't happen to be interested in threesomes, would you?"

I had one foot through the door, but now I'm right back outside. "Nina, we're leaving."

Nina's already walked through the broken-down wall to lay down on a tattered blue couch, laughing so hard that her brown skin has a reddish tint. "No way, no how. This guy's a hoot."

"I suppose I'll take that as a 'no'," the old pervert says with a chuckle. "Can't blame an old man for trying."

"But of course I can," I say with crossed arms.

"Naw, Ah unnerstan'. Jus' cuz yer ol' don' mean ya dick don' work."

"I'm glad at least one of you possesses the empathy to see things from another's..." he coughs, and a burning smell invades my nostrils. "... Perspective. Ahem, sorry about that."

"Apology *not* accepted," I say, but nevertheless enter the house through the door.

"Why are y'all goin' through th' door? Half th' damn's house blown open anyways!"

"A destroyed home does not excuse one from not entering through the door," I say. "It is only proper."

"It appears that the tall one knows a thing or two about etiquette."

I approach the couch Nina's laying on, who sits up and pats the now empty seat next to her. I shrug off the boulder strapped to my back and oblige, immediately finding the furniture extremely comfortable, even more so now that her arm is around my shoulders. "My name is not, 'the tall one', it is Minerva."

"An' Ah'm Nina!" My *girlfriend* says with a wave. "Ah ain't gonna say its nice tah meetcha jus' yet, but Ah guess ya don' seem like too bad o' a guy. Ah 'ppreciate yer honesty, at least."

"Thank you. My name is Cornelius Hopper! You two get comfortable; I will get to work on that tea."

"That won't be necessary. I shall handle that."

"Really, it is no trouble. You two are my guests, and—"

"I insist, dear. Tea should always use a lady's touch." *Besides, I'm not drinking anything this pervert touches. For all I know, he'll slip something in it.*

Cornelius nods. "Oh, I understand now. You have every right to be untrustworthy of my intentions. Not a problem, I will get to work on rolling another magnificent joint. I suppose you two don't smoke?"

Not anything you roll. "No," Nina and I say at the same time.

"That's too bad. Sharing my weed always seems to make me higher. Sharing my tea will have to suffice."

I get to my already sore feet. My my, that backpack was quite heavy. I walk into his kitchen.

I scream. Footsteps echo behind me, and then my mouth is muffled.

"Now what Ah tell ya 'bout screamin'? Whas' all th' fuss 'b—oh." She's evidently seen the decomposed head on a stick perched against the kitchen counter. An eyeball droops from a socket, hanging by a measly string of flesh. "OK, thas' a lil' unsettlin', so Ah'll cut ya sum slack. Still, ya gotta keep it down sugah. Ah'm not in th' mood tah kill anybody tahday."

I remove her hand and whirl around to glare at her. "A little unsettling? Excuse me?"

"This ain't as uncommon as ya seem tah think. Ah had one o' these when Lucio an' Ah hid in th' sewers."

"Seems like you and this Lucio gentleman are pretty darn smart," Cornelius calls from the living room. "You must be new to the Surface, ah, Minerva, was it?"

"Ya, she's only been up here a couplah days."

"Minerva, sometimes we use the corpses of our enemies as a warning to other survivors, almost like a scarecrow on a farm to keep crows off crops."

"Ah couldn't come up wit' a betta analogy mahself," Nina says, pride in her voice.

I fight down more sick. "You two are not finding common ground over something so disgusting."

"Ah think we are, sugah. Hey now, Mistah Cornelius is gonna have mighty dry mouth aftah he gets through wit' that joint. Trytah ignore th' head an' focus on makin' that tea!"

"B-but it smells!"

"No it don'. All Ah smell is *dank*. He probably cleaned out this guy's skull eons ago. Ain't that right, Cornelius?"

"You are absolutely, positively, indisputably, objectively 100% correct," he giggles. "It would be hard to relax if my home constantly smelled of dead person."

"But you're perfectly OK with seeing a dead person when making your breakfast in the morning?" I ask, temple glistening with sweat.

"Of course I am. You can't take two steps without seeing a dead person nowadays. I bet the rest of my rotten teeth you've seen worse on your way here. Am I correct?"

He is, but I'm not willing to admit it. "Where are the tea bags?"

"Check the pantry. You can use my electric kettle to boil the water."

I open the pantry and scan the shelves until I find my prize. I grab the box of tea bags, a smile wide as a mile back on my face. "Nina, have you ever had English tea before?"

"Naw."

"Be prepared for a flavor explosion, dear. Cornelius has my favorite tea, *Celestial Uprising*."

"Thas' neat an' all, but why dontcha hurry up wit' that tea an' get yer pretty lil' self ova here?"

I start boiling water. "A lady never rushes perfection, dear."

"Now don' take too long now, Ah'm already feelin' lovesick."

Heat floods my cheekbones. "Oh, stop it!"

Cornelius chuckles from the living room. "You two are a couple, aren't you?"

"Yessir."

"How long have you two been dating?"

"Less than twenty-four hours," I answer, peeking my head into the living room to share a smile at Nina.

Cornelius gives the joint he's rolling a few licks, then asks, "How did you two meet?"

"Now thas' a helluva long story, Ah dunno if we have the time fer that."

"What do you two have to do that's so important you can't humor an old man for a few hours?"

Nina frowns at me, and I give a shrug. She turns back to him and says, "If ya really wanna know th' whole story, we'll tell ya. No talkin' durin' th' story though."

I giggle. "So it's OK for you to interrupt people during their stories, but not for others?"

"Eeyup."

Cornelius cackles, then takes a long puff. He takes a breath in afterwards, and then blows out smoke with every word he says. "Looks like I'm missing out on a lot of backstory," he says, voice deeper than usual. "Regardless, your condition sounds reasonable, but I will press you afterwards."

Nina waves a cloud of smoke away from her face. "Fine, but if ya blow that stuff towards me 'gain Ah'll smack ya."

He smiles, yellow teeth glistening in the sunlight shining from outside the hole in his home. "My apologies."

X X X

"Is everything you two said really true?" Cornelius asks us. Empty cups of tea and cans of beans rest on the table between us. Even though his eyes are as red and low as ever, he hasn't laughed the entire time. I didn't think someone so high could look ever so serious.

"Every word," Nina says.

Cornelius gets to his feet and walks to the massive hole in his house, looking outside. "How did you lead the Feral to the Chosen's hideout?"

"We killed th' archers guardin' th' entrance, an' then..." she sighs, "we used bits o' their body parts tah lure th' Feral intah goin' unnerground."

My stomach lurches. Even I haven't heard this part of the story.

"I... see," he says.

"What's wrong?" I ask him.

"I used to live there with my family, early after the invasion. But eventually I found out how the Queen was getting our supplies. I confronted her about it, and she told me to keep my mouth shut or she'd kick me and my family out."

Nina cries, "That bitch!"

"Don't call her that, please," I say before I can stop myself.

Nina looks at me like I've grown a third eye, but Cornelius just continues onwards like he hadn't been interrupted. "I told her she wouldn't have to worry about that because we were already leaving. But when I told my wife about what the Queen was doing and said that we needed to leave she declined. She didn't like it, but she wasn't willing to put our children's lives on the line out on the Surface."

Cornelius turns back to us, and then walks back to his seat. He produces a glass jar of weed from his pocket and places it on the table. "I secretly told friends and acquaintances how we were getting our supplies, but they were too scared to make a stand against the Queen. I realized that no one would do anything even if they knew the truth, so I left and made my way back here. I was always bitter towards my family for staying."

He opens the jar, then takes an extra large nug out and rips it to pieces. "I thought I married a woman of moral character," he spits. "I thought I raised my children better than to profit off the suffering of others." He pinches his shredded drugs and tosses it onto a transparent piece of paper. "I don't know how they lived with themselves, knowing every meal they ate was pried from the hands of dead people. But despite my anger, despite my rage, despite their sins, I still loved them. I never wished for this."

"Oh mah God. A-Ah'm so sorry. Ah hope they're alright." Nina's hand squeezes mine. I wish she could transfer her anguish to me, just so we could share the burden.

"It wasn't your fault, Nina," Cornelius says, rolling the paper up slowly and carefully. "Your actions were justified. Many people down there knew what was going on. But not all of them."

"Even if they *did* know, it still ain't right tah kill 'em. In th' end, they were jus' tryin' tah protect their kin too. Ah can't fault 'em fer that. Ah acted too rashly, Ah shouldah—"

Cornelius lights up, but he at least has the courtesy to blow the hit away from us. "Should have what? Let the Queen continue destroying families to provide for the lives of others? The method and collateral damage is unsatisfactory, but the attack itself was most certainly justified. No, my dear, I'd say you are as much of a victim to this as the people who died as a result of your actions. This tragedy is no one's fault but Queen Amity's."

I can remain silent no longer. "Are we going to forget that the Feral are the ones who pushed Queen Amity into making such awful decisions?"

Nina's arm flies off my shoulder like she saw a spider crawling on it. "Ah can't believe you. Th' Feral ain't th' damn issue, Minerva! They're jus' a storm, it's how th' Queen dealt wit' th' storm thas' th' problem. We shouldah all stood tahgether an' fought 'em side by side. If yer Queen wuzn't such a fuckin' coward, we neva wouldah been in this mess in th' first place!"

"She didn't think we could fight them off... I didn't even think we could fight them off!"

"Well, we *can!*"

I start to retaliate, but a cloud of smoke blown my way makes me cough. "Hush, child," Cornelius says with a scowl. "You are embarrassing yourself. While the Feral did push Amity into making some immoral decisions, that does not abstain her from guilt. The amount of people dead as a result of those decisions should speak for itself."

Memories of warm tea parties shared with her Majesty cloud my memory. "She's still a *person.* She just made a few bad choices. We *all* have. Besides, even if you hate her, there is no denying that we will be unable to reunite the two factions without her help. History has already proven that Queen Adelia won't be able to lead the nation all on her own."

Nina and Cornelius glare at me, but still find themselves nodding their heads. "That is true," he says as he lights another joint. Where did this one come from? "Well, politics, aside, you two will need transportation to Edinburgh if you are to save our nation, correct?"

Nina and I share a look, then she says, "What're ya gettin' at?"

"You see that red car outside? It's mine." He tosses a black key towards her. "Now it's yours."

My eyes go wide. "Y-you're going to give us your car?"

"Correct."

"Thas' mighty nice o' ya, Mistah Cornelius!"

"A little *too* nice, I am afraid." I walk to him and drop the key back into his palm. "We can't accept such a wonderful gift. We just met you. To take advantage of your generosity would be criminal."

Nina starts to say something, but Cornelius speaks first. "You misunderstand. This is not a gift; this is my contribution. You two are going to save England, after all. It's not like I was using the car anyway."

"What if you *do* need to use it later?"

Cornelius shrugs and takes another puff. "Won't matter. I'm no use to anyone anyway. This is my last contribution to society."

"Ya don' mean...?"

"Come now, why else would I have been singing at the top of my lungs? I expected a murderer at any moment, be it a human or an alien one. But instead I look outside and see two beautiful young women. I thought I was just high, so I rubbed my eyes, but you two were still there when I opened them. So I opened the door to say hello." He laughs. "This moment, the fact that this conversation is even happening right now, is a miracle. You two are the best thing that's happened to me since I've left the colony. And when you leave, I'll be all alone again."

He takes another puff, then smiles, and it hurts how pure that smile is. "I shouldn't complain. Soon, I won't feel this loneliness. I won't feel anything at all."

"Stop talkin' nonsense, right now! We ain't gonna leave ya all alone. Not completely, at least." She opens her backpack and takes out five books; some hardcover, some paperback, all heavily worn from time's influence and heavy use. "Now these may not look like much, but these books are mah treasure. Ah reckon a part o' me an' mah brother's soul is entwined intah th' pages, we done read 'em so much. Ah can only hope they bring ya half as much joy as they've brought us." She gently places them on the table.

Cornelius's bloodshot eyes water. "I—I can't take this."

"Ah ain't askin' ya. They're yours."

"I have no words." Neither do I.

"How's bout, 'thank you'?"

"This is one scenario where words will not suffice. Please come here, both of you." We approach him, and he looks up at us with a grimace.

"What?" Nina and I ask simultaneously. We look at each other and giggle. Where we even arguing a few moments ago?

"I'm sorry ladies, but I have a terrible case of couch lock. Would you be ever so kind and help me an old man to his feet, please?"

We roll our eyes and each grab ahold of one of his hands. We give a pull, and before long the man is standing on his own two wobbly legs. He wraps his wrinkled arms around our shoulders and pulls us in close. Even though he reeks of weed and sweat, I can't help but smile and hug him back. "Thank you for spending the afternoon with me," he says with such gratitude my throat tightens.

"Thanks fer th' ride!"

I elbow Nina in the ribs. "We enjoyed yer company too, o' course."

"Of course you did." He lets us go and collapses back in his chair. "Do come back and visit, if you ever find yourself in the area."

"But of course, dear."

"Before you two go, I have one more thing to offer you. Nina, if you turn around, you will see my bookstand. Feel free to take any reading material you find interesting."

Nina's the one with wobbly legs now. She leans against me for support looking like she's about to faint. "Are ya an angel or sumthin'?"

"No, I am just a perverted old man who wants to see you bend over."

Chapter 18

CORNELIUS'S CAR IS sleek, sexy, an' cherry red. A cartoon sloth sticker wit' red rimmed eyes gives me a thumbs up from th' trunk window. Ah jus' 'bout find mahself smirkin' despite mah bad mood before Ah toss th' water bottles intah th' trunk, slam it shut, then hop in th' passenger's seat while Minerva gets in th' driver's seat. "Ugh," she says wit' a frown as she waves th' air in frontah her nose. Ah'm boutah berate her fer complainin', but then mah own nostrils flinch unner th' dank assault. *This is definitely Cornelius's car.* "I suppose I can't complain. This is his car, after all."

"Hmph."

She starts th' engine, steps on th' brakes, then shifts us intah drive. We drive through th' maze o' broken machines in silence. Eventually, we're back on th' road. Th' endless desert blurs past us while Ah look tah th' sky. Th' sun is hidin' behin' clouds, givin' th' ordinarily desolate gray sky an orange tint. Th' view ain't half bad. It's like God painted this scene wit' heavenly ink brushes. Ah clench mah teeth. Even wit' our good fortune an' th' fairytale scenery, Ah still ain't fergottin'. Ah still ain't fergottin'.

"Are you alright, dear?" Minerva asks, gently touchin' mah arm. Th' earnesty in her tone makes me clench mah teeth even harder. How could a person so wonderful support sumone so awful?

"No, Ah ain't. Ah'm mad as hell atcha."

"Is it about the Queen?"

"Ya damn right it's 'bout th' Queen. She's a cold-blooded monster an' ya keep tryin' tah defend her! Ah wish Ah could take back sendin' th' Feral down tah yer colony, but Ah still hope one o' 'em ripped her tah shreds."

Minerva keeps her eyes on th' road, but her hands are clutchin' th' wheel. "She was one of my only friends after my parents died. When my face got ruined, I became a rotten person."

"Yer face ain't ruined, Ah done toldcha that."

"

"I didn't think anyone would like me anymore, so I started acting like someone who wasn't likable to justify my destructive mindset. I lost all but one of my friends, well, all the ones who survived I-Day I mean. Whenever I saw them I'd act rotten, and they'd smile and nod at me while I was around but talk bad about me behind my back. I know this because I'd spy on them with my powers. I deserved the criticism, of course, but it hurt that they never told me to my face.

"But the Queen never tolerated my behavior. She treated me just as she always had, as her prized knight she always expected the best from. My scars didn't change anything. But our relationship wasn't me giving my all and she giving nothing in return. She was always there for me when I needed her, be it a shoulder for me to cry on, or just someone to listen to my problems. Despite her terrible actions; I still respect her a great deal."

My heart pumps fiery blood through mah veins. "Yer talkin' like yer in love wit' her! Damn it, she wuz jus' usin' ya fer yer powers. She doesn't really care 'boutcha, she doesn't really care 'bout anyone, not even her own damn sister!"

Minerva says through gritted teeth, "You're assuming *quite* a lot about a person you've never had a single conversation with."

"Actions speak loudah than words."

"This is true." She covers mah mouth wit' her hand.

Ah smack her hand away hard, makin' us swerve on th' road. "Yer really startin' tah get on mah nerves, sugah."

Her fierce blue eyes make me freeze. "You are getting on *my* nerves, dear. Perhaps we should spend the rest of the trip in silence? If we keep talking I just might punch you out again."

Ain't gonna lay a finger on me eva 'gain, huh? "Fine!"

"*Fine!*"

Ah rip open mah backpack an' yank outta book from Cornelius's. Ah flip tah page one without even lookin' at th' cover, an' even though Ah'm starin' at th' words Ah ain't readin'. Ah'm so angry Ah can hardly stand it. Th' words blur unner mah eyes. *Ah can't believe this bitch. Why did Ah kiss her? Why am Ah even wit' her? This ain't gonna work out. Ah'm an idiot. She's in love sumone else, an' that sumone is mah worst enemy.*

Ah sludge through th' first few pages o' th' book, but itsa waste o' time. Ah'm too damn angry tah concentrate. It don' help that Minerva's scowlin' at me every so often, an' when Ah turn tah face her she looks away. We sit in silence fer maybe an hour 'till Ah've had enough o' it. "Stop th' damn car."

"Why should I do that when you're being *ever* so rude?"

"Cuz Ah gotta piss, an' if ya don' stop th' damn car Ah'll piss in here instead!"

"Ugh!" Th' car screeches tah a stop, lurchin' us forward 'fore our seatbelts catch us. "Hurry on with it, then!"

"Ya don' tell me what tah do. Ah ain't yer slave no mo'!"

"You were never my slave, and you know that! Now get on with it, dear, go *relieve* your urinal tract, I'm sure you really have to go on account of your overdramatic, 'Stop *th'* car!'"

"Dramatic?" Ah open th' door an' get out. "Yer one tah talk."

Ah wait fer her tah start yappin', then slam th' door in her face. Ah snicker, drownin' out her muffled rebuttal as Ah look 'round. There ain't a soul in sight, nuthin' but th' same ol' wasteland, so Ah drop mah pants, crouch, an' do mah business. Ah breathe a sigh o' relief, then pull up mah pants an' hop back in th' car.

"Nina, look at me." Ah shut th' door wit' a *slam*, then scowl at her. "I am *not* in love with the Queen.

"Indeed, I was once *infatuated* her. But I was infatuated with the *idea* of the Queen of England, not the actual Queen of England."

"Ya ain't makin' a lick o' sense," Ah say even though Ah get what she means.

"I do not know the Queen like I know you, dear. Before I left the colony, I realized that half of what I know about her is based on lies and half-truths."

"An' ya still defend her an' call her a friend?"

"Yes." We start movin' again, makin' our tires crunch ova th' busted gravel unnerneath us. "You have every right to hate the Queen and be distrustful of her intentions. But please remember that the same person that destroyed your life is the same person who changed mine for the better. The same person who has killed thousands has also saved thousands. In no way does Her Majesty's intentions justify her heinous actions, but there is a story behind every crime, a fact of which I have no doubt you are aware."

Ah give a frustrated snort. "Ah still hate her fuckin' guts, but Ah guess Ah can't let that get 'tween us. An' Ah 'spose yer, ahem, *infatuation* wit' th' royal bitch won't get 'tween us either?"

Th' tip o' her ears are redder thana bowl o' ketchup. "I believe I said I was *once* infatuated with her, not that I *am* infatuated with her."

"Well Ah ain't buyin' it," Ah say wit' crossed arms. "Ya got this weird look in yer eye when ya talked 'bout her."

"A little jealous, perhaps?"

"Ah ain't a lil' jealous, Ah'm a lot jealous."

Now her cheeks are red. "I'm flattered, dear. I believe I have a way to alleviate your concerns while simultaneously proving my very real affection towards you, though I am afraid that would involve me taking my eyes off the road."

"Guess you'll haftah do that latah then."

"I am afraid so. Rest assured, I find it quite difficult to even think about other women when I am in the presence of a specimen as marvelous as yourself. Which reminds me of something I've been meaning to ask you for quite some time now. When did you first realize you were gay?"

"Oh, Ah guess we neva talked 'bout this, huh? Tah be honest, Ah'm pretty sure Ah ain't gay. Yer actually th' first gal tah catch mah eye, so Ah guess that makes me Bi."

"*Really?* But I'm—"

"God damn it, if ya call yerself ugly one mo' time Ah'm gonna slap ya silly. Ya ain't ugly, yer th' mos' beautiful gal Ah done eva laid mah eyes on. Now Ah ain't gonna lie tah ya, those scars sure do look scary when yer pissed off, but when ya smile it's like they jus' melt away. Hell, Ah'll even go as far as sayin' Ah like 'em."

Minerva flinches, so Ah say, "Ah'm serious! They let me know right off th' bat that Ah wuzn't dealin' wit' sum fussy gal who's all bark an' no bite. 'Sides, even ignorin' how dang pretty ya are, yer th' strongest person Ah've eva fought, an' yer kind, generous, honest—Ah—Ah jus' really like ya, OK? So stop talkin' down on yerself. Ah feel like yer insultin' mah tastes or sumthin'."

Th' car screeches tah a stop, an' Ah fly forward in mah seat 'fore mah seatbelt catches me. "What in tarnat—"

Ah can't speak on account o' Minerva's lips pressin' 'gainst mine. Happy fireworks explode in mah brain. Ah smile intah th' kiss, then put mah hands on her shoulder an' push her back. "Simmer down sugah, Ah—" Mo' fireworks. Ah push her back again, a lil' harder this time, refusin' tah let her suck me down a hole o' pleasure that could be th' end o' us both. "This ain't a game. We start foolin' 'round out here an' there'll be no stoppin' us from makin' out on th' side o' th' road all day. An' as much as Ah like ya sugah, Ah ain't tryin' tah get caught wit' mah pants down by sum Feral."

Minerva leans back in her chair wit' a sigh, her face flushed. Her eyebrows are knit together in frustration, but she still puts her foot on th' brakes, switches gears, then puts her foot back on th' gas. "... You raise a fair point. My apologies, for this immature action as well as what I said to you before about knocking you out. I was just angry; I should have never said that."

"Yer damn right ya shouldn't have," Ah say heatedly. Then Ah take inna sigh an' smile. "Butcha ain't gotta 'pologize fer kissin' me, sugah. Ah feel th' same way as you. But you were right earlier when ya said we shouldn't flirt on th' road. We ain't eva safe out here, even less so while on th' move."

"I understand." She starts drivin' wit' one hand, usin' th' otha tah wipe her wet eyes wit' a sniffle. A chill goes down mah spine.

Did mah words really mean that much tah her? Ah purse mah lips, re-livin' her passionate kiss in mah memory.

Heh, Ah guess so.

"I'm sorry," Minerva says, her voice still tight. She clears her throat, then says, "where were we? Before I derailed the conversation to talk about my vain self, of course. Oh, yes, we were discussing your blossoming sexuality."

Ah chuckle at that, though Ah don' really know why. "Well, Ah wuz neva really one fer romance, but every so often a guy at school would make mah head turn."

"Did you ever date one?"

"Nah. Not on account o' not tryin', mind you. See, mos' guys Ah met were nice an' all, but always too nice. It's like they were too scared tah challenge me when Ah acted like an ass cuz they were scared o' losin' me. Kinda ironic, seein' as how their lack o' a backbone wuz th' biggest turnoff o' 'em all fer me. Ah wuzn't lookin' fer a puppet who agreed wit' everything Ah said, Ah wuz lookin' fer a partner who wouldn' stand fer mah shit jus' as much as Ah ain't gonna stand fer their shit. Ah met sum real handsum guys who could make me smile an' laugh, but Ah neva met one who stood up fer themselves. Mah folks said Ah should neva date a man who wuzn't man enough tah stand up fer himself, so Ah neva did." Ah scratch mah chin. "Mattah fact, Ah think Ah started likin' ya aftah ya took that damned bracelet offah me."

"Why is that?"

"Ah asked ya if you would put th' bracelet back on me, an' you said yes even though Ah got all up in yer face an' ya were scared. Ya didn' back off one bit, ya stood yer ground an' told me exactly what wuz on yer mind even though it wuz th' opposite o' what Ah wanted tah hear. Neva met a guy who would do that."

"Wait, so if you never dated any men, did you never kiss one either?"

"Naw."

"I was your first kiss?"

She sounds so dang excited Ah chuckle. "Eeyup."

She turns tah look at me. "That is just..."

"Eyes on th' road!" Ah shout 'fore she swerves tah avoid a crater sized pothole. Ah glare at her, holdin' mah seatbelt real tight.

"My apologies, it's just, well... I'm honored!"

"Is it that big o' a deal?"

"But of course it is!" She rests her cheek in her palm, sighing dreamily. "Oh, this is so romantic."

"Get that love struck head outta th' clouds an' focus on drivin', ya hear?" Ah say, shakin' mah head. "Anywho, what 'bout you? Ya eva date any guys?"

"Never been interested. As a child, whenever my family would watch princess films, I could never get over how pretty they were. My friends would always talk about their favorite male celebrities or cute boys around school, but I was too busy looking at them to notice."

"Ya mustah felt like an outcast, huh?"

"No question. One year in high school, a very shy boy who always looked at me when he thought I didn't see him finally gained the courage to ask me out on a date. I didn't have the heart to tell the sweetie pie no."

Ah suck mah teeth wit' a shake o' mah head. "Ah can see where this is goin'."

"We went to an ice-skating rink and had a swell time. When he dropped me back off at my place he tried to kiss me. I almost let him, just to see if I would enjoy it, but the closer he got to me the more I realized it was an awful idea."

"How come ya knew ya wouldn' like th' kiss? Jus' curious is all."

"Hmm... how do I put this? ... Have you ever kissed a skunk's anus?"

"Hell no, what th' hell is wrong wit'cha?"

"How do you know you wouldn't like the kiss?"

"Shoot, ya got me there. Sorry fer interruptin', keep goin'."

"I pushed him away and told him I was gay. He was the first person I'd ever told."

"How'd ya feel?"

"Good! Well, good and bad, I suppose. Good that I finally told someone, but bad that I had strung him along just because I was confused."

"Ah feel like thas' almos' unavoidable. Yer bound tah hurt *someone* as ya find yerself. It's good that ya stopped him 'fore things got too physical though."

"I agree. He didn't feel the same way, of course. He sat down on my porch, curled up into a ball and started bawling."

Ah chuckle even though Ah know Ah shouldn't. "Aw."

"'Aw', indeed. He confessed that he'd had a crush on me ever since he'd first laid eyes on me. For years he could say nothing as I walked past him time and time again. When he finally gained the courage to ask me out and I said yes, he told me he was the happiest he'd ever been, and he'd gotten even happier seeing as the date had went well. Finding out our relationship from my perspective was strictly platonic broke his heart. He told me he wished I had just told him no from the beginning instead of toying with his emotions."

"Poor guy." Ah mean it, too.

"Fear not, good did come from this monumental tragedy. I apologized for my careless actions and vowed to make it up to him. And that I did, in the form of a great friend. I hooked the two of them up, and they couldn't have been happier."

"Phew, Ah'm glad that story had a happy endin'."

"I as well." She sighs. "I *do* hope they're alright, I have not heard from them since the invasion."

"Ah'm sure they're fine," Ah lie.

"I sure hope so."

Ah start rubbin' mah chin, a question comin' tah mind. "So, let me ask ya sumthin'. Say, Ah—Ah dunno, tripped an' grew a dick. Would ya still—"

We swerve intah th' opposin' lane. "I'm sorry, dear... *what?*"

Ah laugh so hard mah tummy aches, but 'tween gulps fer oxygen Ah say, "Ya heard me right! Say Ah grew a dick. Got a strong jaw line, lost mah boobs, y'know, th' works. Say Ah wuz a guy. Would ya still like me?"

"I... are you considering a sex change, Nina?"

Is that even possible *nowadays?* Ah laugh harder. "Naw, sugah! This is purely a hypothetical question."

"I am afraid I do not have the answer to that."

Ah scoff. "Aw, yer no fun."

"I honestly do not! The Nina I fell for is a woman."

"But Ah'm askin' if Ah suddenly grew a dick, would ya still like me?"

"*Ugh, why* are we having this conversation?"

"Cuz its interestin'. Dontcha think so? Ah mean, Ah jus' found out Ah'm bi. Do ya think yer sexual orientation could change fer me too?"

"Hm. I suppose this *is* an interesting question. Is a compatible personality enough to carry a relationship? Is attractiveness a paramount value in love? The way you worded your question was rather questionable, but I nevertheless see the merit in it now."

"So," Ah ask wit' a grin, "wuz yer answer?"

She spares a glance at me, then her eyes go back tah th' road. "Dear, while I cannot say for certain whether I would leave you or not until it actually happened, I believe the answer would be no."

"Aw, shucks, so ya like me jus' fer mah tits?"

"Do not be ridiculous. Not to insult you, but you have lost quite a lot of cleavage from what I presume to be malnourishment. Assuming they used to be larger, of course."

Ah look down at mah meager chest an' chuckle sadly. "Yer right. They used tah be bigger. Ah fergot Ah lost mah babies... so it's mah ass, then?"

Minerva giggles. "Quite. I am not sure how you managed to retain *that* when you were starving to death. But really, Nina, this question is impossible to answer. Whose to say a Nina with a penis wouldn't be a *different* Nina?"

"Ha! 'Penis' sounds funny comin' from that fancy mouth o' yers." Ah laugh sum mo'. "Penis. *Ha!*"

"That is not very funny."

"Why're smilin' then?"

"Because you make me smile." Ah flush a bit at that, then she says, "That does not mean that poor attempt at a joke had any quality humor in it whatsoever."

"So ya don' think Penina an' Nina would have th' same personality?"

"Pe-nina? Really, dear?"

"Ah know ya wanna laugh."

She scoffs, which turns intah a reluctant titter. "You are ridiculous. And yes, I do not think you would remain the same person if you had a penis. All that testosterone would have to change you somehow."

"Ya, Ah guess yer right. But what if Ah, Ah dunno, took estrogen pills tah balance it out or sumthin'?"

"I am pretty sure you would grow breasts then."

"Isn't that a good thing?"

"Nina..."

"C'mon, jus' roll wit' it!"

Minerva sighs. "I do not find men attractive. I do not think they are ugly, I have found some that I think are quite cute, actually, but in the same way I consider a puppy cute. I am afraid I do not want to have sex with them."

"So, like, what if you were intah bestiality?"

"I think we are done here, Nina."

We spend th' rest o' th' day drivin', only stoppin' fer potty breaks an' tah switch drivers. Th' closah we get tah Edinburgh, th' mo' Ah startah wonder how th' scientists think we're gonna stop th' Feral. They don' really have a weakness, ya jus' hadtah be quick on yer feet when ya fought 'em. Ah look at mah scarred arm, swallowin' spit. *Real quick.*

At sum point Ah mustah dosed off, 'cuz when Ah come to Ah don' recognize mah surroundings. "We've finally arrived," Minerva says, parkin' th' car in frontah an abandoned cabin in th' middle o' th' woods. Ah get outta th' car an' stretch. Behin' us is a murky brown pond that Ah'm guessin' used tah be a beautiful fishin' hole. "Sugah, Ah ain't from here an' even Ah know this ain't Edinburgh."

"Don't be silly dear, this is another hideout the Queen built for us so we'd have comfortable places to stay whilst on the Surface."

"Wait, we get tah sleep in those supah comfy beds 'gain?"

"Yes mamn, assuming no one's in!" Minerva says wit' a hopeful smile.

Ah kiss her. "Maybe th' Queen ain't so bad." An image o' Lucio flashes tah mah mind. "Ah take that back. Ah neva said that, ya hear me?"

"Said what, dear?"

"Thank ya kindly."

We approach th' door. "Hey, so what happens if we walk in here an' it's bein' occupied by anotha couple?" Ah ask wit' a laugh.

"Uh, I suppose we'll just excuse ourselves to the other bedroom, provided there is one," Minerva says, face flushed. She pulls a silver key out of her pocket, then pushes it inside th' door's keyhole. *Click.* "Excellent."

She pushes open th' door an' starts tah hold it open fer me, but then she shakes her head an' walks in ahead. Heh, guess she came tah th' same conclusion as me. As polite as we are tah each otha sumtimes, we'd be out here all night decidin' who gets tah go in first. Ah follow her inside, mah feet creakin' on th' sensitive wooden floor. Th' place is empty aside from two beds restin' 'gainst th' wall. Shit, Ah ain't complainin'. At least we gotta bed.

We shrug off our backpacks an' leave 'em near th' beds. "Hey, is there a mirror ova here?"

"Probably. Why do you ask?"

"Ah wanna see sumthin'. C'mon!"

Ah grab her hand an' drag her intah what Ah think is th' restroom, but itsa barren kitchen. Minerva laughs. "Maybe you should let someone who actually knows where things are lead the way?"

"Point taken."

Minerva leads us intah th' restroom. Th' mirror is dusty as all Hell, but a few swipes o' mah hands an' Ah can see our smudged reflections. Ah trytah turn on th' water faucet tah wipe th' filth off mah hands, but there's no water. Ah groan. "Can't tell ya how many times Ah done fell fer this trick." Ah wipe mah hands on mah jeans, gettin' rid o' mos' o' th' dust, then wrap mah arms 'round her waist an' manage tah peak at our reflections from ova her shoulder. Minerva's reflection responds wit' a shaky smile, her perfectly imperfect face flushed. "What, ya can't handle a lil' dust?"

Ah look at mahself raise an eyebrow fer a sec, realizin' Ah hadn't seen mah reflection fer th' longest time. ... God damn, Ah look like shit.

Ah force a laugh. Th' strangah in th' mirror has a body made o' twigs an' a face made o' stone. "Ah wanted tah see if we looked good tahgetha, but Ah gotta admit Ah can't believe a beaut' like you fell fer..." Ah let go o' her waist tah gesture at mah broken body, "...*this.*"

Minerva's shaky smile has collapsed. She's frownin' hard now, a river o' tears flowin' down her face. Th' sudden cryin' leaves me speechless as Minerva says, "Are you blind? You have the cutest little nose contrasting with your toned face, those freckles are to *die for*, and don't even get me started on those magnificent eyes! You're quite the specimen, Nina, and it is a bloody shame you've shackled yourself to a freak like me."

"Hey!" Ah grab her wrist so she'll look me in th' eye. "Ya don' look like a freak. Ah toldcha that yer th' mos' beautiful gal Ah've eva seen an' Ah meant it!" Minerva starts avoidin' eye contact, so

Ah reach up an' grab her shoulders an' say, "Do Ah look like Ah'm *lyin'* tah you?"

"N-no."

"Then why do ya look so glum?"

"... Because every time I look in the mirror, my chest hurts. I look at you and see how beautiful you are, then I look at me and I just—" She chokes back a sob, an' it sounds so damn sad that mah heart feels empty.

Ah put mah hand on her back. "Ah hate seein' you cry. What can Ah say—what can Ah *do* tah make ya feel betta?"

"I... I do not know, dear." Th' corners o' mah mouth sink wit' mo' weight than *Titanic*. "I really do not! I do not *enjoy* feeling horrible every time I confront my reflection. I would love for you to make everything better, Nina. Perhaps, one day, I will begin to believe your truth. But, for now, I cannot bear to look at myself."

Ah roll mah jaw. "Y'know what? Ah think we're goin' 'bout this th' wrong way. Fact is, Ah can call ya beautiful 'till pigs fly, but 'till ya actually start tah believe it, we ain't gettin' nowhere. Ah can't heal yer wound, Minerva. Th' only one who can is *you*."

She tries lookin' at her reflection, but when she meets her own eyes she winces an' turns away. Ah grab her hand an' pull her outta th' bathroom. "Well, shit, Rome wuzn't built inna day. 'Sides, Ah might not be able tah heal th' wound, but Ah can damn well try. Don' see pigs flyin' anytime soon."

Minerva blesses me wit' a smile that makes mah head spin. How can a person be so beautiful it hurts tah look at 'em? "I can't thank you enough for your kind words, Nina."

Ah shake mah head wit' a sad laugh. "Ah wish ya could know jus' how honest Ah'm bein', but Ah guess you'll jus' haftah take mah word fer it."

"Let me cook you dinner! What are you hungry for?"

Ah grab her wrist an' pull her outta th' restroom an' closah tah th' bed. "Ya, Ah'm hungry, but not fer food."

Minerva raises a sly eyebrow. "Whatever are you hungry for?"

"Yer face!"

Minerva rolls her eyes wit' a snicker 'fore Ah fling her tah th' bed. Ah dive on tahppah her, but mah lips meet an open palm. "Just a moment, dear. I hate to bring this up, truly I do, but about this morning..."

Ah purse mah lips wit' a sigh, feelin' th' heaviness o' yesterday's memories return all at once. "Ya?"

"I... I do not wish to hurt you, dear. Or do anything that makes you the slightest bit uncomfortable. That is the last thing I want to do, believe me. How do I know when I am doing something wrong?"

"Ya neva did anythin' wrong sugah, don' eva ferget that. Ah'll let y'know if Ah'm feelin' uncomfortable, OK? Don' sweat it now. Ah... Ah think Ah only got freaked out this mornin' cuz Ah couldn't see yer pretty face. Maybe Ah flashed back tah last night cuz Ah couldn't see them freaks while they were... y'know."

"I understand. I will not turn invisible again when we are getting intimate."

"Much obliged. Now Ah'm gettin' sick o' talkin'!"

Soon enough, time fades intah obscurity. Ah dunno how long we've been kissin' at this point, an' Ah really don' give a damn. Anotha nuke could've gone off outside, or dozens o' Feral could be surroundin' us as our lips lock an' our tongues dance. Still don' care. We're in our own lil' bubble o' passion an' nuthin's gonna takc mah mind offah her. Ah ain't gotta problem doin' this 'till Ah draw mah last breath—least Ah didn' 'till Ah see tears streakin' down her beautifully scarred face. Ah hop offah her. "Whas' wrong sugah?"

"Nothing, dear. Just keep kissing me, please."

"Not 'till ya tell me whas' goin' on, Ah ain't." Ah kinda wanna tease her 'bout how she cries a lot, but now ain't th' time. 'Sides, both o' us have been through a lotta shit th' past few days, so Ah gotta cut her sum slack.

She sniffles her sharp nose, suckin' a thick drop o' snot back intah her nostril. Ah hold inna laugh as she snatches up a tissue box like her life depends onnit. "Hold on, let me go blow my nose."

Ah raise an eyebrow. "Ya can do that right here, sugah."

"A lady does not produce snot in front of her lover."

"Ya already slobbered all ova mah shoulder, a lil' snot ain't gonna bother me none."

Minerva manages a small smile, blushin'. "P-promise me you won't do anything rash."

"O' course."

She blows her nose, then says, "I'm having such a wonderful time with you, dear. And it's making me feel like a horrible person."

"Why?"

"All my friends are probably dead. Sarah, William, Tyrone, Angel, Queen Amity—they all sacrificed so much for me, and here I am snogging my girlfriend without a care in the world. Does that make me a bad person?"

Hearin' th' names o' only a few people out o' th' hundreds o' people Ah done probably murdered makes mah stomach roll, but Ah manage tah say without throwin' up, "Course not sugah. Ain't no sense in walkin' 'round miserable all day. 'Sides, we literally spent th' whole day travelin', Ah think we're both due fer a lil' relaxation. Ah don' think yer friends would fault ya fer that."

Minerva takes in a shaky breath. "You're right, dear. My apologies, I didn't mean to spoil the mood. I'm just so worried about them. Sarah's pregnant, you see, and—"

Ah trytah tell her, "Be right back," but Ah jus' manage tah spill flicks o' vomit ontah th' sheets. Ah run outside an' throw up. Th' moon's reflection off th' surface o' th' muddy water appears wavy as th' poisonous snake that is guilt slithers 'round in mah chest. A warm hand pats mah shoulder right as mo' sick spills outta mah mouth. Ah wobble tah mah shaky legs, wipe mah mouth off then throw mah arms 'round Minerva. "Ah'm so sorry, gal."

Ah know she wants tah shriek away from me on account o' th' sick, an' Ah'm hella grateful she doesn't. "It is not your fault, dear."

"It is. It wuz mah idea tah send th' Feral down there. When Ah wuz torturin' Zack, he told me he had a family. Ah wuz so mad 'bout Lucio's death Ah didn' even care 'bout what he wuz sayin'. If Ah'd jus' listened tah him, maybe Ah wouldn' have done it."

"Maybe, what if, could have, should have—darling, that mistake is in the past now and there is no way we can reverse that decision. What matters now is that you are doing everything in your power to rectify that mistake."

"That don' stop me from feelin' like an awful person."

"Then what will, dear?"

"Ah—Ah dunno."

"Perhaps dinner and a good night's rest will help, hm?"

Ah jus' stare at th' ground as Minerva drags me back intah th' cabin. "Ah'm sorry. Ah wuz 'sposed tah be listenin' tah you an' Ah end up makin' this all 'bout mahself."

Minerva has a small smile even though her eyes as still wet from worry. "Happens to the best of us, dear, believe me."

"When we get back from Edinburgh, Ah promise we'll get back tah yer colony an' check on yer friends."

"I'm looking forward to our journey back. I can only hope that whatever we find in Edinburgh will be so easily conquered."

Chapter 19

The few buildings that have managed to remain standing look like they've come straight from the medieval times. They've got large melted spires and intricate brickwork that's been defiled by the nuclear toxin. "Well, looks like we're finally here," Nina says from the driver's seat through her gas mask. Like London, Edinburgh had been specifically bombed during the nuclear strikes. But while London's air was breathable in most areas, Edinburgh's air is especially toxic. "Where to next?"

"The Queen told me I would find the scientists over at Old Town, so that's where we're heading. We're pretty close now. I'm excited!"

"Ah ain't."

"Whyever not?"

"Cuz Ah think we're in fer sum bad news, sugah. Ah've been thinkin' 'bout th' Feral eva since we got back from Cornelius's. They really ain't so smart, 'specially if ya can trick 'em intah goin' where ya want 'em tah go wit' jus' a few pieces o' flesh. So how th' hell did they get tah Earth? Sumthin's up, gal."

"It appears as though we'll be finding out just what sooner rather than later." We drive into the once populated city. "Oh, I'm sure this place used to be absolutely beautiful. What a shame!"

When I first got to the Surface, I thought a wave of death had swept over the world. Here, it looked as though Hades himself had personally destroyed the environment. Whole buildings, once tall and strong, symbolizing the artistic wonder of mankind's intellect, were reduced to rubble. We can hear every squish and crunch as our car rolls over mutilated and decomposed corpses. Unintelligible trash like destroyed building materials, tattered clothes and broken toys lay alongside corpses, and the devastating sights went on for miles.

"If 'th' scientists are still alive, they're th' toughest group o' folks Ah'll eva see."

"You can say that again, partner."

We end up parking a little ways away from the X the Queen marked on the map on the side of the street. I get out of the car, stomach performing for an imaginary circus. Nina follows suit, and the two of us hobble over all the debris to a manhole cover. I look to the sky. The sun is nowhere in sight, and the endless sea of grey clouds looks as oppressive as ever.

"This is it," I say, "This is where we'll find the answers we've been seeking ever since these terrible creatures invaded. Are you ready?"

"If Ah were you Ah'd have jus' took off th' cover," Nina teases, nudging my arm.

"Ah, but that is because you lack a flare for the dramatics, which is most unfortunate."

"Unfortunate? Gal, if Ah were as dramatic as you we'd both be dead." We look at each other, presumably sharing a smile. "Truth be told, Ah'm kinda scared as tah what we're gonna find down here. Ah wonder if th' scientists ever figured out who dropped th' nuke on us in th' first place, an' if it's even possible tah do anythin' 'bout it once we know."

"Worthy questions to be answered, indeed."

"Y'know, that pretty face o' yers would go a long way towards givin' me th' courage tah face whateva we're gonna find. Then again, takin' that mask off would probably kill ya, so Ah guess mah imagination'll haftah do." I grab her by the shoulders and press my forehead against hers. "What're ya doin'?"

"This is my replacement for a kiss." We rest for a moment, giving each other strength. "Now let's do this!"

kkkrrooooookkk!

A shockwave bowls Nina over, but I stand my ground. I turn to the side to see a tall Feral with tight blue skin and a bloated and deformed arm shrieking at us. It looks like someone's wrapped the arm up in swollen pepperoni. I draw my blade, throwing a defensive arm behind me.

"Nina, you lift the cover, I'll take care of this beast!"

Amazing how having someone to protect can give you so much courage. I charge the monster right as it shrieks again, revealing a mouthful of crimson teeth. I materialize a barrier and deflect the shockwave sideways. A few chunks of debris sprinkles across my face, but I still slash my blade across the alien's right arm.

I sidestep to avoid the ensuing spray of blood, but its bloated arm comes up. I duck. It's jagged claws slash through the air as I tuck into roll. I turn to face the Feral, and the sight of curly blonde hair lying at the place I just was makes my heart plummet.

I launch myself at the beast with a roar, ramming the Blade of Justice through its stomach. A sticky warmness splashes onto my hands, but I dig the blade through even deeper, all the way up to the hilt. Its anguished howl makes me feel bad, but that sympathy is replaced with determination when I see it slashing at my legs. I leave the sword buried inside it then cartwheel over its bloated arm. A brutal stomp to the back of a knees makes it buckle. I reach my arm around to its stomach, and with a strong pull, lurch out the blade. The Feral gives a horrible croak.

I give a relived sigh only to feel my sword get smacked out of my hands. The Feral has one claw to its stomach, keeping its insides from spilling out, and tries another swipe at me. I duck, but the claw skims my scalp.

I just lost even more hair, didn't I?

I run forward and with all the power of a fashion disaster, launch a drop kick right in its chest. It stumbles backwards as I hit the floor, guts dribbling down its body. I snatch up my sword and slash across its throat. Its vocal sack expands with red—

I turn back to Nina right as it explodes, conjuring up a barrier behind me to block most of the blood from splattering against my person. Nina stares at me, slack jawed.

"Well, what are we waiting for?" I say. "Let's find out how to stop these bastards once and for all!"

Her eyes go wide and darts to something over my shoulder. "Look out!"

Her arm becomes a blur. A silver smudge skims past my person. I whirl around, then cover my mouth to keep myself from vomiting. A baby Feral, smaller than the child I saw in the forest, had crawled out of the bloated arm, its blue skin drenched in blood.

Its mouth is wide open, filled with dozens of tiny teeth, and the only thing that stopped its tongue from stabbing me in the back is the tomahawk cleaved into its skull. Waves of chilling goosebumps ripple through my body. I turn back to Nina, wishing I could see her face. "Y-you saved my life. Again!"

"Ain't nuthin' to it, yer th' one who took out th' big guy. But what in th' hell wuz that!"

I can't bring myself to watch Nina retrieve her weapon. "Perhaps this is why the Feral lack genitalia. They must reproduce asexually."

Nina gives a disagreeing grunt. "That don' seem right. Ah dunno, what Ah jus' saw don' seem natural."

"Well, some species of frogs reproduce asexually, so it's not that uncommon. Besides, they're probably from another solar system, so it would definitely seem out of the ordinary for us."

Nina shakes her head and walks past me towards the manhole. "Sumthin's up. Les' find out what." She turns to look me up and down. "Nice haircut, by the way."

"Give me a mirror!"

She's started climbing down the ladder. "Y'know damn well Ah ain't gotta mirror, an' we ain't got time fer that no how."

I start climbing down alongside her, eyes tearing up. "I must look awful."

"Yeah, th' Feral ain't really fit fer a job at th' salon. But hey, on th' plus side, ya took out that freak without even gettin' hurt. It wuz really cool how ya took 'em out, plus you've still got a really nice ass, so there's that."

"You always know just what to say."

"Yeah, Ah'm pretty great."

My cheeks are hotter than my anger at the death of my beautiful hair. "Be a dear and *stop* staring at my backside. I can feel your eyes burning a hole through the fabric."

"Naw, Ah'm good."

I sigh as we finally reach the underground floor. "Oh my, this place smells dreadful."

Nina grabs my hand. Our fingers interlock as we start walking down the hall, footsteps echoing off the hollow brown and decaying walls. It's quite dark, but thanks to the sunlight beaming from the open manhole cover I can see crusty sewer pipes stretching out in every direction. "Now y'know ya can't smell anythin' wit' that gas mask on, right?"

"Of course, dear," I lie, "but I'm sure it would smell dreadful if we weren't wearing these."

"Mhm. Lissen, Ah hope ya ain't too upset 'bout yer hair."

"I'm trying really hard not to cry right now, if only because I won't be able to wipe the tears away."

"Now th' cut looks bad, Ah can't lie, but don'cha go thinkin' you've lost yer last attractive feature or sumthin'. Like Ah toldcha yesterday, yer th' prettiest gal Ah've eva seen, an' Ah don' eva wanna hear you thinkin' othawise, OK?"

I lean my head against hers. I wish I was smaller than her, so I could lean my head on her shoulder instead. "You really do know just what to say sometimes."

"Don' get too comfortable, sugah. Ah'm only bein' sweet so Ah can get intah yer drawers."

"You just *had* to ruin it, didn't you?"

We reach the end of the tunnel, entering a large open room. Even though it's hard to see, I can tell something has gone seriously wrong. The floor is sticky and wet; every footstep makes a noise like "*slitch*". I purse my lips. "Can we get some light?"

"Ah reckon we ain't gonna like what we see, but sure." She produces a flashlight from her backpack. A beam of light pierces the darkness, revealing my most horrifying sight yet. Dozens of bodies litter the room, men and women with bloody lab coats sprawled out on the floor. Some are missing whole appendages, others have their chests ripped open and guts exposed, others only have one eyeball.

I feel like I just got punched in the face. I topple against Nina, who keeps me upright. We hobble deeper into the deathly room, trying to avoid stepping in fecal matter and other bodily fluids as much as possible. Nina stops in her tracks, grabs ahold of her chest, and a large lump goes down her throat. "Try not tah throw up, ya don' wanna mess up yer gas mask."

My foot squishes against something wet and slimy. I don't dare look down to see what is, but my mind's eye sees a rotted, decomposed lower intestines. "Nina, we have to get out of here!"

"We didn' come all this way jus' tah turn 'round when things got messy. They're answers here, Ah jus' know it."

On tables set at the corners of the room we see vials and syringes filled with bubbly chemicals of all colors. Bloody paperwork is scattered across the tables. At the very back of the room holds a few desktop computers, a considerable number of wires connecting them to three giant monitors on the wall. The wall is lined with steel black folding chairs, though a large leather rolling chair is set in the middle of them. A smaller computer monitor is next to it, alongside a keyboard and mouse.

"Well, this looks like a good place tah start," Nina says. We walk towards the small monitor as she sweeps the beam of light across the room. The is massive; there are several different exits leading to who knows where past the monitor. "Les' jus' hope these scientists weren't as perverted as those freaks at the hotel."

"Ugh, don't remind me. I thought you wanted me *not* to throw up."

Nina hands me the flashlight then shoves the leather chair to the side. She bends over to lean on the table, fiddling with the control panel. "Ah sure hope they've still got power," she mumbles.

I find myself staring at her ass. It's easily the most pleasant thing in sight, but it only takes a second for me to feel sleazy so I avert my eyes to the chair. It's still spinning from Nina's shove, but the front half faces me as it comes to a complete stop.

In the chair rests the corpse of a white man with thick black glasses and spiky silver hair. A significant portion of his throat is missing, leaving behind a gaping hole of exposed arteries and veins. In his lap sits a nude child-like figure who appears no older than ten. She has tight blue skin like the Feral I just fought and a scaly bald head. The child's head twists around like an owl, grinning at me with blood-soaked teeth. Bits of flesh are caught in its diastema. My heart freezes as her alien orange eyes dance with what must be delight.

She pounces from the chair in a blue streak. Silver claws rip through her knuckles stained with tattered bits of her skin. Nina continues fiddling with the control panel as the girl lunges towards her.

The flashlight hits the floor as I jump to Nina's defense. My sword meets the creature's claws in the darkness. Sparks burst like fireworks, lighting up the room for an instant. One shove flings her tiny frame backwards. I yank up the flashlight as she hits the ground on all fours like a cat sliding on ice, dragging her claws across the floor to bring her momentum to a stop. She bounces back up with a wide smile. Bony fangs drenched in red emerge from the roof of her mouth.

I will not fight a child, even an alien one! I thrust my palm out, yelling, "Don't come any closer!" I blink, and when I open my eyes, a large transparent purple orb has surrounded her person. The girl slashes against the orb several times, making her hands a silver blur. My brain feels like it's being juiced like a lemon as the claws rake against the barrier's interior.

The hum of the desktop computers announce Nina's arrival as she steps beside me. "Ah didn' know ya could do that!"

The giant computer monitors overhead illuminates the room in a pale blue light. Some parts of the room are still shrouded in darkness, but I'm not going to risk fighting with one hand. I toss the flashlight aside, then say, "I didn't either."

Our new captive shrieks at a wince inducing volume. Vials explode and a giant crack ripples through the central computer monitor, dimming the room even more. "... Too bad Ah can't see it holdin' fer long. Jeezus, what in th' hell is she?"

"I wish I kn—" I lose my footing as she punches a hole through the orb. A pounding headache makes me caress my temple, but I squint at the hole hard regardless. A bit of purple light shimmers to existence and makes the sphere whole again.

"Yer jus' full o' surprises, ain'tcha?"

I lean against her for support. It feels like a nuclear reactor has exploded in my brain. "Surprises or not, what do we do when she breaks out?"

I can tell Nina's grimacing as she draws her axe. "What we gotta do. This gal ain't jus' a child anymo', sugah."

I grit my teeth as another hole bursts the barrier open. "It's never going to get any easier, is it?"

"'Course not."

The barrier crackles and then explodes in a flush of intense purple light. My head feels heavier than a refrigerator, but I still charge alongside Nina.

Right before we're within striking range a large glob of orange spit shoots from the creature's mouth. Nina and I jump out of the way in opposite directions. My eyes widen in horror. A sizzling hole has appeared in the floor where the spit landed.

The creature hisses at us as we back it up against the wall, weapons clenched. "Jus' give up! It's two on one. Don' make us kill ya!"

She leans back and cackles in what I assume to be laughter. Her voice has an eerie echo and a childlike squeak. For a second I'm afraid we're in for more acid, but then something even worse happens. She raises her claws, jams them through her throat, then, after a moment of struggling, *rips off her own head. Her* decapitated head splutters in the hands of her headless body, then it hurls her smiling face at me. I yelp and duck. Her head sails right over my shoulder.

I turn around and follow the arc of her head as it hits the floor with a roll then spins into the juices secreting from the people she killed. It starts *laughing,* then, dozens of ropey body parts covered in slime burst from under her nonexistent neck, flapping about in an invisible breeze. *"What the bloody hell"* I cry as the slick ropes of flesh morph together and take the shape of her original body at a fantastic rate.

"What th' fuck!" Nina cries behind me.

I spare a glance her way to see a twisted geyser of blood erupting from where the creature's head used to be. Bits of brain matter, teeth, and cartilage emerge from that red jet then swirl together to create a perfect replica of her skull. Two orange pennies appear in her just then empty eye sockets, then expand into wide orange orbs.

I turn back to face my fully regenerated opponent and realize that she could have attacked me while I was looking away. She gives me a delighted smile that's almost cute. I take a step back and Nina does as well. Our backs meet as she yells, "No mo' standin' 'round amazed!"

My heart throbs as I stab at the Replicator. Who wants to kill a child? She makes it clear that she has no regard for my sympathy, leaping over my blade and slashing at my mask. A barrier blocks the blow, but that single swipe shatters it into a thousand pieces. The supernatural buckshot blasts me backwards but I start the motion for a retreating swing. She's kicked me full in the face before my arm can even extend. I spin away with a throbbing head and a mouthful of blood, and by the time I regain my footing she's tearing into me.

She slashes at my throat from the right. I deflect the strike then fall back a single step. *Wait, where'd she go?* I look from side to side, then at the floor.

The Replicator crouches low then springs upwards. Her right shoulder twitches, so I twist my blade to deflect the upcoming slash. In that half-second of movement, time slows down. From the corner of my eye I see her left claw coming up at an angle in between a hook and an uppercut. I shift my blade in time to cover the strike but the gazelle slash still pulverizes my defense with ease.

I lose another step, but this one feels fatal. I fall backwards, probably tripping over a corpse I couldn't see. As I fall, the monster rakes into my left forearm and right leg, tearing through my clothes and skin.

Blood explodes from the fresh wounds as the side of my face splashes into a puddle of urine and waste. I roll over and sit up, using my right hand as support and my left to bat back the creature's never ending onslaught of slashes with my blade. My gas mask's visor is so filthy it's a miracle I'm not dead yet.

Ping ping ping! I wince as I reflect the hardest attack yet, wrist throbbing. I try and scoot backwards, but the icky floor makes my fingertips slip. Something wet gets in my hair as the back of my head crashes into the sticky floor. I drop my sword in stunned pain. It clatters next to me while my ears ring in alarm, but I find myself laughing on the inside. At least I won't ever find out what's in my hair.

I'm still conscious after three seconds, so I open my eyes. Nina's digging her axe into the side of the unsuspecting child's stomach, making the poor creature crumple sideways. She hits the floor next to me, eyes closed and mouth grimacing. Why is life so cruel? Who did this to you—

Her orange eyes pop open and her round iris narrows like a reptiles', then she claws at my face. "No ya don'," Nina says as she crashes her foot into the Replicator's gut. The instant this happens, the Replicator gives me a toothy grin. Then Nina's kick sends her flying across a table full of vials and out of my sight.

I groan in agony, miserable as can be. Nina reaches down to help me up, but my cut appendages feel like they're on fire and my visor's clogged with brown smudges and I don't even know what's in my hair!

"Ah need yer help, sug'," Nina whispers. The blood running down the side of her face glows in the dead cyan light. "Ah can't fight her alone."

Her pleading green eyes fan the fires of my determination. I take her hand and let her pull me to my feet even as my everything screams in agony. The fight isn't over yet. We race towards the alien girl, who lays unmoving on the floor amidst a pile of glass. Her ears are missing, making blood drizzle down the side of her head. Nina raises her axe to finish the Replicator off, but I grab her wrist and yank her backwards.

Two Replicators emerge from the shadows and cut through the space Nina just was. They stand alongside one another while the supposedly original Replicator gets up and stands in-between them. She has a fresh new pair of ears, and the cuts she got from the broken vials have sealed up as if they never were. The three of them charge.

Damn it all.

I thrust my hands out, forming a wide barrier that from my perspective looks like an upside-down U. Our front and sides are protected for one second, buying Nina enough time to draw her bow. The Replicators claw at the barrier with mighty swings so I dart forward.

Right when they tear through the barrier I use The Blade of Justice to cut through a Replicator's thigh, chest, and arm. She falls into three pieces then hits the floor with a messy *splat. Replicate after that, foul creature!*

A *thud* announces the death of the second Replicator. Two arrows have gone through her skull. *Nicely done, darling.* I turn to my other side, and the remaining Replicator has an arrow in her thigh. She yanks it out with a grunt, then smiles. Nina fires another, but the Replicator darts out of the way and slashes at me. My sword and her claws clash again and again, but I'm the one losing ground. It's as if she'd never been shot in the leg at all—her speed is incredible.

My sword gets caught in her left claw. I curse as the Replicator brings up her right claw to slice my throat open, but Nina appears at my side and meets the strike with her axe. She kicks the Replicator away, leaving me free to withdraw my sword. Nina and I's eyes flick towards one another then we strike at the Replicator simultaneously.

She weaves her way through our attack like a leaf fleeing from the eye of a tornado. I turn around to see her standing behind us. Her claws are drizzling blood in the pale cyan light. When did she—

The side of my right arm bursts open. I collapse to one knee; clasping the fresh wound, then find Nina doing the same. Did we just lose?

The Replicator is smiling at something behind us. I throw a glance backwards to see three Replicators emerging from the pile of body pieces I created from one. Ha. We definitely just lost.

Nina throws down a small silver ball. I tackle her to the floor and make us invisible as the smoke bomb explodes. We crawl along at a snail's pace, holding hands and intertwining our fingers. This may very well be the end.

We hide amongst the corpses trying to stay perfectly still. I stare into a dead woman's cold blue eyes and try to remain calm even as her body fluids sink into my clothes. The only thing preventing me from snogging her is a weak glass screen.

I hold Nina's hand tight. I want to tell her how I'll do anything to protect her. I want to tell her how much I care for her. I want to tell her that I wish more than anything for another second with her. I want to tell her these things and countless more, but all I can do is squeeze her hand. She squeezes back right as orange saliva splashes onto the dead woman's face. Hiss. Her face melts like a candle licked by flames. I shut my eyes, but the image is already burned into my mind.

The Replicators are sniffing the air above us. One of them spits somewhere, and another does the same. It sounds like bacon on the grill but it smells like fried human. It's only a matter of time before we're dead. I look back at the woman. Her face is no more—the only thing left is her skull. And her eyes... I stare into the endless black depths and the only thing I can think is: *No. Not to my Nina.*

I leap to my feet, turning visible as I draw my blade. The Replicators cock their heads in unison as if wondering why I've compromised myself.

"Come," I growl.

I don't have to tell Nina anything. Talk is cheap.

I take a deep breath, then close my eyes and clench my blade. I won't let them hurt my Nina. I won't. I hear banging sounds, enraged howls then animalistic whines, and when I open my eyes I see an orb of transparent blackness has surrounded us. Around us lie three Replicators, their claws lying in silver pieces on the floor as they roll around in agony. *Their claws must have nerve ends.* The only thing shielding us from their cries of pain is my barrier.

Nina gets to her feet and puts a shaky hand on my shoulder. "...Wuz wonderin' when you'd do that."

"I couldn't have done it without you, darling."

The still standing Replicator looks at my barrier with what appears to be amused interest. She retracts her claws, then scratches at her chin as if in deep thought. "Well?" I challenge. "Are you going to kill us or not?"

The Replicator picks up the wrist of her howling clone, then presses her palm against the barrier. The clone screeches as my shield rejects her touch, leaving her hands flayed and tattered. The Replicator laughs as her clone collapses and withers on the floor in agony, then, the Replicator walks to the computer at the end of the room.

"What th' hell..." Nina whispers.

The Replicator opens up a typing program, then types: "You two are fun! The tall one especially. I've never run into another metahuman before. I admire your will to live, so on account of us being sisters I'll let you go. But should our paths cross again, don't expect to walk away."

And with that, she raises her claws and tears her body to shreds. Bits of her blue skin and mangled organs go flying like she's running herself through a grater until nothing but a mushy red stump remains. Dozens and dozens of Replicators emerge from the tornado of gore, filling up the entire room.

Each of them crouches and heaves up a corpse three times their size. She might as well be a colony of unkillable super ants. Nina squeezes my hand, and her touch gives me strength. The Replicators walk past us with their prey as my barrier pulses with a strong purple light. A few of them bump against it and get blasted back as if they'd been hit by defibrillators.

The Replicators steer clear of us after that. Soon enough, they've all gone down the hallway and out of sight, dragging every scientist along with them. It's as if they never existed at all. I drop my barrier and almost collapse on the spot.

"She... she got away," Nina groans and leans on me for support. An ocean of blood spreads from underneath us.

"No, my dear... we got away."

X X X

We fiddle around with the control panel and find a universal light switch. Our path now visible, we venture further into the underground city hobbled together like elderly women as we look for a place to shower. Every footstep creates a trail of blood for anyone to follow. The fight is even more terrifying in hindsight—the Replicator could have swarmed us from the very beginning.

As luck would have it, our journey through the underground city has been peaceful and relatively gore free. We enter a surgeon room with white walls and a white floor. In the middle of the room is a long brown table with mean black straps that wouldn't look out of place in a medieval dungeon. "I'd hate to admit it..." I say with a wince, "but this is better than a shower."

We find some suture needles and thread, so we sit on the eerie table and I get to work on stitching us up. Nina is shaking when the needle approaches her arm, but I use my free hand to rub her shoulder. She relaxes a bit, and the rest of the process goes smoothly.

I grab two separate rolls of surgical tape from the cabinet, then hand one to Nina. "We'll use these once we shower."

"OK," she says.

"Are you?"

"No. You?"

"No."

Nina sighs as we make our way out of the room and back into the open-ended city. "That thing almos' killed us. Ah wouldah died withoutcha, y'know."

"Have you already forgotten about how you saved me before we got underground, not to mention you saving me twice during this fight alone?"

"... Eeyup."

We walk into a classroom with a white board packed with math formulas, then a dungeon with a bunch of broken open cages. Just what were the scientists doing here?

The answer to that question will have to wait because we just found the bathrooms. "I've never needed a shower more in my entire life."

"Ya can say that again."

We check to make sure both rooms are clear, and then Nina gives me a hug. "Don' spend an entirety in there now, Ah wanna know what th' hell is goin' on here." She lets me go, then bounces the surgical tape between her hands in a flurry of white. "Ah'll be at th' entrance when ya get out, 'K?"

"OK!"

I step inside my restroom, close the door, then strip off my gas mask and the bloody clothes that stick to me in the most disgusting way. I ransack the cabinets, finding plenty of soap and shampoo, even a change of clothes. Once I'm undressed, I hop in the bathtub and get the water running.

It only takes a second for me to realize that this both the best and worst shower of my life. It's the best because I've never been filthier, but it's the worst because the water really stings when it hits one of my wounds—and considering my whole body is full of those, the shower isn't as pleasant as it could be. I can't even use much soap, which is a criminal offence in of itself.

The bathtub is red by the time I'm done. I step out of the shower, wincing with every step. I practically have to drown myself in alcohol, cleaning spray and bandages before I can get dressed. I'm soon wearing purple doctor's scrubs, and though it's a little high-water, I still manage to make it work. I'm quite amazed at how quickly I've grown accustomed to taking things from dead people, though I suppose I've had quite a bit of experience.

I look in the mirror. My scars are still there, obviously, but looking at them doesn't hurt quite as much. "Yer th' mos' beautiful gal Ah done eva seen," I hear. I smile at myself, but my lips dip when I see my new haircut.

It is completely unsalvageable, a total fashion disaster, a disgrace to my past life as a model. The curls are uneven, like tectonic plates before an earthquake, and bits of my scalp are showing. Through blurry eyes, I tear through the drawers until I find some clippers. *I have no choice, do I?*

Tears hit the sink, and I take a shaky breath before turning it on. The device begins *buzzing*, sending a dreadful chill down my spine. I take aim at my once beautiful hair...

Chapter 20

AH STRAP ON mah gas mask 'fore re-enterin' th' room full o' corpses, holdin' a chair in each hand. Y'know, me an' Lucio done seen a lotta awful stuff in our day, but this tops th' list. Ah keep mah eyes tah mahself as Ah set th' chairs down in frontah th' large table seperatin' me from th' giant monitor attached tah th' wall.

Ah plop down inna chair, tryin' tah relax inna room Ah wuz fightin' in only an hour ago. Ah start messin' wit' th' control panel, tryin' tah get th' image o' th' alien kid nibblin' on flesh outta mah head.

Ah concentrate on th' monitor in frontah me as th' pleasant *hum* o' th' computers starts tah calm me down. Th' monitors are still on th' blue start screen, but Ah haftah type inna password tah get through. Ah type in "password" then click 'enter'. Soon enough Ah'm lookin' at th' desktop's background. Itsa picture o' all th' scientists huddled tahgetha. They're smilin' like it's Christmas Eve. In th' center is th' white guy wit' spiky silver hair an' thick glasses, th' same guy lil' missy wuz eatin' up 'fore she tried tah kill us.

Ah sit there fer God knows how long, wonderin' what th' hell happened tah these people an' whas' takin' Minerva. Ah can't even get mad though; she hates stains worse than Ah hate dishonesty, an' her past two fights have left her lookin' rough. She's still probably in th' shower, tryin' tah pretty herself up as much as she can. Sudden footsteps make me stand at attention an' yank out mah gun. "Whose there," Ah shout, hoppin' outta mah chair.

A bald woman walks in from th' hall, a gas mask strapped tah her face. Ah'm 'boutah take aim, but her voice makes me freeze. "Do refrain from shouting, dear. My ears can only take so much punishment."

"Minerva! Ya look... ya look..."

Her confident posture deflates, lookin' like a comedian wit' a tough audience. "Awful, don't I?"

"Are ya kiddin'? Ya look badass an' beautiful at th' same time! Ah mean, Ah'm still gonna miss yer hair, but not *too* much. C'mon ova here an' gimmie sum sugah, sugah," Ah holler, walkin' towards her wit' arms outstretched. Ah hug her real tight, restin' mah head 'gianst hers. "Ugh, Ah can't wait 'till we get outta here, this is a poor substitute fer a kiss."

Minerva gently pushes me back tah look me in th' eye. "Y-you're not just saying this to make me feel better, right?"

"Who th' hell do ya think yer talkin' to?" Ah ask wit' a wink.

Minerva graces me wit' that heart stoppin' smile. Well, Ah mean, Ah can't see her lips, but Ah can tell she's smilin' from th' way her eyes are crinklin' tahgetha. "Fair point."

We walk on ova tah th' chairs an' sit down. When Minerva sees th' background picture, she sighs an' leans her head on mah shoulder. "Oh my. What happened to these people?"

"Les' find out." Ah hover th' reticule ova a file that says "Eulogy", then click onnit. A video pops up, an' th' white man wit' th' silver spiky hair an' thick glasses bounces intah th' frame, speakin' mo' energetically than Lucio on caffeine.

"Hiya! My name is Dr. Light. Ten months ago, the Queen gave me access to the top scientists of the nation and state of the art technology with two goals in mind—finding out where the Feral came from and how to stop them. Fortunately, we've solved both puzzles. *Unfortunately*, if you're watching this video, we're all dead!" He places his palm ova th' side o' his face like he's tellin' us a secret. "That, or I'm too lazy to tell you everything we've discovered in person.

"Whichever the case, it would benefit us both if I got straight to the point. We know from a report by Fringe Science Inc. done a few years back that our solar system is devoid of any intelligent life forms. This has brought us to the conclusion that the Feral have come from another solar system entirely."

"I knew it," Minerva whispers.

"But they didn't come alone. They *couldn't* have come alone."

"Ha!" Ah nudge mah gal. "*Ah* knew it!"

"We've preformed several autopsies on the Feral and observed their behavior whilst in captivity." Th' video cuts tah three Feral locked up in th' room full o' cages we saw earlier. Two o' 'em are adults, an' one is a kid. Th' parents huddle 'round th' kid, shiverin' in whas' gotta be fear. Fer th' first time it hits me that these guys have families too. Sparklin' rods push through th' gaps 'tween th' cage's bars, then prod th' adult aliens, makin' 'em shriek in agony. They hit th' floor convulsin'. Th' kid tries tah slice through th' bars, but his claws ain't poppin' out. It opens its mouth, but a stumpy tongue is its only defense.

"This is awful! Why, I nev—oh."

"Oh," don' even begin tah describe it. Right 'fore our eyes, th' scientists plunge a blade through th' kid's forehead. It shudders on th' spot, dead. Th' parents pound th' bars so hard th' cage rattles, but anotha poke from th' rods sends 'em right back tah th' floor. Th' video starts playin' fasta like sumone pressed th' fast forward button, an' th' date on th' upper right corner o' th' screen tells me that several days pass. Th' parents don' move an inch th' whole time, clingin' tah one anotha day in an' day out. Every now an' then th' scientists throw inna human limb or two, but th' food is ignored. Then, soon enough, th' parents stop movin' fer good.

Ah pause th' video an' turn tah mah gal, whose back is hunched ova. Is she cryin' behin' that mask? "Are ya alright?"

"No, I am *not* alright. I simply cannot believe we came all this way to meet a pack of psychopathic murdering bastards who kill just to satisfy their curiosity. I can't believe I'm the knight of the Queen who funded this nonsense. This is awful and I hate it I hate it I hate it!"

Wit' every, "I hate it," Minerva stomps her foot down. Ah wanna tell her tah simmer down, but Ah jus' hold off an' let her vent. Ah gotta admit Ah didn' 'xpect these folks would be so damn cruel tah murder a child in frontah it's folks. Ah know th' Feral eat us alive an' all, even killed mah gal's folks, but Ah mean, maybe we're th' only food source fer 'em or sumthin'. Ain't many animals tah snack on aftah th' nuke 'sides us humans. What we jus' saw seemed so unnecessary... Ah can't blame Minerva fer gettin' upset. Still...

"Y'know we gotta finish th' video, right?"

"I know, I know," she sighs. "Just give me a minute, please."

Ah give her as much time as she wants, feelin' sick as Ah digest th' snuff film. Aftah awhile, Minerva says, "I'm ready," an' Ah click 'play' 'gain. Th' video cuts back tah Dr. Light, whose grinnin' like a kid goin' tah an ice cream store. "Fascinating, isn't it? They come from an entire solar system away, and they still possess emotions like happiness and sadness. As you just saw, the parents were so traumatized by the loss of their child that they starved themselves to death. The impact of this decision is huge. You see, the Feral's sense of smell is one of its greatest strengths and weaknesses. Once they catch the scent of blood, they lose all sense of reason and logic and follow wherever the smell leads them."

"So that's how you were able to attack the colony..." Minerva whispers.

"When we gave them food and they resisted eating, they overcame their body's powerful survival instincts. From this and several other experiments of this nature, we've concluded that the Feral are actually remarkably intelligent, with intellect rivaling beings such as elephants and dolphins. But their intelligence is offset by their intense desire for food, especially when hungry. They're not so unlike us."

Ah remember rakin' intah Lucio's face ova a rat an' mah own burns wit' shame. "And yet, even with their intelligence, we know that the Feral could not have made the journey to our solar system alone. They lack dexterity, knowledge of technology, and their need to consume outweighs their need to advance their society through science. Aside from that, the Feral come built in with everything they need to hunt prey. It was only because we lacked claws that we invented the spear.

"So, the question remains: Who exactly helped the Feral get here? We don't know the answer to that question, but the further we get into our research, the more proof we have to validate this hypothesis." Th' video cuts tah th' room full o' cages. This time, th' camera zooms in onnah operatin' table thas' gotta Feral chained up from its legs tah its arms. Th' camera zooms in on its crotch area, where there is only skin. "Upon first glance, the Feral lack genitalia. Why is that?

"Initially, we assumed that they reproduced asexually, but upon further observation, we discovered this was not the case. The Feral have two sexes, just like us. The female genitalia only reveals itself when aroused. As for the males...they've been castrated. All of them."

"What th' hell?" Ah cry.

"There is but one final piece of the puzzle. If the Feral didn't need to create technology to survive, why do they have technology built into their wrists?"

Th' camera zooms in on th' Feral's hairy wrists. A pair o' garden shears hack through th' hair, revealin' a shiny silver speck. "You can't tell from the camera, but a bracelet made from unidentifiable technology is embedded into its skin. Take a look at this!"

A sudden *bang* makes me jump, but Ah realize aftahwards that it came from th' video. Th' air 'round th' chained up Feral distorts an' twists, an' sumone off screen gives a horrible scream. Th' camera cuts back tah Dr. Light, whose wearin' a sheepish grin. "As you saw, the bullet was reflected back as always. But you may have noticed the bracelet vibrating once the shot was fired. This is not a coincidence. The bracelet embedded into their skin is the reason why firearms do not work against them. Any object traveling over three hundred miles per hour is reflected."

Minerva an' Ah share a look, then Dr. Light says, "So now we know that the Feral are not born with an internal force field, the technology that enables the force field is embedded into their flesh." Th' video cuts tah Doctor Light standin' in frontah a chalk board. "So, let's do a quick recap, shall we?"

He uncaps a marker, then turns tah th' white board behin' him an' writes numbers 1 through 3 like he has a grudge against 'em. "1: The Feral are intelligent, but not capable of producing technology. 2: All of the males have been castrated. 3: They have advanced technology embedded into their flesh. Conclusion: *The Feral are as much of a victim as we are in this war!* Another alien race, one far stronger and intelligent, stripped the Feral of their ability to reproduce and shackled them with technology that makes it much harder for humans to kill them.

"Imagine, an entire race forced off their home planet, unable to create a family, with their only viable food source being an intelligent race that fights back. The poor bastards bear no particular grudge against us, nor do they want to take over the world. They're just hungry."

"As cruel as this plan is, it is nevertheless tremendously effective. Whether or not we manage to kill off the Feral, or they manage to eat us all, this mystery race has weakened both parties tremendously, leaving the Earth easy for the taking."

Ah pause th' video again, leanin' back in mah seat as th' weight o' th' news makes mah soul buckle. Ah laugh, jus' cuz Ah dunno what else tah do. "Y'know, when Ah killed eight o' 'em things tah save ya, Ah thought Ah wuz jus' th' mos' badass gal tah walk th' planet. Neva heard o' anyone takin' on that many by themselves. Don' get mah wrong, Ah'd do it again, but now Ah jus' feel like, insteadah killin' vicious, bloodthirsty aliens, Ah jus' killed a pack o' beaten down puppies."

Ah glance at Minerva in amazement, whose coverin' her mask wit' her hands. "All this time, I thought they were our enemy," she says, voice tight. "I hated them for ruining my life and wanted to kill them all. I didn't know how wrong I was."

"Neither did Ah." Ah sigh. "Damn. Things really ain't eva gonna get easier."

"If the Feral was strong enough to send an entire continent sprawling into chaos, how are we going to deal with even stronger aliens?"

"Same as how we deal wit' everythang else. *Deal*."

Minerva nods weakly. Ah want tah comfort her sumhow, but mah head is spinnin' too fast fer me tah even sit up straight. Mah parents lost their lives tryin' tah fight th' Feral 'fore th' nuke wiped 'em out, but they didn' even know they were fightin' th' wrong aliens. They died fer no reason.

Ah give a shaky sigh, suppressin' tears. Minerva grabs ahold o' mah hand. Does she know what Ah'm thinkin? Ah don' say nuthin', but Ah squeeze her hand 'fore pressin' 'play'.

"But not all is lost, Your Majesty," Dr. Light says wit' confidence. "We've discovered a lot about the Feral, and killing them is going to be a lot easier from now on. Knowing that the Feral's defensive barrier was brought about by technology and not biology finally gave us an idea of how to fight back." He reaches intah his lab coat an' pulls outta small black ball 'bout th' size o' a golf ball. "Throw one of these, and upon impact, any Feral within twenty-five feet will have their force field de-activated, finally making guns a viable option again."

Ah nod. *This'll make dealin' wit' herds a lot easier... a shame we gotta slay these innocent creatures though.*

"Each one is built in with a self-sustaining battery, meaning you can re-use them after only a five-minute duration. We call these gems Energizers. But we're not done. We've also developed another type of grenade, one that targets the Feral's sense of smell. When thrown, these will emit pheromones that they will be unable to resist. These make for perfect distractions when faced with unwinnable situations, though they smell particularly horrible." He takes outta white ball 'bout as big as a tennis ball wit' a red button on top. "We call these Stink Bombs. Provided we can distribute them fast enough, these grenades are estimated to improve survival rates by at least 50%.

"You'll find the schematics for both devices at the end of the video, so any scientist can create these special grenades provided they have the materials. But we wouldn't be the top scientists in the kingdom if this is all we invented in a year's time. By pure chance, a large chunk of Super Meteorite landed in our fair city, and an extraction team was able to acquire it. A few years back, a group of scientists in Texas discovered that close exposure to the Super Meteorite granted extraordinary abilities even by metahuman standards. Thanks to their experiment, a woman named Cynthia Alegit became one of the most powerful metahumans in existence; granted the ability to move objects with her mind.

"With all due respect, Your Majesty, any one of your knights would be annihilated by that woman. We need stronger metahumans; one's capable of fighting armies of Feral all on their own. Unfortunately, it appears that none of our scientists, including myself, have the metahuman gene. The metahuman gene is a catch all term we use to describe whatever biological differences metahumans have from normal humans that enables them to interact with the Super Meteorite, which grants metahumans their powers.

"We never had enough time to study metahumans closely enough to figure out just how their bodies differ from normals, but one thing we do know is that children and young adults are much more susceptible to the Super Meteorite than adults. Whilst growing up, the brain is very malleable, which is our best guess as to why there are many young metahumans and few adult ones. Fortunately, we had one young volunteer at hand: My beautiful, brave little girl Lucy."

Th' camera cuts tah a young gal, no older than nine, wit' short black hair bound inna ponytail, thick black glasses, an' an adorable smile too wide fer her face. She's lyin' in bed, a copy o' *Ender's Game* restin' in her hands. Mah heart throbs. *Ender's Game* wuz one o' th' books Ah gave Cornelius, one o' me an' Lucio's favorites. Speakin' o' mah brother, if he wuz reincarnated intah a white gal, Lucy would be a dead ringer. That giant smile, th' way her feet kicks up an' down on th' bed, th' way she giggles tah herself 'fore flippin' th' page—th' sight is too much.

Ah pause th' video, but th' fresh wave o' hurt still pushes me back intah mah chair. Too many memories come back all at once—th' time Ah took him tah th' mall so he could get his first galfriend th' perfect valentine's gift, th' time he cheered mah name so loud durin' a rodeo competition Ah lost, th' time he clapped harder than anyone durin' mah last theater play in highschool, that night we found sum weed in an abandoned house after th' invasion. That night wuz one o' th' best nights o' mah life. We stayed up 'till th' sun rose talkin' 'bout ma an' pa, wonderin' what they were up tah in heaven, tellin' each otha stories 'bout how crazy they were, like th' time—

"What's wrong, dear?"

"N-nuthin'. She jus' reminds me o' Lucio, is all."

"Oh," Minerva says, pattin' mah hand.

"He wouldah loved ya, y'know. Really wouldah loved ya."

"I know, sweetie. I know."

Ah choke back a sob as Ah remember that Ah'm th' last Eagleheart all ova again, which is really fuckin' irritatin'. "Sorry. Ah'm 'sposed tah be stronger than this. Don' mind me none."

Minerva gets outta her chair an' sits on mah lap. She's tall an' heavy as hell so o' course it hurts, but Ah don' say nuthin'. She strokes mah gas mask in th' best an' worst possible way, makin' me feel warm an' weak an' needy. "Tell me, Nina. When I cry, do you consider me weak?"

"No!"

"So why do you feel that way when you cry?"

"Cuz... Ah dunno."

"Perhaps I do? Maybe you hold unrealistic expectations for yourself, and constantly failing to meet those expectations leads to lower self-esteem and endless frustration?"

Ah press mah temple against hers. "Stop bein' so damn smart, ya make me feel stupid."

"Stop being so darn charming, dear, you make me feel dull and uninteresting." She rubs mah shoulder gently, then gets up an' sits back in her chair. "I hope I wasn't too heavy."

"'Course not."

"You're an awful liar, Nina. Shall we finish watching the video?"

Ah shake mah head an' press play once again.

"Lucy, buttercup, could you do me a favor," Dr. Light asks.

Lucy reluctantly looks up from her book, glarin' at th' camera, then at her father. "Depends on the favor."

"Could you, pretty please, do the trick again?"

"But *Daddy*! We've been running tests all day. Can't I read a book in peace for once?"

"I know, buttercup! Just one more time, *please*? I'm going to show this video to the Queen, and I want her to know just how brilliant you are."

Lucy puffs her chubby cheeks, makin' me smile. "All right Daddy, but this is the last time!" She grabs a page an' folds a corner, bookmarkin' th' page fer latah. Then she rolls out o' bed, landin' on her feet an' shiftin' her body tah th' side. She clenches her fists an' squints her eyes real tight.

Ah nudge Minerva. "She looks like she's constipated."

She giggles an' slaps mah arm. "Stop it!"

Ah'm 'boutah start tappin' mah foot 'gainst hers, but what Ah see next takes me outta a flirtin' mood. "Oh, *Jeezus*."

Th' camera focuses on Lucy's side profile right as a hand drippin' red reaches out from Lucy's back. Her whole body starts shakin' wit' concentration, an' anotha hand emerges, thena foot, then anotha foot. It looks as disturbin' as you'd 'xpect, makin' me feel like Ah jus' fell through an elevator shaft. Ah'm glad th' camera ain't lookin' directly at th' hole. A perfect replica o' herself emerges from her backside—ugh, Ah mean her *actual* back as Dr. Light's cries, "Brilliant, brilliant!" he says, clappin' his hands all th' while.

Lucy blushes while mah face gets jus' as red. "That *bastard!* He mutated his own flesh an' blood."

Minerva rubs th' tahppah mah hand. "I considered the possibility, but I didn't want to believe it."

"You can go back to your book, buttercup. Thanks again!"

The original Lucy smiles weakly, then plops back on her bed. She reaches for her book, then stops midway, instead goin' fer a pillow. Lucy's clone grabs Dr. Light's hand, askin', "Happy now?" wit' a smirk.

"Very. Come along, buttercup, we have more tests to run."

Lucy's clone groans, but leans her head 'gainst Dr. Light's arm, jus' like Ah used tah do wit' mah Pa. Ugh, Ah swear, this fella made mah skin crawl worse thana dozen spiders. He looks intah th' camera, sayin', "Lucy's clones are entirely self-aware, perfect duplicates of my perfect little girl. After around thirty minutes to an hour, they explode into a cloud of smoke, as if they were never there."

"I'm right here, you know," Lucy's clone says, though she jus' seems amused by th' whole thing.

Dr. Light rolls his eyes. "Lucy can only make three clones at the moment, though we suspect this number will change drastically as her abilities grow stronger."

He leads her intah th' surgery room me an' Minerva were in earlier. Th' clone's face falls. "I'm not going to like this, am I?"

Dr. Light shakes his head "no".

Th' clone goes silent but doesn't resist as scientists strap her up tah th' evil brown table we sat on earlier. Right next tah her rests a Feral wit' a filthy, bumpy-all-ova arm that looks jus' like th' Feral Minerva fought this aftahnoon.

"Oh, *my...*" Minerva whispers.

Dr. Light exchanges nods wit' an Indian woman, who takes outta butcher knife so big Ah can't help but feel sorry fer all th' animals Ah done butchered on th' farm back home.

"Let us observe the vast differences of durability between my daughter's clone versus a Feral we have experimented on." Th' Indian woman hands th' knife ova tah Dr. Light, who raises it ova th' clone's exposed arm. Dr. Light strokes th' clone's face, tears comin' tah his eyes. "Are you ready, sweetie?"

"No."

"I'm sorry."

He raises his knife—

"*Stop it!*" Minerva shouts. Ah close th' video, an' turn tah her right as she draws her sword.

Ah jump in frontah th' blade's path tah th' computer. "Don' do anythin' rash! Destroyin' all their research ain't gonna do nothin' but screw us ova. We need tah grab th' schematics fer th' grenades, remember?"

"... Fine." She sheathes th' blade, then pounds her clenched fists against th' table, rattlin' th' desktops. "This man is a *monster*." Ah'm jus' as pissed as her, but Ah don' see how pourin' gasoline onnah forest fire is gonna help anyone. Ah reach tah stroke her hair but then remember it ain't there no mo', so Ah grab her hand an' stroke her palm instead. "He's already dead sugah, ain't nuthin' we can do 'bout it now."

"I'm just—I can't believe..."

"Ah know sugah. Ah know."

We sit there for a while tryin' tah digest a tragedy onnah whole new level.

"He mustah been really desperate."

"And look where that got him and his team. Nothing but death."

"Ah don' disagree. Do ya wanna finish th' video?"

"No. We know what happens next anyway. He spliced in experimented Feral DNA into his daughter, and then she killed them all."

"Ah guess so." Ah sigh, both at this situation as well as realizin' that Dr. Light didn't mention th' nuke once durin' th' entire video. Looks like th' scientists dunno who dropped th' nuke either. Maybe

Ah'll never know who's responsible fer mah parents' death. Ah neglect tah mention any o' this tah Minerva, not wantin' tah upset her any more than she already is. Best course o' action is tah distract her. "So what do we do now?

Minerva reaches intah her pocket an' pulls out a flash drive. "Let's copy the video onto this and see if we can find the documents for those grenades they made. Then we are getting the hell out of here."

Chapter 21

WE'RE DRIVIN' BACK tah Minerva's colony when we decide tah visit Cornelius. *Maybe he wants tah come wit' us?* If his family survived th' attack, Ah'm sure he would want tah see 'em. We knock on th' door smilin' at each otha, but th' smell o' blood makes mah smile go away quicker thana fart in th' wind.

We run through th' hole in th' wall an' intah th' kitchen. We find him lyin' on th' floor across froma woman. Both o' 'em have guns in their hands an' holes through their chests. Minerva clings tah mah arm, shakin' an' tearin' up. Ah walk back intah th' livin' room an' look at th' couch. *Ender's Game* is lyin' there. It must've been th' book he wuz readin' 'fore he got ambushed. Ah stop on th' page he bookmarked, then laugh.

"What's funny," Minerva snaps.

"Ain't that sum shit," Ah ask wit' tears in mah eyes. "He died right before he could get tah th' twist."

Chapter 22

I collapse on the swing set with as much melodramatic weight as I can manage, grabbing ahold of the chains to my side. I feel rather cheery despite the moody grey sky overhead. "Oh, Nina. Do you remember how we first met?"

Strong hands push my back, sending me skyward. "Uh, we tried tah kill each otha here?" The wind tickles my naked head as I soar back to Nina, who pushes me once more. "'Sides, that couldn't have been mo' thana week ago. Huh, now that Ah think 'bout it, weren't these swings broken last time?" She pushes me again, higher this time, and I can't help but giggle with glee. "Ah ain't gonna lie tah ya sug', yer angelic voice jus' made mah heart skippah beat."

"Oh, *stop it*!" I squee. "But, correct, I do believe the swings weren't in working order last week. Why do you suppose they went through the trouble of repairing it?"

"No clue." She spends another few moments pushing me. The chains to my sides whine as I fly higher, smiling blissfully all the while. I think back to simpler times, when father and mother would take turns pushing me at a park like this when I was just a child. Oh, how I missed them!

"I wish my parents could have met you," I say with a sniffle.

"Ah wish ya couldah met mah folks, too," Nina says, her next push noticeably weaker than the last. When I drift back to her, my head gently bumps against her stomach, bringing me to a stop. She wraps her arms around my shoulders then rests her chin on my head.

"T-this is where my parents died, you know. But it is also where I met you. The best and worst moments of my life all happened here. Isn't that funny?"

"Minerva..."

We sit there for the longest time, conversing in our silent language. Eventually, Nina breaks the spell.

"D—Don'cha think it would be a good idea tah go ahead an' figure out whas' goin' on? Y'know damn well Ah enjoy yer company, but Ah don' think now is th' right time fer a play date."

"... Could you wait here with me for a moment, please?" I whisper.

"O' course," she coos, letting go of me. She sits on the swing set next to me. "We can wait 'slong as ya like."

She grabs my hand gently, rubbing her hard thumb across my knuckles every few seconds. I take a deep breath, basking in the warm presence that radiates from her like the sun. The chains to our sides creak as we sway back and forth, back and forth, back and—

"Are ya 'fraid o' how yer friends will react tah yer new do?" Nina asks, running her hand over my bald head. It is not quite as sensitive as before, but I still shiver at her touch.

"No, I am afraid they won't be around to react to it."

Nina sighs. "Ah know sugah. Jus' tryin' tah lighten up th' mood."

"Well, it is not working."

"Are ya mad at me?"

"No," I lie.

"Yeah, you are. Look, Ah'm sorry. Ah really am!" she says, her voice cracked.

I meet her eyes so fast I get whiplash. "Is sorry going to bring back my friends?"

She looks away. "We don' even know if they're dead."

"Yet."

She stops her slow and steady swinging, and, putting her head down, starts drawing a lazy 's' in the dirt with a foot. "Ain't nuthin' else Ah can say otha than sorry, sugah."

"Oh, what the bloody hell am I doing?" I stamp my feet down, bringing the pendulum that is me to a stop. I place my index finger and thumb under her chin and turn her towards me. I get lost in those brilliant emeralds, and within them I find myself.

"Listen to me. No matter what we see down there, no matter what I say or do, I'm telling you now that none of this is your fault. I am sorry I took out my troubles on you. That was very irresponsible."

Nina sighs again but takes ahold of both of my hands and rests her forehead against mine. "Ain't nuthin' ya need tah 'pologize fer. Now, Ah might be wrong, but it seems tah me like yer ready tah face th' truth."

"Correct." We stand up, united once more as we walk towards the cabin. Nina tries to open the door, but it is locked. Are there people inside? I think I hear someone moaning... She's about to front kick the door into splinters, but I grab her wrist and knock her knuckles against it instead. "See? It isn't as hard as you may think, dear."

"Maybe not, but it sure as hell is mo' boring."

I kiss her cheek. "You silly girl."

Frantic rumbling can be heard from within the cabin. There are definitely people inside. I turn invisible and draw my sword, just in case. I pat Nina's back and whisper, "I'm right here, darling."

"Couldn't ya have patted a lil' lower?"

I feel myself redden right as the door opens. A tall, muscular black man with one arm has a gun pointed at Nina. He puts the gun down before I can cut off his other arm. "Oh my God, Nina! You're alive!" He envelops her in a hug. I fight off another vision of me hacking off his remaining arm while he says, "Zis is unbelievable! Ve zought you vere dead."

"Jeezus, Pete! Yer gonna snap me in two."

He lets her go with obvious reluctance. "Chinwei, get over here! You've got to see zis."

"One second," a lady with an American accent says from inside the cabin.

"Ah, you'll have to excuse her. Ve vere, um, slacking on ze job, if you know vhat I mean."

Nina chuckles, shaking her head while Chinwei groans, "Peeete!"

She pops up at his shoulder, clothes wrinkled and sweaty. She's a petite Asian woman with short and wavy black hair. A shallow scar cuts across her left cheek. Was it a knife fight, or a grazed bullet? Either way, I'd kill to trade scars with her. As the couple gets closer I realize just how badly they reek of sex. … And yet the woman still pulls Nina into a hug.

I feel my face scrunch up in disgust as she says, "Holy shit! It really is you."

"Vhat, did you zink I vas talking to a ghost?"

"No, but, c'mon Pete, we attended her funeral! It's just a little hard to believe, is all."

Chinwei finally lets her go, and I absentmindedly wonder if they even bothered to wash their filthy hands before touching my Nina.

"Well, come on in! Queen Adelia will be thrilled," she exclaims.

Nina follows them inside. Pete starts to close the door behind them, but I stop it from closing with my foot. He looks up in bewilderment, and at that precise moment I turn visible. "Boo!"

Pete yelps and falls over, scrambling for his gun, but Nina kicks it out of his reach. "Sorry! This is jus' mah galfriend's idea o' a practical joke."

"My apologies," I say with a giggle, stepping inside the cabin. I close the door and lock it behind me as I say, "The opportunity was too good to pass up."

"Another metahuman!" Chinwei says. "A pleasure to meet you." She helps Pete to his feet; then holds out her hand. I study the sweaty appendage momentarily, and then take it with a suppressed sigh.

We shake hands. "It's a pleasure to meet you two as well," I say, trying my best to mean it. Now that I'm looking at her face to face, I remember that this isn't my first-time meeting Chinwei. She was the one who spread our archer's limbs throughout the colony, drawing the Feral inside.

I suppress a shudder. This friendly little lady is a cold-blooded murderer. So why haven't I attacked her? Because the same can be said for my Nina.

I hold out my hand to Pete, who gives me a firm but gentle shake. "My name is Minerva. If I might ask, Chinwei, what is your power?"

"I make people spontaneously combust through vibration."

"... I see."

She laughs, though I don't detect any venom in it. I guess she's used to other people being surprised at her powers, even other metahumans. "So, how did you two meet?"

"Oh, we met when she was invading my home, so I tried to cut her head off."

"Vait, you're from zis colony?" Pete asks.

"That is correct. To sum up a long, convoluted story, after we fought, we decided to team up on an important mission from Queen Amity. And now we're back." A familiar bubble of terror expands in my chest, though it's larger than ever before. "I *do* hope you haven't slaughtered her alongside all of my companions."

Chinwei's eyes narrow. "I'd say we kept casualties to a minimum, considering the circumstances. As for your so-called Queen, she abandoned her people and escaped like the coward she is. I can't say for sure whether or not she died, but I sure as hell hope she has."

Ever since the attack my chest has felt like it's got a two-thousand-pound weight strapped to it. Chinwei's words are the spotter that lifts the weight off my chest, even as they throw my heart on a treadmill.

"I'm well aware that Queen Amity has wronged you, all of you, and the rest of the Ignored. But that does not mean she deserves to die."

"Says *you*," Chinwei says, with Pete nodding in agreement. "You don't what we've been through. You don't know what she's done to us. She doesn't just deserve death, she deserves Hell!"

These primitive single-minded naïve idiots! I grit my teeth and step forward, but Nina puts her hand on my chest and pushes me back. "Nina," I growl.

She grins but has the decency to at least blush. "Sorry," she says. "Anyway, y'all gotta stop this nonsense. Whether th' Queen's dead or not don' mean nuthin' right now." She puts her hand on my shoulder. "We're here tah check on yer friends, right? 'Sides, there's anotha Queen we can deliver this information to." She takes her arm off my shoulder and steps between the Ignored and me.

"Now y'all are all good people. Ain't no need tah start fightin' one anotha ova a difference in opinion. Th' Chosen an' Th' Ignored have both hurt each otha, but th' past is in th' past. Whas' done is done. So stop lookin' back an' start lookin' forward. Everyone cool?"

I look at Pete and Chinwei, whose eyes are softening under my gaze. On our journey back here, Nina told me all the awful things the Chosen had done to her and people she knew. Perhaps these two inspired some of her tales of horror?

I take a deep breath, and then smile at them. "I apologize for losing my temper. Forgive me?"

"Ah, no, zere is no need for apologizes. I'm sure all of us have good reasons to be upset, but zat does not mean ve need to be cross vith one another. Zank you for ze reminder, Nina."

She waves off his thanks while Chinwei says to me, "I thought you were scary when you popped into existence right in front of my love. But you have a beautiful smile. It must have knocked Nina right off her feet."

I blush while Nina nods in affirmation. "What Ah tell ya, sugah? Smile so good make a woman change teams." I roll my eyes until she wraps her arm around my shoulder and kisses my cheek, which makes me so happy I could just cry.

"After I got these scars, I never thought I would feel pretty again. Thank you, Nina."

"Yer gonna thank me fer tellin' ya th' truth? Thas' jus' what Ah do, sugah."

The urge to rip her clothes off and eat her for breakfast is strong, but this is neither the time nor the place. Besides, I've never been one to approve of overly affectionate gestures done in the presence of others.

Pete and Chinwei smile at us, shaking their heads. "Going from vorst enemies to lovers in a little more than a veek's time—you can't make zis stuff up."

"C'mon, Pete," Chinwei says, wrapping her arm around his, "let's show our new friend how a real Queen acts. I'm sure you'll love her."

I stop smiling. "I saw a little girl get eaten alive by Feral your Queen sent down to a colony of civilians."

"Uh, that wuz mah idea, sugah," Nina says, studying the floor like it's a fascinating specimen.

"I am aware; however, you first proposed this idea to Queen Adelia, correct?"

"Uh, yeah?"

"And she provided the resources and manpower that made your plan possible, correct?"

"Uh... yeah."

"My point still stands, dear."

"Sharp as a bayonet, zis one. You should know, Minerva, that ze first zing ze Queen did, after ze Feral died and ve restrained ze knights, vas to get down on her knees and apologize to every single citizen in ze colony. Personally. None of us knew zis was a civilian colony. Queen Amity told her sister zat she planned to be surrounded by ze strongest knights in ze country, so ve assumed a heavier attack vas necessary. It vas a mistake—a grave one, but a mistake neverzeless. As for ze little girl, did she happen to have red hair?"

I can almost hear her bones being disintegrated again. "…Yes," I manage.

"Chances are, her name was Scarlet Hopper."

"… Hopper?" I turn to Nina. "She must have been Cornelius's granddaughter."

"W—what?" Nina legs start quivering. She presses her back up against the wall and slowly crouches down. "Aw, *fuck*. Ah killed his granddaughter."

"Wait, you two are familiar with Cornelius?" Chinwei asks.

"Correct, we met him on our way to Edinburgh," I say, looking sadly at Nina. She's curled up into a fetal position. I sit next to her and try to hold her hand, but she jerks it away.

I feel like I just swallowed a grenade.

"Sorry, Ah…" She reaches for my hand, stops, and then crosses her arms. "Sorry."

I stand up and walk away from her, closing my eyes tight. "Not a problem, dear."

Pete and Chinwei share awkward glances, then Chinwei asks, "Did he tell you he had family here?"

"Yes. We visited him again on our way back from Edinburgh to see if he wanted to come back here, but he'd already lost his life in a firefight. To think that he would die a day after we met..."

"Zat is quite awful."

"Indeed. What did you want to mention about his granddaughter?"

"When ze Queen vas apologizing to ze Hoppers, zey apologized too. Cornelius had told zem zat zeir happiness vas built on ze corpses of others, but zey never left ze colony. Zey interpreted ze loss of zeir child as a bit of divine retribution."

"I violently disagree with that sentiment," I spit.

Pete raises his hands defensively. "I'm not saying I agree eizer. But zat's how zey see zings."

"... I'm not sure I understand why you are telling me this. Is it supposed to make me feel better that the Hoppers forgave the Queen? An innocent child still died."

"She wouldn't be dead if they had left the colony," Chinwei says.

"You don't know that! The Surface is dangerous. Cornelius left the colony, and while I applaud his moral fiber, he died too. The colony would have been perfectly safe if Queen Adelia hadn't attacked this place."

"Have you forgotten zat your people have been slaughtering foreigners zis vhole time? Ve only attacked as retribution for ze people your faction killed, one of zem being your girlfriend's brozer!"

All of the fight sucks out of me, like oxygen in the vacuum of space. "You are right. We threw the first blow."

"An' our counterpunch killed innocent people, children," Nina says. "Ah only helped in th' attack tah stop mo' families from bein' killed, an' all Ah did wuz cause mo' pain."

"Don't you remember what Cornelius said? There was nothing you could do *but* attack," I say. "It's not like you knew you were attacking civilians. You corner a dog and it's bound to bite back."

"Are ya callin' me a bitch?"

"Oh, stop it, darling!" I walk over and try to help her up. When she sees me approaching, she immediately stands up. Another stab to the heart makes me flinch, but I try not to take it personal. Nina would never do anything to hurt me intentionally. You don't risk your life to save someone just to treat them badly a few days later. It would be a farce to say I was dying to know why she wouldn't touch me, however.

Before I can overthink things to the point of panic, Chinwei pats me on the shoulder. "We've spent more than enough time arguing. I'm sure you want to make sure your friends are OK."

"Correct."

Pete removes the scrap hiding the vault's metallic wheel, and then twists it open. He and Chinwei hold hands as they walk down the stairwell. I turn to Nina. Her hands are in her pockets and her expression is as soulless as an unpainted canvas. I feel sick with the knowledge that Sarah, William, and the others might be gone forever, but this time I don't even have Nina's comforting touch to put me at ease. For the first time since I met Nina, I feel alone.

Walking down the stairs makes me feel like I'm descending into my own personal hell. It is only when

I open the doors to the colony that I start to feel somewhat at ease. Teenagers are stripping the walls of its bloody spring paper, replacing it with a fresh winter theme. Near the entrance is a massive ornate shrine made of wood. On it rests dozens of framed pictures. Paper mache flowers and sealed envelopes rest on the floor of the shrine alongside several kneeling children.

Nina and I run over to it, and then stare hard at the plaque that reads, "In loving memory of..." which goes on to list at least fifty names. As I scan down the list, my heart sinks lower and lower. It appears that Scarlet Hopper wasn't the only child causality. Nevertheless, by the time I've read and re-read the list, I've calmed considerably. In fact, I'm smiling, which makes me feel awful because I'm essentially standing in front of a gravesite. The dark thought does not strip the smile from my face, however, because none of my friends have died.

Sarah, William, Tyrone, Angel, the other knights... they are alive. I sink to my knees in relief, tears coming to my eyes.

"Ya alright, sug'?" Nina asks softly.

"I am quite well at the moment, dear, though I admit I would be better if your arm was around me."

She won't look me in the eye, so I let it drop. I watch her as she drops to both knees next to the children, promptly going into a praying position. I suppose we will have to discuss this in private... whatever "this" is. "Well, I am thrilled to see that my friends are alive," I say. "Are we free to roam the premises, or is the colony under totalitarian control?"

Pete scoffs. "Of course not. Ze only mandatory rules ze Queen auzorized vas physical and mental zerapy at regular intervals. Ve haven't been here very long, and many civilians are claiming zat zeir day to day life is much more interesting that it vas before," he says with an upturned nose.

"How do you know they didn't say that out of fear," I challenge.

"Because—"

"If y'all don' stop th' damn arguin' an' let me pay mah respects in peace, Ah swear tah God..." She stops yelling once she realizes that she's freighted the children, who shake in their boots. Nevertheless, the message has been received loud and clear.

"My apologies."

"We're sorry," Pete and Chinwei drawl.

Nina grunts and grumbles, then goes back into praying position. Pete, Chinwei and I smile at one another, though I can't say exactly why.

"Well, Pete and I've got to be on our way. We promised to help cook dinner." The couple approaches the kneeling Nina. Chinwei pats her shoulder while Pete pats the other, murmuring something that sounds vaguely French into her ear. They start walking towards the kitchen, then stop suddenly. "Oh, and Minerva?"

"Yes?"

"I know we spent most of our time together at each other's throats, but it really was a pleasure to meet you, and I'm not saying that just to be nice. I don't know Nina as well as I'd wish, but you seem like the perfect partner for her." Pete nods along with his girlfriend's words, smiling politely.

I resist the urge to try and grab Nina's hand, not wanting to feel the cold burn of rejection again. "It was nice to meet you two as well. You are very cute together, and Pete has the most charming accent," I say with the most genuine smile I am capable of giving.

They return my smile then head out on their own path. I turn to Nina, who's done praying and looking as miserable as ever. Her arms are crossed tight and her bottom lip sticks out a fraction.

"I want to introduce you to my friends and speak with Queen Adelia ASAP to determine our next course of action, but you do not seem to be in a very sociable mood. Would you like to relax in my room for awhile?"

Nina doesn't say anything, but she does nod slowly. Her eyes dart towards the shrine momentarily, then her bottom lip quivers, making my heart race with agency. "Let me hold your hand, dear. *Please.*"

She looks at me with eyes as tired as old moss, then she holds out her hand. I grab it, and after making sure no one's looking, turn us invisible. I lead her to my old room. We see plenty of familiar faces along the way and I'd love to at least say hello but getting Nina to a private place is my top priority.

I find myself a bit nostalgic as I stand in front of the door to my room. A quick scan reveals that no one is watching, so I turn us visible then knock on the door. When there is no response, I decide to open it, assuming the room is vacant. A woman with short, wavy hair the color of snow and eyes like granny smith apples is lying on my bed, flipping through one of my romance novels with evident boredom. She doesn't look up when Nina and I walk in, her eyes glued to the book.

"Sorry Queen Adelia, the answer's still no. I'm not helping you train a bunch of civilians. They've got no guts, and—"

"A-Angel?" I say, taking a tentative step forward.

The hefty book falls on her face with a *slap*. Angel bolts upright and stares at me with puffy eyes. "Minerva!" She jumps to her feet. "You're alive!"

She practically bowls me over with a hug, but Nina's supportive hand presses against my back to keep me upright. I hug her back with a smile. "I never thought I would say this, but I am glad the Feral did not eat you alive. I was very, very worried about you."

She holds the hug a bit longer than I deem necessary, complete with back rubbing, wobbling, and a heavy sigh. When she lets me go, she plops her hand on my bald head with a *slap*!

"Ha! There's no way I was going to die, chrome dome!" I remove her hand, thoroughly unamused as Angel plops back on my bed and continues, "Not until you came back to me. Not until I apologized for every disgusting thing I said to you over the past year. Not until..." She takes a deep breath, clenching her fists. Then she looks up at me with a daring smile. "Not until I finally told you how I feel."

The world goes sideways. All those mean nicknames, her aggressive antagonism, the relentless glaring... they all make some type of sense now, in a grade school crush kind of way. "Oh, dear."

Nina flashes past me quicker than a thunderclap. "Howdy," she exclaims with newborn vigor. She holds out her hand to be shaken. Angel takes it with a raised eyebrow then a wince as Nina's firm grip shakes her around like a test dummy in a car crash. "Ah'm Nina, Minerva's *girlfriend.* Nice tah meetcha!"

Nina stumbles a bit as Angel slithers her hand away, probably using her intangibility powers to escape Nina's clutches. "A pleasure," she says through gritted teeth.

"Hey, maybe if ya hadn't spent th' past year treatin' mah gal like shit you'd be wit' her insteadah me. Ah mean, nuthin' says, 'Ah like ya', like teasin' 'em ova a traumatic experience, right?"

"Nina, dear—"

"Honestly, when she told me what ya said tah her Ah swore tah mahself Ah'd beat ya half tah death."

Angel slowly rises. "Care to try your luck?"

Nina chuckles darkly as I step in between them, heart ramming. I never imagined two women would fight over me after I got these scars. As exhilarating as this is, I have no desire to see Angel get her wings ripped off. "Ladies! Let us be civilized."

"Relax sugah, Ah ain't gonna do nuthin'. Look, it seems like you've got sum apologetic words tah say, an' Ah respect that, so Ah'm gonna let ya speak tah her in private. But don' try no funny business now, alright? Ah'm basically trustin' ya wit' mah life."

A harpoon of happy impales my heart and zips me towards Nina. I wrap my arms around her waist and pull her in, nuzzling the back of her neck with a content sigh. My chest feels so light she might as well have injected me with helium. "I would have liked to hear these words half an hour ago, but, nevertheless, they are *greatly* appreciated, dear."

Nina chuckles awkwardly, mumbling, "Ah'm a might sorry 'bout that. Ah'll explain latah, not that anythin' really excuses what Ah did."

"Correct," I agree, but still tickle her rib cage.

She giggles then pushes my hand away. "Hey now, not in frontah company." I look up to see a solemn Angel, complete with clenched teeth and averted eyes. My face meets my palm. She has been right in front of me this whole time. I had forgotten she was here and had basically just confessed her feelings for me. And here I was being all lovey dovey. How scandalous!

"Lissen, Ah'mma let y'all talk in peace. Minerva, can Ah hop in yer shower? Ah feel filthier thana pig rollin' 'round in its own—"

"Yes! Yes you may."

Nina shakes her head, squeezes my hand then walks into the bathroom. I am enchanted by her figure until she slips from my world. Then I turn to Angel. "My apologies, dear, I didn't—"

Angel lunges. I back step and hurl a fist. Angel's jaw blasts sideways, sending her sprawling onto my bed like a human pretzel.

"What in the bloody hell do you think you're doing," I hiss, not wanting to alert Nina next door and get Angel killed. "Did you not hear a word my girlfriend just said to you?"

Angel slowly untangles herself and sits up, caressing her now red cheek then curling into a delicate little ball. "I did. And I don't give a damn." I scowl, but before I can tell her off she looks me in the eye and declares, "Minerva, I'm in love with you."

I stare at her for one long moment. Then, time stops. The Earth makes a full loop around the sun. New stars are born as dead ones become white dwarfs. An entire species evolves from a single cell organism into a complex masterpiece of biology capable of producing mind-bending technology. All the while, a storm of an unimaginable scale brews inside me.

"... You *dare?*"

Angel does not move. Everything goes black.

My internal boom box cranks to full volume. "*You dare?*"

She flinches as a vomit of emotion cascades from my mouth with the force of a busted fire hydrant. "You've known me for a year and spent every waking moment ridiculing me, treating me like a freak, an enemy, and you want to say you're in *love* with me? Nina has known me a little more than a week, and in that time frame has saved my life thrice!"

"*I—*"

"*More importantly*, she has treated me with respect, been there for me, made me feel pretty again, a feat that should have been impossible thanks to people like you! She has taught me more about love then I've known my whole life. If you compare your feelings for me to her again I won't just punch you, *I'll end you.*"

Angel's bunched up ball gets even tighter, then starts quivering. Anger finally spent; I sigh. "Ah, my apologies. The ludicrousy of your statement just flipped the 'righteous fury' switch in my brain."

Angel makes a ragged chuckle between sobs, and then looks up to smile at me with red rimmed eyes. I manage to return her smile even though her eyes remind me of certain elderly man sprawled out on the floor with a puddle of dried blood spread out underneath him. "What's funny?"

"That was the most half-assed apology I've ever heard."

"Well I am not really sorry for anything I just said, I just felt obligated to apologize because seeing you cry made me feel bad."

She laughs again, sobs subsiding. "You know why I like you? No matter how much I tried to tear you down, to break you, you kept bouncing back stronger than ever. It's like nothing I ever said or did even fazed you. When I think of a true knight, you are the person to come to mind."

I sigh again. While her words were flattering... "That was just a mask, Angel. Every insult you threw obliterated my self-esteem bit by bit. Every time you called me Scarface, the more I couldn't stand to look at my reflection. The entire basis of your infatuation with me is based on a lie. Why on Earth would you possibly degrade the object of your affections to such an extreme, anyway?"

"I didn't know why being near you made me so crazy. You'd make me flush, give me goosebumps, make my heart skip beats. I was already jealous because you were Queen Amity's favorite, so I thought I was just angry at you. When I realized how much I liked you, I was ashamed of being attracted to a woman. I guess I thought that my feelings would go away if I tried to hate you."

"Nina is not gay, you know. She is bisexual."

"You mean she's confused?"

My eyes narrow. "No, I mean she is bisexual. You just found out you are attracted to women, how would you feel if someone belittled your genuine feelings for mere confusion?"

"… I guess you're right."

"I *am* right, thank you very much. As I was saying, Nina is bi, but that is a newly discovered fact. Apparently, I am the first woman she has been attracted to."

Angel gives me a bitter smile. "I bet that makes you feel like hot shit."

"It was quite the pleasant surprise, to be sure. But my point is that Nina didn't fight her feelings. She found out something new about herself and just rolled with it. I didn't even know she was bi until a few days ago."

Angel nods, and then swallows spit. "… If I had reacted like Nina did when I found out I liked you… do you think we could have been something?"

"That is an impossible question to answer, even on a purely hypothetical basis. The only Angel I have ever known has been a vicious, cold-blooded bitch." I cough into my fist. "No offense to your present self, of course."

Angel swallows again, voice tight. "That… that makes sense. Um, I guess this won't give you any solace, but I really am sorry for the way I acted. Really."

"I know you are, dear," I stand up. "Come here and give me a hug."

Angel springs to her feet, and I hold up my palm. "Be aware that if you do anything courageous, my fist will stand in for my blade."

"R-right."

Angel takes a timid step forward, and I close the gap between us with an embrace. When she pulls me in tight and begins to shiver, I feel awkward and resort to back pats. Over her shoulder, I see the bathroom door open to reveal a dripping wet Nina. An angry eyebrow shoots to the heavens, but a hasty thumbs up and a few flicks of the back of my hand is enough to get her to silently close the door and give us privacy.

"I never thanked you for making me leave when the colony was invaded. Thanks to you and the other knight's sacrifice, I was able to meet Nina and complete the mission Queen Amity bestowed to me. So... thank you."

Angel mumbles, "No problem," and brings me in closer. I rub her back for another moment then gently pry her off.

"Do you know where Tyrone is? I would like to thank him as well."

Angel sits back on my bed, looking a bit glum. "Oh, he's not here. He left the colony with some of the Ignored. Sarah, William, and other physically disabled people are with them."

"What? Why?"

"This isn't just a civilian colony anymore. Queen Adelia is making this place a training base."

"But why?"

Angel shrugs. "She says all of our civilians are under-equipped to handle any type of threat, and that is why their assault worked so well. And she's right. We wouldn't have lost so many civilians if they could actually defend themselves." I purse my lips. "She sent away the people who couldn't fight to someplace more secure. Tyrone went with other members of the Ignored as extra security."

"Always the gentleman," I say. "Do you know where this colony is?"

"No. You would have to ask Queen Adelia."

Nina strolls back into the room, dry now. "Ah can't wait fer ya tah meet her, Minerva. She's great!"

"Hm. What do *you* think about her, Angel?"

"Honestly? She's brilliant. Tough as tits, too. When she was apologizing to everyone, I challenged her to a spar. I told her she didn't deserve to lead us knights. How could she just stroll into our home, kill our friends, chase our Queen away and expect us to roll over and kiss her feet just because she apologized?"

I nod along with her words, smiling.

"So we started sparring. At first, she let me wail on her, but when I told her to fight serious... I don't even remember what happened after that. She came at me so fast I didn't even have time to turn intangible. For a Normal to obliterate a metahuman like that... she earned my respect immediately. And the fact that she let me give her a black eye just so I would feel better doesn't hurt either."

Nina wraps her arms around my shoulders. "Y'all metahumans are tough, but y'all rely too much on yer powers. Spend too long out on th' Surface an' you'll be so strong that sumthin' like supahpowers won' even make ya flinch."

"Nina, dear, you were positively *terrifying* our first encounter. I thought you were going to kill me."

"So did Ah. Butcha neva gave up. Ah'm glad Ah didn' kill ya."

"As am I."

We smile at one another until Angel coughs softly. "I'd better excuse myself. I'm sure you two would like some privacy."

She goes up and motions to the door, but stops herself and turns around. "Nina, you should know that I tried to kiss Minerva when you left the room."

An alarm bell rings in my brain while Nina just nods. "Not surprised. Bein' attracted tah Minerva usually equates tah losin' yer sense o' self-preservation. Now, do Ah haftah slug ya or did Minerva already give ya one fer?"

"She delivered the message loud and clear," Angel says, pointing to her reddened cheek.

Nina winks at me. "Great," she says, then lumbers to her feet and clasps a hand on Angel's shoulder. "Lissen, Ah 'ppreciate yer honesty, but Ah don' need tah tell ya what Ah'mma do tah ya if ya try sumthin' like that 'gain, right?"

"No, I get it. And I apologize. But I don't need to tell you what I'll do to you if you hurt her, right?"

Nina howls with laughter, smacking her hand on Angel's shoulder. "Ah like you. Apology accepted, an' point taken. Friends?" She holds out her hand to be shaken once more. Angel, with one hand rubbing her shoulder and a tight grin, takes Nina's hand. The two women shake hands, making me smile. Angel gives me a nod over Nina's shoulder, and then excuses herself.

Nina turns around, smiling a smile that does not begin to reach her eyes. "Minerva, Ah'm sorry. Ah didn' mean tah push ya away earlier."

"Then *why did you?*"

Nina flinches, stammering out, "When Ah found out 'bout Cornelius's granddaughter dyin' cuz o' me—"

"It. Was. Not. Your. Fault."

"Stop it, Minerva!"

This time, I flinch.

When we make eye contact again, Nina grabs the side of my arms and says, "Ah killed those people. Me. No one else. Mah idea. Mah plan. Mah sin. This isn't like what happened wit' you an' that pregnant lady." My stomach flips at the memory. "That wuz self-defense, see, an automatic self-defense mechanism. But me? Ah planned this. Ah chopped off people's limbs while they were still alive. Ah watched 'em bleed out, then used their body pieces tah lead innocent aliens tah their deaths. Ah know yer jus' tryin' tah help, sugah, butcha can't let me run away from mah problem."

"I... OK," I finish weakly. *It is not her fault. It is not!*

Nina sighs deeply, and then says, "Sorry fer snappin' atcha like that. But, uh, when Ah found out Cornelius's granddaughter died cuz o' me, Ah jus' felt filthy. Felt like mah whole body wuz drenched in th' blood o' all th' people Ah killed. Didn' want ya tah touch a dirty gal who'd—who'd already been touched."

Speechless.

I flash forward, then say, "Close your eyes."

"Don' touch me," Nina chokes out. "Don'—"

"Close your eyes, dear."

She complies, trembling like a newborn. I caress her face as gently as possible, smiling sadly. In a way, Nina reminds me of a beautiful glass statue. Looking at her is enough to make my heart stop, but I can't be *too coarse with her, lest she shatters. I bring my lips closer to her as slowly as possible, as if my body were submerged in molasses. I think about how her laugh sounds like Beethoven. I think about how her smile shields me from my worst demons. I think about how she risked her life for someone she just met, someone who embedded glass into her temple, someone who punched her out, someone who shackled an electric bracelet to her wrist, all because we were friends. Then I kiss her. It is nothing dramatic. No tongue, no heavy petting, just the most affectionate peck I can deliver.*

IMAGINE BUNGIE JUMPIN' froma thousand feet intah a mountain o' th' purest cocaine in th' world, snortin' as much as ya could inna single breath. Th' rush ya got from that experience wouldn' be half as good as th' rush Ah got from Minerva's delicate kiss.

She pulls away jus' as Ah wuz hopin' she'd come in closer. Ah look up as she wraps her arms 'round mah neck. Her gaze pierces mah soul. Ah can't breathe, so Ah guess Ah'm dyin', but thas' OK cuz she's real, she's right here, an' nuthin' else mattahs.

"Ah'm sorry. Ah'm sorry."

"Shh..." She pulls me in an' coos as she rubs mah back gently.

Ah push her back a bit so Ah can look th' biggest ocean in th' world. "No. Ah wuz so busy feelin' sorry fer mahself that Ah rejected yer affection. That ain't right, an' it sure as hell ain't right fer it tah take anotha gal tah get me tah come tah mah senses. It's like, it's like Ah'm seein' ya as a toy—Ah won' play wit'cha by mahself, but if anotha kid wants tah play Ah get all territorial." Ah scoff. "What in th' blue blazes is wrong wit' me?"

Minerva laughs in that condescendin', "you silly girl" kinda way that should piss me off but instead makes me smile. "While I will not say I approve of your actions, I do not condemn them. After all you have been through, it is only natural you would not feel touchy-feely all the time. Relationships aren't about never disappointing your lover. Rather, they are about sticking with them *in spite* of their disappointments. Our bond is far too strong for a few petite squabbles to get in our way. Isn't that right, sweetie?"

Ah bring her in close an' muffle outta "yes". Ah hold her, fergettin' that awful night at th' hotel fer a lil' while. "Y'know, Ah'm glad we ran intah Angel."

"And why is that?"

"She wuz a great reminder that yer one helluva catch. If Ah keep takin' ya fer granted, sumone else'll snatch ya up."

She laughs that condescendin' laugh 'gain. "Perhaps this is entirely presumptuous, dear, but as far as I am concerned, you are mine, and I am yours."

My brother's last words echo in mah head: *"Ya gotta find anotha family. No mattah how long it takes."*

"Minerva?"

"Yes?"

"Don' let go o' me."

"I'm here, darling. Until I draw my last breath."

A ragged chuckle escapes mah tight throat. "Yer so dramatic."

Chapter 23

I fall asleep into a sobbing Nina's arms, awaken a few hours later, then stumble out of bed like an alcoholic late for work. I've begun my journey to the bathroom when Nina clutches my wrist. She's still asleep, mumbling to herself, "Lucio... don' go..."

My heart sinks like a car underwater. I want to smother her with hugs, but I do not wish to awaken her, so I plant a ghost of a kiss on her forehead instead. Her frown dissipates and is replaced by a small smile. The grip on my wrist loosens, and her now relaxed arm sinks back into the soft bed. I feel like a superhero for the first time, and my powers have nothing to do with it.

I walk into the bathroom, and then take my time in the shower, letting the warm water wash my problems away. I am terrified about Sarah, William, and Tyrone's safety, but that issue seems so far away in my heated chamber of isolation. The water feels magnificent on my scalp. I dare say I will miss this sensation once my hair grows back. I never thought my new hairstyle, or lack thereof, would have any positive impact, but I am nevertheless pleasantly surprised.

I leave the shower just before my skin gets ickly pruney. A thought strikes me with the force of a lightning bolt thrown by Zeus himself. With a schoolgirl's giggle, I leap to my cabinet. As expected, my make-up is right where I left it. Angel said that when she thought of a true knight, I was the first thing that came to mind. While I was flattered at the compliment, the truth was that my combat arsenal consisted of concealer, foundation, eyeliner and lipstick.

I prepare myself for battle with expert precision, using each weapon to the best of its abilities, but never using one for too long. Once, as a child, I raided my mother's purse and piled on as much make-up as possible. It was then that she taught me, while holding back laughter, how, when it came to make-up, less is more. That lesson of restraint was crucial during my time as a model.

I am finished with my ritual within ten or fifteen minutes. My my, the beautifying process is infinitely quicker without hair. I look at my reflection with a satisfied smile. *"Ya ain't ugly, yer th' mos' beautiful gal Ah done eva laid mah eyes on."* I will *never* forget those words, and I shall cherish them until the day I die.

Surely if I looked pretty then, I look even better now. Wearing white flats, white spandex pants, a white tank top with an exposed midriff, *ElecTrick Sex* blue lipstick with a dab of black lipstick in the middle, and a bit of black eyeliner, I feel both cute and dangerous! My scars are still there, obviously, but they aren't quite as prominent. *Hell, Ah'll even go as far as sayin' Ah like 'em. They let me know right off th' bat that Ah wuzn't dealin' wit' sum fussy gal who's all bark an' no bite.*

You know what, Nina? I like my scars too. The woman in the mirror looks strong and confident, and I couldn't be happier.

I hear Nina shuffling around next door. My heart starts pounding, harder than times I walked the catwalk or times I was photographed by professional photographers. Nina is a very practical woman. I do not know if she will appreciate the aesthetic value of make-up and fashion and such. Before I go back in the room to greet her, I take a moment to laugh about how ridiculous this is. With the other girls I dated, I was worried about them seeing me without make-up. With Nina, it is the opposite.

I take a deep breath, and then open the door. She has her back turned to me, rummaging through my bookshelf. "Hey, Minerva. Ah see yer book collection is pretty varied."

"Ah, sarcasm," I grin, leaning against the doorway with my arms crossed. "It sounds exquisite coming from you."

"Wow, I thought yer sarcasm detector wuz broken. Didn' think you'd catch that. Neva seen so many romance novels in one place before!" She turns around, her head in a book. "'A spike o' pain impales my soul,'" she reads with a chuckle. "Sounds like sumthin' you'd..." we make eye contact, and then the book hits the floor. "...say. Wow."

Uh-oh. "W-what do you think, dear?"

She slowly walks forward, holding her palm out as if she wants to touch me but isn't sure if I'm real. I am more than a little nervous when she reaches me. She wraps her arms around my waist then looks up at me with a smile wider than the diameter of Jupiter. "Ah gotta tell ya, Minerva, Ah knew this day would come eventually. 'Xcept, in mah head, you'd come outta th' restroom lookin' like a clown, an' Ah'd give ya this whole speech 'bout how Ah liked ya *au natural.* But Ah gotta say, you look

amazin'. Ah mean, you always do, but god damn!"
She squeezes me tight, wielding far more strength
than what should be possible for someone so skinny.
"Gimmie sum sugah, sugah!"

She pecks me on the lips, and when we break
apart, her lips are stained blue. "Huh. So thas' what
lipstick tastes like."

"Do you like it?"

"Let me get anotha taste." Another peck. "Hm. Ah
think Ah like th' natural taste betta."

I smile, taking out my pocket mirror and dabbing
more lipstick on where needed. "That compliment
was well played, dear." I close the mirror, and then
stuff it back into my irritatingly small pocket. "If
you'd like, I could give you a complete make-over. It
would not take more than five minutes, I promise!"

"Sorry sug', make-up ain't mah style."

"Please?"

"Naw, Ah'm good."

"But you'd look simply marvelous, even more so
than you do now."

"Heh. You kinda sound like mah Ma. She always
wanted tah doll me up. An' Ah'll tell ya what Ah
told her fer years: Ecnope." Her smile dips. "Wish
Ah'd let her do it at least once 'fore she passed,
though." She looks away and clears her throat once,
twice. "Sorry," she says in a raspy voice.

"No apologies needed," I say with a heavy heart.
"Do you wish to talk about her?"

"Naw, Ah don' feel like takin' a trip down memory
lane right now." She clears her throat again. "So!
Whas' th' plan fer th' rest o' th' day? Ya ready tah
meet Queen Adelia, or do ya want me tah meet yer

friends? Ah'm pretty interested in meetin' this William feller. Seems like ya mightah killed me aftah our fight if ya hadn't met him."

I purse my lips, thinking. "Perhaps. But, unfortunately, you won't be able to meet him anytime soon." I tell her about how Queen Adelia is transporting the physically disabled to another colony.

Nina raises an eyebrow. "But why?"

"Queen Adelia is going to turn my home into a training facility. We shall be having words with her, of course."

"What're ya plannin', sug'?"

"I would have dressed formally if we were to talk over tea. Are you ready to go?"

She grimaces as if she has smelled something foul. "Ah 'spose Ah can't talk ya outta this?"

"No. This is between me and her."

She sighs. "Then Ah guess Ah'm ready tah go."

"Excellent. Oh!" I grab The Blade of Justice and strap it to my waist, just in case. "Almost forgot this gem."

"Where'd ya get that thing, anyway? It's as sharp as it is fancy."

"A gift from Queen Amity," I coo.

She crosses her arm with a huff. "Figures."

X X X

Nina and I hide in the shadows of the bleachers while Queen Adelia concludes a lesson the two of us hadn't heard the beginning of. Surrounded by hundreds of curious faces, Queen Adelia stands calm in the center of the gym room, her royal aura oozing confidence. She wears a dark green long sleeved crewneck top and black spandex pants. Her black hair is done in a messy ballet bun.

"Let me reiterate: Combat with Feral should be avoided at all costs. Their powerful sense of smell can be exploited but make no mistake—the Feral are intelligent creatures capable of trickery and deception. However, should you find yourself in an unavoidable fight with them, keep these tips in mind."

A member of the Ignored turns on a tennis ball machine maybe six, seven feet away.

"The Feral's primary means of attack is its tongue. You have three options to avoid this. The first is a sidestep or a roll." The Ignored fires two consecutive balls. The Queen sidesteps one and rolls out of the way of the other. "It is the safest option, but it also possesses its own risk. The Feral's next move might be another tongue strike, and you may not be fast enough to avoid it a second time. The second option you have is removing the tongue."

Another ball spits out. A knife flashes into her hands. A blur of movement later, the ball, now cut in two, falls at her feet. Everyone starts clapping, including Nina, making me roll my eyes.

"Settle down, now," she says with a small smile. "This is another good tactic, though the downside is that you will have to fight it up close afterwards. There is one more tactic you could use—it is simultaneously the most dangerous and most effective tactic, so if you use it you have to be very, very careful."

Another ball flies. Without taking her eyes off the crowd, Queen Adelia catches it. She can't possibly mean... "If you grab the tongue, the Feral will retract it, bringing you face to face with it instantaneously. And once you're close—" She leaps forward and stabs her dagger into the space next to the machine. "You finish it in single blow."

Someone says, "Um... that sounds dangerous and neigh suicidal. No offense, Your Majesty."

"Well, that's because it is. A friend of mine attempted to show me this trick in the midst of battle, and he didn't get a chance to show me again."

"But you've tried this. And it works?"

"Absolutely. Only the tip of the Feral's tongue is sharp, the rest of it is soft and therefore safe to grab. I wouldn't be showing you this if it weren't an effective tactic. But it *is* dangerous."

I scoff and turn to Nina. "This woman is crazy. Grabbing a Feral's tongue? Insanity."

She gives me a wicked grin. "It is. An' guess what? Ah did it."

"You grabbed a Feral tongue? Why? I cannot picture something more disgusting." A vision of a room full of decaying corpses disagrees with that statement, but I keep it to myself.

She kisses my cheek. "Tah save ya, doofus."

I pull her in close, nuzzling her. "Do tell."

"I wuz fightin' eight at once, remember? Ah hadtah be quick on mah feet. Face it: Queen Adelia's got experience an' skill. Ya sure ya wanna tangle wit' her?"

Private tea parties after lunch. Monday movie nights. Late night talks, early morning training.

Queen Amity is one of the closest friends I have ever known. And now she is gone. "I have to, Nina. I have to."

Queen Adelia instructs members of the Ignored to supervise civilians as they practice, then takes her leave. Nina and I follow her out, still invisible. As the three of us make our way to the exit, several acquaintances hurl compliments at Queen Adelia. "Very informative lesson, Your Highness."

"It was really neat how you cut that ball in half, Queen Adelia!"

"You're gorgeous. What are you doing tonight?"

She laughs at that last one, making a swift exit before someone else can ask her out. I scowl at the traitors. This woman killed people. Barely a week has passed, and suddenly she is magically forgiven for her sins? It is not right, and I will *not* stand for it.

We continue following her for a few moments, but when Queen Adelia turns into the next hallway, Nina says, "What're ya waitin' fer? Ya gonna challenge her tah a spar or what?"

"Not yet, dear. I cannot break her nose if she is a good person."

"So... whaddya propose we do? Follow her 'round 'till she does sumthin' vaguely villainous?"

"Why of course dear."

She lets go of my hand. Someone walking by blinks hard, stares at Nina, rubs their eyes, and then walks away. "You can't be serious!"

I turn visible, shocked at Nina's disgusted expression. "But I am. What is the issue? She won't even know we are there."

"Maybe cuz it *ain't th' right thing tah do?* If ya wanna know 'bout her, why don'cha jus' talk tah her?"

"How will I know she's being truthful? I want to see what kind of person she is in the dark."

Nina flinches and shakes her head. "You an' Ah got tah know each otha by talkin'. Ya didn' need tah spy on me tah find out what kinda person Ah am. What yer sayin' don' make no sense. 'Sides, what yer 'bout tah do shows what kinda person *you* are in th' dark, Minerva." I frown at that, then she says, "Ah'm disappointed in you, sugah. Usin' yer powers tah stalk people is jus' 'bout th' least lady like thing you can do."

My stomach churns with shame. "B—but good has come from my, um, stealth missions. For example, Sarah—"

"Th' ends don' justify th' means," she snorts. "Least it don' fer me. Y'know damn well what yer doin' ain't right, Ah can see it on yer face."

I look away. "So... you won't accompany me?"

She snorts again. "'Fraid not. But yer a grown woman an' Ah ain't gonna tell ya howtah act. Jus' know Ah don' approve on *any* level." She sighs then pecks at my cheek. It is the most lackluster kiss I have ever received in my life, a stark contrast to the usual grandiose kisses she bestows me. "Look, Ah'll be in yer room when ya get back. Hopefully then you'll have come tah yer senses. Maybe then we can talk tah her like, y'know, *every otha person on th' planet.*"

I vanish from the world as she turns away from me. But even though I cannot be seen, I have never felt more exposed. Nevertheless, the need to prove that Queen Adelia is not as great as everyone says far outweighs my indignity.

I dart into the hallway I last saw the Queen. A wisp of black hair disappears into the kitchen. Calm that I hadn't lost her, I tip toe into the kitchen to find Her Majesty conversating with Pete and Chinwei. A shiny silver plate cover rests on the table next to them.

"Wow, that smells simply wonderful, you two," she says. "Great job!"

"Heh. Don't thank me, thank Pete. The man knows how to bake a cake!"

Pete nods. "I learned a zing or two as a chef in France. Iz no big deal!"

Queen Adelia chuckles, then picks up the plate. My stomach grumbles a bit. I wonder what's under that cover? "I appreciate your modesty, as well as your hard work. Both of you."

The flabbergasted couple starts tripping over themselves. "Oh, it's nothing, Your Highness," Chinwei says.

"Always a pleasure to serve you, my Queen," Pete says.

"Please, just call me Adelia. You are my friends, my equals. I don't need to be put on a pedestal all the time."

"After all you've done for us, Queen Adelia, it's hard to take the comment about us being equals seriously. That said, I am honored to be considered your friend," Chinwei says, with Pete nodding along.

Queen Adelia sighs. "After all we've been through together; you two are more than just friends to me. But if you *insist* on putting me on an unneeded pedestal, I suppose there is nothing I can say to convince you otherwise. Thanks again for your hard work."

"Mamn!" The two snap into a salute. Queen Adelia sighs again, then walks towards the civilian's chambers. She knocks on the door to chamber 476. After a beat, the cute youngster Timothy opens the door.

"What the bloody hell do you want," asks the pre-adolescent, his voice cracking.

"I, um, brought you something." She takes off the cover of the plate, revealing the most delicious cake I have ever had the pleasure of seeing. "I was hoping we could talk over tea and dessert." It is glazed to perfection with white frosting. Little drizzles of chocolate surround a dozen strawberries that lie on the circumference of the cake. It's a simple and elegant design. If Nina and I ever get married, I simply *must* have Pete bake our wedding cake!

The smell is so intoxicating I just about snatch it from the Queen's open hands, but before I can Timothy smacks it to the ground. Her expression of shock no doubt mirrors my own.

"You killed my mum! I will *never* forgive you. Some fancy cake won't change that." And with that, he slams the door shut. Queen Adelia stares at the door for one long moment. Then, with a heavy sigh, she walks away. She enters the supply closet, then emerges with a broom, dustpan, a mop, a bucket full of water and a *caution: wet floor!* sign tucked under her arm.

She goes back to the destroyed masterpiece and the broken pieces of plate scattered across the floor in front of Timothy's room. Then, she begins to clean.

I watch her perform the mundane task with awe. She did not have to do this. She could have easily gotten one of her followers to do it for her, so why?

An Ignored walking by asks Queen Adelia to let her finish it up. Queen Adelia says, "Sorry Betty, but this is my mess, thus, my responsibility to clean it up."

Once the floor is spotless, Queen Adelia returns the supplies to the closet. She then visits the restroom, but I at least have the decency not to follow her *in there.* I perch against the wall outside of it, deep in thought.

Nina is right. I am completely, totally out of line for this. And yet, the more I see of Queen Adelia's good nature, the hotter the angry flames within me burn. If she really is remorseful for her actions, what am I to do? Punching someone who is already wracked with guilt is not justice, it is senseless violence. If Queen Adelia is a good person then I no longer have a visible target for my rage.

The Feral are just as much of a victim as we are in the war. As for whatever alien race that's pulling the strings, I do not even know what they look like, nor where to find them. Being upset and having no one to blame is simply dreadful, and I refuse to—

Queen Adelia makes a brisk exit from the restroom. Her eyes are red and puffy. She hastily pulls up her sleeve, but before she does, I get a peek at a tan arm mapped with dozens of deep cuts. Even with that split-second visual, I can tell that the wounds aren't Feral inflected.

Yes, I believe that settles it. I am a disgusting person.

X X X

AH'M FLIPPIN' THROUGH one o' Cornelius's books when Minerva returns from creepyville. "So," Ah start, not lookin' away from th' book, "didcha see her twirlin' her mustache like th' connivin' villain she is?"

"No, I merely saw something I should not have seen," she says. Her voice is so glum that Ah look up. Ah've seen cancer patients wit' mo' joy on their face than her. "I am an absolute bugger for my juvenile behavior."

Ah dunno what that means, but Ah don' have tah. "Eeyup."

"Will you ever forgive me?"

Ah snort. "Naw, Ahmma hold one mistake ova yer head 'till death. 'Course Ah fergive ya, sug'. Ah hope you know Ah'm not tryin' tah take th' moral high ground or sumthin'. If Ah could turn invisible, maybe Ah'd do th' same thing. Ah mean, who wouldn' want tah know what otha people *really* thought o' ya when you aren't around?"

Minerva purses her full, electric blue lips. "Maybe that is why people call some metahumans superheroes. It is not our powers that make us super. Rather, it is the restraint not to abuse our powers that make us so."

"Wooooow," Ah drone, "Thas' *deep*." It is, but Ah ain't gonna give her an easy time aftah what she jus' pulled.

Minerva nods solemnly. Whelp, looks like her sarcasm detector is broken again. "One day, I would love to meet The Cube and Samurai Kid. They were the first metahumans, after all. I am sure those two could teach me a thing or two about being a hero."

"Thas' a long shot, Minerva. How do we know they ain't dead? 'Sides, they're a continent away. How many pilots do ya think are alive right now—betta yet, how are we even gonna get our hands onnah plane?"

"... Fair point. Still, a girl can dream. You said you and your brother met Samurai Kid, correct?" Ah nod. "What was he like?"

Ah chew mah bottom lip, tryin' tah clear up th' dense fog surroundin' th' memory. "Uh, he struck me as a supah humble guy. Lucio wuz bouncin' 'round, so exited tah meet such a big celebrity. He kept ramblin' 'bout all th' good things Samurai Kid did—how he'd jailed human traffickers, stopped robberies, y'know, supahhero stuff. But he wuz really excited 'bout th' time Samurai Kid went intah a burnin' day care center tah save sum kids trapped inside."

"He sounds pretty amazing."

"Definitely," Ah say. "Th' crazy thing is that all he'd eva do in response tah th' praise is wave it off."

"Hm... remind you of anyone?" Minerva coos.

Ah see where she's tryin' tah go wit' this, but Ah don' take th' bait. "No. Anyway, y'know how ya can compliment sumone an' they say, 'It's nuthin' butcha can tell they're proud o' themselves? Wit' Samurai Kid, ya really got th' sense that he really meant that all he'd done wuz no big deal. Lucio asked him how he could be so nonchalant 'bout his deeds, an' he got all serious, crouchin' down tah look mah brother in th' eye. He told him that all he did wuz th' right thing. He said that if Lucio wuz in his shoes, he'd trust that he'd do th' right thing too, so all that he'd accomplished wuz nuthin' special."

"My my, quite the modest fellow. He really reminds me of someone in this very room!"

"Lucio really liked that answer, an' once he got his autograph he scampered off in excitement. Ah shook th' man's hand an' thanked him fer his kindness, but he told me that he meant every word an' that no thanks were necessary. Even though he smiled as he said it, Ah could see this deep sadness in his eyes. Whateva inner demons he wuz battlin', Ah sure hope he vanquished 'em."

"Oh, now I want to meet them even more!"

Ah sigh. "Look, jus' don' get yer hopes up. Are ya ready tah talk tah Queen Adelia now?"

Minerva coughs. "Ah, I don't think she is particularly interested in visitors at the moment. Perhaps we should wait an hour or two?"

Ah wanna know exactly what she saw, but askin' her would be jus' as bad as bein' there when she wuz stalkin' her. "OK, sounds good."

"Oh, good heavens, Nina!" Minerva sighs, lyin' 'cross her bed inna half-competent seductive pose. "What*ever* shall we *do* to pass the time, hmm?"

Ah go back tah Cornelius' book, which wuz startin' tah get *really* good. "Ah gotta idea in mind."

Minerva sighs.

Chapter 24

WIT' MINERVA AT mah side, Ah knock on th' door tah Queen Adelia's chambers. "Give me a moment," calls a startled voice. Minerva an' Ah share a worried glance. Ah wonder again what Minerva saw, but Ah bite mah tongue 'fore Ah can ask.

Ah grab ahold o' her hand, tryin' tah steady mah nerves. If Ah felt bad fer sendin' th' Feral down tah th' colony, Queen Adelia hastah feel worse. When she talked 'bout th' men she lost durin' th' Feral horde attack, Ah could see th' grief on her face. Knowin' she killed innocents durin' th' attack has gotta weigh down on her soul—Ah know from experience.

Th' door opens. Fer a split secon', Ah see her polished, professional smile at Minerva. Then, when she sees me an' recognition dawns on her face, a genuine smile shatters her mask. She steps forward, 'bout tah throw her arms 'round me, then takes a step back. "Oh, where are my manners? It is *wonderful* to see you again, Nina. M-may I give you a hug?"

Ah chuckle. "Sure."

She embraces me like a long-lost daughter. "We thought you were dead. We even held a funeral for you."

Ah'm taken aback, but Ah still rub her back in her circles, jus' like Ah did tah Ma when she wuz upset. "It's OK. Ah'm alive, an' neva betta." She lets go o' me, messagin' mah arms like she's makin' sure Ah'm really there. "Oh, just *where* are my manners today! Who is your friend?" she asks, noddin' at Minerva.

"Ah wuz jus' gettin' tah that. This beaut' here is mah girlfriend Minerva. Ah met her when Ah wuz attackin' th' colony from th' back entrance."

Her eyebrows shoot up, then she gently takes ahold o' Minerva's hand. "Oh, my. I've heard lots about you from my sister, Minerva Henswood. She is *quite* fond of you."

Minerva shoots me a smug smirk as she shakes Queen Adelia's hand, which irritates th' livin' shit outta me. "Oh?"

"Yes." She rubs her temple, lookin' pained. "This is *quite* the scandal; I'll have you two know. Queen Amity's prized knight dating Queen Adelia's promising new recruit? They're going to make a movie about this one day. I can see it now—Romeo and Juliet: Lesbian Edition."

Ah kinda wanna tell Queen Adelia Ah'm bi, but Ah'm too busy laughin' wit' 'em tah care.

"Come on in, you two. I will make us some delicious tea."

"Oh, marvelous!" Minerva says.

"On one condition, that is. I want you two to tell me the whole story. I expect healthy doses of action, intrigue, and romance."

"Oh, you'll get that, Yer Highness. An' mo' gore than ya can ask fer inna horror film."

"Do not bother with formalities here. I haven't known you for long, Nina, and you even less so, Minerva, but I hope I can call you both friends."

"Alright, Adelia," Ah say. "Les' get this tea party started."

X X X

"I'm sorry, can you give me a quick recap of *everything you just said?*" Adelia says wit' a sigh. "This is a *lot* to take in."

"When we got to Edinburgh, all the scientists were dead. We logged onto their computer and found out that the Feral came here with the help of aliens of unknown origin. That unknown race is using the Feral as expendable soldiers. Essentially, the Feral are victims of this war as well."

Adelia caresses her temple. "So the creatures that threw our country into chaos are just pawns in a bigger chess game?"

"Yes. The real threat has yet to come."

Adelia sits perfectly still, takin' calm, even breaths. Ah get th' feelin' she would be inna fetal postion if we weren't in th' room.

"Hey, th' trip wuzn't a total waste. We got these neat grenades that can disable th' Feral's force field, an' ones that can distract 'em wit' th' smell o' blood. We've got sum on us right now, an' we even brought th' schematics so y'all can make mo' grenades once we get th' right materials."

"The scientists have estimated that these will increase survival rates to up to 50%." Minerva says. "These grenades are definitely a game changer."

Adelia seems tah calm down a bit. "Alright, those sound helpful. Did they discover any new ways to defeat the aliens?"

"Not quite," Minerva says. "The scientists created their own metahuman. The lead scientist, Dr. Light, experimented on his own daughter. He exposed her to the Super Meteorite and spliced Feral DNA into her, creating a cannibalistic monster that turned on the scientists and killed them all."

Adelia looks ill as she sinks back intah her couch. "Where is the metahuman now?"

"We dunno."

"And you say she is extremely powerful?"

"Yes," Minerva says. "It took all of our strength just to survive. She could replicate herself, and who knows how many copies she can make at once? If she got hungry and stumbled across a colony..." she shivers. Ah wrap mah arm 'round her shoulder, tryin' tah calm her down.

Adelia's eyebrows furrow. "So, we're up against aliens leagues smarter than the Feral and a one girl army who happens to feed on human flesh. What, pray tell, is the plan to deal with these threats?"

Me an' Minerva frown at each otha. "Uh, we wuz hopin' *you* would have a plan."

Adelia sighs. "Well, I suppose what I am doing now will have to suffice. The training must intensify if we are to survive. In a few months' time, everyone in this colony will be a fully trained solider."

"Adelia, forgive my questioning, but there are children here. Why were they not transported to the safe house with the disabled Chosen?"

"Because they aren't disabled. They need to know how to fight more than any of us."

"But... they're merely children."

Adelia's eyes flash. "*And?* You've been on the Surface. Do you think the Feral care if the human they eat is a child? Do you think the *rapists* care because the victim is a child? Such a helpless victim would probably turn them on more! My sister spent the past year babying every civilian in this colony, and it's made you all *weak*."

"Now hold yer horses Adelia, Minerva is th' strongest person Ah've eva fought."

"Let us say, hypothetically, that Minerva is *not* an extraordinarily powerful metahuman, and just a normal knight. How would she have fared in battle then?"

Ah look tah mah side, starin' at her glistenin' sapphires. Minerva answers th' question fer me: "She would have killed me."

Adelia nods. "I admit that it is rather superfluous to call you weak. If that were true, Nina would have killed you, regardless of how strong your powers are. But do you see the point I am trying to make? Nina spent every day for the past year fighting for her life. Meanwhile, people here were watching movies, sipping tea and doing math homework. Imagine, if you will, that some other organization with ill intent had attacked the colony instead of us. Every last person here would be dead."

Th' silence that followed wuz jus' 'bout as loud as an explosion in space.

"No more pampering," Adelia says. "We're living after the end of the world. Math is a great and all, but we're going to need to teach these children something a little more substantial if they are going to survive on the Surface."

Minerva whimpers, "Oh, *fine!* Point made. Now then, I believe it is *our* turn to ask the questions."

Adelia gets up an' starts brewin' anotha batch o' tea. "Ask away, dear."

Minerva flinches at "dear" fer whateva reason, an' then says, "Firstly, where is the safe house for the disabled?"

"It's at a hidden Ignored base near Buckingham Palace."

"*What*? Why there, of all places?"

"Buckingham Palace is the most secure place in all of England. Booby traps surround the block, keeping Feral and bandits at bay on a day-to-day basis. Some of my knights previously lived in the palace and joined the Ignored. Those knights are accompanying the disabled Chosen to the safe house, ensuring that they avoid the traps and any other threats."

"Tell me if I am incorrect, but do you think Queen Amity would be there?"

Adelia sighs again. "There is a very strong possibility my sister fled there, assuming she didn't die on the way. In fact, I initially thought she would be cowering there—that was her original plan. That colony is far more protected than this one. I suppose I'll never know why she wasn't there from the start."

"Why not?" Minerva asks. "You are acting as if you will never see her again. What will it take you for you to reconcile with Queen Amity?"

Adelia snorts like a hog. "Reconcile with her? Dear, the next time I see her it will be a challenge not to kill her where she stands. I have spent the past year witnessing the results of her terrible actions every single day. I don't think I have it in me to forgive her."

"But... she's your sister!" Ah facepalm. *Aw, she's done it now.*

Adelia springs tah her feet. Her knees slam intah tea table, knockin' a cup sideways an' shatterin' th' delicate glass. "You think I don't know that? I grew up with her! I idealized her just as you do now. No one on this planet loves her as much as I do. And that is precisely why I want to kill her."

"That is known as a paradox, *dear*."

"Of sorts, yes. But I am sure you understand where I'm coming from, Nina."

Ah think 'bout Lucio. Durin' that year we spent tahgetha, he would drive me crazy half th' time. He'd be a smart ass at th' worst times, an' then be all sensitive when Ah'd snap at him. Sumtimes he'd wake me up wit' his cryin, otha times from laughin' at a book he'd read a billion times. It wuz like, bro, is it so hard tah getta room? Still, even though he drove me crazy half th' time, now that he's gone it feels like Ah lost a piece o' mah soul Ah'll neva get back.

Ah blink, rememberin' Ah'm still in Adelia's office. Mah friends are lookin' at me like they've jus' found out Ah'm a rape victim. *Ugh, that analogy couldah been a lil' less accurate.*

"Oh," Ah choke out, coughin' tah clear up mah tight throat. "Sorry y'all," Ah cough again. "Jus' got lost in thought. Yeah, Ah know what ya mean Adelia. How ya can love an' hate a siblin' at th' same time."

Adelia nods slightly. "When we were youths, Adelia was a courageous, kind and generous young soul. Her younger self would be disgusted by the kind of person she has become, and so am I."

Minerva goes, "Hmm. What do you suppose made her change?"

"Citizens showed her no respect whatsoever. While people were struggling to put food on the table or get through school, she was lying on a million-pound mattress eating fish and chips. People resented her for being royal and rich, and they made it known to her. When she went and bought her new identity, she got to experience what life was like as an ordinary citizen. Her private political views, such as reduced border control and lowered taxes, were the exact opposite by the time she regained the throne. I suppose the new perspective she gained made her more cynical. There is definitely merit to the idea that there aren't enough resources for everyone. But I still won't forgive her for what she's done."

"Surely you don't agree with packing thousands of people in facilities that can barely contain a few hundred?" Minerva asks.

"What will happen when we run out of food sooner rather than later?"

"We'd all kill each other. Again, I understand why my sister did what she did, but that does not mean I can agree with it. Some of my people have been through Hell because of her decision. I can't just let that slide."

"Very well," Minerva says, "How do you propose to defeat an entire alien race we know nothing about with only—and I'm being generous with my numbers here—*half* of England's forces behind you?"

Adelia frowns fer th' first time. "We'll manage." Minerva swallows spit, then looks at me like she's drownin' an' 'xpectin' me tah toss her a life jacket.

Ah sigh, then clear mah throat. "Uh, Adelia, Ah've got jus' as much o' a reason tah hate yer sister as you do. Least Ah think so. Ah mean, she took th' last member o' mah family away from me, y'know? But even Ah admit..." Ah tighten mah grip on Her hand, "that Minerva's right. There ain't no way we can handle anotha alien threat on our own. We need th' Chosen's help."

Adelia starts grittin' her teeth. "But so many of them are despicable, evil people. Take my sister, for example. When we attacked, she sealed the emergency exits and trapped her civilians with us just so she could get away! She doesn't value your lives. If she can't value her own comrades there's no way she can work together with us."

Minerva scoffs. "We don't know if Queen Amity was the one who did that. Just because it happened and it benefited her doesn't necessarily mean it was by her orders. Many of the Chosen would have gladly sealed the exit if it meant her escape. Your Majesty with all due respect you're painting the worst possible picture for your sister because she hurt you in the past. I understand that she's made many mistakes and has hurt many of the people who you call family now, but do you really think your sister is downright *evil?*"

Adelia purses her lips an' wit' a sigh, shakes her head no.

"We know fer sure that we can't trust all th' Chosen. But remember what ya told me that night at th' gym? We all stand tahgetha, an' we all fall tahgetha. Ya can't let yer family drama get in th' way o' yer philosophy, or in th' way o' yer country's survival."

Adelia nods calmly at mah words. "You're right. Both of you." She takes anotha sip o' her quiverin' tea cup. Then she hurls it 'gainst th' wall. *Crash!* Minerva clutches mah hand right as mah heart jumps intah mah throat. Drops o' tea an' bits o' shattered glass go flyin' as Adelia hollers, "*Bloody hell!* You're right. I'm going to have to work with the monster I vowed to vanquish. She caused my people so much harm, tore this country apart... but she's still my sister. And I still love her."

Her tight posture uncoils, an' then she collapses intah her chair. Usin' her elbows tah prop herself up, she buries her face in both hands. "Damn it all. I'm sorry, you two, I didn't mean for you to see me like this."

"Now there ain't no reason tah feel ashamed o' bein' frustrated."

"I'm the bloody Queen of England. I'm supposed to have my emotions in check at all times."

"Hmm... I seem to recall you saying we needn't bother with formalities here," Minerva quips.

"'Sides, right now, ya ain't th' Queen o' England. Yer jus' Adelia."

Adelia smiles at us. "Thank you, you two. Would it be questionable to ask for another hug?"

"Not at all," Minerva exclaims, wit' me noddin' alongside her. We all stand up an' hug. Ah smile as mah gal an' Ah bring her in closah—then frown. We'd held Cornelius like this a day 'fore he died. Whose tah say th' same won' happen tah Adelia? Ah fight tah keep a smile on mah face when Ah let her go. Ah'm sure she'd normally figure sumthin's off wit' me, but she's gotta be so torn up by th' news bomb we jus' dropped on her that she doesn't notice.

"Well then! You'll have to excuse me, you two. I've got a lot to think about as of now. Perhaps we can have tea again sometime tomorrow?"

"Sounds great! We'll get outta yer hair."

Ah startah walk out when a thought comes tah mind. "Hey, can Ah ask ya sumthin'?"

"Anything," Adelia says, interlockin' her fingers unner her chin.

"How come ya held a funeral fer me?" Ah ask heatedly, though Ah dunno why. "We only knew each otha fer one night."

Adelia chuckles. "Is it so hard to believe that I grew to care for you in such a short time frame? You're my friend, Nina, and that's all there is to it. I am very glad you aren't dead."

Mah face is hot as Ah digest that, then Ah toss her a grin an' start walkin' out again. On mah way out Ah see Minerva noddin' politely at Adelia, then from mah peripheral vision Ah see her startah follow me out. 'Fore Ah can close th' door behin' us, Adelia calls out, "Oh! And Nina?"

"Eeyup, thas' me."

"I'm sorry about what happened to your brother. But I'm glad you were able to start a new family."

Ah wipe mah eyes, an' then smile at her. "Thanks. Ah mean… thanks. Ah 'ppreciate it." We grin at one anotha 'fore Ah close th' door.

Minerva locks her arm 'round mine an' says, "That went about as well as it could have."

"Truth," Ah say, puttin' a jolly pep in our step.

"So! What is our plan for the rest of the evening? Shall we visit the library, or relax in the theater?"

"Actually, Ah wuz hopin' fer a lil' action."

"*Oh, my.* Um."

"N-not *that* kinda action, sug'. It's jus' that we've been lyin' 'round all day talkin'. Ah could use sum activity is all. Ya said y'all gotta gym here, right?"

Minerva giggles, makin' mah arm hum. "I'm not sure whether or not I'm happy or disappointed you weren't referring something more... intimate."

Ah groan, fightin' back a blisterin' hot blush. "Minerva!" Ah groan.

She giggles sum mo'. "You seem flustered," she says, tickilin' mah rib cage.

Now Ah'm drownin' in lava. "Quit it, missy!"

"Oh, but you're just so fun to tease! Any*who*, to answer your question, we do indeed have a gym available for public use."

"Well sug', are ya ready tah get ripped?"

"A lady does not 'get ripped', dear, they merely get toned. Alas, I am afraid I have to use the little girl's room."

"How'd ya go froma woman tah a gal in less than five seconds," Ah ask wit' a chuckle. "Alright, do ya want me tah wait outside th' restroom or met ya at th' gym?"

"Oh, you can meet me there darling. I appreciate you asking, however."

"Eeyup," Ah drawl, unwrappin' mah arm from hers. "Oh, wait, how do Ah get there?"

Minerva giggles. "Just go down the hall and take a right. It'll be the first door on the left."

"Thank ya kindly. See ya soon." Ah kiss her cheek, an' then Ah'm on mah way. As Ah walk, Ah take in th' area. Ah dunno if Ah'll eva get used tah walkin' on grass in-doors, but Ah guess itsa nice touch. Th' halls are mostly empty, but th' place doesn't feel lonely. You'll see a couple or two roamin' th' place, wit' a few kids runnin' 'round without a care in th' world. Ah can hear bits o' music comin' from people's rooms. Sum o' th' songs are depressin', which ain't a surprise considerin' what these people have seen aftah a year o' peace, but a lot o' 'em are pretty upbeat.

Ah head on intah th' gym. It's a big ass room wit' glossy wooden floors an' blue walls, an' it's bustlin' wit' activity—people are liftin' weights, or usin' a buncha fancy work-out machines, doin' yoga, whateva. Mah head is buzzin' wit' thoughts, so Ah jus' slide onnah pair o' boxin' gloves, square up a punchin' bag, an' get tah work.

Ah can't help but wonder what mah life would be like if Lucio an' Ah had spent th' past year here insteadah out there on th' Surface. Fer one, he probably wouldn' be dead. Ah wouldn' be so damn skinny, either. On th' otha hand, that year on th' Surface really toughened me up, an' if anythin' were tah happen tah this place, chances are Ah wouldn' be able tah defend mahself, an' me *an'* Lucio would be dead.

A flurry o' jabs smack th' bag 'round 'fore a front kick blasts it backwards. When th' bag returns fer anotha beatin', Ah twist intah an elbow strike. Ah tuck intah a roll, avoidin' an imaginary strike, then leap ontah th' bag 'fore drivin' mah knee intah it. Then, Ah'm back tah jabbin'.

Plus, would Ah have even met Minerva inna peaceful place like this? Ah mean, sure Ah mightah *met* her, like bump intah her or sumthin', but would we have actually talked? Ah feel like th' only reason we started talkin' is 'cuz we kinda had to. We're so seemingly different from one anotha Ah probably wouldn' have given her a secon' glance had we met. But even so, Ah wanna believe...

Ah kick th' bag backwards 'gain, but 'fore it can return tah me delicate white fingers grab ahold o' it from both sides. Minerva peaks her head out from behin' th' bag, smilin' like Christmas came early. "My my, you're really getting into this!"

"Gotta lot on mah mind is all. Ya plannin' on keepin' th' bag still fer me?"

"Correct. No need to hold back on my account!"

"Alrighty then!" Ah slug th' bag sum mo', workin' back intah a rhythm. "Hey, Minerva?"

She grunts as Ah pound th' bag within' an inch o' its inanimate life. "Yes, dear?"

"Les' say Ah spent th' past year here steadah out on th' Surface. Do ya think we would still be tahgetha?"

"Mmm..." She's silent as Ah tenderize th' bag like a slab o' meat. "I hate to say it, but perhaps not! I feel like we met each other at the time where we needed each other most. Your brother had recently passed, and you found companionship from an unlikely source. As for me, I needed someone to accompany me on the most dangerous journey of my life, at a time where I felt most insecure. Had the mission Queen Amity gave me not bound us together, we probably would have just got on each other's nerves had we bumped into one another, then not spare the other another thought."

Her words suck th' energy outta mah blows. Minerva seems tah sense this, so she pushes th' bag towards me. Ah catch it wit' a start. Minerva winks at me, then hops on both feet like an out-boxer. Soon, she's circlin' 'round th' bag, peltin' it wit' elegant right jabs. *Heh, Ah fergot she wuz left-handed.*

"You seem... disturbed at my response, dear."

"Ah gotta admit Ah'm a bit disappointed," Ah say wit' a small smile.

"Why is that?"

Ah pause fer a moment, listenin' tah th' metronome o' Minerva's punches. "Eh, Ah dunno, maybe Ah'm too much o' a romantic."

Th' bag quivers like Lucio aftah he saw *Alien*. "Never thought I'd hear you say those words, dear. And that's coming from *me*."

"Laugh it up, sug', Ah jus' figured you'd say we'd always be tahgetha—on account o' us bein' soul mates or sumthin'."

Ah brace mahself tah catch anotha blow, but th' bag ain't shakin' no mo'. Minerva peaks 'round th' bag, lookin' at me wit' eyes brighter thana eight carat diamond. "T-that's remarkably sweet, dear." She pecks me on th' lips, makin' th' world spin, then she's back tah punchin' 'fore Ah can regain mah footin'. "If it's any conciliation, I do hope we'd beat the odds. But even if we didn't, it hardly matters. In fact, perhaps I'd prefer it if we didn't!"

Mah stomach drops like Ah hate rocks fer lunch. "Why?"

"Let us say, hypothetically, that we had access to the multiverse, where we could see all the different realities and our fates within them."

"Damn gal," Ah chuckle, "are we really gettin' that deep intah this?"

"Hold on now, I'm going somewhere with this. You see, in all those different realities, we may have only ended up together here. Perhaps our love," mah heart pounds *extra* hard at 'love' "won't transcend time and space, but doesn't that make what we have even more special?"

"Ah... Ah ain't quite followin', sug'."

Th' rhythm o' Minerva's punches get mo' methodical, like she sizin' up an invisible opponent. "Ugh, this is *quite* hard to put into words. How do I put this... on the surface, our varying personalities and dialect quite possibly could have pushed us apart. But because of select, delicate circumstances, we ended up becoming lovers. If anything in the past happened differently, like your brother not passing, or me not befriending an abusive alcoholic, we wouldn't have met, or I might have killed you after our fight... are you following me so far?"

Mah head is startin' tah hurt, partially cuz th' conversation has gotten all, Ah dunno, metaphysical, an' partially cuz Minerva punches *hard*. "Uh... sorta."

"I am not a religious woman, Nina. But if anything would make me believe in a higher power, it would be meeting you."

Ah've been piecin' tahgetha a puzzle eva since we started this conversation. But that last part is th' missin' piece. Ah push th' stupid bag outta mah way an' hold her close. "Ah... damn, gal, yer beautiful, y'know that?"

She smiles. "I do now."

Ah kiss her, then force mahself tah let her go. People are startin' tah look at us, an' while Ah don' give a damn what they think, Ah'm sure that our public displays o' affection is sickenin' from outside our transparent bubble. "Les' hit th' treadmills. Ah gotta lotta energy tah burn off now."

"I can think of vastly more satisfying ways of expending that energy, you know."

Ah grab her hand an' speed walk tah th' damned machines, mah face burnin' sumthin' fierce. "So could Ah, but Ah'd rathah not eat mah dessert durin' breakfast."

Minerva giggles. "Wow, I thought you were only sweet to me because you wanted to, how did you say it... 'get intah mah pants'?"

Ah chuckle. "Ah only said that tah blow away th' cloud o' sentimentality we were in. Fact is, Ah ain't got no sexual experience, an' Ah sure as hell ain't ready fer that anytime soon. Right now Ah'm mo' interested in gettin' tah know yer brain steadah yer body."

"My my, you really are a romantic! Perhaps I can recommend you some of my reading material?"

Titles like, *The Temptation of The Lover* an' *The Touch of the Lonely Moonlight* flash in mah memory, th' same ones Ah saw on her bookshelf. "Uh, les' jus' get tah runnin'."

Chapter 25

AH STEP OUTTA th' steamin' restroom, a wet towel ova mah shoulder. Minerva's brewin' her fiftieth cup o' tea tahday, her back tah me. Ah wrap mah arms 'round her waist, inhalin' her perfume. "Ah tell ya, aftah a year o' bein' filthy as a hog, showerin' neva gets ol'."

Minerva turns around an' pecks me on th' cheek; her weak smile shakier thana bridge durin' a thunderstorm. Ah raise a brow. "Whassup, sug'?"

She turns off th' tea pot an' grabs ahold o' both o' mah hands. "I have terrible news, darling. C-could you take a seat with me?"

Ah raise an eyebrow. *Whas' she up to?* "... Sure."

She continues tah hold mah hands as we take a seat on th' edge o' her bed. She takes a deep breath, thena purple sphere surrounds us. Mah eyebrow hits th' ceilin'. "Whas' goin' on?"

Minerva takes anotha deep breath, which is really startin' tah grind mah gears. "While you were in the shower, I visited Adelia for some of those exquisite tea bags. On my way back, I..." *anotha* deep breath, "I saw Zack."

Blink. "Ah'm sorry, *what?*"

"I saw Zack, Nina. He looked like an empty sack of flesh, a moving corpse with no soul. It was... quite the shock."

"H-he killed mah brother, Minerva." She don' say nuthin', jus' rubs her thumbs ova mah knuckles smoothly. "Ya really think this barrier's gonna hold me back?"

She tightens her grip. "Nina. *Please.*"

Ah chuckle. "Neva thought Ah'd say this, but Ah need ya tah let go o' me. *Now.*" Minerva looks me in th' eye, then slowly nods. Th' barrier 'round us dissipates. "Whas' his room number?" She don' say nuthin', so Ah growl, "Minerva."

"... A216."

"Thanks," Ah grunt. She throws her arms 'round me, then kisses mah cheek. Ah smile at her but pry her off neva-th'-less. Ah strap on mah belt o' deadly goodies, an' Ah'mma 'boutah leave when Minerva says, "Wait!"

Ah don' turn 'round tah look her in th' eye. "Yeah?"

"We aren't on the Surface anymore."

Ah nod, but still open th' door an' step intah th' hall. A kid walkin' by points at me, screams, then runs away. Ah shrug, then take a-gander at Minerva's room number. A198. Th' door next tah it is room 200. So Zack's room should be right down this here hall. Thas' pretty convenient. Mus' be God givin' me a sign Ah'm doin' th' right thing. Ah start walkin' tah his room, but at th' end o' th' hallway, a tall an' dark figure has popped intah view. He wears a black stetson an' a brown jacket that says "Police" on th' front. He darts towards me; his hand at his waist, but when he makes eye contact, his worried face is replaced by a warm smile.

"Nina," Pete says, "vhat are you up to, young lady? You're scaring ze children."

"Ha! They would make th' big black guy security." Pete rolls his eyes wit' a smile, then Ah say, "Anywho, Ah'm gonna have words wit' th' bastard that killed mah brother."

Pete's eyes shoot tah mah waist. "Vhat are you planning to do?"

"Whaddya think?"

Pete takes a small sidestep, now standin' directly in mah path. "Let's be rational about zis, Nina."

"He killed mah brother. There ain't no reason tah be rational."

Pete sends a worried glance ova mah shoulder. Ah turn 'round tah see a small group o' civilians lookin' at me in fear. "Can ve talk about zis somewhere private, please?"

"Ah ain't got time tah talk, Pete."

"*Nina*," Pete groans. "Can you just do zis for me? Please?"

Ah remember th' night we met, how he told me not tah be 'fraid when Ah wuz 'boutah lose mah mind wit' fear aftah seein' how bloody th' church wuz. If he could show a strangah such kindness, th' least Ah could do wuz honor our friendship wit' his simple request, even if Ah wuz on th' verge o' gettin' mah revenge once an' fer all. "*Fine.*"

Pete sighs wit' relief an' knocks on th' nearest door. A red eyed teenager wit' a bad case o' bed hair opens th' door a few moments later. "Hm?"

"Hi!" Pete flashes his police badge. "I'm sorry, may ve use zis room for but a moment? We have important zings to discuss in private."

Th' kid scratches his ass wit' one hand an' checks his watch wit' anotha. "You got five minutes, mate." He goes back tah his bed, grabs his covers an' a pillow, then exits th' room wit' a proud fart. Pete starts closin' th' door, but 'fore it fully shuts Ah see th' kid toss his pillow on th' floor, lay his head onnit an' wrap his covers 'round himself.

Ah chuckle. "He mus' be tired."

Pete shakes his head. "Listen, if you kill zat man now, that'll make ze ozer civilians zink zis place isn't a home but a battleground. Zese people have seen enough death in ze past week. Let Adelia know vhat he's done, and I assure you justice vill be served."

"This ain't 'tween nobody but me an' him. Pete, Ah like ya. Yer mah friend. Ah didn' wanna unnermine yer authority in frontah th' civilians, but Ah'm tellin' ya here that if ya get in mah way yer gonna regret it." Pete grits his teeth. His hand flashes towards his waist, but now he's lookin' down th' barrel o' mah pistol. "Sorry, Pete, but Ah'mma need ya tah gimmie yer gun."

Pete chuckles nervously. "You're not going to shoot me," he says, though th' way he says it sounds like, "You're not going to shoot me, *right?*"

"No, Ah ain't." Ah take th' gun outta his face, then holster it. "Then again, you ain't gonna shoot me neither, so this whole standoff is pointless." Ah turn tah open th' door, but he grabs me by th' wrist. Ah pull back wit' mah full body weight, an' it's jus' enough tah tip th' gentle giant towards me, puttin' him off balance.

Ah slam intah him wit' everything Ah got, makin' him bust his ass on th' floor.

He rubs his hindquarters in surprise as Ah warn him, "Don' let mah size fool ya, sug'. Ah can still whoop yer ass." Pete crosses his one arm 'cross his chest, lookin' like an ovasized toddler 'boutah throw a tantrum. "Don' gimmie that look. You an' Ah know damn well it ain't right tah let this guy roam 'round aftah all th' shit he's done. Mah brother wuzn't th' only life he took, Ah assure ya!"

"I don't doubt your vords, but zat doesn't mean you can just take matters into your own hands. Ve aren't on ze Surface anymore! Vigilante justice cannot work wiz ze law in place. Say you kill zis man. Vhat are we supposed to do zen? Let it slide? Vhat happens when ze next person kills someone? Z'ell think zat zey won't be punished because you veren't. And vhat about—"

"Alright, alright," Ah say, holdin' mah hands up. "Ah get it."

Pete's eyes go wide. "So you von't kill him?"

"Naw, Ah'm still gonna kill him. But Ah ain't gonna resist arrest."

He shakes his head. "I can't let you do zis."

Ah clench mah fists. "Don' make me fight you."

"You know I'm not ze only security officer, right?"

"Butcha ain't gonna call 'em."

"Vhy not? You'll beat me up?" He gets tah his feet an' towers ova me, flexin' his impressive muscles. Damn. Ah talk a big game, but Ah really jus' caught him by surprise jus' now. Ah doubt Ah could beat him in a straight up fight.

"No, you ain't gonna call 'em cuz Ah'm yer friend an' yer gonna do me a solid an' keep yer mouth shut while Ah take care o' business. Once Ah'm done wit' that scumbag, y'all can have yer way wit' me." Ah hold out mah hand. "We square?"

Pete slowly nods, but he don' take mah hand. "*Fine.* But vhatever punishment you get, it'll push you avay from Minerva for vho knows how long. Is that vorth it?"

"Minerva can wait fer me tah get outta jail or whateva. She'll probably be able tah visit me too. But Ah can't wait tah finish what Ah started an' kill that son o'va bitch."

"Yer beautiful, sis."

Ah storm outta th' room 'fore Pete can say anythin' else. Ah step ova th' teenager sleepin' on th' floor then stomp ova tah room A216. Ah pound th' shit outta th' door. An enraged voice answers, "Who the hell is it?"

"Th' gal who stabbed ya in th' eye!" Ah roar back.

Ah hear th' worm scramblin' behin' th' door. Everything goes red. Ah kick th' door down. Zack is 'cross th' room onnah bed. He's aimin' a shaky gun at me, but Ah've already hurled mah knife. It jams th' barrel right as he pulls th' trigga. Th' gun explodes in his hands, makin' bits o' blood an' skin go flyin' from his hands. He screams. A punch tah his eye patch shuts him up. He slams ontah th' floor on his shoulder.

Ah take out mah gun, lick mah dry lips, then say, "Sorry Ah didn' kill ya before. Torturin' ya wuz wrong. Ah ain't gonna make th' same mistake 'gain." Ah take a deep breath. "Ah'm finally avengin' ya, brother," Ah whisper. Right before Ah pull th' trigga warm arms wrap 'round mah waist.

"Minerva, Ah'm 'boutah kill this guy. You really wanna see this?"

"I do not. However, I feel that it is my responsibility to be here at this crucial moment."

"Suit yerself," Ah say wit' a shrug. Ah re-aim th' nozzle at a squirmin' Zack's heart, then Minerva tugs at mah elbow, throwin' off mah aim 'gain. "*What?*"

"Look at him, dear."

"Minerva, if yer tryin' tah convince me not tah kill him, jus' *leave* alright!"

"*Please*, Nina. Just look at him for one moment."

Ah roll mah eyes, but still look at him. Mah punch tore a hole in his eye patch, revealin' a crusty eyeball wit' a slit down th' middle. Th' slit Ah made. Mah stomach flips as Ah glance at his left hand, where Ah blew off his pinky finger. Th' hand is wrapped inna bloody white cloth, lookin' unnatural as all hell. Zack's glares at me from th' floor, lookin' like he's gotta terminal illness. "Was having my wife and kid eaten alive not good enough revenge for you, bitch? You killed my family and took my fucking *bike*. If you're going to kill me, get it over with already. I'm already dead, anyway!"

He covers his disgustin' face before breakin' intah heavy sobs that wrack his entire body. Ah raise th' gun tah put him outta his misery even as Minerva hugs me even tighter from behin'. He looks so pathetic that killin' him would feel like Ah'd be doin' him a favor, an' doin' this bastard a favor is th' last thing Ah wanna do. "Do ya wanna die?"

"... Yes," he whispers.

Ah toss him his ol' gun. It clatters next tah his breathin' corpse. "Then jus' kill yerself."

ina leaves the room, tears streaking down her cheeks. I turn back to Zack, heart dropping when I see him jamming the pistol down his throat.

"Zack! What on Earth are you doing?"

He looks at me with glazed, lifeless eyes.

"Don't!"

He slowly takes the pistol out of his mouth. "Why not?"

"Let me tell you a story, Zack."

"I'm not in a story telling mo—" I turn invisible, dart towards him, and then swipe the gun from his hands. "Hey!"

I turn visible again, then say, "Do not, 'hey' me! If you are going to kill yourself, do it out on the Surface. No one wants to clean up your disgusting, rotting corpse."

He grunts, "Fine", and motions to get up, but I push my hand forward. A barrier corners him against the back of the wall. "You're not going anywhere. You're going to listen to what I have to say before you do *anything* foolish, otherwise you will taste the sting of my blade. Understood?"

"Bitch—"

The barrier gets smaller, crushing him against the wall. He cries out in pain. I sigh, and then snap my fingers. The barrier shatters into nothingness. Zack collapses on his knees, breathing hard.

"As I was saying—Nina is my girlfriend."

"You're fucking that piece of—"

"Do *not* insult her. As I was *saying*, I met her when she was attacking the colony. On your bike, no less. I defeated her and took her to one of our safe houses."

"Why didn't you kill her?"

"Tyrone, a fellow knight, had run into her on the Surface awhile back. He told me that the Bell Brothers attacked her brother, so she killed them. She let him go but warned him that if anyone tried to hurt her brother, she would kill us all. How could I kill someone who'd been wronged by my people? She was attacked first; everything afterwards was retaliation."

"Look, I was just doing my job," Zack grumbles. "If anyone killed her brother, it was Queen Amity, not me."

"Nazis said the same thing when they were being tried for the Holocaust. Have you no spine? You could have just told her no."

"Sure, but then what would I do with my day?"

"I don't know; perhaps *spend time with your family?* You realize that if Nina was able to feed her brother before he *starved to death*, he might not have died, and then the colony would have never been attacked. Your family would probably still be alive."

"I'm sorry; I thought you were trying to talk me *out* of killing myself."

I sigh. "Forgive me, I got sidetracked. Anyway, when Nina found out the attack she planned killed innocent people, she tried to kill herself. But I gave her a reason to keep going." I tell him about the mission Queen Amity gave me, and how Nina and I eventually got romantically involved.

"Why should I give a shit about *anything* you're saying right now?"

I take a deep breath and resist the urge to crush him against the wall again. "Right now, you are exactly where Nina was a week or so ago. You can kill *yourself and die a heartless murderer who offed himself to save others the trouble, or you can find a new reason to live. Perhaps you can start helping people instead of hurting them."*

"What's in it for me?

"Not dying as something worse than rubbish?" I ask.

Zack slowly nods, and then asks, "Why are you helping me? I ruined your girlfriend's life."

"Because every life is precious. Even you deserve a chance at redemption. Nina's actions lead to the death of dozens of innocents, but has helped me obtain information that will save thousands of lives. You have the same opportunity to do good as she did. I do hope you don't let it go to waste."

Zack nods again. "Hey, where's my bike?"

I sigh. Did anything I just have any effect on him at all? "It's gone. Some scavengers stole it from us."

Zack groans. "I told that girl not to put a scratch on my ride, and she ends up losing the whole damn thing. I hate her." He clenches his fist, then cries out when his nails dig into his flayed hands.

Ugh, I can't tell if he's more upset over his family dying or him losing his bike. "Listen, I'm going to get the nurse. Are you going to be alright?"

"Yeah, it's fine." He looks at his bloody hands, as if noticing the injury for the first time. "Thanks for the talk. I think I just found something to live for."

He sounds genuine, so I smile at him. This is the third suicide I've prevented. I'm getting good at this! "Wonderful!" I confiscate the gun then open the door and start walking out. "You have a great night." I start to close the door, and then say, "I'm sorry for what Nina did to you. One day, she just might apologize to you."

He scoffs. "Whatever. I won't forgive her no matter what she says."

I frown at the pure hatred in his voice. "You realize that if you lay a finger on her it will be the last thing you do, correct?"

He chuckles. "Yes."

I turn and glare at him. *I could blow his brains out and make it look like a suicide, easy.* The vicious train of thought makes me flinch. *I can't kill someone over something they* might *do. Besides, Zack is nothing but a harmless man full of spite. Nina's defeated him twice now, and I'm sure I can too. I have nothing to worry about. Killing him would only give me more nightmares, and I've got enough of those as it is.* I exit the room and walk towards the nurse's office.

X X X

I collapse on the bed next to Nina with a sigh. For one long moment, we just stare at the ceiling together. The only sound in the room is our slow, steady breathing. Eventually, Nina croaks, "Is he dead?"

"No. I convinced him not to kill himself." Nina groans, and my heart sinks. I turn to look at her, but her eyes are still on the ceiling. "Please don't be angry with me!"

"Ah ain't. It's jus' like you tah see th' best in people. Ya probably didn' want him tah die a worthless coward, right?"

"You know me too well."

"Ya pulled th' same shtick on me when Ah wanted tah die, too. So what happens tah him now?"

"I just got done speaking with Queen Adelia. She said she doesn't feel right punishing anyone here for their past sins."

"Why?"

"She told me that her actions killed Zack's family, and further retaliation on her part would be immoral."

Nina pounds the mattress, then rolls away from me. "Easy fer her tah be objective when it wuzn't her brother that wuz killed, damn it!"

I grab her hand, running my thumb across her palm. "She also said that if you ended up killing him, the most severe punishment you would get would be incarceration. You would be made an example of in the public's eye—however; my invisibility would ensure that the punishment would be more like a slap on the wrist."

Nina tense hand relaxes a bit. "Guess she meant it when she called us friends."

"Indeed. Personally, as welcome as it is, I find her condition highly unprofessional. How is she to earn the Chosen's trust if she's so clearly biased towards the Ignored?"

"Ya dunno how many Chosen colonies she's been tah 'round th' country. It's gotta be hard fer her tah have much sympathy fer th' same group o' people who've had a hand in suppressin' every single one o' her civilians."

I contemplate her statement for but a moment. "I can see that."

Nina rolls back around to look me in the eye, only it feels like she's staring straight into my soul. "Yer so beautiful it hurts."

It feels like I've just swallowed a mountain. "I—I'm sorry, what?"

Nina laughs, which soothes my heart better than any violin. "Guess Ah can fluster ya sumtimes."

My face is burning so hot I fear I will burn my make-up off. "What, pray tell, brought on such a magnificent compliment?"

She kisses me softly. "'Jus' you bein' you, sug'. 'Fore ya got here, Ah wuz sulkin' in here all on mah lonesum. Killin' Zack ain't gonna bring back mah brother, an' realizin' that jus' made me feel hollow. Got me thinkin' 'bout Lucio an' mah folks, y'know? Ah mean, Ah'm th' last Eagleheart. Mah entire family is gone. Ah started feelin' so sad Ah remembered why Ah wanted tah die a week ago. We'd already completed our mission, why couldn't Ah jus' off mahself now?"

My vision starts swimming. I take in a sharp breath, but before I can remind her of her promise not to kill herself, she kisses me again. "Ah ain't done yet, sug'. So Ah'm thinkin' all this, feelin' 'bout as lost as a sheep inna wolf's den, then you walk intah th' room, takin' care o' business, bein' as sincere as always, an' Ah remember why Ah'm still alive, why Ah wanna stay alive, why breakin' our promise would be th' stupidest thing Ah could eva do. Minerva, yer th' best thing thas' ever happened tah me, an' when yer by mah side Ah know Ah can face any demon. Ah love you."

She smiles that simple smile, running her fingers across my bald head. I choke back sobs, my heart skipping five beats. I feel like I've gone into cardiac arrest twice in the past sixty seconds. "I—you—" My throat closes up, tight. She chuckles even though she's literally rendered me speechless. Bloody hell, even if I could speak, I don't think I would be able to come up with words sufficient enough to convey just how much her words mean to me, if such words exist in the first place! The only thing I can do is kiss her, hold her until I lose consciousness, where I do the same in my dreams.

Chapter 26

AH STRETCH ON th' cloud Ah'm layin' on, then scratch at mah full breasts wit' a lazy smile. *It's good tah have mah babies back.* Ah wrap th' thick, warm covers 'round mah body, comfy as all hell. It's like Ahmma sausage an' th' covers are a pancake. Ah chuckle, then throw th' covers offah me. "'Nerva, where are ya? Ah need tah see that smile 'fore mah mornin' rituals are complete!"

Minerva steps intah view, her curly blonde hair drippin' wet. A purple towel that hides too much is wrapped 'round her body, obscurin' mah view from what Ah'm sure is a beautiful sight. "Good morning, dear," she says, a coy smile on her lips.

Ah bite mah bottom lip. "It ain't nice tah be a tease, 'specially so early in th' mornin'."

She struts forward, oozin' confidence wit' every step. Ah sit up right as she greets me wit' a kiss on th' lips. Ah push her back wit' a *giggle*, then cough an' turn mah laugh intah a hearty chuckle. "Aw, gross! Ah haven't even brushed mah teeth yet."

"And yet, you still taste magnificent."

"That hadtah be th' best lie you've eva told. Sumone's tryin' tah get laid tahnight."

"Darling, I've been trying to, ahem, 'get laid', for the past month!"

"Well, ya might jus' get yer wish tahnight." Ah smack her bum, an' she gives a pleased, "oh!" Ah lie back on th' bed, then throw th' covers ova mah head.

"Oh, Nina, I'm afraid sleeping in isn't an option today. We're supposed to meet Adelia at 11, remember?"

"Aw, shit!" Ah throw th' covers offah me an' hustle intah th' shower. Ah'm clean as a whistle in unner five minutes. When Ah get out, dressed in blue shorts an' an orange shirt, 'Nerva's lyin' on th' bed, givin' me this sultry look that makes mah legs quake. At th' angle she's lyin', her breasts are spillin' outta her low-cut purple blouse.

"A-are ya ready tah go?"

Minerva winks at me 'fore rollin' outta bed an' ontah her feet, th' frills o' her long purple skirt rustlin'. "Ya betta stop teasin'' me," Ah say, hookin' mah arm 'round hers. "We might not make it tah Adelia's chambers."

"Perhaps that was my intention," Minerva says, eyein' me as she buttons up her blouse wit' one hand. Ah swallow air an' lead 'Nerva outta th' room, usin' mah foot tah shut th' door behin' us. We walk down th' familiar corridor inna pleasant silence, only steppin' tah th' side tah let a group o' joggers pass by. In th' past two months, th' group o' baby faced civilians had finally grown a lil' stubble. Mandatory escapades tah th' Surface reminded these folk that our safe haven wuz jus' a temporary slice o' heaven inna world that'd turned tah Hell. If th' colony wuz attacked 'gain, Ah reckon there won' be even half th' casualties as there were last time.

We knock on th' door tah Adelia's chambers. "C'mon in, y'all," she shouts inna terrible imitation o' mah voice. Minerva giggles while Ah bite back a laugh, bustin' th' door open wit' what Ah hope is a convincin' frown. "I'll have you know that I am *quite* offended at your absolute *disregard* of my culture through the *butchering* of my *charming* southern accent! Come forth, put your dukes up, as it were!" Ah challenge, raisin' mah fists an' bouncin' 'em tah a soundless rhythm. "We shall end this verbal conflict with a physical altercation!"

Fer a moment, th' room is silent. Minerva gaps at me while Adelia, sittin' behin' her desk, looks petrified, her teacup frozen mid-sip. Th' two women slowly turn tah look at each otha, then back at me. Then, laughter.

"B-bloody hell!" Adelia shouts, bangin' her fist on th' table. "That was incredible. Where did you learn to speak formally?"

Ah examine mah fingernails, then rub 'em 'gainst mah shirt. "Took theater in high school. Wuz inna few plays. No big deal."

Ah'm actin' all nonchalant, but Ah'm glad Ah wuz able tah getta rise outta 'em.

"Why don't you speak like that all the time?" Adelia asks. "You sounded *quite* posh."

"Cuz that ain't me. That accent is reserved fer th' stage an' cheap laughs."

"But your accent is so strong it can be hard to understand you at times."

"Ah guess you can say Ah speak th' way Ah do cuz itsa good judge o' character. When people write me off jus' cuz Ah speak differently than them, that lets me know Ah'm dealin' wit' sumone that ain't worthy o' mah time. Ah mean, if we meet an' ya don' make th' effort tah unnerstan' me, why should Ah try tah unnerstan' you?"

Adelia nods in unnerstandin' while Minerva says, "Mm, I understand that reasoning. You raise some fair points. Personally, I found myself misjudging you because of that accent, and that made me see some problems with myself that I wouldn't have seen otherwise. Now that I've gotten to know you so well, I have to say that I wouldn't change anything about you, especially that impeccably charming accent of yours." She offers me her elbow, which Ah hook wit' mah arm. We take a seat tahgetha in frontah a beamin' Adelia.

"Tell me, ladies, how have you been enjoying the past two months?"

"Best two months o' mah life," 'Nerva an' Ah say at th' same time. We laugh tahgetha while Adelia's smile dips slightly. "Wow. Could you both tell me why, one at a time, please?"

"Guess Ah'll go first. Adelia, me an' mah brother spent a year out on th' Surface. Lucio starved tah death while Ah got anorexic. Every day wuz a livin' Hell. We were *always* low on supplies. Imagine bein' constantly hungry an' thirsty fer 365 days straight, wit' no idea o' where yer gettin' yer next meal. Didn' help that there wuz always a Feral or Chosen 'round th' corner. Lookin' back onnit, it wuz a complete miracle that we eva survived 'slong as we did."

Ah remember a time when Lucio an' Ah stumbled 'cross a vendin' machine buried unner sum rubble. It took us a few hours tah unearth it an' flip it ova. All we found inside wuz a few bags o' chips, but we still cried like we'd gotten a reservation fer a six-course meal. Mah chest throbs, but th' pain o' losin' mah brother ain't *quite* as painful as it wuz two months ago.

"Here, Ah ain't gotta worry 'bout starvin' tah death. Combine that wit' th' fact that everyday Ah wake up tah *this* gal's smile, an' it's impossible fer these two months *not* tah be th' best o' mah life."

Adelia's smile has dipped even lower. "And you, Minerva?"

"I honestly do not have much to say. I lived here for a year after the invasion, so the perks of the colony are welcome, but not unexpected. The person that has made these two months so special is Nina, period. When we first started dating on the Surface, our mission from Queen Amity took priority over our relationship. This colony has given us a luxury few people can afford—the ability to feel like a normal couple in the aftermath of the apocalypse. We've been able to watch movies together, work out at the gym, feed each other meals, all without having to look over our shoulders every five seconds. Nina's made these past two months an absolute joy."

Ah'm smilin' hard at that, but Adelia ain't. Ah decide tah bite th' bullet. "Alright then, why're you askin' all this?"

Adelia sighs. "To remind myself that you two both have your own lives, your own ambitions. What I'm about to ask of you is entirely unfair, after all. This is 100% voluntarily, and you should not feel obligated to assist me in this ordeal."

"So, what, do ya *not* want us tah do whateva it is ya want us tah do?" Ah ask, startin' tah get a lil' annoyed.

"To be honest, I don't! Which is precisely why I asked you two to tell me how much you've enjoyed these past two months. If you accept this mission, you have my word that the future has nothing but hardship for the both of you. Your good times will be all but over."

"I believe you should let *us* decide that," Minerva says, huffin'. "Now then, what is it that you need done?"

"Very well," Adelia sighs, then gets up an' starts pacin' th' length o' th' room. "I've been keeping it hush hush, but we've taken over Buckingham Palace."

Minerva flinches. "*What?* Since when?"

Adelia's proud smirk takes me aback. "A month ago. We've gained so much momentum that this task was almost no problem. We'd already made a base near the palace two months back, taking it over was as simple as adding men to the pre-existing forces and unleashing a surprise attack." Her smile dips a bit as she says, "Casualties were minimal, but we took a crucial piece from my sister."

"Why lose lives over an arbitrary piece of territory?" Minerva asks.

Her smile is gone. "My initial reasoning for the attack was that we needed the space. And we do. Our forces have grown significantly. Previously unseen survivors have joined us, as well as prior Chosen. We couldn't fit everyone in here forever, and if you combine that with the fact that I wanted to strip away my old home from Amity, it made for quite the alluring target."

"I can't say I grew up in the palace as you do, but I spent a lot of time there with Adelia and definitely considered it a home away from home. I am not sure why you decided it was necessary to spill blood there."

"Because I'm human, Minerva. I claim to be a wise leader of the people, but I'm just another fool." She takes a sip o' her tea. "I saw my sister during the attack. I... I aimed my pistol at her. She ran away before I could make the biggest mistake of my life. She looked so *scared*. I almost killed her because of this territorial toddler mentality. And that is why I've called you two in here.

"Ever since you two found out the Feral are being manipulated by a higher alien race, I've been sending Ignored out to the Surface.

As disgusting as it is, I found myself re-watching Dr. Light's presentation to my sister quite often."

Minerva shivers. "Uh, just hearing that cunt's name sends chills down my spine."

Ah ain't mad at her, Ah've re-watched it a few times too. "What caught yer eye?" Ah ask, rubbin' 'Nerva's back.

"He brought up the question of how the Feral got here. Some people claim they saw Feral dropping from UFO's, others say they came from Hell. Either way, the string of nuclear attacks that decimated the country afterwards should have wiped the Feral out for good. Yet they still remain. Why do you suppose so?"

"Ah ain't got a clue. 'Nerva?"

She twirls her index finger 'round a loose strain o' hair. "The aliens must have a way to send the Feral here, unbeknownst to us. But no one's spotted UFO's since the invasion, at least as far as I know. How could they possibly send Feral here without any of us seeing?"

"You're thinking too logically," Adelia says. "You have superpowers. The fabric of our reality has changed for good. Think outside the box."

"OK, how 'bout an interdimensional portal?"

Adelia's smile is back in action. "Precisely. I believe when the aliens first arrived, they used the Feral as a distraction. While we were busy fighting, they could have set up portals right under our noses."

Minerva's eyebrows furrow. "If this is true, the idea of starving the Feral out was incredibly foolish. Assuming there are a lot of Feral on the alien's home planet, killing them off isn't an option either. We can kill as many as we like, but they'd just send more Feral through, while we keep losing men. Our best option is to find the portals and destroy them."

"Agreed," Adelia says. "The problem is that when I send Ignored to the Surface to search for portals, they don't come back."

"Whyever not?" Minerva asks.

"We have my sister to thank. The Chosen aren't stupid enough to try and take back this colony *yet*, but they *have* surrounded the colony's circumference as of a week ago."

"An' ya didn' think we should know 'bout this? Jeezus, what if sumone got hurt? 'Nerva an' Ah jus' went up tah th' park yesterday wit' th' kids."

"We're keeping a close eye on the park and all exits. No one's going to get hurt. Besides, you two have done more than enough for our country. I felt that it was none of your concern. After all you two have been through, I couldn't put such a burden on you."

"So why are you asking now?" Minerva asks.

"Because, sadly, I've run out of options. Between the palace and the other colonies the Ignored have occupied, I've spread my forces too thin. The Chosen have us out numbered and out gunned. I'm radioing in support, but I know this will only invite more meaningless bloodshed. This idiotic civil war, this petite squabble for land and resources will doom us all. It needs to end before these mystery aliens decide to strike with something even deadlier than the Feral."

"Whaddya want us tah do?"

"Find my sister. We believe she's taken residence at a luxury hotel not far from Buckingham Palace. I've prepared a peace treaty for her if you agree to go, but I do not know if my words will be enough. To be honest, our best chance of ending this war is *you*, Minerva Henswood."

"Why do you say that?"

Adelia sighs. "Amity *adores* you, Minerva. Amity and I weren't exactly close after she stole the crown from me, but we still talked casually on occasion. She told me that you had top marks in metahuman training academy *and* normal school simultaneously. She was positive that you were the knight with the most potential in the entirety of England."

"I—wow. That is quite flattering." Minerva's blushin', an' now mah blood's boilin'. Ah bite mah tongue tah keep mahself from sayin' sumthin' stupid.

"I was wondering why my sister decided to stay here instead of going to Buckingham Palace. But now that I think about it, she probably stayed because you were here."

She fans at her face, fannin' mah jealously without even knowin' it. "Come to think of it, she *did* ask me if I wanted to switch colonies early on. But I refused to leave. I wasn't going anywhere without Sarah, who wasn't going anywhere without going anywhere without William, who *couldn't* go anywhere because he had just lost his legs. You understand."

"I do. Minerva, you're the best chance we've got at ending this civil war. With the Ignored and Chosen acting as one, we can focus all our efforts on stopping the aliens. Nevertheless, this is *not* an order. You are free to spend the rest of your days here as you wish."

"Queen Adelia, I've come to value you just as much as I do your sister. When I became a knight, I pledged to protect England with my life. Whether you or Amity requests my services, your wish is my command. I will gladly venture to the Surface and deliver your peace treaty to Amity."

Minerva drops tah one knee in frontah a teary eyed Adelia's desk, then looks expectantly at me.

Ah sigh. "Look, aftah spendin' two months here, Ah've come tah realize how Chosen can sit 'round an' relax while people outside are starvin' tah death. It's hard tah care 'bout otha people's problems when yer safe, even if yer happiness is built onnah mountain o' corpses. Ah like tah think Ahmma lil' betta than yer average Chosen. Ah've still got plenty o' sins tah atone fer, anyway." Ah hook mah arm 'round Minerva's, then haul her tah her feet. Ah hold out mah hand in frontah Adelia. "Yeah, Ah'll help 'Nerva reach yer sister, 'slong as they don' fuck when we get there."

Minerva scoffs while Adelia wipes a tear from her face, ignorin' mah hand an' going in fer a hug. "You two are the most selfless individuals I have ever met. Thank you."

We hug her back, an' then let her go. "When do you wish for us to leave?" Minerva asks.

"Ah, whenever you wish. But preferably, by the end of the week."

"How 'bout we jus' leave tahmorrow, sug'?"

"My my, someone's eager."

Ah shrug. "Look, sooner we get this shit ova wit', th' sooner we can come back here an' relax."

"You raise a fair point. I agree to your terms—on one condition."

"Whas' that?"

She whispers in mah ear. Ah get so hot Ah feel like Ah'll melt right through th' floor. Adelia coughs, *loudly*, her face as red as mine feels. "Ahem, yes, well... I'll let you two get right to it." She coughs again, as if coughin' will make this any less awkward.

Ah trytah say sumthin', but Adelia coughs *again*, then sits on her desk an' makes a big deal o' shufflin' through paperwork. Minerva giggles an' drags me outta th' room.

"Ugh, Minerva, why ya gotta do that?"

"Because teasing you makes for brilliant comedy."

Ah roll mah eyes. "Says *you*."

Me an' 'Nerva spend th' res' o' th' day like we would any otha. We finish our latest novel ova breakfast, hit th' gym, train civilians in hand tah hand combat wit' Angel, then have story time wit' th' kids. Aftahwards, we lead 'em up tah th' Surface, then watch 'em play at th' park as th' sun goes down. Sum Ignored stand guard behin' us, sharin' a chat unner th' miraculously clear blue sky. Meanwhile, 'Nerva an' Ah hold hands onnah bench as th' kids push each otha on th' swings or run 'round in circles, excited wit' th' simple pleasure o' *bein'*.

Minerva rests her head 'gainst mine. "Y'know, Ah'm glad we got tah see lil' Timothy smile. He wuz so distraught aftah his mother's death Ah thought we'd neva see it."

"It's good to see *you* smile, dear."

Ah raise an eyebrow. "Ah'm always smilin', right?"

"Doesn't make your smiles any less special." She kisses mah cheek.

"Golly gee, ya sure know howtah make a gal blush," Ah say earnestly. *Huh... dejavu.*

Minerva clears her throat. "Um, Nina. In preparation for... tonight, I was wondering if you'd like to have a glass of wine or two with me during tonight's film?"

"*No.*"

Minerva takes her head off mine tah look me in th' eye, raisin' an eyebrow. "Whyever not?"

"Ah've seen too many o' mah people fuck themselves over cuz o' alcohol. Mah Uncle drank himself tah death, remember? 'Pparently it's a myth that Native Americans are genetically predisposed tah alcoholism, but Ah don' care 'bout that. Ah already promised mah parents Ah'd neva drink a day in mah life durin' mah uncle's funeral, an' Ah'm many things, sug', but Ah ain't a liar."

"I... see. Very well then, it matters not! I do not need alcohol to get in the mood; I merely suggested it so you'd be relaxed during your first time."

Ah *almos'* ask, "How many gals have ya slept wit'?" But then Ah realize that it don' mattah none. 'Nerva couldah slept wit' dozens o' gals fer all Ah care. All that mattahs is that she's wit' me now, an' no one else.

Ah chuckle. "Sug', as beautiful as you are, Ah reckon there ain't no drug that'll keep me calm when Ah see ya in yer birthday suit."

She kisses mah cheek 'gain. "I can hardly wait!"

We watch 'em play fer anotha half hour, then head back inside. We catch a supah lame film alongside everyone else in th' cafeteria. While everyone else is eatin' sandwiches, Pete wuz nice enough tah give us roast chicken wit' broccoli an' carrots on th' side. Itsa great meal fer our last night here—jus' a shame th' movie is so lame. Itsa generic rom-com wit' nuthin' new—same ol' characters, same ol' plot devices an' contrived circumstances. Ah swear, all these romance films are th' same.

'Nerva's cryin' at th' predictable endin', as usual, an' that at least makes me chuckle. Aftah th' film, we help wash dishes fer maybe half an' hour, then retreat intah 'Nerva's rom. At this point, we usually kiss an' cuddle 'till we fall asleep.

Not tahnight.

Ah open th' door an' walk intah our room. Minerva grabs me by th' shoulder an' flips me 'round. "What in th' blu—" She cuts me off wit' a *hard* kiss. Now Ah'm in alien territory. Her kisses are usually gentle, comfortin' pecks o' affection. This one's *hungry*, almos', wit' passion so intoxicatin' Ah'm taken aback. Th' last time she kissed me like this wuz right after we'd met Cornelius, when Ah'd told her she wuz beautiful an' tah stop callin' herself ugly. Back then, we'd been on Th' Surface, an' Ah had tah put a stop tah things or risk us getting' hurt. But there ain't nuthin' stoppin' us now.

A fuse sparks in mah chest. Wheneva Ah'd see people makin' out in films, Ah'd wonder why they'd get all dramatic. One moment they're smoochin' softly, th' next they're down each otha's throats. Now Ah get why. Th' way 'Nerva's kissin' me right now, its gettin' hard tah breathe. But if Ah hadtah choose 'tween oxygen an' Minerva's kisses, Ah'd go wit' th' latter inna heartbeat. Ah'm drownin' in her essence, meltin' intah her. By th' end o' th' night, we'd be One.

Minerva strips off her top an' unclasps her bra so fast she's gotta have set a new record. Seein' her full breasts makes mah heart *pound* an' mah fingers itch. Her nipples look harder than th' great wall o' China.

Jeezus, is this really happenin'? If Ah'm dreamin, God, don' wake me up!

"W-wow," Ah choke.

Minerva blushes so hard Ah'm 'fraid she'll burn herself out. "We're just getting started, dear." She slowly swings her hips 'round, dancin' tah music Ah can't hear. She turns 'round wit' agonizin' slowness, bends ova, spreads her legs, then, uses both thumbs tah reach unnerneath th' damned skirt blockin' mah view. Lacy purple panties slide down acres o' pure, flawlessly sculpted white legs. She kicks 'em off, revealin' a huge wet patch in th' unnerwear's middle. Th' smell o' her arousal hits me like a kick tah th' nose, an' th' fact that her exposed sex lies jus' beyond a thin piece o' fabric drives me ova th' edge. Ah reach out tah lift th' skirt up, but a barrier explodes intah existence an' blocks mah hand.

"Ah-ah-ah!" Minerva coos, standin' tah her full height an' waggin' her index finger, not even turnin' 'round tah look at me. "No touching. Yet." Ah stare at her bare back, burnin' th' image intah mah mind. Its like Ah'm lookin' at a movin' work o' art. *Hey, that sounds kinda romantic!* Ah open mah mouth tah say jus' that, but then Minerva makes mah heart stop. She slowly lifts th' skirt up, jus' barely givin' me a glimpse o' her sex 'fore th' skirt hides it once mo'. If Ah weren't wet before, now Ah'm drenched.

"Y'know, Ah didn' fall fer ya *jus'* cuz you've gotta beautiful heart."

"Oh?" Minerva asks, struttin' towards me wit' th' walk that she must've mastered on th' catwalk. When she reaches me, she wraps her arms 'round mah neck an' assaults me wit' a kiss so good mah head spins.

"Yeah," Ah say, wrappin' mah arms 'round her waist. It's funny, as good as her boobs look, Ah can't tear mah eyes away from hers. "It's also cuz yer sexy as fuck."

Minerva flashes me that magic smile. "Alright now, no more talking!" She grabs mah shirt wit' both hands, an' wit' a mighty yell, rips th' damn thing in half.

"H-holy shit!" Ah cry as she unclasps mah bra, pushin' me back towards th' bed wit' kisses. She pushes me ontah it once mah bra's off. Feelin' mah naked back on th' soft sheets makes me shiver. Minerva collapses on tahppa me. She kisses mah neck, caressin' mah breasts at th' same time, which feels *good*, but it *shouldn't*, cuz

Ah'm surrounded by men an' there's fingers on me an' *in* me an Ah'm bleedin' *down there* an' Ah'm drownin' Ah'm drownin' Ah'm—

"*Stop!*" Ah cry, voice cracked. Minerva pulls back, horrified. What th' fuck? Am Ah in th' hotel room, or am Ah wit' Minerva? Whas' happenin' tah me? Why am Ah cryin'?

"Are you alright?" Minerva asks, bless her soul. She strokes mah face, brushin' tears away wit' her thumb, jus' like she did when Ah told her how much Ah missed Lucio. Then those men—

Mah entire body shivers. Minerva pulls her hand back but its not her fault its not her fault its not her fault she can touch me Ah swear Ah *want* her tah touch me cuz *Ah love her* but she *can't* touch me cuz Ah'm *filthy* an'—

Ah hug mahself, tryin' tah pull mahself tahgetha as mah brain rips itself in two. This wuz supposed tah be a special moment 'tween jus' us, an' Ah'm thinkin' 'bout sumthin' that happened months ago.

"Ah dunno, Minerva. Ah dunno."

Chapter 27

YOU DON'T *HAVE* to go to the Surface, you know." Ah crack open an eye. Ah'm lyin' on Minerva's shoulder. Her eye bags are darker than black. She constantly wraps an' unwraps her finger 'round mah hair, starin' at me like Ah've gotta terminal illness.

"Why wouldn' Ah wanna go?" Ah croak.

Her eyes flash so bright Ah'm fully awake now. "Must I really say why not?"

Couldn't perform one time (but what if) *an' she's already givin' me shit!* "Maybe ya do!"

Minerva stops playin' wit' mah hair, bitin' her quiverin' bottom lip. Ah sigh. "OK, OK, truce," she says. Ah sigh again, right 'fore a surge o' rage rushes through me. *Why do we even gotta have this conversation? Why couldn't Ah make love tah her?* "Wh-who th' hell are ya gonna take wit'cha anyway!"

"I do not know," Minerva says somberly. "Angel, maybe."

"Ah don' trust her," Ah growl. Minerva raises an eyebrow. Ah wave mah hand. "Don' get me wrong, Angel's mah friend an' Ah trust her not tah, y'know, make a move or anythin', but Ah don' trust her tah keep ya safe. Not up there." Ah take inna shaky breath, grabbin' her hand.

"Ya dunno how much Ah care 'bout ya, sug'. If anythin' happened tah ya, Ah couldn't..." Ah take inna breath that don' begin tah fill mah lungs. Minerva clasps her hands 'round mine, an' mah broken soul becomes whole again. "M-Minerva, ya gotta know that Ah *wanted* ya last night. A—Ah didn' freak out 'cuz we were movin' too fast, or 'cuz Ah wuzn't ready, or *anythin'* like that. It weren't yer fault, OK?"

Minerva sighs. "I am aware that it was not I who subjected you to such horrors."

"Ah dunno, sum o' yer books are pretty horrifyin'," Ah say, nudgin' her side.

Minerva frowns. "I'm serious. The fact that it was my loving touch that brought back such an awful memory makes me feel so guilty it physically hurts." She's holdin' a clenched fist tah her chest an' hangin' her head.

Ah tuck a loose strain o' her soft hair behin' an ear. "Well, don' be baby! If anyone should feel bad, it would be me. Last night couldah been really special. An' Ah fucked it all up." Ah bite mah bottom lip. "Ah'm sorry, sug'. Ah wanted tah make love wit'cha. Ah wuzn't strong enough tah ferget."

"Maybe that's part of the problem, dear. You want to forget what happened to you, but those events are burned into your subconscious." She chews her bottom lip, makin' that face she makes when th' gears in her head start whirlin'. "You've only had these flashbacks twice so far—once the day after it happened, and of course last night. The first time it happened, you said you flashed back because you remembered not being able to see the people touching you. And last night, you must have flashed back because I touched you the same place they touched you.

"Nina, you are living proof that time does not heal all wounds. If we don't tackle this issue head on, years can go by," (but what if) "and we still won't be able to reach the next level in our relationship. You—a-and I," she chokes, "must accept the fact that you were sexually assaulted. We can't pretend it didn't happen anymore. Maybe once we digest the truth, we can finally move on with our lives."

Fer a split secon', Ah trytah think back on that night at th' hotel.

Next thing Ah know, Ah'm inna fetal position, an' Minerva's curled up 'round me like she's a mouse an' Ah'm cheese. Ah'm shakin' all ova, sweatin' like a hog, but inhalin' her flowery scent makes mah heart finally slow down. "A-Ah don' think Ah'm ready."

"Hey," Minerva says sternly. She grabs mah chin wit' those perfect little fingers, tiltin' mah head up so Ah gotta look her in th' eye. "As usual, you are not treating yourself fairly. The expectations you hold for yourself are charming, but still ridiculous. You cannot expect to recover from being molested in only two months, and come to think of it, neither should I. I shouldn't have pressured you into making love so soon, knowing you were still dealing with this issue." She looks at me like she's a bitch an' Ah'mma fat, juicy steak, an' then kisses mah cheek. "That said, one cannot fault me for being eager."

Ah chuckle! How can she make me laugh when Ah couldn't breathe an' Ah'm surrounded fingers everywhere—Ah shake mah head, erasin' th' past wit' th' smile 'Nerva gave me. "Stop flatterin' me."

"Never." She kisses mah cheek again. "You have to realize, dear, that this whole situation is not your fault. Not one bit."

Ah dunno why, but Ah start tearin' up. *Gah, this gal has made me such a sap.* "Ah guess a part o' me feels responsible fer it. If Ah hadn't lead us intah th' hotel—"

"Do you remember *why* you were so adamant on going to the hotel?"

"... Ah think Ah wuz feelin' really tired."

"You lost a lot of blood that day," Minerva says, grabbing my scarred arm with one hand and stroking it with the other. Ah got that scar savin' her life from th' Feral. "How can you blame yourself for wanting to sleep in a bed? You didn't will those people to come into our room and assault you. Those people made an awful decision, and that decision has nothing do with us being there. It's not your fault, Nina."

Ah keep repeatin' her words tah mahself ova an' ova again in mah head (not yer fault), 'till Ah hopefully actually startah believe it. "You said before that Ah couldn't be 'xpected tah recover from bein' molested in two months. What happened tah th' whole, 'time doesn't heal all wounds' bit? If that weren't th' case then why does it mattah how much time passed?"

"Well, the phrase is still true, but that doesn't mean time can't *help* heal the wound whatsoever. If we compare your mental anguish to a physical injury—let's say being molested is like being stabbed in the stomach." Ah nod. "Right now, accepting the truth will be like giving you a blood transfusion, while time slowly slaps a... a really big band-aid on the hole in your stomach so you don't bleed out."

Ah manage tah crack a grin. "A really big band-aid?"

"Forgive me, dear, it's early in the morning. That said, this whole talk has only further illustrated why I can't let you get hurt again. I refuse to allow it! Stay here, where it's safe. *Please.*"

"*No.* Ah'm comin' wit'cha, like it or not."

Minerva scowls, an' suddenly th' sweet angel Ah'm spoonin' turns intah an angry demon. She sits up an' bellows, "This is *unacceptable.* Do you not trust me to complete this quest? Do you really think I will let *anything* prevent me from coming back to you? A hundred Feral, a million metahumans—I'd cut through them all to see your face again. I *won't* die, and you *will not* accompany me." She clasps her hands 'round her face. "You looked so *broken* last night, Nina. For a moment, you looked like you were having the time of your life."

"Ah wuz," Ah whisper.

"The next, indescribable pain washes across your face. D-do you know what it's like to see someone you love go through so much suffering?"

Ah think o' Lucio's face as he starved tah death. "Yeah," Ah say softly.

"Then you know exactly why I'm not letting you go."

"Thas' really sweet, 'Nerva. Really. Butcha can't stop me from goin' wit'cha." Ah smile at her as Ah say this, but she ain't smilin' back. She gets this weird look in her eye, an' then *leaps* off th' bed. In that split secon', Ah realize exactly what she thought: *I can.*

Ah roll outta bed right as sumthin' hard smacks th' spot Ah jus' lay. Ah catch mah fall on th' floor, then spring tah mah feet. Minerva's disappeared.

"What th' hell do ya think yer doin', sug'?" As Ah say this, Ah back mahself against th' wall, eyes bouncin' 'round everywhere.

Ah've gone intah huntin' mode, jus' like Ah did th' first time we fought. Jus' 'cuz Minerva's invisible don' mean she can't be found.

A sock moves a centimeter, so Ah flash forward. Ah barrel intah th' invisible woman, smashin' through her barrier like its paper machete. We hit th' ground, but Ah'm on tahppah her. Ah grab her wrists an' pin her arms down. Minerva's fierce, fast, an' a metahuman wit' incredible power. But Ah grew up onnah farm liftin' shit all day so Ah'm stronger than her. Funny how far hard work can take ya, huh?

"Pa taught me everything there is tah know 'bout huntin', sug'."

She struggles against me, tryin' tah raise her hands, but it's no use. Ah keep her arms in place, jus' smilin' down on at her. She's neva looked mo' adorable. While she wuz consolin' me, her eyes were gentle an' soothin', like moonlight reflected in sapphire. Now that she's all determined an' pissed, it looks like a tsunami has formed in her eyes. Ah lean in, close mah eyes, an' kiss her deeply. Th' fight in her limbs dies almos' immediately. When we break apart, her lips are pursed, as if she jus' got through sayin', "Wow," an' her eyes are still as th' ocean.

Y'know, Ah'm not so good wit' words. But seein' 'Nerva like that, as beautiful as eva, made mah heart swell. Mah whole relationship wit' her goes sumthin' like this—Ah'mma deflated balloon, see, an' she's helium. So she's been fillin' me up eva since we met, an' Ah jus' now popped. "Ya wanna know why Ah'm goin' tah Hell wit'cha? Nuthin' up there can hurt me as much as bein' apart from you will. Ah love you, Minerva." Her face keeps th' exact same expression, lookin' so beautiful it hurts; only now tears are streamin' down her face. Ah kiss th' tears away wit' a smile. "So what time do ya wanna leave?"

Chapter 28

AH HEAR 'NERVA step outta th' shower while Ah put onnah long sleeve orange shirt, thena thick brown jacket. Y'know what Ah think is funny," Ah ask her, hopin' mah voice bursts through th' walls seperatin' us.

"What's that, dear?"

Ah slip intah a battered pair o' jeans Ah borrowed froma sparrin' partner, then strap on mah tool belt, already packed wit' weapons an' anti-Feral grenades. "Yer barriers are strong enough tah reflect bullets. But fer sum reason, Ah can break through 'em. Why is that?"

Minerva steps outta th' bathroom, a cloud o' steam envelopin' her curvy figure in fog. She's wearin' anotha purple jumpsuit, though this one is insulated an' has thick white lines goin' down her arms an' legs. Her sword is attatched tah her waist by holster. "I do not know."

"Ah think Ah do." Ah tuck her wet, short curly hair behin' an ear, an' then tap her temple. "It's yer *will*. When yer deflectin' bullets, ya know you've gotta put a lotta energy intah th' barrier, cuz, y'know, itsa *bullet* an' no one wants tah get shot. But if Ah come atcha wit' a punch, ya don' put as much effort intah th' barrier."

"I *suppose* that's true," Minerva says, cradlin' her chin wit' her thumb an' index finger.

"Not convinced? Th' one time Ah couldn't break yer barrier wuz when Ah had a knife tah yer throat."

Minerva shudders. "That was the scariest moment of my life until we met Lucy."

Hearin' Lucy's name makes *me* shudder, but Ah shake it off. "Butcha stopped me, remember? Yer barrier wuz so strong mah knife shattered."

"That's absolutely true," Minerva says, examinin' her fingernails.

Ah roll mah eyes wit' a chuckle, then ask, "Come tah think o' it, when didcha realize ya could make barriers? Ah swear ya told me at first all ya could do wuz turn invisible."

"Correct. Actually, I believe I only found I out could create barriers the day before I met you."

"Intrestin'... *whoa, wait a secon'.*" Ah plop down on th' carpet, sittin' cross legged wit' mah arms crossed.

"... What—"

Ah hollup mah palm. "Wait a sec, Ah'm thinkin' o' sumthin' *huge.*" Ah squint mah eyes, then cross mah arms closa tahgetha. *If Minerva could turn invisible first, what does that mean? Don' it mean sumthin'? Ah know it does. C'mon dumb brain, work.*

Ah pop off th' ground, smilin' so hard mah lips are sore. "So y'know what that means, right?"

"What?"

"Yer powers ain't invisibility, it's usin' barriers tah make yerself invisible, or tah defend yerself, or *who knows what else!* You can do *anythin',* sug'."

Ah kiss her cheek an' bring her in fer a hug, but when Ah've pulled away she's frownin' hard. "I make for one pathetic knight."

Ah frown back. "Ah *don'* agree. Why're ya talkin' nonsense all o' a sudden?"

"You've spent more time thinking about my powers than I have. I spent the last two months improving my swordsman ship, cooking and make-up skills, neglecting the one thing that makes me special these days. If *you* had my powers, you'd make a better knight!"

"Now you stop right there missy. Yer powers don' make ya special, an' yer looks don' either. Th' thing that makes you special, th' thing that makes ya beautiful, is yer heart. 'Sides, Ah don' want powers anyway, so if Ah had 'em Ah doubt Ah would use 'em."

"It's not often I catch you in the midst of a lie, Nina," Minerva coos. "Though I do appreciate your flattery."

Mah face burns. "OK OK, ya got me. Ah really don' want powers, but if Ah had 'em yer damn right Ah'd use 'em!"

"Whyever would you not want powers, though?"

"'Cuz they make ya complacent. Ah've fought at least a dozen metahuman by this point, an' ain't one o' 'em, 'sides you an'—" Ah shudder again, "*Lucy*, have beat me inna fight."

"That's more metahuman than *I've* fought! I never realized how much happened to you that year on the Surface."

Ah shrug. "Powers make people cocky. Lotta metahumans think they're betta than everyone else, so when they see a Normal they don' 'xpect much o' a fight. By th' time they realize they need tah fight serious, Ah've already got mah foot in their face."

"But you've fought Angel and the other knights plenty of times, and they never win. How do you do it without powers?"

"Shoot, ain't nuthin' to it sug'. Once Ah see a power, Allsah gotta do is think 'bout how Ah can use it 'gainst 'em tah win. Th' only problem is when yer fightin' a metahuman fer th' first time, 'cuz ya dunno what they can do. Lucy whooped our ass 'cuz we'd neva seen anythin' like her. If we ran intah sumone like her again who actually took us serious from th' onset, well, we'd definitely be in trouble."

Minerva shakes her head. "I disagree." She closes th' gap 'tween us an' holds me so tight Ah can't really breathe. Ah smile anyway. "You know what I love about you?"

"Mah fat ass?"

She pulls away jus' in time fer me tah see her cool smile. "That goes without saying, dear. No, what I love about you is your drive. When you fight, you use absolutely everything in your power to win. I've let my metahuman abilities make me complacent, but you can't afford to. You are constantly pushing yourself to the limit." She stands up, sapphires steelin' 'fore my eyes. "The next time I engage in battle, I pledge to fight with newfound vigor. I won't let you, Amity, Adelia or *myself* down. I greatly appreciate the advice, dear, I shan't let your words of wisdom be wasted!"

"Minerva?"

"Yes, dear?"

"Ya don' gotta be so dramatic."

X X X

'Nerva an' Ah sit in Adelia's office, holdin' hands. Adelia sits behin' her desk, restin' her chin onnah bridge she made wit' th' back o' her hands. Her smile is happy, but curious. "You two seem... different."

"Different how?" Ah ask.

"It's hard to put my finger on it. It's a good different, though! You both look ready for anything."

"Long as this gal's by mah side, there ain't nuthin' Ah can't handle."

Minerva looks down, flushin' as she gives mah hand a reassurin' squeeze.

"That's great to hear!" Adelia says. "I'm confident the two of you will make it back safely." She coughs intah her fist. "Um, speaking of your Quest. On the subject of transportation... Cornelius's car doesn't work anymore."

Ah facepalm. "God damn it, its th' starter, ain't it?" Adelia nods. "Th' ol' fart told me he started it every once an' a while tah keep it runnin', bless his soul. Shouldah took that advice."

"Do you have a vehicle you could loan us for the journey ahead?" Minerva asks.

"Unfortunately, I do not. However, when I was asking around the colony for assistance, someone volunteered their vehicle."

"My my, that's quite generous of them! Whom do we have to thank?" Minerva asks.

Adelia opens her mouth to respond, but there's a knock on th' door. "Um... I suppose it's too late for introductions at this point." She looks at me like Ah jus' told her mah dog died. "This is going to feel sudden, you two, but please remember that this man volunteered his services and is expecting nothing in return. Please, do not act rashly."

Ah look at Minerva in confusion, but she looks jus' as baffled. Sumone knocks on th' door, makin' Adelia sigh. "Come in, Zack."

What.

Th' door opens, an' there he is. His shoulders are straight an' he keeps his head held high wit' a bashful smile. He looks like a jolly pirate.

Th' band-aid on his hand ain't there no mo'. Ah stare at th' hand wit' no pinky, shudderin' as Ah remember th' exact moment Ah blew it off. Ah can see his eyes slammin' shut as blood bursts from th' wound, feel th' bits o' blood an' bone splatter mah clothes, can hear his agonizin' scream. Ah'm boutah flip shit when Minerva starts rubbin' her thumb in circles on mah palm. Th' warm sensation pries me outta fear's cold grip, yankin' me outta th' past an' throwin' me intah a place Ah don' even unnerstan'. "Why are you here?"

He looks at me wit' his one brown eye. Ah can't tell what th' hell he's thinkin'. "I owe you an apology." Ah stare at him, lookin' fer th' slightest sign he's lyin'. But so far, so good. "Let me," he takes a breath, "let me tell you about myself."

Ah see mah brother's face, an' Ah'm jus' 'boutah give him what fer, but Minerva's holdin' mah hand an' doin' that circle thing an' Adelia's watchin' so Ah jus' set mah jaw an' brace mahself fer a whole lotta bullshit. He takes a deep breath, then says, "My wife Kyra and I spent years saving up for this brilliant house." He leans back agiant th' door, eyes driftin' tah th' ceilin'. "We had a garden in the backyard, which Kyra loved. She planted apple and orange trees, and just about every morning we'd have fruit salad for breakfast. I built my little girl, Sophie, her own playground set, so she'd bring her friends over and they'd run around and play and..." He sighs again, shakin' his head.

A wave o' guilt washes ova me, but Ah hide mah feelings behin' a scowl. "Ugh, where was I going with this?" He snaps his fingers. "Right. So, when the aliens invaded we had to leave our home and come here. I felt so damn worthless, like I wasn't a man. I couldn't protect the home we worked so hard for, couldn't protect my daughter's smile. I pushed my family away when they needed me most, all because of my insecurity. Before I could fall into depression, Queen Amity offered me a job."

"Ya really gonna call killin' people an' stealin' their stuff a job?" Ah cry.

Zack raises his hands. "Hey, that's the way she presented it. I knew what I was doing was wrong, but I really did think I was helping the colony. Her Majesty herself offered me something I perceived to be meaningful when I felt the most useless. So I took the job. And I admit it, I had fun."

Ah nod, rememberin' how he talked tah his pardners when they shot a couple at th' science museum. "Ah know how you feel 'bout killin' people, an' Ah'm glad yer honest 'bout it an' all, but Ah don' see why yer tellin' me all this. What're ya tryin' tah accomplish?"

Zack scratches unnerneath his eye patch. "I don't know. I suppose I want you to sympathize with me. Thought we'd share some common ground."

"Ah ain't nuthin' like you!"

"Are you sure about that? Tell me you didn't enjoy killing Chosen. Tell me you didn't enjoy torturing me."

"Sure it felt good when Ah wuz doin' it. But now Ah've got nightmares out th' ass jus' thinkin' 'bout all th' people Ah killed. Ah feel terrible a lotta th' time, would be worse if Ah didn' have this here angel lookin' aftah me."

'Nerva smiles at me while Zack says, "Whose to say I don't feel the same way? When I built that bike and put on that helmet, I wasn't Zack anymore. I was a *warrior* doing Her Majesty's dirty work. When you attacked the colony, I bet you wore the helmet too."

"So what Ah wore a helmet! What does that prove?"

"Wearing a helmet or a mask whilst committing terrible deeds is kind of like creating your own separate persona to put the weight of your crimes on," Minerva says.

"Ah don' get it," Ah drawl even though Ah definitely do. Ah'd read 'bout this in a psychology book, but they didn' know that.

"When I first met you, I thought of you as 'Killer'. When I knocked Zack's helmet off, you became 'Stranger'. Make sense now?"

"Eenope."

Minerva scoffs, an' outta th' corner o' mah eye Ah see Adelia smilin' wit' a shake o' her head.

"Face it," Zack says, "We're more alike than you say."

Ah guess mah *mask ain't foolin' no one here.* "So what if we are!" Ah snap. "Ya think Ah'll fergive ya jus' cuz o' that?"

"I'm not here for forgiveness. I'm here for atonement."

He reaches intah his pocket. Ah leap up, hand flashin' tah mah tool belt. He plucks outta black key, an' then tosses it at me. Ah catch it, then sit back down wit' a blush. "Uh, whas' this fer?"

Zack's glare moves from me tah Adelia. "Wait a second, didn't Her Majesty tell you why I'm here?"

Ah resist th' urge tah glare at her too. "Well, she mentioned that sumone had volunteered a ve-hicle fer us, but seein' ya kinda made me ferget why Ah wuz even here in th' first place." Ah turn tah Adelia. "Don'cha think ya couldah handled this a lil' betta?"

She flushes. "My apologies. Zack knocked on the door right as I was about to explain things, and I thought it rude to keep a man doing us such a monumental favor waiting."

"Did he really," Ah ask, "or didcha jus' wanna see how things would play out without yer interference?"

She coughs intah her palm. "I see your bullshit detector hasn't lost its touch."

"Yers neither," Ah say, winkin' at her. Ah turn back tah Zack. "Looks like Ah misunnerstood yer intentions. Fer you tah show such generosity aftah all Ah've done tah ya... Ah 'ppreciate it. Really. An'..." *Yer beautiful, sis.* Ah take inna deep, shaky breath, an' then let it out. Then, graspin' Minerva's hand, Ah let it go. "Ah'm sorry 'bout everything. 'Bout tourtin' ya. 'Bout killin' yer kin. 'Bout tellin' ya tah kill yerself. Ah'm sorry."

Sumthin' ripples 'cross Zack's face. Anger? Resentment? Relief? Whateva it wuz, he hides it behin' a convincin' smile, then says, "I really was going to kill myself, you know. But Minerva saved my life and convinced me I had something else to live for."

"And what, pray tell *is* that purpose?" Minerva asks wit' a gentle smile.

Zack licks his lips, "I... haven't decided yet. But whatever I do, I won't be able to do it if I'm dead."

Ah narrow mah eyes. Why wuz he lyin' all o' a sudden? He meets mah eye, then looks away. Ah'm boutah ask why he's actin' fishy, then Ah shake mah head. How am Ah gonna grill th' guy whose givin' us a free ride?

He coughs a bit. "Well, my work here is done. But before I leave, I want to make one thing clear. Like I said, I'm not here for forgiveness. And I'm not here to forgive either."

Ah nod. "... Maybe we ain't so different aftah all."

"I can only hope that my gift to you helps Her Majesty in some way." He briefly drops tah one knee, then bows an' leaves th' room.

Ah turn tah Minerva. "Well, Ah'll be damned. Looks like yer generosity paid off."

"I'm just glad he is alive and not hurting anyone," Minerva says. "That is more than enough pay off for me."

Adelia smiles. "As usual, I can see why Amity was so fond of you."

Minerva blushes while Ah roll mah eyes. Adelia clears her throat. "Ladies, this is your *final* chance to back out. Are you positively sure you're up for this?"

'Nerva an' Ah nod in unison. "Les' jus' get this ova wit'."

Adelia nods grimly, then hands us a map, a radio, an' a golden sealed envelope. "I've traced a route from here directly to Amity's colony. Shouldn't take more than a few days at most. Use the radio to contact me at least once every 24 hours. If you don't, I will assume something happened to you two and will assemble an assault team immediately."

Ah nod, but Minerva shakes her head. "That sounds incredibly foolish, Adelia. What happens if the radio breaks, or we lose it, or something of that nature? You musn't be rash."

Adelia crosses her arms. "Well, how am I supposed to know if my friends need help?"

"Trust that we won't need it. We survived our last journey together, just the two of us. If you send Ignored to attack Chosen, you'll just make the fighting worse, and we'll be one step closer to an all-out war. Worst case scenario, Nina and I die on the Surface. All you have to do is call back every Ignored you have at your disposal and send them back here. That way, you'll best be prepared to defend yourself when Amity retaliates."

"Sure, but my best friends will be *dead*." Ah purse mah lips, heart heavy. "Everyone here treats me like a Queen. You two are the only ones who treat me like a person. I refuse to let you two get hurt up there, especially on my orders."

"We'll be *fine*," Ah say, but Ah might as well be lyin'. Ah'm still not 'fine' aftah our last adventure, an' that wuz months ago. Adelia glares at me, which Ah guess is her way o' tellin' me tah shut up. It works.

"You *better* be. If Amity's troops so much as scratch you two, she won't be the one to start the war."

ina and I walk hand and hand to the colony's exit. We say our goodbyes to friends and acquaintances on our way out. They look at us as if we're on our way to the electric chair, but I'm not afraid. I can't be.

Once we reach the entrance, I use my hand to cover my mouth.

Oh, my.

The children we've baby sat for the past two months are all standing at the exit, alongside Angel, Pete and Chinwei. A banner is drawn across the top of the door, and on it reads: "We love you, Nina and Minerva!" alongside crudely drawn versions of ourselves holding hands. Dozens of little red hearts cover the edges of the banner, and healthy doses of glitter ensure that every eye in its proximity is ensnared in its flashy trap. I place a hand over my thriving heart, smiling at the little ones.

"Alright, who planned this," Nina asks with a smile so bright it almost hurts to look at.

"No one in particular," Chinwei says, though she keeps darting her eyes in Pete's direction. I turn to thank the gentleman, but he's holding a cake that looks so delicious my mouth salivates at an unprecedented level. When I met his eye, he winks at me, and I wonder how in the bloody hell he discovered my secret weakness—caramel. Someone taps me on the shoulder. I turn around to see Adelia's smiling face, a party popper between her lips.

After a far too brief hour of tea, cake, and fun, Nina claps her hand on my shoulder. "We stay here any longer, an' Ah ain't goin' nowhere."

I nod at her, then start the goodbye process once more. Little Timothy approaches me, his head hung. "Will I ever see you again?"

I see a room full of corpses and a little girl with tight blue skin licking her blood-stained lips. "Of course, dear," I say, the lie burning the back of my throat. I'm not sure if I'm being confident for his benefit, or mine.

Timothy's tiny nose scrunches up and he runs off, leaving me frowning at his back until he disappears around a corner. I suppose his late mother once wore the same mask I'm wearing now.

I consider following him, but Angel steps into my path. "Are you sure I can't come with you two? You know I'm an asset in battle."

"I'm aware. However, should we fail and Amity foolishly attacks the colony, Adelia will need all the help she can get. Besides, three people will attract even more Feral to us, and we only have so many grenades. Also, I don't think I can keep three people invisible for long. Aside from that—"

Angel cuts me off with a laugh. "Alright, alright! I can see I'm not wanted."

"Angel, dear—"

"Relax, I'm just teasing. Come here." She opens her arms. I walk forward and we embrace. This time, I don't feel the suffocating hold that alludes to unfulfilled desires. Instead, I feel the simple warmth of a worried friend.

She pulls away with a sad smile. "Please, stay safe."

"I... I will try my best."

Chapter 29

*A*h'm drivin', an' thas' final!"

I smile. *"If you insist, dear."* Works every time.

Nina sits on the bike, and I slide in behind her. I wrap mah arms around her waist, and then smile into her back. It's cold out, and although my jumpsuit is keeping me warm, Nina's touch is always welcome. "You know, as intimidating as Zack's previous bike was, I much prefer its aesthetic design. It had *quite* the personality. This one is... pretty bland."

The motorcycle is a beat-up, dusty old thing, with a color that frankly looks like dried fecal matter.

"Now don' look a gift horse in th' mouth, sug'." *She presses hard on the gas, and then yells,* "Ya feel that? This baby might not look th' part, but it's jus' as fast as th' last one. Zack didn' fuck us ova, thas' fer sure."

I tighten my grip on Nina, and then turn us invisible. While I can no longer see Nina, the bike is still visible. I frown, and then close my eyes. I imagine a circle expanding from my very core, growing larger until it envelops the motorcycle below us.

When I open my eyes, we're completely invisible, save for the trail of dust spilling behind us. "Really, dear," *I say, trying to sounds casual while yelling,* "you musn't be so loud. Remember, there are supposed to be Chosen somewhere around here."

"Yer right, Ah'm sorry! Jus' got ova excited is all."

"Not a problem, dear." *My eyes narrow as Nina passes up a turn.* "Where are we going? You were supposed to take a right back there..."

"Ah know, sug'. Ah'm takin' ya sumwhere special first."

"I—alright then!"

Where could we possibly be going? I can't think of a plausible dating spot in a nuclear wasteland.

I watch the destroyed landscape blur by with great disinterest. All you can see for miles on end is a cloudy grey sky, brown, scrap, brown, a decayed corpse or two, brown, brown, brown. I sigh. Mother Nature could really use an exterior designer.

I blink. "Um, Nina?"

"Whassup sug'?"

"Do you believe in God?"

"Ah... dunno anymo'."

"But you used to?"

"Yeah. Then my whole family died an' Ah fell in love wit' a woman."

I yell over the wind, "What does your sexual orientation have to do with believing in God?"

"Well, Ah guess it don', but it sure as hell goes 'gainst mah faith. Ah grew up goin' tah a Christian church, an' now Ah'm a day tah day sinner who couldn't be happier."

"But how is loving me a sin?" I cry. "What makes our love any different?"

"Nuthin', really. But we can't reproduce, so Ah guess th' Bible counts our relationship as a sin?"

"But some heterosexual couples are unable to reproduce as well. Does that make their relationship sinful too?"

"Yes? No? Ah dunno sug', Ah don' really get th' Bible's logic mahself. What 'bout you?"

"I also do not know."

"What 'bout before all this?"

"I was an atheist. Never thought our existence was anything more than an incredible coincidence."

"So what changed?"

"You know the answer to this," I shout with a smile. "I met you."

The statement hangs in the air, then Nina hollers, "Hold on tight!" She pulls back hard on the handlebars. I cry out, losing my concentration. We're visible now, and I see the front wheel pop off the pavement and go skyward. My stomach bounces on the trampoline that is my lower intestines, then does a triple front flip as it launches itself right into my esophagus. From my peripheral vision, I see a group of blurry men emerging from a collapsed building, riding by on horses. One of them points to us, and another raises a rifle.

The bike's front wheel hits the pavement with a screech. Nina stomps on the gas right as a thunderclap nearly ruptures my ear drum. A bullet whizzes by us, but before they can fire again we're invisible. I can hear them cursing all the way from here, but another building passes between us and we lose eye contact. We say nothing for a minute or two, just in case we're being followed. Once I'm sure they're out of earshot, I explode.

"What on Earth were you thinking, dear? You could have gotten us both killed!"

Nina chuckles. Well, I suppose I cannot *hear* her chuckle because of the wind rushing past my ears, but I can feel her stomach and ribs vibrate, which is just as good.

"Yeah, Ah'm mighty sorry 'bout that. Didn' see those fellers. Wuz tryin' tah be romantic is all."

"And *what*, pray tell, is *romantic* about doing a *wheelie* on a *cracked* road going *80 miles per hour*?"

Nina chuckles, *again*. "Yeah, that wuz pretty stupid. Ah dunno, sug'... but it wuz fun, right?"

I sigh as loudly as humanly possible. "I *suppose* it would have been *somewhat* enjoyable if we hadn't gotten shot at."

"Y'know that feelin' ya get when yer stomach flips, like when yer onnah roller coaster ride or doin' a wheelie at 80 miles an hour?"

"Ah, yes, the feeling of imminent death. *Quite* romantic."

"Heh, haven't seen ya this pissed inna while! But, well, what Ah'm tryin' tah say is..." she sighs, "When Ah see yer smile, when Ah hear yer laugh, everytime we kiss... Ah get that feelin'. I-inna good way, o' course. So, uh, thanks fer th', y'know, makin' ya wanna believe in God thing."

"Oh, *Nina*," I squeal, hugging her tight, "That was quite romantic. Although I must admit the roller coaster analogy would have been sufficient."

"Haha, yeah. Anyways, we're here."

We park a little ways away from a metro station's entrance, still invisible. There are two Feral in sight, so I spurt us with perfume just in case they catch our scent. One is an adult, closely inspecting one of the two skulls on a stick at the entrance. It nibbles on the skull from all angles, but there's not a scrap of flesh to be found. The adult looks at the child next to it in what must be pity.

The child lies sprawled across the dirt, its long, dry tongue sticking out and its little chest heaving. The poor thing coughs, once, twice, and then has a croaking fit so fierce its entire body shakes. Then it goes still.

The remaining Feral shakes the little one's corpse, hard, but gets no response. It leaps to its feet, clicking furiously. It grabs both skulls and then smashes them against its own head. The skulls explode into dust as it collapses to the dirt, mumbling in a language I can't understand but can hear the sorrow in. Making whimpers so pathetic my heart sinks, it grabs ahold of the dead child's claw, exposes its throat, then—

I look away, but I can still hear the Feral chocking on its own body fluids. Nina jumps off the bike, unstraps her bow from the headrest then rushes over. I blink, then dart to her side, reaching her just in time to see two arrows go straight into the Feral's brain. When the creature goes still, she sighs with relief, then, after a few strong pulls, lurches the bloody arrows out of its forehead. She wipes the arrows off in the dirt, and then sticks them back in her quiver. When she turns to me, her face is stained with tears.

"When Lucio died, Ah thought Amity wuz th' mos' evil person in existence. How could she let mah brother starve tah death? What did we eva do tah her? But then, when Ah wuz lookin' at th' food cellar unnerground, Ah kinda got where she wuz comin' from. Ah mean, Ah still hate her guts, but Ah unnerstan' why she shut us out. There really ain't enough resources fer th' whole country tah share.

"Then, when we saw Dr. Light's lil' video, Ah thought, OK, now *this* guy is evil. Experimentin' on aliens y'know are innocent, experimentin' on yer own god damn daughter, how do ya get worse than that?" She sighs. "Ah couldn't wrap mah head 'round it, so Ah rewatched th' video a couple o' times."

"How could you bear witness to such awful events a second time?"

"Ah wuz too damn curious tah be scared." She wipes her eyes. "Ah don' unnerstan' people. An' Ah wanna. So, uh… God damn, where th' hell wuz Ah goin' wit' this," she asks with a sniffle.

"You were telling me about Dr. Light," I say, grabbing her hands. I smile at her, even though what we just saw makes me want to go back home already. Nina lets out a sigh, then faces me with a smile.

"Thanks sug'. So, uh… when Ah rewatched th' video, Ah started tah feel fer th' bastard. Queen Amity threw an entire nation's survival on Dr. Light and his team. If they couldn't find a way tah stop th' Feral, we would all be fucked. Ah ain't gonna say Dr. Light ain't a piece o' shit, but… th' piece o' shit loved his daughter. He jus' chose tah save th' world ova savin' Lucy. Reckon he's one o' 'em self-sacrificin' hero-types, like Samurai Kid."

I nod, understanding where she was coming from, but not quite sensing the point of the matter. The blood underneath us is oozing towards my shoes, so I lead us back towards the bike.

"Ah'm sayin' all o' this tah tell ya that Ah unnerstan' that sumtimes good people do terrible things when th' world pushes 'em intah a corner. But whoeva th' hell did this," she says, points at the corpses behind us, "ain't gotta soul. We gotta stop these bastards, Minerva. Fer us, *an'fer th' Feral.*"

"I absolutely agree, darling. I absolutely agree."

We stand there for a moment, holding hands while the Feral's corpse twitches underneath us. I shudder, thinking about how close Nina came to suffering the same fate.

With another sigh, Nina stops moving. She tugs at my hand, leading us back towards the figurative and literally bloody metro stations. This horrid place is sending hellish chills down my spine!

"C'mon, sug'. Ah got sumone Ah want ya tah meet."

She guides me past the Feral corpses and down the metro station. As my world slowly shifts from desolate brown to absolute blackness, a thought comes to mind. "Those skulls at the entrance... Am I right to believe they were all that remained of the Bell Brothers?"

"If they're th' idiots who attacked me an' Lucio wit' that Tyrone feller, then yeah, that wuz them. Ah wuzn't kiddin' when Ah toldcha we put th' corpses o' our enemies out like scarecrows. Keeps mos' folk away."

As we descend the stairwell and enter a hallway, darkness swallows us whole. I am unafraid. Nina is the only light I need.

She pauses, making my nose bump into her shoulder. "Apologies," I say, not entirely meaning it because of where my hand ended up. She chuckles as she, from the sound of it, starts playing pat-a-cake with the wall. I'm about to ask her what she's doing when she drags me *through* the wall—there must be a crack I couldn't see.

I think I know where I am now.

She lets go of my hand. I hear a soft thump, and a zipper opening. There's a *click*, and the room is suddenly illuminated. I turn to Nina, who's wielding a sword of light that pierces the darkness.

I suppose a literal *light* is not unwelcome.

The room is filthy. Candy and chip wrappers litter the floor alongside the skeletal remains of rats, mice, and other small creatures. A crusty old mattress is in the corner, and on top of it are torn open, smelly pillows. I look at the poor excuse for a home in absolute disgust. A cockroach skitters across the pillow, making me yelp like a hurt puppy and cower behind Nina. Even though I can't see her face, I know she's rolling her eyes. "C'mon sug', even Shaggy ain't afraid o' bugs."

"I am not Shaggy, dear. And even if I were, I could not afford the obscene amount of pot he smokes."

We laugh, but then I see Cornelius's corpse in my mind's eye and stop. Nina has stopped laughing, too, and she breaks the sad silence with a tired voice that says, "C'mon ova here, sug'."

We walk to the corner of the room. Nina kicks some trash out of our way with relish, and then plops down on the floor in front of a few books.

"I'm not particularly comfortable with sitting down in a room crawling with bugs. N-no offense, of course."

"Ah ain't offended. But it would really mean a lot tah me if you'd plop a squat wit' yer gal real quick." I frown at the hideous floor, looking for a sign of other creepy crawlers. Nina looks up at me with those big green eyes. "Please."

I sigh. "Very well." I take a deep breath, remove my backpack, then, 'pop a squat' on the floor. My backside is not immediately ravished by horrendous insects, so

I suppose this isn't quite as bad as I expected. However...

"Why are we sitting on the floor, darling?"

Nina goes still for a moment. Then, her shoulders hunch and quiver. I turn away before my heart can break and look at the strange sight in front of me. There are three books against the wall. Two are standing upright, maybe twelve inches apart from one another, and the third lies on top of the others horizontally. On top of the third book is an upside down brown stetson, and inside rests a small, dusty white urn. I stare at the bizarre podium for another moment, and then realize its purpose as a makeshift shrine.

Nina takes a deep breath, and then says, "Hey lil' brother. It's been awhile, huh? Ah-Ah can't put intah words how much Ah've missed ya. Feels like Ah've lost a piece o' mah soul Ah ain't eva gettin' back. Tah be honest, losin' you hurt even worse than it did when we lost our folks. Ah mean, Pa an' Ma lived long lives. They built their own business. Fell in love. Got married. Had kids, traveled. But yer life wuz jus' gettin' started. Don' make no sense a plum idiot like me survived while a genius like you died."

"Do not call yourself an idiot again, dear," I growl.

Nina wipes her eyes, flashes me a tired smile, then wraps an arm around my shoulders. "Lucio, Ah'd like ya tah meet mah galfriend Minerva. Neva thought Ah'd be introducin' ya tah a gal 'stedah a guy but... thas' how it goes Ah guess. Y'know, ya, ya told me tah find sumone that makes me happy. Well, Minerva's that person. She's really special tah me, an' Ah really wish ya couldah met her." Her voice gets tight. "Y'all wouldah gotten along so well. Both o' y'all are so smart. Reckon th' two o' y'all couldah saved th' world had it not pushed y'all apart."

I wipe my eyes, grab Nina's hand and kiss her cheek. As an only child, I cannot possibly understand what it's like to lose a sibling *on top* of already losing one's parents. The only thing I can do is be there for my Nina, and be there I shall.

"But Ah ain't here jus' tah introduce y'all. Lil' brother, tahday Ah had a lil' chat wit' th' man that killed ya. Or, well, th' guy Ah've been *sayin'* killed ya. A guy who Ah used as a target fer mah rage, basically. Cuz, y'know, even though he took th' last bit o' food from us, ya mightah still died anyway. You were so skinny... ya looked like a god damn Holocaust victim." She laughs, *hard*, and I hold her close before the laugh turns into full blown sobbing with cries of sadness so deep the very depths of your soul is burdened with complete sorrow. I feel like I'm drowning, but I keep my head above the water, for Nina's sake. What good am I, as a lover, if I cannot bear my lady's sorrow without being crushed by the weight?

I stroke her soft hair, rub her muscular back in circles, and hold her for an eternity until the sobs finally subside. For once, I am grateful I am large enough to hold her in my arms. Nina is one tough lady, but even she needs to be cradled every now and them.

She sniffles in my arms, her brown skin tinted red. "Feeling a little better, sweetie?"

"Thanks tah you, yeah." She kisses me. My brain explodes, but puts itself back together the moment she pulls away. "Dunno what th' Hell Ah'd do without ya, sug'."

"I can say the same for you."

We smile at one another, and then Nina turns back to Lucio. "Lil' brother, what Ah'm tryin' tah say is... Ah can't blame anyone fer yer death. Not me, not Amity, not Zack, not th' Feral, not even th' bastards who sent 'em here an' caused all this. You were a great person, an' sumtimes great people die fer no reason. Ah hate it, Lawd knows Ah hate it, but thas' jus' th' way things are. So, Ah'mma do ya a favor, lil' brother. Ah'mma let ya go."

She stands up, and I follow suit. She grabs the urn, and then places the stetson on her head. She nods at the books, and I nod back then place them in her backpack. I zip it up as Nina walks to the doorway, then turns to take one last look at her old home. Then we ascend to the Surface.

The sun smiles down at us, making the Feral's blood glisten in its holy light. We step over the corpses once more. Nina opens the urn and flips it upside down. A gust of otherworldly wind blows by, making her brother's ashes swirl around her. I gasp as Nina adjusts the stetson on her head, her silky black hair bellowing in the wind. "Goodbye, little brother."

She turns to me with a sniffle, her emerald eyes twinkling as waxy tears roll down her cheeks. Her smile is so warm my heart has melted.

"Nina."

"Yeah?"

"You've never looked more beautiful."

Her rejuvenated smile is brighter than a billion suns. She leans in, then—

The sound of roaring thunder makes me flinch. It's as if God himself cracked a whip across the desolate gray sky.

Nina stumbles backwards, eyes wide. She gives me a confused smile. "Minerva?" Her hand goes to her stomach and comes away red. She sways on the spot, but I catch her before she can fall next to the Feral corpses.

"Minerva?" she mumbles again. My arms are (no) warm and (impossible) wet. I look up and see four men on horseback, all of them with rifles aimed at me.

This can't be happening. So why am I screaming?

Chapter 30

Oh, will someone shut her up?" One of the horsemen shouts over my sobs.

"With pleasure," another grunts.

Minerva, you are a knight. Get ahold of yourself, woman!

I stop bawling and gently lay Nina next to the Feral. "Minerva?" she croaks.

"Hold on, dear. Just hold on," I say, standing to face the four horsemen of the apocalypse. I thrust both hands forward. A large purple square explodes into existence before the horsemen fire once more. The bullets ricochet off my barrier with loud *pangs.*

"M-Minerva? Wuz... wuz happenin'?"

"Don't talk!" I shout, not turning to look at her. Maybe a dozen feet away, I see them reloading their rifles. One of them smiles grimly when they see the barrier, a cigarette between his lips and a black baseball cap on his head.

"Well well well, it's Minerva Henswood herself! I knew you were a metahuman. And it appears that the other rumors were true as well: You joined the Ignored. I'm looking forward to killing you."

The other men laugh. "Judas!" one cries out while another says, "Scarface!"

"Queen Amity will have your heads," I spit through clenched teeth.

"She'll never know," Black Cap snarls with a triumphant grin. "Pincer formation, gentlemen!"

The scumbag charges forward, quickly clearing the distance between us. Two horsemen approach me from my left, the other two from the right.

"Minerva?" Nina moans softly. Indescribable rage blinds me. As if I ever needed to use Queen Amity's name for protection. These men shot my valentine. I'm going to kill them all.

Black Cap fires another round at my barrier. After so many bullets, the barrier starts to crack under the pressure. He laughs, taunting, "You're making this really easy on us, you know that?" My vision goes red. I wave my arms together, as if embracing myself. The barrier turns 90 degrees. I no longer see a transparent purple square, but a thin line of purple light. It is as if I just turned a sheet of paper facing me sideways.

"Yer powers ain't invisibility, its usin' barriers tah make yerself invisible, or tah defend yerself, or who knows what else!"

I roar, throwing my arms out. The light bursts forward with impossible speed, a cloud of dust sprouting in its wake. It slices through Black Cap and his horse, splitting them both right down the middle in an explosion of blood, guts, and flesh. I stare at the strange sight, absentmindedly creating two barriers the size of doorways to block bullets hitting me from the sides. The two halves of both creatures slither to the ground simultaneously. Their inwards slowly spill out, horse intestines sliding around a still throbbing human heart.

"Shit! Take her down!" One of the two approaching from the right says. I glare at the scumbags as they fire once more. I prepare to hurl a barrier at them like a ninja star—but there were four of them! I keep my right hand steady, keeping the barrier still as I look around for the missing member.

He's not to my left anymore, he's right in front of me! The man with goggles charges forward, using one hand to hold the reins on his brown horse and another to aim a revolver at me. I thrust out my left hand. A purple sphere encapsulates his head. I pay his muffled scream no mind and wave my arm as if I am cutting through air. His heads tugs sharply to the side, making his foot get caught on the stirrup as he falls off his horse. I dismantle the barrier right before his head smashes into the ground. I turn to face the two approaching from the right as I hear Mr. Goggles's neck *snap*.

A blonde-haired horseman is upon me, wielding a black machete. He's rode around the barriers I made on my right. He swings, but I roll to the side and narrowly avoid a swipe that would have lobbed off an ear. He continues riding past me, yelling, "I'll get you next time, bitch!"

I turn fully to face him, drawing The Blade of Justice. "We shall see!" I charge, but the sound of another gunshot makes me flinch. My newly formed barrier has already cracked from the impact, and one more shot is all it takes for it to shatter. I'm wondering if they're suddenly using a different caliber of bullets when something punches into *my arm!* I stumble, lightning bolts of sheer agony runs through my right arm and rebounds through my body but it doesn't matter because *Nina.*

Machete Boy is coming around for another swing. I leap as high as I can, then create barriers underneath my feet, creating a path as I run on air. Machete Boy swipes at my ankles, but I front flip over him, dragging my blade across the side of his neck. I hit the ground with a roll, jostling my ever-exploding arm.

Blackness overwhelms my vision. I'm so very tired...

Nina

I bite my bottom lip so hard I bleed, and the pain there is enough to distract me from the hellish fire burning in my right arm. My vision returns in time to see the man I just slashed galloping off. Even awhile away, I can see a geyser of blood bursting from his throat's side.

I stab my sword into the dirt, then thrust my left palm forward, placing a barrier between me and the last remaining horseman—the one who shot me.

He raises his rifle, but my eyes catch his brown ones. The barrier in front of me is a shade of royal purple, but as I glare at the man it turns into obsidian black. I don't care what kind of bullet he's using, it won't penetrate this barrier, and if I focus right, I bet I can reflect it right back at him. He drops the weapon.

"I—I, I didn't mean—" he falls to his knees, his face twisting in regret. "Minerva, please. Don't kill me, please," he cries, then starts sobbing.

I laugh. He already knows I won't show him mercy. I slice my arm horizontally, cutting the air, sending my barrier spinning towards the man's neck at a wicked angle. The black bolt of light slashes through his neck so fast my eyes can't even follow the fatal cut. Bodily fluids erupt from where the man's head used to be, coloring the poor white horse underneath him red.

I hear guts slop down on the horse with a disgusting slap. The horse whines, then, raising both forelegs, gallops off in the distance, dragging its headless master off with him.

I hobble back towards Nina as fast as possible, cradling my right arm. It feels like the bullet went clean through. I spare a micro glance back at the head of the man who shot me. His eyes are bulged in horror, still alive with fright. Heh. I've been told the brain still retains its consciousness for a few minutes once decapitated. If this is true, I can only hope he enjoys suffocating to death.

I reach Nina, whose chest is still moving up and down. I smile, vision blurring. "Thank God. Thank God." I pick her up. She is far heavier than she was two months ago, and the strain on my right arm is immense, but I do not care. Nina is alive (for how long?) *Stop that. Nina is alive!*

I take her down the stairwell, being ever so careful as to not slip.

"Minerva?" she whispers.

"Don't talk, my angel."

I carry her back into her old home, and then gently place her on the disgusting mattress. The pain in my arm lessens somewhat, making me sigh with relief. My sigh is cut short when I notice the red pool spilling from underneath Nina, glistening in the darkness. I cover my mouth.

"Hey, Minerva? Ah think Ah got shot."

She laughs, and then stops suddenly. "Hey, don' cry. Ah hate it when ya cry."

"I told you not to talk, dear," I say, wiping my eyes. I rip open my backpack and snatch out some of Nina's rope, our flashlight, and the first aid kit. I create a hook tipped barrier the size of a pencil, and then stab *its bottom into one end of the rope. I climb onto the bed, careful not to disturb Nina, and then break the tip of the barrier into the ceiling. I lightly pull on the rope, and the barrier holds, so I use the rope to tie a knot around the flashlight. I turn the device on, and the makeshift ceiling light does its job admirably. I get off the bed, and, trying to avoid using my right arm as much as possible, I open the first aid kit. Its silver contents smile up at me with gleam.*

My trusty scalpel! I grab it, then slice open her shirt.

"Ya not—ain'tcha gonna ask me tah dinner first?"

Bloody. Fucking. Hell. I scramble with the kit, taking out supplies through swimming vision, damning my right arm for slowing me down. Damn it, do I take out the bullet first, and then give her a blood transfusion? Or should I just give her the transfusion and leave the bullet for—

What am I even doing!

I yank out the radio Adelia gave us, thankful I hadn't already put on my latex gloves. "Adelia, this is Minerva. We've got an emergency!"

As I speak, I take out gauze pads and press them against Nina's wound. She grunts. I apologize wordlessly, and then wince as blood soaks through the material immediately. My fingertips are hot, wet, and sticky.

Static, then, "Adelia here. What's happened, friend?"

Do human beings really have this much blood in them? "Nina and I've been shot. We're in the metro stations underground a few miles north of the colony. You'll see Feral and human corpses just outside where we're hiding. Please hurry!"

"*What? We're on our way. Give us ten minutes, max. Just hang on, you two. Do whatever you can to stay conscious!*"

"*Yes mamn. If you can, find someone with type O-negative blood. I have to give Nina a transfusion.*"

"*Bloody hell.*"

"*Yes. Please hurry.*"

I decide to leave the surgery to our medic, and instead focus on keeping Nina alive. I grab a tube tail ended by a needle and jam it into my right wrist's radial artery, and then try to transfer the opposite end of the cannula into Nina's median cephalic. But as the apparatus gets close to her, Nina's cloudy eyes bulge with awareness. "Booooy howdy, what do ya think yer doin' wit' that needle?"

My arm my arm my arm my arm my— "Giving you a blood transfusion, dear."

Nina's eyes travel to the hole in my arm. "But... you got shot too."

"No matter. It is my fault you were shot in the first place. Now just *let me—*" I motion to inject her, but she inches away from me. We both groan.

"It weren't yer fault. Ah wuz th' one who did that stupid ass wheelie. Ah caught their attention."

"But if I had defeated you back home, we wouldn't be in this situation right now."

Nina smiles widely, her white teeth-stained red. "Even if you *did* beat me, when Ah woke up Ah wouldah just followed ya tah th' Surface by mahself. This wuz *mah* choice tah make, not—hey!"

I grab her by the wrist, and then start rubbing the inside of her elbow to see the vein. She struggles against my grip, but the bullet wound has sapped much of her strength.

"Let go!"

"No." I inject her with the cannula.

"Ya—ya don' even know mah blood type. Hell, even Ah dunno mah blood type!"

"Irrelevant. I'm a universal donor, blood O-negative."

Nina motions to remove the contraption, but I grab her hand with an iron grip. "Ya can't do this, Minerva. Look at yer arm. Look at yer clothes! You've gotta be bleedin' jus' as bad as Ah am."

"False. You were shot in the stomach, while I was shot in the arm. You've lost much, much more blood than me. Besides, Adelia is on her way with supplies and more blood. I'll be fine." My throbbing arm says otherwise.

"Ah can't let ya die so Ah can live."

"Well, I'm not living without you. Now *this*, darling, is *my* choice, not yours."

Nina groans as my blood drips into the tube and slowly slips into her bloodstream. "Shouldah known that would come back tah bite me in th' ass."

A dizzy spell takes my brain for a loop. I lean my head back against the wall, grabbing my dear's hand. I try to give her hand a reassuring squeeze, but what strength I had is gone. It feels like a firework has exploded in my arm, setting my nerves aflame. I curse under my breath, then, to take my mind off the pain, say, "You know, I was about to follow through with why meeting you has made me believe in God, but then you did that wheelie and I lost my train of thought."

Nina laughs, and then starts coughing hard. When the coughing stops and she pulls her hand away, it is dripping with blood. "Aw, shit."

Indescribable panic chokes my throat. I try to ask her if she's alright—*fool, the answer is clearly no*—but no words come out. Nina smiles, wiping streaks of red away from the corner of her mouth. "Y'know, Ah believed it when ya told me ya loved me, but seein' that look on yer face…"

I grab my face and close my eyes. This can't be happening. This can't be happening!

Nina grabs my hands and brings them both down to her lap so I have to look her in the eye. "Now you…" she winces. "Now you lissen here. Yer already givin' me blood. Ain't no need in worryin' now. You've already done all you could do. So go on an' finish what ya were gonna say an' help me take mah mind offah this pain."

I wipe my eyes, sending a shockwave of agony that ripples from my right arm and into the rest of my body. Curse muscle memory! "I once saw this brilliant film called *Before Sunrise*."

"Lemme guess. It wuz a rom com?"

"Close, but no cigar. It was a tried-and-true romance."

"So, what wuz it about?"

"Well—"

"Wait, lemme guess!" I roll my eyes with a small smile as she says, "B-boy an' gal meet, start datin', then break up durin' th' second act ova sum asinine misunderstandin'. Then th'," she swallows, then makes a face, "ugh, blood tastes gross… anyway, th' gal starts tah leave th' city, but th' guy meets her at th' airport an' declares his love fer her!"

I half-chuckle. She manages to be amusing no matter the circumstance. "I see that, even whilst sustaining a life-threatening injury, you *insist* on interrupting my story. At any rate, you were correct on only two observations; the fact that the protagonists consists of a male and a female, and the fact that they do indeed 'hook up'." Nina has another coughing fit, so I gently rub her back as I say, "However, I do not feel that you deserve any credit for these observations, seeing as though a male and a female hooking up is portrayed in at least 95% of media."

"Ah know..." She winces again with a tight smile, "Ah know damn well ya pulled that statistic outta yer ass."

"Perhaps. So, *as I was saying*, the film is about an American man visiting Vienna. He meets a woman on a train, and they hit it off immediately. The problem is that the man is moving back to America the next day. Undeterred, they decide to spend the rest of the day together before they part the morrow."

"So, what, th' whole film is them walkin' 'round th' city an' yappin' all day?"

"Correct."

"That... actually sounds kinda interestin'. Ah mean, its got potential tah be boring as all hell, but Ah'd be willin' tah watch it wit' an open mind."

"Quite. At any rate, the reason why I bring this up is because there is some fantastic dialogue midway through the film. The woman says something along the lines of, "I believe if there's any kind of God, it wouldn't be in any of us, in you, or in me, but just this little space in between."

"Wow. Thas' pretty deep. Reminds me o' a Bible verse... think it went sumthin' like, 'No one has ever seen God. But if we love each otha, God lives in us, an' his love is brought tah full expression in us.'"

My eyebrows hit the ceiling. "I can finally see why Sarah is so smitten with that book."

"There's a lotta love in that book, hidden in between sum o' th' bigotry an' hate." We're silent for a moment. "Hey, 'Nerva."

"Yes, dear?"

"Fer th' past few minutes, Ah've been in so much pain Ah can't even begin tah describe it. Ah'm sad tah say that Ah'm happy that mah body has started tah go numb. But, y'know that feelin' ya get when yer doin' a wheelie?"

This time, I don't wipe my eyes. "Yes."

"What ya jus' said 'bout God bein' 'tween us... it made me feel that way." Her eyes start to close. "Ah guess if he really does live in our love, then Ah'll see you in heaven."

I just about slap her full in the face to keep her conscious, but something tells me violence just isn't the answer this time.

"Nina," I say with utmost seriousness, trying to blow through the hazy pain clouding my mind. "You have to stay awake. The doctors are going to need to ask you questions."

"No Ah don'," Nina says drowsily. "Ah only stayed alive cuz o' you. An' now Ah can feel yer blood flowin' through me." She yawns. "God's here wit' us right now, an' he's tellin' me there ain't no way Ah ain't seein' you in heaven."

I tilt her chin towards me, purse my lips, and then call upon the Lord to keep my Nina alive. When we break apart, both of us are crying. "Open your eyes, dear. I need to see your eyes."

Nina groans, but cracks open both of her eyes. "Feels like there's *boulders* on my eyelids. No wonder Lucio didn't make it. But... Ah should be seein' him soon."

Seeing those normally sharp eyes so groggy and unfocused makes my throat so tight I should be incapable of speech, but I push through the pain. "Nina, you listen to me. There may be a God, but I don't think there's a Heaven. The lives we live can either be a brief utopia, or a relentless Hell, or something in between—but once our lives are over, they're over. So stay awake, Nina, fight for every precious second we get to spend together. Because once you close your eyes, you may never see me again."

Nina takes in a deep breath, then croaks, "*Shit.* Ain't that a damn shame?"

It looks like she's standing at death's door. "I don't want you to go, baby."

"Ah don' wanna go either. But at least Ah spent mah final moments wit'cha." She coughs, sending a violet splash of red flying onto my already stained jumpsuit. "A—Ah can only hope th' memories Ah gave ya last a lifetime."

I grab her hand with both of mine, and then press her against my heart. The tube connecting our physical forms is overflowing with my love. "I wouldn't worry about that, dear."

I kiss her deeply. When I pull away, she graces me with that heart stopping smile, her brilliant emeralds still shining despite being trapped in broken jewelry. Then, she goes still.

No. Please, no... I put my hand on her wrist.

My world just ended.

END OF VOLUME 1

ACKNOWLEDGMENTS

Although this book has been edited an incalculable number of times, most of the script was written in 2014-2015 when I worked at the now deceased Fry's Electronics. My coworkers Jarvis Sampson, Julio Tuck, Jonah Camba, Taylor Bradberry and Susan Huerta were absolutely instrumental to the writing process. As Ryuiskhi07 once wrote, it takes two to create a universe. By listening to my unending rambling, providing feedback to the latest chapter, and suggesting directions the plot could go, they helped develop the universe you're holding in your hands. I cannot thank them enough for their support and friendship!

I hired Marissa van Uden to edit the first quarter of the novel, and she did a wonderful job giving me the keys I needed to unlock this story's full potential. You've played an indisputable role in my development as an author, and I thank you for that.

Alice Sanner drew the lovely cover to this novel and I couldn't be happier with her work. Find her on Instagram @a1i.star

Big shouts out to my entire family for their unending support. My parents helped cultivate my love for reading and writing and this novel wouldn't exist without them. Each of my siblings supported me in their own unique ways and I'm eternally grateful for that.

As you may have noticed, there is a huge gap in time between when the book was written and the time of publication. The journey to get this story published was a long and arduous one. If it weren't for my wonderful prereaders Daniel Garvey, Hoa Nguyen, Jeremy Jean-Jacques, Ally Theft, Keith Garmond, Oziel Briseño and Phillip J Polk I have no doubt this novel would've faded into obscurity. Thank you all for giving me the confidence I needed to put this story out into the world!

Lastly, I'd like to thank You for buying and reading my book. I put my everything into this and your support is greatly appreciated. Sorry not sorry about the gut punch of an ending~

ABOUT THE AUTHOR

If you couldn't tell already, I'm a born and raised Houstonian. I infused a lot of Nina's punctation with the day-to-day language I hear in the city. By reading this book, you've absorbed just a small piece of what my lovely city has to offer. Be sure to give it a visit, but don't stay—this place is crowded as hell.

Anyway, I've been writing for as long as I can remember, but Nina and Minerva is my first published work. If I'm not writing I'm probably playing video games, watching anime, or out dancing. You can follow me on Twitter @lilcrossv2 or send me an email at cycross@sbcglobal.net. Thanks again for reading Nina and Minerva and be sure to pick up volume 2 when it's released in 2023!